more . . .

"A great read! These characters are truly believable and you find yourself sitting on the edge of your seat waiting to see what happens next. This is not your typical vampire read, and that is very refreshing."

—*RoundTableReviews.com*

"A saucy, witty read filled with spicy romance and dry humor. Vampires go chick-lit and this tale makes for a delightful and humorous read. Definitely one to add to your paranormal shelf."

—*ParanormalRomanceWriters.com*

"Michelle Rowen . . . takes the vampire world and turns it from scary and dark, to goofy and fun. Not an easy task, I am sure, but one Rowen attacks nicely . . . I haven't laughed so hard in a long time . . . The humor in this tale is absolutely priceless . . . and totally makes this light read worth your time."

—*RomanceReaderatHeart.com*

Also by Michelle Rowen

Bitten & Smitten

Angel with ATTITUDE

MICHELLE ROWEN

NEW YORK   BOSTON

Warner Forever and the Warner Forever logo are trademarks of Time Warner Inc. or an affiliated company. Used under license by Hachette Book Group, which is not affiliated with Time Warner Inc.

Book design by Stratford Publishing Services
Cover design by Diane Luger

Warner Books
Hachette Book Group USA
1271 Avenue of the Americas
New York, NY 10020

Printed in the United States of America

First Printing: August 2006

10 9 8 7 6 5 4 3 2 1

ATTENTION CORPORATIONS AND ORGANIZATIONS:
Most WARNER books are available at quantity discounts with bulk purchase for educational, business, or sales promotional use. For information, please call or write:

Special Markets Department, Warner Books, Inc.
1271 Avenue of the Americas, New York, NY 10020.
Telephone: 1-800-222-6747 Fax: 1-800-477-5925

To my sister,
Cindy

(Sorry, no chimps in this one, either.)

Acknowledgments

Thank you . . .

Melanie Murray whose skills as an editor are truly heaven sent.

Jim McCarthy, my guardian angel of an agent who is always there with great advice or a kind word when I get a little neurotic. It happens.

Bonnie Staring and Holly Biffl, my cherubic beta readers. You rock.

To the ladies on the Warner e-mail loop who have answered my newbie questions with patience and grace. You are some of the warmest and friendliest women I've ever met.

And lastly . . . to Hugh Jackman. Thank you for being so damn hot.

Angel with
ATTITUDE

So You're A Fallen Angel . . . Now What?
Golden Scroll Edition 2.1

Your misdeeds in Heaven have led to this unfortunate situation. You only have yourself to blame, but here are a few guidelines that may help to ease your way.

Do

- Find somewhere safe to live.
- Eat regularly. Three meals a day is standard for human sustenance.
- Study the behavior and interactions of other humans so you will be able to fit in with them. Suggestion: watch television and go to the movies. Also, observe real humans in everyday activity.

Do Not

- Tell anyone you are a fallen one. They will not believe you, and probably will think that you are simply insane. Don't say we didn't warn you.

How Do You Return to Heaven?

You don't. But do your best to make the most of your situation. Be good. Help others. Do good deeds. At the end of your human life (approximately 70 years), you may have balanced the scales for whatever you were originally expelled for. It is unlikely, but you never know about these things. However, if you die by natural or unnatural causes before this balance has been reached, the doors of Heaven will forever be closed to you.

Warning

Be wary of any stranger who takes an interest in your safety and well-being. Tempter Demons are assigned to lure fallen ones to Hell for an eternity of torturous servitude. TEMPTER DEMONS ARE VERY DANGEROUS. Their methods are underhanded and almost impossible to resist. You will know one when you see one. Remember to: JUST SAY NO! Do not let your guard down when confronted with a Tempter or you will regret it. Big time.

Good luck! You're going to need it.
The Management

Chapter One

—⌇—

Falling out of Heaven is the easy part. It's *landing* that's difficult.

Luckily—or unluckily, as the case may be—someone up there had a strange sense of humor. She could have landed anywhere in the earthly realm. Pavement, grass, the middle of the ocean . . .

. . . MarineLand in Niagara Falls. Or, more precisely, the *killer whale tank* at MarineLand.

Plop.

The cold water jarred her from her free-fall daze and she thrashed about, eyes wide. What just happened? She'd been reading a scroll. A golden scroll somebody had thrust into her hands. Something about the rules of being a fallen angel, and then . . . then what?

She swallowed a large mouthful of water and started to choke before she slipped under.

And then somebody pushed me.

Somebody pushed her out of Heaven.

Son of a b—

She bobbed above the water and gasped for air before going under again. Then suddenly she felt herself forcefully yanked above the waterline. Somebody had hold of her upper arm. *Ouch.* An extremely tight hold.

Her first impression of being a human? *Pain sucked.*

The large black-and-white killer whale—*where did it get that name from, anyhow?* she thought with growing panic—nudged her leg curiously as she was dragged out of the tank. She could hear applause and cheers from somewhere, but her vision was too blurry to see more than just shapes and colors.

"Miss? What exactly do you think you're doing? Is this some sort of joke?"

She opened her mouth to respond with, "Mahhhhh." This actually meant: "I need to go back to Heaven. There's been a huge mistake. Somebody, anybody, help me!," but her first incomprehensible word was followed with a, "Bahhhh."

The blurry dot of a human peered closer at her. "Are you okay?"

She knew enough to shake her head. No. She wasn't okay. Not even close to being okay.

"Where did you come from?"

She blinked at the human, then pointed up. He followed the direction of her finger, then looked at her with confusion.

"I . . . I . . . fell from . . . ," she began, happy she could finally speak, but then abruptly shut her mouth.

What had the golden scroll said? *Do not tell anyone you are a fallen one . . . Don't say we didn't warn you.*

She rubbed her eyes, which helped make the human, who turned out to be a uniformed security guard, a little less blurry, then wracked her equally blurry mind for something to say. Anything. "I . . . I . . . was skydiving. My . . . chute didn't open."

She couldn't believe her ears. She'd just lied for the first time. And actually, it sounded pretty good, all things considered.

The applause slowed, and a male voice shouted above the crowd: "Dude! She's, like, totally naked! Get the camera!"

She swallowed and looked down at herself. "Uh . . . *nude* skydiving. It's the latest thing. Haven't you heard?"

The security guard was having a difficult time keeping his attention fully on her face and his expression turned skeptical. "Nude skydiving. Right."

Okay, maybe she wasn't as good a liar as she'd thought.

"Where am I?" she managed.

"MarineLand." At her frown of confusion, he continued, "In Niagara Falls."

Niagara Falls. That meant that she just fell . . . to the *Falls?*

She looked up at the clouds and shot whomever might be watching a very dirty look.

"What's the date today?"

"Are you kidding?"

"I wish I was. Date? What is it?"

"It's September the thirtieth. A Saturday. Good enough?" He eyed her warily. "What's your name?"

She knew this one. She didn't seem to have anything else, but she did have a name. "It's V-v-valerie. Valerie Grace."

He frowned, then reached into his pocket. "Then this must be yours. I was just about to turn it in to lost and found."

It was a small, black leather wallet. After closer inspection, she discovered it contained a birth certificate with her name on it and a hundred dollars in cash. There was also a torn piece of paper with the handwritten words "Paradise Inn" and an address.

The security guard tapped the paper. "That motel's just around the corner. Are you staying there?"

It hurt to think. "I . . . I guess I might be."

Somebody approached from behind and was trying to slip something over her head. Remembering what the scroll said, she instinctively began to fight against whomever or whatever it was. "Demon!" she shrieked. "Get away from me!"

"No," the security guard assured her. "It's only a T-shirt, Ms. Grace. To cover you up. I think the crowd has gotten enough pictures today, don't you think? Why don't I get a taxi for you? Then you can go back to your motel and maybe . . . rest a bit?"

She clutched his arm. "Have you seen any demons? They're very dangerous. I have to get back to Heaven as soon as possible. This is all a horrible, horrible mistake."

The water in the tank had been very cold and she started to shiver as the sun disappeared behind some clouds in the otherwise clear sky.

The guard eyed her strangely. "Let's start with the taxi, shall we?"

Get hold of yourself, Valerie, she commanded herself. The golden scroll was right. Anyone who listened to her would think she was insane. She'd been human for only five minutes and even she could see that.

She nodded at him and tried not to cry.

This was a mistake. She hadn't done anything to warrant this. She had to go back. They'd take her back, wouldn't they? She'd *always* been an angel, it was all she knew. All she ever *wanted* to know.

The security guard shuffled her through the swelling crowd. As they passed a group of four leering teenage boys, he confiscated a digital camera to their loud and angry protests.

All a mistake.

Huge.

She got in a taxi and left MarineLand headed for the Paradise Inn with three things to her name. A complimentary BOOM BOOM THE KILLER WHALE oversized T-shirt, the security guard's home phone number ("we should get together for drinks when you're feeling better"), and the absolute, unwavering determination to get back to Heaven as soon as *humanly* possible.

You've got to be kidding me, Val thought with despair. *Is this part of my punishment, too?*

The taxi had let her off in front of a run-down motel just off the main strip of Niagara Falls. She stood in place in her oversized T-shirt, her long, wet blond hair hanging like a drippy curtain over her right shoulder, clutching the wallet against her chest, and just stared at the Paradise Inn.

All Val had ever known in her existence had been Heaven. And Heaven, as was common knowledge, was perfect. Whatever one's idea of perfection was, that is how Heaven became to suit them. Beauty as far as the eye could see, clean and comfortable and flawless in every way.

This, however, was a whole other story.

The Paradise Inn had seen better days. To say the least. It was run-down, with roof tiles missing and a big crack in the tacky fifties-style sign. It looked tired and old and only days away from being demolished.

Val closed her eyes for a moment and tried to think of Heaven. It wasn't cold there, for one thing. Always the perfect temperature. She never felt alone because there was always someone with her or very close by. She felt needed there, not discarded like a bubblegum wrapper. She knew what to expect and that there was nothing to fear there. And, also . . . also—

She frowned. She knew what it was like, how great it was, but as she tried to picture it, the images in her head started to become a little fuzzy. She opened her eyes again and swallowed hard, feeling a wave of panic flood her as she saw where she really was.

It was one thing to be abandoned, when it was so obviously a mistake, but to be led to an obvious dead end like this?

Her bottom lip wobbled. Maybe the nice cab driver—who had seemed so surprised to pick up a half-naked woman that he didn't even complain about the fact she was slightly soggy from her unexpected nosedive into the tank—would take her somewhere better than this. Somewhere appropriate where she could think about what she was going to do next, in comfort and luxury.

She turned back to the cab just as it pulled away from the curb.

"Wait!" she called, but it was too late.

She swallowed hard. The street was fairly busy. She could see another yellow taxi in the distance. She raised her hand as it approached.

But it didn't stop. Instead it drove right through a puddle, drenching Val in a small tidal wave of cold water. She sputtered and wiped at her face.

Her bottom lip began to wobble again.

She turned back around to face the motel.

PARADISE INN. VACANCY.

Lucky me, she thought. *There's a vacancy. Woo-hoo.*

Just then, she heard a strange sound. She frowned and listened, then turned around to see that it was squealing tires. A rusty Volkswagen Jetta came to a screeching halt next to her. The passenger door flew open, and a man flew out who hit the sidewalk hard. The door slammed shut and the car sped off.

The man got to his feet, brushed off his faded jeans, and yelled, "Claire, baby! Come on . . . I didn't do anything wrong!" He sighed heavily, and turned to glance absently at Val. "My girlfriend. She's the jealous type. No reason to be though." His gaze slowly tracked down Val's wet BOOM-BOOM-THE-KILLER-WHALE-T-shirt-and-nothing-else clad body. "Well, hello there, beautiful."

She looked at him warily. He was pleasant looking. A few inches taller than she, and with brown hair that was definitely receding. He smiled, which slightly showed off his crooked teeth and she noted that his brown eyes were friendly. She felt goose bumps form on her arms and took a step back.

"You're a demon, aren't you?" she asked quietly.

"I'm a what?"

"Demon. Please leave me alone. Don't come any closer."

He stared at her blankly, then laughed. "Is that what

Claire called me before she took off? She's so cute. Must be a new pet name."

Val frowned at him, not sure what to think or do next.

He wagged a finger at her. "Don't I know you?"

She shook her head and shifted her bare feet nervously against the cool sidewalk.

"No, I know you. Those legs. Unforgettable." He snapped his fingers. "I've got it. That strip club down on Barrister Road . . . What's it called again? . . . Booty Call? Yeah, that's it. You're a strip . . . er"—he cleared his throat—"I mean . . . *exotic dancer.*"

"Booty *what?*"

"Not that I go there anymore. Nah. Me and Claire, we've got something special between us. She's the best thing that's ever happened to me." He sighed and stared off in the direction of the speeding Jetta.

Val glanced in the same direction. "Claire is the woman who just threw you out of her car?"

He smiled dreamily and leaned his shoulder against the Pardise Inn signpost. "That's the one."

"And . . . you think I'm a . . . an exotic dancer?"

"Nothing to be ashamed of, gorgeous. Noble profession."

"I'm not." Val looked down at herself to note that the now wet T-shirt was, in fact, see-through. She crossed her arms. "*Seriously.* I'm not."

"If you say so," he grinned. "What's your name, gorgeous?"

"Valerie Grace."

"I'm Reggie." He reached out to shake her tentative hand. "Now if you'll excuse me, I need to . . . hey, you can let go now."

She clutched his hand. "I need to go back. You have to help me."

"Ow! You've got a grip on you, you know that?"

"I don't belong here." She swallowed hard and realized she was tearing up again. This man seemed nice enough. He couldn't be a demon. He would have tried to tempt her by now, and she certainly didn't feel very tempted, if that was worth anything. And if he was a demon, well, he seemed like a very nice one who meant no harm. He'd help her, wouldn't he? Grabbing the nearest thing seemed like her best course of action. The nearest thing, in this case, was his hand. Currently turning purple.

"So if you don't belong here, then leave! My hand! Alone!" He yanked away from her and looked at her warily. "Where are you from, anyhow?"

"Heaven." She sniffed, ran a hand under her nose and tried not to cry. She turned her gaze away to stare at the seedy motel.

"Heaven." He frowned. "Is that another strip club? What town is that in?"

"It's not a strip club." She was about to tell him about what happened to her. That they'd kicked her out of Heaven for no reason. That it was a huge mistake because she'd never done anything to deserve this kind of treatment. She was a great angel! Her last job review had even said so. And management always did very detailed report scrolls. What had hers said again? She thought about it and came up blank. She frowned. Why couldn't she remember?

She wiped a tear away. "It's been a really bad day. That's all. Sorry for freaking out a bit."

Reggie shook his head. "The beautiful ones are always

a bit nutty. My girlfriend is, too. Totally understandable. Probably your time of the month, right?"

"My what?"

He waved his hand. "Forget I asked. So, are you staying here?" Reggie nodded at the motel.

She swallowed. "Not if I can help it."

"Then what are you doing here?"

She pulled the ratty piece of paper out of her wallet and showed it to him. He squinted at it, then took it away from her.

"Oh, you must be here for the job," he said.

"For the what?" She glanced at the paper and was surprised to see that the motel name and address wasn't the only thing written on it anymore.

It also had "B. Barlow," and "1:00 P.M." on it. It hadn't said that before, she was almost positive. Then again, since her plunge, she hadn't really been thinking clearly.

"I'll let him know you're here," Reggie said, and before Val could say anything, he headed for the center section of the U-shaped motel, where a sign read MANAGER'S OFFICE.

Her immediate thought was to run away, to flee, but where was she going to go? She needed somewhere safe to stay. Somewhere she could think about what to do next. Figure out how to get in contact with somebody Up There to help sort things out. So she could go back.

She crossed her arms protectively in front of her, shivering from being wet for too long. Before she had a chance to have second thoughts about not running away, Reggie emerged from the office with a white-haired old man who eyed her curiously as they approached.

"You're here for the job?" the old man asked her.

Reggie snatched the paper out of her hand and showed it to him before she could say anything. Not that she knew what to say.

The old man looked up from the paper, crooked a white eyebrow, and smiled at her. A warm, friendly smile that made deep lines fan out from his blue eyes. "That will not do for a uniform, I'm afraid, young lady."

Val looked down at herself, feeling embarrassed for the first time. "This, I, uh . . ."

Well, that sounded intelligent, she thought.

"It's a pleasure to meet you . . ." He stretched out his hand and seemed to be waiting for something.

"Her name's Valerie," Reggie piped up.

She stepped closer to the motel and out of the way of two young boys riding skateboards. They stared at her lack of clothes with wide eyes as they passed by.

At least they don't have a camera, too, she thought.

"Valerie," the man continued. Then she found that she was shaking his hand, finding it as strangely warm and comforting as his smile. "I am Bartholomew Barlow. I look after the Paradise Inn."

She nodded stiffly. "About the job. I don't really know—"

"My former employee unfortunately has left us. With no notice. I've had to manage on my own for several weeks, and I fear I'm too old, too tired, to continue without assistance. Your help would be greatly appreciated."

Reggie nodded. "Lisa was gorgeous, too. Didn't even say good-bye before she took off."

Mr. Barlow finally let go of Val's hand and she felt oddly bereft. "I'm not sure I'm what you're looking for."

"Nonsense. You'll do just fine. Though, I'm afraid I'm

unable to pay very much. This isn't the busy time of year around here. At the moment we only have a few tenants."

"I live here permanently," Reggie added. "Barlow cut me a great deal. Until Claire lets me move in with her, that is."

Barlow turned his gaze to the other man. "Speaking of deals. I believe you are behind on your rent."

Reggie glanced at his wristwatch and tapped it with his index finger. "Will you look at the time? I have somewhere I need to be. Nice meeting you, Valerie."

Val watched the back of his head moving away as he scurried along the sidewalk. She turned her attention back to the kindly old man.

"It's not the money, I . . . I just don't think I'll be here very long."

"Here in Niagara Falls?"

She was about to say "on Earth," but stopped herself. "Yeah, here in Niagara Falls."

"You don't like it here?"

"I don't belong here. There's somewhere else I need to be."

He nodded. "Homesick. I understand completely. If you would like the job for as long as you're here, I would certainly be willing to work something out."

"Why are you doing this? Offering me a job?"

"Because I am in need of a maid. And you are here. Perhaps you'd like to go back to wherever you're staying and give it some thought?"

She almost smiled at that, but then realized that it wasn't very funny. "I don't have anywhere to stay."

"No?" He appeared to mull over a thought. "Well, you are welcome to use one of my rooms for as long as you care to. Like I said, there are plenty available. Freshen up. Change your clothes." He crooked his eyebrow again at her choice of wardrobe.

She pulled the small amount of T-shirt material down as far as she could. "Would you believe me if I told you I didn't have any clothes?"

She waited for the inevitable questions that she was certain she wouldn't be able to answer properly. *Why don't you have anywhere to stay? Why don't you have any possessions . . . suitcases . . . friends . . . family?* But he didn't ask any of that.

"I see," Barlow finally said. "Then perhaps, if you agree to work for me for a while, I can arrange a small advance on your first paycheck. Help to get you settled? How does that sound?"

Frankly, it sounded too good to be true to her. Was he a demon? She eyed him warily. *Is this how they approached to try to lure her to Hell?*

But he hadn't approached her. She'd approached him.

She stared at him for a moment longer, expecting there to be a catch. Expecting him to suddenly turn cruel or lewd. But he simply regarded her with mild interest and a warm expression on his wrinkled face.

She finally put her thoughts into words. "Why are you being so kind to me?"

"Because I can be. We all fall on hard times now and then. I certainly have."

She felt the almost overwhelming urge to give this kind stranger a hug, but she didn't. Instead, she gave him a big, heartfelt smile, her first one, and it felt very good.

She looked at the motel again, and it didn't look quite so bad anymore. It was run-down and old and needed a fresh paint job, but she was welcome there. As she walked into the courtyard leading to the manager's office, she suddenly *felt* welcome there. An odd feeling of warmth came over her, taking the chill away as she followed Mr. Barlow. She exhaled slowly. This would have to do until she figured out how to get back to Heaven.

She frowned suddenly

"Wait a minute," she said. "Did you say you need me to be a *maid?* As in a 'cleaning rooms' and 'making beds' maid?"

He turned and nodded at her. "That's right."

She sighed, but continued to follow the old man. It could be worse, she supposed. She could be working at *Booty Call.*

Chapter Two

—∿—

A nine-year-old little girl was going to solve all of Valerie's problems. Well, all of her problems were really only one, extremely large problem. But the important thing was, after two months stuck in the earthly realm, she'd finally found somebody to help her.

Two months. She could hardly believe it. Working as a maid at the Paradise Inn, which included, as she'd predicted, cleaning rooms and making beds. Also, cleaning toilets, which was just absolutely disgusting. Not the work for an angel, that's for sure. Not that she could entirely remember what she had and hadn't done as an angel anymore. Details were still more unclear than she'd like them to be. But she knew that it beat being human any day of the week.

So that's what she'd done. Worked as a maid. Tried to be friendly to people she met and not give away what she truly was in case they'd think her insane. Tried to cope the best she could with her situation.

She also tried to do as many good deeds as she could. The golden scroll had said that that was one way to get back on Heaven's good side. Even though she was positive she hadn't done anything worth getting thrown out for, she wasn't taking any chances. She helped little old ladies cross the street, she returned stray dogs to their homes, she picked up trash from the sidewalks. Whether these were considered good deeds, or just being helpful, she wasn't sure.

But she'd soon find out. Because tomorrow was the day she'd fix everything.

The nine-year-old girl who was the answer to Val's problems was actually a psychic, and through hard work and a good chunk of luck, Val had an appointment with her. Tomorrow. She'd channel somebody Up There and then Val could ask what went wrong and how she could fix things as soon as possible. Two months was more than enough time for her to decide, most definitely, that while there were certain elements to being a human that weren't entirely distasteful—although she'd be hard pressed to give any examples at present—it was not something she wanted to be for any extended amount of time.

She'd been extremely lucky, too. Two months and she hadn't run into any of those alleged Tempter Demons the golden scroll had so adamantly warned against. She'd kept a vigilant watch, too. Most nights losing a ton of sleep shivering and shaking, waiting for some nasty demon to pounce on her and carry her off to Hell. But nothing happened. No pouncing. She figured the seeming lack of interest in the demon community proved her situation was all an unfortunate error. She must have been off demon radar. And that was just fine by her.

Val sneezed and wiped her nose on her sleeve as she walked along the darkened street. Bad head cold, her first one. At first she'd panicked, thinking it would kill her, but then remembered that colds were mostly harmless—just incredibly annoying. She was on her way back to the Paradise Inn after a midnight drugstore run in the chill of early December. She needed NyQuil. It was nice to have a goal that was easy to accomplish. Plus, it was on sale. Buy two, get one free. She'd bought ten just in case.

How did she get the cold in the first place? From a good deed gone bad: attempting to save a jumper from throwing himself over the Falls only resulted in getting her wet. And being wet in below-zero temperature was a surefire way of getting majorly sick.

She learned something new about being human every day.

The falling snow stung her face and she gathered her thin, hooded sweatshirt closer. A pathetic sight to say the least. The self-pity she felt was almost palpable and completely uncontrollable. She stopped walking for a moment and pulled out a notebook from the pocket of her hoody and opened it up.

"The only snow in Heaven is on the Heavenly Slopes ski hill."

She let out a long breath. Just reading from what she'd dubbed her Heavenly Memories Notebook put her mind at ease. It was immediate stress relief. Every memory of Heaven that came to mind got written down in the book, just in case she forgot. And, sadly, her memory was getting worse with every passing day. She figured it had to do with having a human brain. It simply couldn't possibly hold all the wonders that she'd experienced as an angel. That had to be the reason. She kept the notebook with her at all hours of the day while she tried not to feel sorry for herself.

Well, not any more than absolutely necessary.

Luckily, with it being well after midnight by then, there wasn't an audience for her extreme misery.

The immediate goal was to go back to tiny room seventeen at the motel, chug back the cold medicine, get into bed and pull the covers up over her head. She might get up sometime early the next afternoon and watch a soap or two before her all-important, most certainly life-changing, appointment with the psychic. She had to get her quota of TV viewing in. One thing she had to admit she enjoyed about being human was watching television—it was an excellent place to study realistic human interaction—as suggested in the stupid, golden scroll. In fact, she liked it so much, that when she got back to Heaven she wanted to get cable Up There so she could keep up with *Days of Our Lives*.

The motel loomed in front of her, its VACANCY sign a tacky beacon in the darkness. It was only a few blocks away from the drugstore, a distance that felt three times as far when feeling sick as a dog in the sub-zero temperature.

She felt a sneeze coming on. Or maybe she was going to throw up. Maybe both.

She was so not going to miss any of this. The sickness, the cold weather, the way her back hurt in the morning from the lousy mattress in her room. But it was only for one more night.

Tomorrow she'd fix everything.

She heard something then. Voices. She stopped walking and turned around. It was a man shouting obscenities from around a corner. He sounded angry.

Then she heard a woman's voice. Smaller, meeker,

pleading with him, but Val couldn't hear what she was saying.

Without thinking, she found herself moving toward the voices.

A large man, roughly the size of an obese grizzly bear, had a woman up against the brick wall by her throat.

"There. Try to get away from me now, bitch."

"Let me go," the woman sobbed. Flakes of snow swirled around the dark alleyway from the cold wind.

"Lemme think about that." He cocked his head to one side. "No."

"Why? Please! I didn't do anything to you."

He grinned. "Little girls shouldn't be out late at night. The big bad wolf might get them and eat them up." He moved closer to her face and snapped his teeth.

"Excuse me," Val said as she ran a hand under her clogged nose. "Do either of you happen to have the time?"

His head whipped around in her direction, his eyes wide. She'd surprised him.

"Time for you to mind your own business," he growled. "Get lost."

Val gritted her teeth and tried to look brave. "Why don't you let her go and we can all get lost?"

His eyes narrowed. "Go away. I mean it."

The woman had taken this small distraction as her one opportunity. She sank her teeth into his hand and when he released her with a loud yelp of pain, she kicked him in the shin and ran away, her high-heels clicking against the icy pavement.

Val's good deed for the night was accomplished successfully. She hoped somebody Up There was keeping track of these things.

She turned around just as a hand clamped down on her shoulder. The obese grizzly bear roughly turned her back to face his furious expression.

"I thought I told you to mind your own business?" he snarled.

She stood her ground and tried to ignore the sick, sinking feeling in her stomach. "Look, I don't want any trouble."

"Could have fooled me. Looks to me like you're *looking* for trouble. Looks like you want to know what I do to people who get in my way."

He dug his fingers into her upper arm, pulling her close enough to get an unpleasant whiff of his dollar-store cologne. It didn't quite make up for the putrid stench of his breath, though. She was almost thankful that her nose was nearly stuffed shut from the cold.

His black eyes narrowed. "You owe me now."

"I owe you?"

"You let her escape. I didn't get her purse or anything else. You owe me."

Val gasped as his grip tightened. "I don't have any money."

He stared down at her for a few moments before his scowl turned into a lecherous grin. "Maybe we can work something out, pretty thing." He licked his thin lips and moved his face toward hers.

"Forget it." She slapped him across the face hard enough to make her hand sting.

The grin vanished and his expression darkened. "Who said I was giving you a choice?"

Before she could make another move to protect herself, he clamped his sweaty hand over her mouth. Her ankle twisted as he dragged her farther into the alley and she dropped her bag of cold medication so she could fight him with everything she had—but it wasn't going to be enough. The guy was strong and built like a truck. She felt fingers of panic squeeze her already rapidly beating heart.

He pushed her up against the wall behind a Dumpster and took a step back to get a better look.

"Yeah, this is gonna be good. Blondes are my favorite." He licked his lips.

Val held her hands up in front of her. "You do not want to do this."

"Why not?"

She tried to slow her breathing down so she could put together complete sentences. "Just look at me. I'm sick. I've got a very bad virus. Incredibly contagious. And . . . and I haven't showered today. Yuck, right?"

"You look pretty damn good to me."

"You do *not* want to do this."

He grinned to show her his broken, rotted teeth. "Oh, yes I do. Trust me on that."

And then he was on her. She lashed out with the only weapon she currently had—her fingernails. She got him across his cheek and a watched a line of crimson appear. He stepped back to touch his face, stunned for a moment when he saw the blood on his fingers.

"You're gonna regret that," he said. And she believed him. She really did.

He hit her hard across the face, hard enough that she sank down to the ground, ears ringing from the force of the blow. He grabbed the front of her sweatshirt and pulled her back up to her feet as if she weighed nothing at all and her already injured ankle turned the wrong way. As it snapped she felt pain shoot up her leg like a lightning bolt.

He clutched her throat and pressed her up against the brick wall, hard and fast enough to knock the wind out of her. His fingers closed tighter around her windpipe and he started to squeeze. She stared at him, eyes wide, but after a moment things began to go blurry . . . to fade away. She stopped clawing at him like a wild animal and her hands fell slackly to her sides.

This is what she got for trying to help somebody out: she was going to die. Her good deeds suddenly flashed in front of her eyes. No, she hadn't done enough. And saving that kid the other day from the Pomeranian that was looking at him funny probably didn't even count. This horrible man was going to kill her and she hadn't had enough time to fix things yet. To make Heaven take her back. They *had* to take her back . . . had to . . .

Suddenly, he released her. As she sank down to the ground in a heap, sputtering for breath, she watched him rise into the air. It struck her as odd, but her brain wasn't making logical connections at the moment. He looked down at Val with surprise before he flew backward and slammed against the other wall of the alley, then fell to the snow-covered ground.

Unconscious.

A dark shape moved before her eyes. She blinked and tried to focus on it and saw it slowly condense into that of a man. He crouched down in front of her.

"Are you okay?" he asked.

She coughed. "Do I look okay?"

"Not especially."

It took another moment before everything completely

came back into focus. The man held his hand out and she grabbed it. He pulled her up to her feet, a movement that was met with a gasp of pain as she realized just how hurt her ankle was.

"Did he harm you?" the stranger asked with a frown.

Standing, she could see he was much taller than her five and a half feet. Well over six feet, she estimated. He wore a serious expression on his shadowed face and a long leather jacket over dark clothes. From what she could see in the dim light from a nearby street lamp he was very handsome.

Movie-star handsome.

At least, he was the best-looking man she'd seen outside of the movies or TV. He almost didn't look real.

But maybe her mind was playing tricks on her. She was so disoriented and congested that she couldn't be certain her eyes weren't deceiving her. She swallowed hard and coughed again, realizing that she couldn't even feel her nose for how plugged up it was.

"That man wanted to kill me." She frowned and looked over at the mugger, still out like a light. Humans made no sense at all. Fascinating creatures—sometimes—but completely incomprehensible.

"Your ankle is broken." The stranger's gaze had lowered and he was studying her foot.

She grimaced, the pain was intense. "Yeah, I guess I'd better make a quick trip to the hospital. Just my luck. And here I thought I was going to get some sleep tonight for my big day tomorrow."

Maybe one of those nice doctors from the TV show ER *might be available,* she thought absently.

He looked directly at her then. His eyes were light. In

the darkness she couldn't tell which color, but she felt almost hypnotized as he held her gaze. He smiled and a weird sensation came over her. Woozy. Uncertain. Awkward.

Incredibly attracted to a man she's never seen before.

She shook her head to clear it. *Weird*.

"Let me take a look at it for you," he said.

Val shook her head. "Really, that's not necessary." But he'd already sunk to his knees and pulled up the right leg of her track pants, and was now running a warm hand down her calf. "Oh, well, okay then. If you insist."

Had she shaved her legs recently? She couldn't remember. She thought so. She'd tried out that depilatory lotion stuff. According to the packaging, it was supposed to last longer than just shaving. She was finding human maintenance to be extremely time-consuming, and in the case of the lotion—a bit goopy.

You didn't have to shave your legs in Heaven. Hair-free. All the time. If you wanted to be, that is. She frowned. Maybe she should add that tidbit to her notebook in case she forgot. She patted her pocket to feel the reassuring outline. Still there.

The cold wind touched her face and she was surprised that it didn't bother her. She looked up at the clear dark sky, at all the stars above, and wondered if anyone from Heaven was watching her right now. And, if so, what were they thinking?

All these thoughts helped distract her from the touch of the stranger's warm fingers as he probed her ankle. If she hadn't felt so uncomfortable with her current position, pressed up against a cold brick wall with an unfamiliar handsome man caressing her foot, she probably wouldn't have needed to distract herself. But there it was. She sniffed and felt in her pockets for a Kleenex, but came up empty. She probably should have bought more when she was at the drugstore.

After a moment she attempted to clear her throat. "How's it going down there?" Her words came out a little croaky.

"Just another moment. Almost got it."

"Almost got what?" Then she gasped and braced herself against the wall. "What are you doing?"

A warmth was spreading across the top of her foot and around her broken ankle. He'd slipped off her running shoe and had one hand on either side of her foot, raising it slightly off the ground. But it didn't hurt. Not at all. In fact it felt really good, all warm and tingly. Too good, in fact. She knew she shouldn't feel this good with some unknown man in a dark alley.

The stranger finally rose to his feet.

Val tried to smile at him and felt her cheeks twitch nervously. "Okay, well, that was . . . um . . . interesting. I think I need to leave now."

"Try the ankle."

"What?"

He smiled at her. "Your ankle. Try to put your weight on it."

She did, tentatively. When that didn't hurt she put all her weight on it. Then she hopped up and down on it. It didn't feel broken or even slightly sprained anymore. She stopped hopping.

And glanced at him with a small frown.

"How did you do that?"

His smile widened. "Do you feel better?"

Her frown deepened. "Yes."

"Then, you're welcome."

"I didn't say thank you."

"You're still welcome."

She glanced at the unconscious thug on the ground and her eyes narrowed. "How did you managed to launch him way over there, anyhow? Who are you, Batman or something?"

The handsome stranger's smile held. "No, Valerie, I'm not Batman. Unless you'd like me to be, of course. I'm sure I could scare up a cowl and cape if I needed to."

She tried to swallow the nervous lump forming in her throat. "How do you know my name?"

You will know a Tempter Demon when you see one.

A flame flickered to life in his hand. He held a lighter and with it he lit the cigarette he'd removed from his jacket's inner pocket. Val watched the tip of the cigarette glow red, a flickering glow that lingered in the stranger's eyes longer that it should have. "I know all about you, Valerie. Sorry it's taken me so long to show up. I was . . . unavoidably detained. Have you been waiting for me?"

Tempter Demons are assigned to lure fallen ones to Hell for an eternity of torturous servitude.

She racked her brain. What else did the scroll say?

Eat regularly. Three meals a day is standard for human sustenance.

That wasn't going to be very helpful.

She pressed her hands together to stop them from shaking. And she'd thought having to deal with a mugger was the worst thing that could happen to her that night?

The demon smoked his cigarette and waited patiently for her to find her voice again. But her voice had gone on vacation. Somewhere warm, with palm trees.

Just one more day, she thought miserably. *I only need one more day.* Why did he have to show up now?

Of course he was attractive. All Tempters were. In Heaven she'd heard all sorts of tales about demons from the other angels. She'd listened with distracted amusement, never thinking she'd ever have to personally face one. Otherwise, she might have paid more attention to what was said. Taken some notes, maybe. But, she knew Tempters had to be tempting. After all, it was their job, wasn't it?

How could she have been so out of it not to see this coming? Was she *that* sick?

TEMPTER DEMONS ARE VERY DANGEROUS. Their methods are underhanded and almost impossible to resist.

"Take it back," she finally said, her voice weak but present and accounted for.

"Take what back?"

"What you just did to my ankle."

He took another drag of his cigarette, then flicked it against the wall. "I don't know what you mean."

"I know what you are. I don't want to owe you anything. Take it back. Make it broken again. Please."

He smiled and tried to meet her eyes. But her eyes were shy—they weren't prepared to meet anyone tonight. Or maybe ever again.

"What I did was a favor for you. I expect nothing in return. Is it so wrong that I don't want to see you hurt?"

Val managed to laugh at that. Just a little. It came out sounding jerky and pathetic. "Right."

"My name is Nathaniel." He took a step closer to her.

She took a step back and felt the brick wall, cold and

unyielding behind her. "I'm happy for you. Leave me alone."

The demon pulled something out of his pocket. A cell phone. He flipped the lid open, pressed a few buttons, and looked at the display screen.

"According to this, your last name is Grace." He looked up from the phone and those dangerous eyes of his tried to catch her in their weirdly hypnotic gaze. "Valerie Grace is a very beautiful name."

"I'm going to leave now. Don't try to stop me."

He frowned, creasing that handsome face into a semi-serious expression and cocked his head to one side. "But we have so much to talk about."

"No, we don't." She tried to keep the fear that filled her chest from showing in her words.

"Yes, we most certainly do."

"No," she managed to put more emphasis on it this time. "We really don't." Her head ached, and she was overcome with exhaustion. She attempted to walk past him but he moved to block her escape.

"You don't belong here, Valerie."

"You're absolutely right. I don't. That's why I'm going back."

"To Heaven?" A grin appeared on his perfect lips. "Are you, now? And how are you going to manage that, little angel?"

Is he mocking me? she thought with a sudden jab of disdain.

"Because this is all a mistake, that's how. And I'm going to fix it. So you may as well not waste your time with me."

"A mistake, huh?" His grin widened. "Are you so sure about that?"

"Positive. I didn't do anything wrong." Her throat hurt as she said it. Her memories had grown so faulty that she was no longer positive that was one hundred percent true. However, he didn't have to know that, did he?

"If you haven't done anything wrong than you needn't be afraid of me."

"I'm not afraid." She jumped as he took another step closer to her. "I'm *not*."

"In fact, I can make things so much better. Just listen to what I have to offer and perhaps you won't need to spend another two months in a frozen wasteland like this."

She crossed her arms. "What part of 'I'm going back to Heaven' didn't you understand? Besides, I hear Niagara Falls is beautiful in the springtime. Lots of tulips and happy tourists. Not that I'm going to be here to witness it, that is."

She had to get out of there. From what she remembered about Tempters, they preyed on the weaknesses and insecurities of the newly fallen—loneliness, fear, naïvité. And, she had a very long and detailed list of human weaknesses that he could poke at, right at the top of which seemed to be her immediate need for a Kleenex.

"I can give you beauty for all eternity," he said. "You'll never be cold or alone, or want for anything ever again."

"Right now I want to be cold and alone. Please, just go away." Her voice caught on some unexpected emotion and she forced herself to keep from crying. She swallowed hard.

His brow furrowed and he took a step back at her expression. And as suddenly as his change of mood came on it disappeared, replaced by a confident, drop-dead sexy grin curling up one side of his full lips as he shook his head.

"I can't leave you alone, Valerie."

Don't look at him, she told herself.

She wondered what had taken him so long to show up. It would have made more sense for a Tempter to arrive early, while the fallen were still fresh and gullible. But she'd had two months to adjust to the unpleasantness of being human, albeit kicking and screaming, so there was no way he was going to tempt her.

No way.

Do not let your guard down when confronted by a tempter or you will regret it. Big time.

Then she made the mistake of fully looking into his eyes. Grayish blue, that was the color. He'd moved fully into the light of the lone street lamp so she could see him a bit better. Grayish-blue eyes framed with thick, dark lashes. Chiseled cheekbones led down to full lips. A square jaw with the slightest indication of a cleft. He looked like an angel, but she knew he was just the opposite. The balance. The flip side. And he was trouble.

He reached forward and stroked his fingertips along her cheek. She didn't try to move away and it wasn't just because she was pressed up against the hard wall. His touch left behind a warmth that made her entire body tingle, much as her foot had, but this time it seemed more . . . more *something*. He traced a finger along her bottom lip, probably feeling the remnants of the Chap Stick she'd applied before leaving her safe motel room to go on her fateful trip to the drugstore.

She couldn't stop staring into his eyes, and noticed her head was starting to feel fuzzy.

Just the head cold, she told herself. *Ignore it. Ignore him. Push him away right now.*

But she didn't. As she looked into his eyes she began to wonder if maybe he was right. What if they didn't take her back? What if she was stuck in this awful place? And not just Niagara Falls—the earthly realm in general. Full of its sickness, disappointment, pain, and misery. Maybe there *was* a better way. And if this beautiful stranger was by her side, then how bad could it possibly be?

No, what was she thinking? She didn't honestly believe that, did she? Was he using some kind of demon mojo on her? Maybe it worked like a few cocktails, loosening her inhibitions so she'd agree to something she wouldn't normally. And, if so . . . that was *totally* cheating.

"Just say the word, Valerie." His lips were only a few inches from hers. He moved to push the long, light blond hair out of her eyes and tuck it behind her ear that he then whispered into. "I can take you away from all of this."

Hmmm. The word. What was the word again?

He's a demon! her brain hollered. *And he's cheating. Demon mojo, remember? Ignore what he's saying. Get away from him right now!*

Abracadabra? Hocus-pocus, maybe? No, that was two words. What word was Nathaniel talking about?

Then it came to her. She knew what the word was. The only word that truly counted. And she could say it. So easily. So very easily.

Y-E-S.

"Say it." His voice was warm, open, soothing, and oh-so-tempting, as he leaned back to look at her. "And I will make all your troubles disappear."

She nodded slowly, trying to breathe him in through her stuffed nose. But as she opened her mouth to speak the word that would make it all better, to stop her pain and loneliness and suffering once and for all, she felt something rising inside of her—from deep within.

Deep inside her nostrils, that is.

Oh no, she thought. But it was too late.

She sneezed all over him.

Chapter Three

The expression on the demon's handsome face turned from romantic perfection to sheer disgust. He stepped back, wiping his face furiously with his sleeve.

Valerie wiped her nose on her own sleeve, feeling embarrassed.

"I have a cold," she explained.

He glared at her. "That is *disgusting*."

"Tell me about it."

"You sneezed on me."

She considered apologizing but decided against it. "Yes, I did."

"You could have warned me."

She shrugged. "It just came on. I didn't expect it. I'm sick. I sneeze. That's what humans do."

"It's disgusting."

"You said that already. Allow me not to bother you with my disgusting germs any more this evening." She turned to leave. "I think we're finished here."

He reached out to grab her shoulder. "We're not finished. Far from it."

Val shrugged his hand off her. "Oh we're finished, alright."

"You would choose life as a human—illness and discomfort, slaving away at a job you hate?"

She scowled at him, "I don't hate my job. Much."

He looked down at his cell phone and pressed a couple of buttons. "Let me tell you a little bit about yourself, Valerie Grace. You work and live at the Paradise Inn here in Niagara. You earn a very small salary in return for your free lodging. You consider very few people your friends, and you haven't shared your secret with anyone." He looked down at her. "No one to trust? Or no one you think would believe you?"

She didn't reply. He made her newly human life sound pathetic. Too bad it was all true.

"You try your best to be a good person, doing good deeds for whomever will let you, helping little old ladies cross the street and such." He laughed. "Good deeds, huh? Do you think they"—he pointed up—"care what you do anymore? After they've abandoned you? Turned their backs on your fate? But I'm here now. I can help you."

"I'm doing just fine on my own, thanks so much."

He was regaining his composure after the sneeze incident, slowly but surely, and he flashed her one of his wooze-inducing smiles. "You were just about to say yes to me only a moment ago."

She paused. Unfortunately he was right about that. Her sneeze must have been divine intervention, interrupting what would have been a terrible mistake she would have regretted for the rest of eternity. At least she'd like to think of it as divine intervention. But sometimes a sneeze was just a sneeze.

"That was a moment ago. Ancient history. Go away."

His smile vanished. "Stubborn girl. Why are you making this more difficult than it has to be?"

"I'm not a girl."

"No." His gaze tracked down her body again and she suddenly felt naked in front of him. "Definitely not a girl. A grown woman. What must it be like to be suddenly thrust into the form of a beautiful woman with needs and desires such as you've never known before? It has to be very difficult for you." He breathed the last few words against the side of her face, a warm touch in the cold night.

She shuffled away from him. "I get free cable. Don't worry about me, I'm managing just fine. I don't care what your stupid phone says."

The mugger groaned from the other side of the alley and pushed at the ground in an attempt to get up. Nathaniel grinned at Val, then closed the distance between him and the mugger in a step to grab him around the throat, lurching him to his semiconscious feet.

"And what of this pathetic creature? Would you have been doing just fine if I hadn't stopped him? What nasty things do you think he had planned for you, Valerie?"

"Dude!" The mugger blinked his eyes rapidly as Nathaniel increased the pressure on his windpipe. "What . . . are you . . . doing?"

"It would be better for everyone if I take care of this matter permanently," Nathaniel said. "Make sure that he never tries to hurt you ever again. Consider it a gift, just like the ankle."

She watched with growing horror as the mugger's eyes began to bug out, his face turning an unpleasant shade of purple under the street lamp. His feet raised off the ground so the only thing holding him up were Nathaniel's crushing hands. He began to twitch.

"Stop it," Val said softly, but she was ignored, the demon's attention now focused on his new entertainment.

She walked toward them. "Stop it!"

Nathaniel frowned. "Why should I? He's scum. He deserves to die."

"Let him go. I mean it."

One thing she remembered from being an angel was the knowledge that every human life was precious. Everyone deserved a chance to change. She frankly didn't care what her attacker had tried to do. She didn't care what kind of a person he was, she wasn't going to stand by and let Nathaniel murder him just to prove a point.

She clawed at Nathaniel's hands, then balled her fist to hit him hard in the shoulder. "Let him go!" she yelled.

"You truly want me to let him go?" Nathaniel's amusement at her feeble attempts to stop him was obvious.

"What are you, deaf? Yes!"

"Very well."

The demon threw the mugger to the ground. He stayed on his knees for a moment, relearning how to breathe, then glanced up at them, the fear naked on his face.

"Leave my friend alone," Nathaniel said. "Or I'll find you and finish what I started here."

The man blinked a couple of times, then scrambled to his feet, backing slowly out of the alley while nodding like a lunatic. Then he turned and scampered away.

Nathaniel looked at Val and smiled.

She didn't return the expression. "I'm not your friend."

"I let him go, just as you wished."

"It wasn't a wish, it was a request. Now I request, yet again, that you leave me alone."

"I can't do that, I'm afraid."

"Why not?" She felt so frustrated with the situation that her eyes filled with tears.

He hesitated for a split second. "I . . . I just can't. And you're wasting your breath in asking, so you may as well stop." He stepped toward her and managed to capture her in his gaze again. Even with the knowledge that he was a dangerous demon assigned to lure her to Hell, she couldn't resist staring into those gorgeous eyes.

Helpless.

Afraid.

Ever so slightly turned on.

No, scratch that, she thought. *Just the first two.*

"I'm going back to Heaven," she said firmly.

"No you're not. You're going to be with me. I'm going to take you to a place that can be whatever you want it to be. Don't be fooled by what you've heard. It's wonderful, really." He pressed her up against the wall, his body a hot line against her own. "Just say the word, little angel."

Not good. Not good at all.

She sniffed. "I do need to tell you something . . . Nathaniel."

"Yes? I'm listening."

"I'm . . . I think I'm going to sneeze again."

He took an immediate step back, letting go of her completely.

But there was no sneeze. She didn't like to lie if she could help it, but in this case she was willing to let it pass.

Nathaniel looked very confused, then fixed her with a

small scowl. "You don't have to make this so difficult, you know."

"Neither do you. You can just move on. Leave me be. I'm sure there are others for you to tempt."

He shook his head. "I don't understand this. You should already be mine."

"No, I shouldn't be."

He frowned at her. "This isn't over, you know. I'll be back."

"I won't be here."

He gave her a smile that looked forced, since the frown still furrowed his otherwise perfect forehead. "Oh, yes you will. See you soon, Valerie Grace."

Then he vanished in a column of flame.

She scooted over to pick up her dropped bag of NyQuil and clutched it tightly to her chest as she stood all alone in the alley for a moment. She knew he wasn't lying. He'd be back. She had a suspicion that demons never gave up easily. If they failed on an assignment, there would probably be hell to pay.

Hell to pay. She was so funny.

She laughed until it turned into sobs that echoed softly off the cold brick walls.

Heaven had to take her back. She didn't want to have to face Nathaniel ever again.

"What do you mean I can't come back?" Val wailed.

"What part of 'you can't come back' don't you understand?"

The voice was small, girlish and childlike, but it spoke in a commanding, matter-of-fact manner.

"But—"

"The answer is final."

Val stared at the child psychic, through whom she was speaking to an angel by the name of Garry—assistant guardian to the gates of Heaven. He did most of the PR work Up There. They were acquaintances. Friends even. They'd, at times, commiserated about their Heavenly jobs. Garry usually complained that he was still only the "assistant" guardian after an eternity of doing the same job. Val simply listened and smiled. That's why she was thrilled that he was the one Seraphina ended up channeling. But now he spoke to her in a condescending, businesslike manner, very unlike the way a friend should sound.

Maybe the memory of her relationship with Garry was faulty, she thought. Lately her memories had been faulty a lot, and were fading quicker than she ever would have expected. She was depending on her notes to see her through this until things went back to normal.

And her chance to get back to normal was right here, sitting cross-legged in front of her.

The nine-year-old psychic wore a pink Powerpuff Girls T-shirt on top of blue jeans that had little daisies embroidered on the pockets. Her blond hair was done in perfect ringlets. She sucked on a lollipop—purple for grape-flavored—before the lights had dimmed and she'd gone into her white-eyeballed trance.

Up until then Val wasn't sure this was all for real. But the white-eyeballed thing would be pretty hard to fake.

The office they sat in was more like a lounge, if a child had designed it with a very high budget. A big screen TV sat opposite them hooked up to several high-end video game players. The couch Val sat on looked like a large fluffy pink flower. The carpeting was white and pink and

green, with swirls and dots. The air freshener smelled like
licorice.

Despite the odd surroundings, there was no doubt she
was talking to Garry. Val's memory was iffy, but she felt
certain it was him. The question was, why was he giving
her such a hard time?

"Garry," she leaned over so her gaze was in line with
Seraphina's white eyeballs. "Come on. We're buddies,
right?" She waited for confirmation but there was nothing. "There's got to be something you can do."

"There isn't."

"But I didn't do anything wrong!"

The eyeballs blinked. "Really? Is that what you think?"

"Of course."

The eyeballs shifted back and forth as if the little girl
were reading something. "No, the scrollwork is all in
order. You were kicked out for a very good reason, Valerie. A very good reason indeed."

This news felt like a slap in the face. "What? What did
I do? Whatever it was, I'm sure it was just an accident."

The eyeballs rolled. "This was no accident."

"What was it?"

"Okay"—a corner of Seraphina's rosebud mouth
twisted up—"I'll give you a hint. There are seven of them,
and you're guilty of one. A big one."

She shook her head, which had started to throb.
"Seven? Seven *what*?"

"Come on. You know this."

"Stop playing games with me, Garry. I mean it."

"Seven . . . *sev* . . ." Garry sighed when she didn't
immediately pick up on his verbal clues. "Gosh, Valerie,
you used to be way brighter than this. Being human really

dumbs you up, doesn't it? *Seven deadly sins.* You know, the Big Seven?"

Her mouth dropped open. "But an angel can't commit a deadly sin or they're . . ."

"Uh-huh. Bingo."

She racked her brain. A deadly sin? Her? Impossible. "Which one?"

"I'll give you another clue."

"Garry, this is getting annoying. I don't know how long I'll be able to keep this channel open and I need you to—"

"It starts with a *P.*" Seraphina grinned perfect little white teeth.

"P?" Val thought about that, and ticked off the sins one by one in her mind. Not greed, or gluttony, or sloth . . . she certainly kept busy enough Up There to not be accused of laziness . . . not wrath or envy . . . not lust . . .

She paused on that one. No, she hadn't met Nathaniel until *after* she'd fallen.

But that was beside the point.

"Pride?" she finally said. "Are you kidding me?"

Seraphina nodded her head and her flaxen curls bounced jauntily. "You got it. But being that it's the only *P* sin on the list, it was a bit of a gimme."

"Pride?" she repeated, incredulously.

"You know what they say about pride, don't you Val?"

She shook her head, feeling numb.

"It comes before a fall. Get it? A fall?"

Val wondered, if she wrapped her hands around the little girl's neck, would Garry feel it in Heaven? She managed to restrain herself.

"Yes," Garry continued after he'd finished chuckling at his less-than-amusing joke. "According to your file, the pride you felt doing your angel duties, especially after winning the angel-of-the-month award a while back, was enough to get you tossed. Sorry, I'm just reporting what it says here."

Her notebook was out on her lap and she jotted down what he was saying. "I really won the angel-of-the-month award?"

He sighed. "Yes. I can't believe that you don't remember that. You went on and on about it for ages."

"And what exactly did I do again? My job?"

A heavier sigh now. "After the humans came through the gate and finished with me, you showed them around Heaven. Made them feel welcome. Listened to the stories of their lives without looking too bored."

She nodded as she listened and wrote. She remembered that. She'd always found it interesting, fascinating even to meet her assignments and help them adjust to their new and perfect afterlives—and more than happy that she hadn't had to live on Earth as a human, too, after hearing their stories—but to say she took pride in it . . .

Well, she did feel she did a very good job. And, hello? Angel-of-the-month award?

But, was that pride?

Geesh. It wasn't like wrath, or anything. Pride was such a tiny little deadly sin. Barely even worth noticing. Hardly something to warrant such a miserable punishment.

"It's not all that bad," Garry's words cut through her thoughts. "You've always seemed so enamored by the humans, interested in the lives they'd lived . . ."

"It doesn't mean I wanted to become one," she cut him off. "Like, *ever.*"

"Well, you should have thought about that before the whole *pride* thing."

"Garry," she said, and hated that there was a distinct whine to her voice now. "You have to do something. If I was too proud I'll make up for it. I don't want to be human. It's horrible. You have no idea what it's like down here. It's rainy, miserable, desperate. I'm sick, too. There's phlegm. There's no phlegm in Heaven. Phlegm is a very bad thing. And . . . and I'm scared. Garry, I'm so scared and lonely and—" She broke off.

And there's a really hot demon who wants to add me to his collection.

Seraphina pursed her little lips and Garry spoke. "There's nothing I can do. The scroll's official."

She frowned. "Has anyone been keeping track of my good deeds? It's not just to kiss up, either. I'm like a machine of goodness. That old lady I helped cross the street the other day? That should be worth something. I still have the bruise from where she hit me with her cane. But she made it to the other side in one piece and that was a very busy road! And, come on, the whole killer whale tank thing? Was that your idea? I won't hold a grudge, I promise!"

"There are worse punishments than being human, you know."

She sighed. Her words were wasted on him. "Easy for you to say."

"Hey, maybe in seventy years when you've helped enough old ladies across the street you might be forgiven. When you, you know, *die*. Other than that, I'm not seeing any other way for you to get back here."

"This is not helping. I want to speak to the boss. Is he available? Can somebody get him?"

Seraphina's eyes widened. "Are you kidding? He is very busy, you know. Besides, speaking to fallen ones is not something He would be interested in doing. Ever."

"Can't you just make an exception? For me?"

"No way. Not a chance. Look, Val, got to go. No offense, but I can't spend all day talking to a fallen one. My review's coming up." Seraphina's eyes began to close.

"Wait . . . Garry, please . . ."

Her eyes snapped back open. "Yes?"

Valerie sniffed, and it wasn't from only the head cold anymore. Her eyes stung with tears threatening to fall. "Please, there's a Tempter Demon after me. He wants to lure me to Hell. You have to help me. How can I make him leave me alone?"

A grin spread across her face. "A Tempter? For real? I've heard stories, and all, but never seen one. Is it true that they're incredibly good-looking?"

"Garry!"

"Sorry. Look, here's the drill. Demons exist for the same reason angels exist—to maintain the balance between good and evil. I can't do anything about it. Nobody can. It's all up to you to resist this demon no matter what he tells you. Do so and he'll eventually give up." Seraphina blinked. "Although, it's just a theory."

Val pressed her lips together, hard. She wanted to beg, but she wouldn't let herself. She was about to say something else, anything else to keep the connection between her and Garry open, but Seraphina closed her eyes and she knew that was it. It was over.

She exhaled, a long shuddering sound.

Seraphina blinked her clear blue eyes, shaking the remainder of her trance away.

"Thirsty!" she yelled.

The door opened, casting a beam of light into her eyes, which had become accustomed to the darkened room. The silhouette of Becky, Seraphina's redheaded, business-suited assistant entered, carrying a can of 7Up with a pink bendy straw. She handed it to the little girl who snatched it away and took a sip. Becky glanced at Val.

"I trust everything went well?"

It was thanks to Becky—though perhaps *thanks* wasn't the right word—that she'd been able to make her appointment with the highly booked child psychic. Appointments with Seraphina had a four-month waiting list. She'd met Becky through her brother, Brian—an amateur wizard who owned a local comic book store where she'd gone to buy an issue of *Batman* after liking the television show so much. He'd taken an immediate liking to her. Kind of like when a dog takes a liking to someone's leg, as she'd witnessed happen to poor Reggie the other day just outside of the motel. But Brian was fairly harmless, and his sister just happened to work for Seraphina. Opportunity presenting itself in mysterious and, in this case, *geeky* ways.

Val stood on shaky legs and tried to give Becky an equally shaky smile. "Not as well as I hoped it would."

"That's too bad." Becky glanced at the girl with a look that could only be described as fearful. "I'm so sorry. Was she being difficult?"

"No, she's very good. It's just that—"

"You," Seraphina said.

They looked at her.

"You." Seraphina nodded at Becky.

She forced a smile. "Yes?"

Seraphina held up the can of pop in her tiny hand. Her fingernails were painted bright pink. "This isn't diet. I wanted diet."

Becky sighed. "But, you don't *need* diet. You're not *on* a diet."

The little girl narrowed her blue eyes. "Are you arguing with me?"

"No. I'm just saying that—"

"I want diet." She stamped her foot. "Get me a Diet 7Up *now*."

Becky shrugged at Val. "Duty calls."

"NOW!!"

She practically jumped as Seraphina shoved the full can of pop at her and, without another word, scurried out of the room. Val turned her wide-eyed gaze toward the little girl whom she decided just might be related to Lucifer himself.

Seraphina smiled up at her. "You're an angel."

Val's eyes widened. "What did you say?"

"An angel." She plunked her Powerpuff Girls–attired self down on the plush sofa in the middle of the room. "But you're not anymore. I have an angel Barbie doll, you know."

"You know I'm an angel?"

"My Barbie has big wings. White ones. With sparkles."

"How do you know I'm an angel? Did you hear everything I said to Garry?"

"Who's Garry?" She scratched her arm absently.

Val crouched down in front of the girl. "This is wonderful! I haven't been able to tell anyone else, you know, because they'd think I'm nuts. But for you to know I'm an angel—I feel so relieved that somebody knows. This is so wonderful! What do you know about angels? Can you help me out? Do you know how I can go back to Heaven?"

"What color were your wings?"

Val frowned and grabbed her notebook, shuffling through the pages for a moment. "Actually, I don't think I had wings. Nope"—she tapped the page where she'd written "No Wings"—"I didn't."

She looked disappointed. "Why not?"

Her frown deepened as she searched her brain for the information she knew she possessed and then shuffled forward a few more pages in her notebook. "Um . . . not all angels need them. Only the ones that travel a lot."

"Travel where?"

"Wherever they're needed. Heaven's a big place. Bigger than you could ever imagine."

"Cool."

"So do you think you can help me?"

"What?" Seraphina looked distracted. And a bit bored.

"You know, I'm an angel and I want to go back to Heaven," Val was feeling a bit frustrated talking to the little girl. "Can you help me?"

"Nope."

"Why not?"

She shrugged. "Don't wanna."

Val stood up. "You *don't wanna*?"

"Nope."

She glanced over at the door. "Well, that's not very nice, is it? Maybe I can get Becky to say something to you to make you behave a little more politely. How long does it take to get a can of 7Up, anyhow?"

"It's not over."

"Darn right it's not." Val continued to stare at the closed door.

Seraphina suddenly grabbed her wrist and she turned back around. "The time has come. The change must be made."

The girl's eyes were fully white again and she stared at Val with a blank expression on her face. Her iron grip was strong enough to bruise.

"Garry?" Val grimaced from the pain. "Is that you again?"

"There is one like you to help ease your way. And another who is not like you, though you may believe differently."

"Garry? What are you talking about?"

"Fragments of light once fell to the ground like snow. You must watch and protect it. Beware of those who prefer the darkness, though one is drawn to the light. The balance must be made right."

"Garry? Why are you rhyming?"

Seraphina blinked, her eyes remaining entirely white, then sighed heavily. "No. I'm not Garry. Are you listening, or what?"

"Sorry. Please continue. What were you saying about snowflakes?"

"Fragments of light as snow. It's a metaphor. Maybe you should be writing this down."

"Good idea." Val produced a pen and turned to a blank page in her notebook. "Please continue."

Whomever Seraphina was now channeling nodded. "Follow what is stolen to find the answers you seek. Trust your heart, Valerie Grace."

"Who are you?"

"That isn't important right now. What is important is that you trust your heart."

Val blinked and stopped writing for a moment to look up at the girl. "If I trust my heart can I come back to Heaven?"

Seraphina sighed again but didn't answer the question. "To recap: making changes, another like you, darkness drawn to the light, follow what is stolen, maintain the balance, yada yada. Got it?"

"I think so." Valerie's wrist really hurt now from being clutched by the incredibly strong possessed child. "Anything else?"

"No, that's about it. I can't tell you everything, you know. Good luck. You're going to need it."

She blinked and finally let go of Val's arm, just as the door opened behind them.

"Sorry it took me so long." Becky had a rosy flush to her cheeks and was breathing heavily. "I had to go all the way to the downstairs fridge to get this."

Seraphina, her eyes back to normal, clapped her hands happily and took the new can of pop, this time the bendy straw was blue. Val frowned at her. The little girl didn't seem to remember what just happened. Very strange.

What *had* just happened? Who had she just spoken to? And what on earth were they babbling about?

She wasn't exactly sure. But all of this dealing with psychics and angels was making her thirsty.

Chapter Four

———～———

Val sat, shivering like a nervous Chihuahua, on a park bench by the edge of the Falls and stared at the lightly falling snow as if it would start talking to her any minute.

She was supposed to guard snow?

Metaphor. Pieces of light as snow.

What was that supposed to mean, anyhow? It was just snow.

And what had Seraphina said about darkness drawn to the light? *Stupid.*

Everything is stupid, she thought. *Including myself.* Especially for thinking she could find an easy answer to all of her problems. Served her right for watching so much television in the last two months. On TV, everyone's problems got wrapped up in the course of an episode, and if it was going to take two episodes, there'd be a "to be continued" tag, letting the audience know to hang in there.

Her "to be continued" had been put on indefinate hiatus. No happy ending in sight. No promises. Not even a comforting *maybe.*

And Garry was supposed to be her friend? Some friend. Even as she thought it, she knew she couldn't blame him for her troubles. She'd been kicked out for the reason he'd given her. Pride. Okay. Didn't make sense to her, but at least she had a reason.

That still didn't mean she was giving up.

It didn't mean she was making peace with being a human. No way.

But for the time being she was going to sit on her bench, slowly turning into a blond Popsicle, and feel very sorry for her sad self. Maybe she could be decorated like a Christmas tree. She could become another one of Niagara's tourist attractions. Sounded like a plan.

A couple walked past her with bright shiny smiles on their faces, colorful scarves at their necks. They gave off a "we're totally in love" vibe. If Val had any extra money she would have bet all of it that underneath their clasped together gloved hands were wedding rings bright and shiny enough to match their smiles. Newlyweds, probably. *Isn't that just the most adorable thing?* she thought.

Blah.

"Hey gorgeous," a familiar voice said to her left.

She forced herself to look up. "Hi, Reggie."

He crossed his arms. "Yeah, you look *really* happy."

"That's funny, because I don't *feel* really happy."

"Well, then it's good that I was being sarcastic." He studied her for a moment, then shook his head. "You're lucky you're naturally hot, because you look like hell today."

"Gee, thanks a lot."

"Why are you sitting here all alone?"

She nodded at the Falls. "I'm considering throwing myself over."

He laughed. "I think there's a law that says you can only do that once a month. You already had your chance."

She scowled at him. "That was to help somebody."

"You mean the guy you pushed into the water and almost killed? The one we had to convince not to press charges against you?"

"He was trying to kill himself."

"He was a tourist taking a picture. Or didn't you notice the camera? And the wife? And the kids?"

"I was just trying to help."

He smiled. "I know, and that's what I adore about you. You're always helping people. But you got to realize that some people just don't want any help. Even if it's from a hot blonde. Realize that and you'll save yourself a lot of trouble."

She frowned. A change of subject would be a good idea.

"Where's Claire?" she asked. "Aren't you two joined at the hip?"

Reggie seemed to back away a bit at the mention of his girlfriend's name. "Oh, Claire? *My* Claire? She's . . . she's around."

"I'm sure she is."

His eyes got big. "You've seen her? Where?" He looked around nervously.

Val stared at him. "Oh no. What did you do *this* week to get her mad?"

He took a deep breath and let it out slowly so she could see a puff of frozen air appear as if he were smoking a cigarette. For a second it reminded her of Nathaniel.

"It was a total misunderstanding," Reggie said.

"What was?"

"She thinks I cheated on her."

"Oh?" She raised her eyebrows. "Why would she think something like that?"

He rubbed the side of his face, a nervous gesture, and looked away.

"You didn't," Val scolded. "You cheated on Claire? How could you?"

"I didn't cheat. Not technically, anyhow."

"Not technically? What does that mean?"

"I was at the casino." He gestured with his head toward the direction of Casino Niagara. "I'd had a few beers. I won a hand of blackjack and I sort of gave the dealer a big kiss. Tongues *may* have been involved."

"You kissed a blackjack dealer."

He looked sheepish. "Got her number, too. But I've already thrown it away. I never would have called her. It was just one of those things."

Val took a deep breath. "Well, that sounds fairly harmless. Just a mistake."

"Harmless if Claire's friend hadn't been walking past. Told her everything. Embellished some stuff. Now she wants to kill me."

She shook her head. "You really shouldn't have kissed the dealer."

"But she was so hot."

"You're not helping matters."

"I'm a rat. I'll admit it. When I've got a good thing, I'll always do something to screw it up. And Claire is the best thing that's ever happened to me."

"You need to tell *her* that. Apologize. Take her out for dinner. Fall to the floor and beg her forgiveness."

Reggie shook his head vigorously. "No way. I'm not seeing her until she's calmed down. She's a witch."

Val rolled her eyes. "You're the one who played kissy-face with a blackjack dealer and *she's* the witch? Sure, that sounds like a fair assessment."

"No, I didn't mean it as an insult. She *is* a witch. Like 'eye of newt' witch? She has a ton of books on the subject that make me very nervous. If she finds me in her current state of mind . . . well, let's just say I prefer my genitalia in its current configuration."

"Claire is a witch?" She was surprised Reggie seemed ready to believe it—full-fledged humans rarely accepted oddities unless they were shaken right in front of their faces on a regular basis.

The fact that Claire may or may not have been a real witch didn't scare Val in the slightest. There were more paranormal elements in the earthly realm than most humans knew about. In fact, there was a special section of Heaven where witches and other non-evil creatures like werewolves went to after death. The angels called it the "Hair and Scare" area, but just among themselves. Besides, most witches were very salt-of-the-earth and do-no-evil gals. No green faces and broomstick-riding. At least, for the most part.

Although thinking her boyfriend was a cheater might make any girl go a little green in the gills. Broomstick optional.

"Witchcraft is her latest hobby," Reggie said nervously. "She's been buying candles like crazy lately."

"Scented?"

"Some."

"Then I don't think you should be out in the open like this. You should probably hide."

"Yes. Hide. I'm going to go hide now. At the casino."

"I'll see you back at the motel later."

He nodded. "Do you think you could talk to her?"

"Huh?"

"Talk to Claire. She likes you. Just tell her that I was a rat but I didn't mean to do anything wrong, that it was a big mistake. That she's the only one for me. Say something nice, all pretty and poetic and sincere. Make it up if you have to."

"And why would I want to do that?"

He paused, brow lowered, then he looked at Val with a smile. "Consider it your good deed for the day."

She stared at him for a moment before she burst out laughing. "You have a lot of nerve asking me to do this."

"So that's a yes?"

"I'll talk to her. But you'll owe me big time for this."

His smile widened. "And will you throw her over the Falls if she tries to hurt me?"

"Do you want me to?"

He opened his mouth to say something, but must have had second thoughts. "Of course not."

"Good answer."

"Val, maybe if she doesn't take me back, you and me should go out some time. There's a little place in Tonawanda that has great lobster."

"Please tell me you're kidding."

His smile held but he didn't say anything else.

She pointed in a direction far away from her. "Go."

He went, but looked over his shoulder to blow her a kiss first.

What a jerk, she thought. But she was still smiling. He'd managed to pull her out of her current funk a little bit. Kicking and screaming, but she did feel better.

She was sure it would pass.

Val trudged back to the Paradise Inn, which was a ten minute walk up Clifton Hill, past wax museums, souvenir shops, restaurants, and around the bend.

On the way back she'd come up with a plan. And she was going to follow through with it right away before she chickened out.

There was one person in the earthly realm whom she'd come to trust completely. Somebody who'd never been anything but nice and kind and warm and thoughtful with her. Somebody who'd made the past two months of being human nearly bearable.

Even though he made her clean rooms.

Mr. Barlow. She absolutely adored the old man. She was going to tell him that she was a fallen angel. He would believe her, she knew it. Then she'd have someone who knew what she was—the fact that Seraphina also knew was, sadly, little comfort to her—and help her get back. She wasn't sure exactly how he could help, but getting this huge weight off her mind would be a wonderful thing.

It made perfect sense to her.

Her stomach growled. She hadn't eaten all day. She would talk to Barlow, clear her mind, then head over to McDonald's for dinner.

That was the plan.

She moved past the rickety old patio furniture strewn about in the small courtyard in the middle of the U-shaped motel, sidestepping the pool that apparently hadn't been in working order for more than five years and was currently covered by a thick layer of leaves and snow. She marched right to the manager's office, her plan clear in her mind, and pushed open the door. A little bell above it jingled. Nobody was at the desk.

"Mr. Barlow?"

No answer. She could hear soft music coming from his living area behind the office on the other side of a beaded curtain, so she moved toward that and pushed the curtain aside.

Barlow's living room was small. Drab carpeting. A beat up La-Z-Boy armchair was positioned in front of a television with rabbit ears. A few copies of *Reader's Digest* sat on the chipped coffee table. The room felt comfortable, but old and tired.

At the moment, though, there were a couple of things in the room that *didn't* look old and tired. A balloon, for one. Red and shiny and tied with a long yellow ribbon that trailed down to the floor. Printed on the balloon was HAPPY ANNIVERSARY. It was a smear of color in the colorless room.

Barlow himself sat in the armchair, staring at Val in surprise. The pretty woman holding a cake and standing in front of Barlow didn't look surprised. Which was odd since she was topless. Val would have expected a half-naked woman carrying a cake would look surprised that someone just walked in on her unannounced.

They all stared at each other for a moment as the radio played "Do Ya Think I'm Sexy?" by Rod Stewart.

Val finally averted her gaze. "Awkward," she said aloud. "Sorry, I didn't know you had company."

"This is"—Barlow gestured at the woman—"Alexa. She's . . . um, a friend of mine."

"I can see that," Val glanced briefly at the woman. "I've, uh . . . never seen you around here before."

Barlow cleared his throat. "No, Alexa hasn't visited me for several months."

"Charmed," Alexa said. She put down the cake, then retrieved her blouse from the floor.

"I, uh, wanted to talk to you. But—" Val glanced at the balloon, then again at the now thankfully dressed Alexa, "I'm thinking it can wait a bit. Should I be saying 'happy anniversary' to you today?"

Barlow's gaze shifted to the woman, then he sighed heavily and shook his head. He stood up from the chair, walked over to the ribbon, and pulled the balloon down from the ceiling.

"Not necessary," he said, then popped the balloon between his palms.

Val jumped at the sudden noise. "Bad balloon?"

He let the limp piece of rubber fall to the carpet.

Alexa was now pouting. "Baby, why did you do that?"

He rolled his eyes. "How many times do I have to ask you not to call me 'baby'?"

Her pout deepened.

Val was very confused. Barlow was an old man, easily in his mid-seventies. His face was deeply lined, and his eyes always looked as if they'd seen too much and just wanted to stay shut. His hair was thick but white, just like his eyebrows, and he wore black-rimmed glasses. She'd seen a few pictures of Barlow in his twenties, and he'd been a hottie in his time. That time had passed.

Now he was a nice, harmless old man.

A nice, harmless old man who had a gorgeous woman who didn't look a day over twenty-five calling him *baby*? Maybe he was filthy rich and she just didn't know it.

But as confused as she was by the two of them, it was none of her business.

Val shifted nervously from one foot to the other. "I'll just get out of your hair and let you get back to . . . whatever it was you were doing."

"Are you all right?" Barlow asked, his brow wrinkling even further.

She shrugged. "I've been better. I'll talk to you later." She glanced at Alexa again. "If you aren't too tired, that is."

Alexa grinned at her. She was really gorgeous with long, raven-colored hair, a tight black skirt, and four-inch spiked heels that showed off mile-long legs. Creamy flawless skin, full red lips. The woman positively glowed.

And I clean toilets, Val thought.

"I'll call first," she said.

"Valerie—" Barlow began as she turned away. "Uh . . . very well. We'll speak later."

"Valerie?" Alexa repeated. "As in, Valerie *Grace?*"

Val glanced at her. "That's right."

She smiled. "*Very* interesting."

"Alexa . . ." Barlow's voice held an edge of warning. "Leave her alone."

Her smile widened. "Valerie, dear, would you care for a piece of cake?"

Val's stomach growled. The cake did look pretty tasty.

"Well," she glanced at Barlow. "So . . . uh, you didn't tell me. What's the occasion? Whose anniversary is it, anyhow?"

"Ours." Alexa moved toward the cake and started cutting it up with a big knife.

" 'Ours,' as in who?"

"Me and Barty. It's our fiftieth anniversary." Alexa slipped the first piece of chocolate cake onto a paper plate and brought it to Val.

She frowned with confusion. "Fifty what?"

"Alexa," Barlow growled. "I'm warning you."

She laughed. "Fifty years of being together."

"Fifty years?" Val shook her head. "How is that possible?"

"Valerie, dear." Alexa smiled and shook her pretty head. Val looked into her eyes and saw the flames dance behind them. "Haven't you figured it out yet? I'm Barty's assigned Tempter. He's a fallen angel just like you."

Chapter Five

—∽—

"Huh?" Val squeaked. "He's a what?"

"A fallen angel," Alexa repeated. "You look surprised."

Val stared at Barlow with wide eyes. He was a fallen angel just like her? When did that happen? Did she miss the memo? No, it was impossible. She would have known something like that, wouldn't she? Sense it somehow?

A fallen angel just as she was.

And Alexa was a demon just like Nathaniel?

No way.

Barlow didn't say anything to either deny or agree with what Alexa said. He went back to his armchair and sat down heavily.

Val's mouth felt dry and her heart pounded hard and fast.

Alexa looked at her appraisingly. "So I see that Nathaniel hasn't succeeded yet?"

"What?"

"Nathaniel. He must have made contact with you by now. Didn't he manage to sweep you off your feet?"

Val turned her stunned gaze to the beautiful demon. "Not even close."

"Is it perhaps that he's simply not your type?" Alexa walked a slow circle around Val, looking her up and down, then smiled. "I find that hard to believe. He's quite something, don't you think? Tall, dark, and handsome. A voice that melts against your skin like chocolate. Full lips meant to be kissed. A body meant to be worshipped. But if he's not your type . . ." She trailed off expectantly and raised an eyebrow.

Val swallowed. There was no way she was going to admit that everything Alexa had just said was true. She'd only been human for two months, but if she had to admit to having a "type," then Nathaniel was it. But, nope. She wasn't going to admit that. "He's not, okay?"

Her smile held. "Then perhaps *I* should pay you a visit some time, instead. It would be my pleasure."

"Alexa," Barlow said. "That's enough."

She moved her flame-filled gaze from Val's to look at the old man. "I was simply trying to be helpful."

"I find that difficult to believe. Just go away."

She pouted, and her hurt expression didn't look completely put on. "But it's our anniversary."

He stood up quickly to stare at her, but started coughing so violently that he had to cling to the side of his chair. Alexa rushed to his side.

"Baby, are you all right?" She murmured, stroking his hair, his arm, his back. "It's okay. I'm here."

Val frowned at her and felt a flood of concern for Barlow. That was not a healthy cough.

He finally got it under control, straightened up and shrugged her hands off him. "I'm fine."

"No you're not."

"I said, I'm *fine*."

Alexa sniffed and looked at Val who was surprised to see tears in her eyes. "He won't admit it to anyone but he's gravely ill."

"Alexa," he growled.

She shook her head. "You are. You can't fool me. I can see the disease eating away at you. I've tried to ignore it, but I can't anymore. I won't ignore it. You're sick. You need to use my gift before it's too late." She moved toward him again, but he held his hand out to stop her from getting any closer.

"I'm not promising anything. Leave."

She sniffed. "I'll return."

"I know."

She glanced at Val. "Try to talk some sense into him, would you? He can either finally agree to come with me and I will take care of him and ensure nothing bad ever happens to him, or he can make use of the key. There isn't much time left."

Val opened her mouth to say something, although she wasn't sure what, when Alexa disappeared behind a column of flame leaving Barlow and her alone.

He'd pulled a handkerchief from his pocket and coughed into it some more. When he took it from his mouth Val could see a spot of red on it. Her heart clenched.

"You need to see a doctor."

"No doctors. I'm fine. Just a bit of a cold is all," he murmured and wiped his mouth. "Sounds like your cold has cleared up finally. It was a bad one, wasn't it?"

It was true. Ever since Nathaniel healed her ankle last night, her head cold congestion had become less and less . . . congested. She felt almost completely healthy again.

"You're a fallen angel?" she blurted out.

He didn't say anything for a long moment. Then finally, "Yes, I am."

"And you knew who I am? What I was?"

He nodded.

She let out a long, shuddery sigh. "Why didn't you tell me?"

"There was no reason to."

At first, Val felt incredibly angry that he hadn't told her. Two months and he hadn't said a word when it must have been obvious how distraught she was over her situation. But the anger passed as soon as it had appeared, replaced with a overwhelming wave of complete and utter joy.

A wide smile spread across her features and she ran to him to hug him tightly. "This is so wonderful," she gushed. "I'll never forgive you for not telling me, but now I know. Now everything is going to be better."

Barlow struggled to free himself from Val's grasp and crooked an eyebrow at her. "Is that so?"

"How long have you been here, anyhow?"

"Fifty years."

"And you've known Alexa for that much time?"

"She made her presence known to me almost immediately."

Val's mind raced. "And in all that time you've been able to resist her?"

He looked thoughtful. "I suppose I'm a very stubborn person. Once my mind was made up that I did not want to buy into her fictional tales of how perfect an existence I would have in Hell, there was nothing more she could say to me that would have convinced me otherwise. Frankly,

I'm quite surprised that she's never given up despite my absolute determination to deny her. Now I must simply tolerate her attentions."

Val almost grinned. "Yeah, that must be difficult. She's so ugly."

"I won't say that it hasn't been difficult at times. And I'll admit that I've come close to allowing her to affect me—to tempt me. Mostly in my younger days. But I will say that I am lucky. Demons are gifted with the ability to charm their prey to a certain extent. It's similar to hypnosis. It isn't enough to make the fallen one agree immediately, but it can tilt the scales to the Tempter's benefit. Thankfully I have been mostly immune to this particular demon ability."

Val nodded her head. "Yes, I think Nathaniel tried something like that with me last night. Made my head all cloudy. Made me think that being tempted might be a good thing." She frowned. "I should be mad at you, you know. You could have warned me."

"If you were meant to be tempted, than you would have been. No warning would have made a difference. I am proud that you were able to resist him. Very proud indeed. But you've only seen him the once? Do you think you'll be able to continue in your resistance?"

Resistance is futile, Val thought.

Star Trek. Very addictive television show.

"Probably. I mean, yes. Definitely. No problem whatsoever." She sighed heavily. "What's the deal with these Tempters, anyhow? What's in it for them if they bring one of us over to the dark side? I don't get it."

Barlow cut himself a piece of the anniversary cake and began to pick at it. "It's their job. Tempters tempt."

"I don't want to see him again," Val said. Would she be able to resist him again? She thought she would. But fifty years? That was too much. Barlow was obviously much stronger than she was, or ever would be. "I want to go back. I didn't have any problems like this in Heaven. It was perfect and wonderful, and I loved my job . . . not that I don't like working for you, but it's not the same. I know my memories are fading. They probably fade on purpose so we don't miss it so much, right? Is that how it is? Well, I don't want to forget! I don't want to forget any of it. Now that I've found you, we can go back together. There has to be a way."

Just thinking about it made tears start to well up in her eyes and she fought to hold them back, but it was too late. Big salty tears coursed down her cheeks like the Falls themselves, and she found that Barlow was hugging her, patting her on the back, and telling her everything would be okay while she sobbed against his shoulder.

Finally, she released him and took a step back. "Sorry. I don't know why I'm even bothering anymore. There's obviously no way to go back. It's all just a waste of time. You've been here for fifty years and you're still here. Maybe I need to just give up. Accept being human. Maybe it's not as bad as I think it is after all."

"Oh, it is," Barlow said, as he tucked a long strand of Val's blond hair behind her ear in a fatherly manner. "Being human sucks the big one, pardon my language."

She sniffed. "This is not helping."

"Sorry."

"So you're saying it's useless. That I should just give up."

"No, I'm most certainly not saying that. We're going to go back to Heaven. The both of us."

Val's eyebrows shot up. "What did you just say?"

A grin cut through Barlow's wrinkled face. "Alexa just gave me a very interesting anniversary gift. A very interesting gift indeed."

She felt a weird sensation begin to well up in her chest. It was either indigestion or hope. And since she hadn't eaten her piece of cake yet, it was probably hope. "What was it?"

"What Alexa said before she left. About either coming with her or using the key . . ."

"Yes?"

"She was referring to a very special key, the key she just gave me as a gift . . ." He trailed off and his grin grew wider.

"Mr. Barlow, I'm about to explode. Tell me!"

"Alexa has given me the Key to Heaven for our anniversary."

Val leaned back. "The key to *say-what-now?*"

He looked amused at her reaction. "You heard me. I have the Key to Heaven. I can use it whenever I wish."

She couldn't believe what she was hearing. "But I thought the Key to Heaven was just a myth . . . like when everyone used to talk about a piece of Heaven falling off and disappearing eons ago. Fiction."

"It's not a myth. Lucifer made the key before he was cast out of Heaven. His backdoor access, if you will, so he could sneak back in. The key is quite pretty, too. Rather smaller than you'd think. With the incantation to open the doorway etched into its golden surface. Alexa is quite generous. The gift wrapping left a little to be desired, but I'm certainly not going to complain."

"But," Valerie still couldn't believe that it could be true. "If it's not just a myth, then why didn't Lucifer ever use it?"

"He never used it for one very simple reason. He lost it."

"He *lost* it? No way."

"People lose things all the time. Just like socks. I tell you, Valerie, I don't have one matching pair anymore. I really should make a trip to the mall."

Could it be true? Could she allow herself to believe that something like this was possible? She answered both questions with a resounding *yes*. This was wonderful. Fabulous. The best news she'd gotten in two long months.

"Wait a minute," Val said suddenly. "Why would a Tempter Demon give a fallen angel something that would help them go back to Heaven? Doesn't that defeat the entire purpose of what she does?"

"Yes, it certainly does. No argument. And if her superiors ever find out about her gift she would be punished severely and mercilessly." He suddenly got a faraway look of concern on his face. "But Alexa cares for me. In her own way. After all of these years, I truly believe that she is more interested in my well-being and happiness than fulfilling her mission to tempt me."

Val snorted at that. "Sure she is. And Nathaniel wants to take me out shopping for a two-carat diamond solitaire. I'll send you the wedding invites as soon as they get back from the printer."

"Sarcasm is not necessary, my dear."

"I can't help it. This is just too wonderful. I don't want to be disappointed when it all turns out to be a big fat lie."

"We'll find out tomorrow."

"Find out what?"

"How well the key works. I plan to use it tomorrow to go back to Heaven. And you're welcome to come with me."

Tomorrow. Val didn't think she'd heard a more beautiful word. Wait, she could think of one. *Today.* *Today* was an even *better* word.

"Why don't we, I mean *you,* try it now?" she asked. "Why wait?"

"I am very tired. And it's late. Before I re-enter Heaven I would like to be well rested. I'm quite sure there will be many questions asked when we return unnannounced."

"But—"

"Valerie," he cut her off. "It's *my* gift. We'll use it tomorrow. Patience is a virtue, you know."

She sighed. "Okay. But early tomorrow."

"I'll be waiting." He smiled at her and she couldn't help but return the expression.

Tomorrow. She was going back to Heaven *tomorrow.*

She could hardly wait.

Barlow had given her half of his anniverary cake, which she ate almost all of while watching TV in her room. It was *delicious.*

She made a list in her ever-present Heavenly Memories Notebook of things she wanted to do before she went back. There was really only one thing on the list: *Say good-bye to Reggie.* She'd miss him. He was a good guy. Hopefully he'd be able to work things out with his girlfriend.

After taking a quick shower, she got into her warm

flannel pjs—another thing she liked about being human, as they were quite cozy and comfortable. Then she slipped under the covers of her bed, propped the pillows up behind her head, and used the remote control to click off the television.

Just then there was a knock at the door.

Val sighed. Then she salt bolt upright in bed, thinking that it must be Barlow wanting to use the key that night.

She swung her legs out of bed, hurried over to unhook the chain lock, and twisted the handle to open the door.

"Mr. Barlow—" she began with a big smile on her face.

Nathaniel leaned against the door frame, cigarette in hand. He gave her a sly smile.

"Hey Val," he said. "Did you miss me?"

Chapter Six

—⌒⌒—

Val slammed the door in his face.

She was *so* not ready to deal with the demon tonight. Or ever again, for that matter. This time tomorrow, she'd be long gone and wouldn't have to face Nathaniel ever again. She decided to ignore him. After a while he'd realize she wasn't going to open the door again and he'd go away.

She turned around.

Nathaniel was sitting on her bed.

"Mind if I come in?" he said and held out a paper bag. "I brought you some chicken soup for that nasty cold of yours."

She backed up against the door. "Go away."

He sighed and put the bag down on the floor. "Here I go and give you some time to yourself. Some time to think about the things I said to you last night, for you to realize that there really is no other choice than to agree to come with me, and this is the greeting I get? Very impolite, little angel. I'm shocked."

She scowled at him. "Okay, how about this? Go away. *Please.*"

He looked around at the room. "So this is the little corner of the earthly realm you've carved out for yourself, is it?" He picked up a pink bra she'd tossed on the bed before her shower. "Very nice."

She moved close enough to snatch the bra away from him. "Get out of here. You can't tempt me. I don't care what you say. I'm serious."

He stretched his long, lean frame out on the bed and put his hands behind his head. "Oh, you're *serious*. Then that changes everything."

She ignored the smirk he gave her.

"Can I ask you a question?" Val moved back and leaned against the closed door, trying to make herself look as relaxed as possible while having a drop-dead gorgeous demon with ulterior motives spread across her bed.

He cocked his head to the side. "Ask anything you desire."

"Why are you doing this?"

"Doing what?"

"I've practically begged you to leave. It should be obvious that I'm not going to fall at your feet and beg you to take me to Hell. Why can't you go tempt somebody else instead? Somebody who'll appreciate your efforts more than I will."

He regarded her for a moment, and propped himself up on one arm against her pillow. "Because I care about what happens to you. I don't want to see you here in the earthly realm. You despise it. I can tell. Say the word and I can make it all better. You will be treated like a queen where I take you, you will serve no one but yourself."

"No."

The grin fell slowly from his face. "No?"

"That's right." Val swallowed hard and tried to keep her face expressionless. "And don't bother trying any of your demon mojo on me. It won't work. Alexa says you're next to impossible to resist, but I'm resisting just fine, thanks so much."

A shadow crossed his expression. "You've been talking to Alexa, have you? Why am I not surprised?"

"What do you care? I'd think anyone would want the rumor that they're hard to resist spread about themselves. It's sort of like the rumor about men with big feet." Val refused to look down at Nathaniel's shoes. "She said you're hard to resist when you *try* to be. What's that supposed to mean? Does it take a lot of effort?"

He ignored the question. "Is she still fixated on Bartholomew Barlow?"

Val crossed her arms. "Maybe she is, maybe she isn't. Now, let's recap, shall we? I want you to leave. Right now. And don't come back. Ever."

He lay back on the bed and laughed, but it didn't sound happy. It sounded scary. "And what makes you think that anything I do is up to me?"

She frowned. "What?"

He sat up suddenly and met her eyes directly with a fierceness that made her take a step back. "Why are you being so difficult? It's never been like this in the past. Why now, when it's so important that you come with me?"

"So important? What are you talking about?"

There was a long moment when he said nothing, just stared at her so intently and silently that Val could hear her heart drumming wildly in her chest. Then finally, "This doesn't have to be a bad thing, my little angel."

"Yes it does. And don't call me that."

He raised an eyebrow at her. "Why not?"

"I'm not an angel anymore." *Well, not until tomorrow,* she thought absently.

His mouth twisted into an unpleasant grin. "Oh, I'm well aware of that. You're a bad, bad girl. That's why you got sent down here. And that's why you're getting a visit from your friendly neighborhood demon. And I don't give up that easily, angel. Not when it counts."

She frowned. "Something wrong?"

"Pardon me?"

"You don't seem to be in a very good mood. In fact, I'm not feeling tempted in the slightest tonight. Is your concentration off? Did somebody pee in your brimstone this morning?"

His eyes narrowed, but after another long moment of silence between them he started to laugh again. This time it didn't sound scary at all. It sounded very good and made her stomach tingle warmly.

"We're a lot alike, you and I," he said. "I think I have an idea of what you're going through right now. What you're feeling. That's why I can help you."

"Is that right? How so?"

"I used to be human. A long, long time ago. Then I was given a chance to be something . . ." He paused and seemed to search for the right word. ". . .Better. And it is much, much better. And what Alexa said about every woman unable to resist me? It's all true. I was chosen for this job for very specific reasons. I'm very good at it."

The warm tingles in her stomach began to travel downward. Was it the sexy tone of his voice? Was it the fact that he seemed so interested in her, even if it was only a lie? Or was he using that demon mojo again to influence her?

Tomorrow. She clung to the word. It would get her through tonight.

She gave the demon a sour look and ignored the tingles. "That leaving thing I mentioned earlier? How about that?"

His confident expression slipped slightly, and he stood. Their gazes locked.

"What makes you so different from the others?" he mused aloud.

Val stood her ground and held his gaze. She wasn't going to be anything but cool, calm, and collected. After tomorrow, she'd never have to see him again. Bye-bye, demon-boy.

"No one can resist forever," he said, his words fierce, as if he was trying to convince himself as well as her.

"Go"—Val's eyes widened as he came toward her—"away."

Then he kissed her, hard enough that her lips felt bruised, and moved his hand to the back of her head to tangle it in her long blond hair. Val's hands were free so she could start fighting against him.

Any minute now.

Why wasn't she fighting him?

Damn.

Her first human kiss. Right there in her motel room, with a handsome demon who crushed her body against his as if it were going to be the last kiss for either of them. And it was. This was the last time she'd ever kiss him, kiss anybody. She was going back to . . . back to . . .

Where was she going again?

Her lips parted to him, and she felt his tongue against hers as she kissed him desperately, giving in to it totally and completely. She melted against his firm body, wrapping her arms around him, just as he broke off the kiss and backed away from her. Val blinked up at him, feeling dazed.

"See what I told you?" he said, and she could have sworn his voice caught on the words. "Even *you* can't resist me. Till next time, little angel."

He vanished in a column of fire.

Even as she cursed him, her lips still tingled with the warmth from the kiss. She tried to wipe the feel of him away with the back of her hand.

Evil bastard.

The next morning, after spending the night tossing and turning and subsequently having very strange dreams about herself, Nathaniel, and Barney the purple dinosaur, Val woke to somebody yelling her name. She sat up and stared around the empty motel room. The chicken soup Nathaniel brought had tipped over and leaked out onto the carpet. *Crap.* The digital clock on top of the television read 11:15 A.M.

Double crap. She'd slept in.

"Valerie!"

She rubbed her eyes and swung her legs out of bed, moving as fast as she could to the door. She unhooked the chain, turned the lock, and opened it up to peer outside.

Nothing.

Val rubbed her eyes again and stretched into a big yawn, chalking the sound up to her imagination.

Then she felt something rub against her bare foot. She looked down.

It was a rat, whiskers twitching, looking up at her with

little black, beady eyes. She screamed, scrambled back from it, and slammed the door shut.

How *disgusting!* It was enough that she had to deal with the two cockroaches that had set up house in room eighteen the other day, but now the Paradise Inn was infested with rodents?

Add that to the list of things about being human that sucked, she thought. Near the top.

She cracked the door open again and looked out. The rat was gone. She sighed with relief.

"Get back here, you bastard!" a female voice yelled from her right.

A girl in a McDonald's uniform, no coat, was tearing through the motel's courtyard, narrowly missing falling into the leaf-covered pool. She held a baseball bat, two-handed, and didn't look like she was off to the ballpark.

Val recognized her immediately, mostly due to the fast-food uniform since her face was wrapped in a big orange scarf. It was Reggie's girlfriend, Claire.

Oh no, Val thought. With her current bat-wielding stance she was probably looking for Reggie, furious about his slight indiscretion. She'd planned to talk to Claire girl-to-girl today and try to help smooth things over before she did anything crazy, but it looked like it might be a bit late for that.

In a way it was good. Any later and Val might have already been gone. This way she could help smooth things over between the two before she and Barlow used the key.

Val slid into her fuzzy pink slippers, pulled a thin green jacket on over her pajamas, and emerged into the bright, but not too cold outdoors.

"Claire," she called out, but was ignored. Claire had

gone over to the small, black Dumpster near the manager's office and was hitting it with the bat, which made a resounding *gong* sound each time.

Val pulled the jacket closer to her and, nimbly as she could, made her way over to the woman. The last thing she wanted to do was get Claire more agitated. She could do without getting inadvertently hit in the mouth with a baseball bat. She stayed back a few feet.

"Claire!" she said louder. "What are you doing?"

Claire's shoulders tensed, and she stopped banging on the Dumpster for a moment. She turned around, a tense smile in place, breathing hard.

"Hi, Val. How's it going?"

"Okay. You?"

"Great, just great."

"So, uh . . . what are you doing?"

She sniffed, and Val noticed her eyes were red. "What does it look like?"

"It looks like you're beating up the garbage."

She laughed. "Good way to put it."

"O-kay. Listen, why don't you and me go get a coffee or something?"

"Can't. Have to work. I start at noon." Her gaze left Val and tracked down to the ground. "There you are, you little prick . . . trying to sneak away? Ha!"

Val frowned at her. "What are you—"

"Coward!" she cried out. "Get back here and face me like a man!"

She took off toward the pool.

Obviously Claire had gone insane. Sad, really. Val watched her run a circle around the pool twice before she spotted what the woman was after.

The rat. It was running like a miniature race horse, staying just a few steps ahead of her. Every now and then she'd bring down the bat with a loud *crack,* then shriek with dismay when she missed her mark.

The rat broke its circle and started coming toward Val. Right toward her. She tried to step out of the way, but it darted behind her slipper. She turned and it followed, one paw on the fuzzy pink material.

"Get away from him," Claire said and Val looked to see she was directly in front of her with the bat raised above her head.

She held up her hand. "Claire, take it easy. We'll put out a trap. One of those humane traps, of course, and maybe we'll take it someplace where it can have a nice long and happy life. Do you know if they accept rats at the Toronto Zoo?"

Her eyes were wild. "I'm going to kill him. Move away now."

"No!" the rat said. "Don't let her hurt me, Val!"

Okay. Hold on, Val thought.

The rat said *what*?

"He cheated on me," Claire said. "And now I'm going to kill him."

Val looked down, eyes wide. "Reggie? Is that you?"

The rat was practically hugging her slipper. He looked up, whiskers trembling. "See? I told you she was a witch."

"Oh, wait a minute." Claire lowered the bat. "I think I understand what's going on here."

Val blinked at her. "Well, that makes one of us. Please explain."

"You're the other woman."

"I'm the what?"

Her eyes narrowed. "I'm going to kill *both* of you."

Claire raised the bat again. Val opened her mouth but all that came out was a little *ahhh* sound. Then Claire dropped the bat, put her hands over her scarf-covered face, and started to sob.

Val let out a long sigh of relief and looked down at Reggie.

"I told her I was a rat." He shrugged his rat shoulders. "She agreed with me."

"Obviously."

He scurried away from them without another word.

Val kicked the baseball bat away, and crouched down next to Claire. "It's going to be okay. And just for the record, it was only a kiss. And it wasn't with me." She put her hand on Claire's shoulder and she tensed, pulled her scarf away so she could wipe her face, and stood up.

"You can have him."

"I don't want him."

"He's all yours. The jerk."

She turned away, giving Val her back.

"You need to change him back," Val told her.

Claire spun back around, her tear-filled eyes full of pain. "But he's exactly what he is now. A rat. Now he can't fool anyone else into believing he's a wonderful, caring man who loves them." Her bottom lip quivered.

Val didn't have a response for that. "I had no idea you were so powerful."

"Neither did he. Maybe if he'd known what would happen he wouldn't have been so stupid."

"Well, maybe—"

"You tell him that." Her voice cracked on the words.

"That he was stupid. And now he has to live with his mistakes."

Before Val could say another word, Claire turned her back and stormed out of the motel's courtyard.

Super, she thought. Now a witch thought she'd slept with her boyfriend. That was one McDonald's she wouldn't be able to go to anymore.

Val frowned. Not that it mattered since she was leaving. But she'd miss her McChicken sandwich. Another okay thing about being human. And the french fries were pretty good, too.

Reggie had disappeared, and she gave up looking for him after a few minutes. She went back to her room, mopped up the spilled chicken soup, which unfortunately made her think about Nathaniel and his visit last night. Then she pulled on a pair of dark jeans, a plain white tank top, and a big, warm purple cardigan. She brushed her hair, washed her face, and wiped the sleep out of her eyes.

Time to go home, she told her slightly bleary-eyed reflection. She hoped Reggie would be able to sort out his bizarre girlfriend issues without her help.

She considered asking Barlow to wait a bit on their trip. To make sure everything worked out. But decided against it. She didn't want any possibility of seeing Nathaniel again. She didn't even want to spend any more time thinking about the evil jerk. The fact that when she closed her eyes she could still feel his body against hers was definitely *not* a good thing.

She had to get out of there.

She pulled on a cream-colored winter coat, and the last

thing she grabbed was the notebook with her pages upon pages of scrawled memories, lists, and reminders. She decided to take it along with her as a souvenir of the two months stuck on her earthly vacation.

Val left the motel room and headed to the manager's office, hearing the bell jingle as she pushed open the door. Nobody was behind the counter so she started for the beaded curtain, but stopped when she heard voices. Raised, shouting voices. And then a loud cracking sound that made her jump.

The beaded curtain whipped to the side and she saw Alexa standing there with a wild look on her face.

"Valerie! Please. You have to help. You can't let him have it."

"Have what?"

She raised her clenched fist and opened it to reveal a small, golden key. She met Val's gaze and shook her head. "This is all my fault. All of it. Protect Barty. Help him. Do whatever it takes to—"

There was another cracking sound. Alexa jerked forward and her eyes widened. Flames gathered at her feet, and slowly moved up her body. It was kind of like when Nathaniel chose to make his dramatic exit, only slower and somehow much, much scarier.

"No." Alexa turned to look at whatever was behind her. "You backstabbing bastard. I won't let you do this—"

But then the flames picked up speed and engulfed her. Val heard her scream; a loud, piercing, painful sound that was abruptly cut off. The key fell to the ground and came to rest in the middle of a circle of black ash. Alexa was gone.

Val couldn't believe what she'd just witnessed. She'd heard stories of what it was like, but to see a demon vanquished—destroyed in front of her eyes, reduced to nothing but ash—chilled her right to the bone.

But who was responsible? Or what?

She looked up, eyes wide, as the curtain parted before her.

Chapter Seven

—✦—

Val didn't recognize him. He was medium height, thin, with blond hair and hollow cheeks. Vivid blue eyes. He wore black leather pants and a tight blue shirt that showed off his sleekly toned upper body. He stared at her for a moment before a smile spread across his painfully handsome features—a cold, thin smile that froze her inside as fire lit up his eyes.

Another demon, she thought as fear washed over her.

The blond demon crouched down to pick up the golden key and brought it to his lips to blow off the bits of ash. Bits of Alexa. Then he rose to his feet.

Val didn't move, couldn't move, but her heart beat against her ribcage like a trapped animal.

He raised an eyebrow. "Valerie, right?"

She opened her mouth but nothing came out.

He held the key between his thumb and middle finger. "Do you know what this is?"

Val swallowed hard. "A key."

"Such a small word, isn't it? For such an important thing?" He grinned. "That Alexa, quite the wily one. Didn't make even a mention that she had something so precious in her possession. And to give it to her little fallen angel boyfriend. Cute, isn't it? Love certainly works in mysterious ways."

"Who are you? What do you want?"

His grin widened. "Well, isn't that sweet of you to ask. My name is Julian. And I just got what I wanted."

"You're a demon."

He looked down at himself. "Does it show?"

Val glanced at Alexa's ashes and felt anger rise inside her. "Only in that you're obviously evil and heartless."

He mock pouted. "You wound me."

"I'd like to." The tremor in her voice didn't give her words as much impact as she would have liked.

He licked his lips and studied her for a moment. "I think I like you. No wonder Nathaniel wishes to keep you all for himself."

That gave her a chill. "You know Nathaniel?"

He grimaced at the name. "Unfortunately. I wonder what he'll say when he learns what I've done to you. Knowing him as I do, he may be relieved you've been taken off his hands."

Her breath caught and she took a step back, clutching her notebook to her chest.

Julian cocked his head to one side, staring at the little book. In a motion quicker than she could see, he snatched it away from her. "What's this?"

"Nothing. Give it back."

He flipped through the pages and laughed. "Isn't that adorable. How long has Nathaniel left you to your own devices that you've been able to make such extensively useless notes about your former home?"

Tears stung her eyes. "Give that back to me or I swear I'll . . . I'll . . ."

"You'll what?" He raised an eyebrow and extended the book to her. She reached out to grab it just as it exploded into flame, a small fireball in the palm of Julian's hand that, when gone, left no trace of the book behind. "You'll do nothing, that's what you'll do. You're powerless against me, fallen one. Never forget that."

Her notebook. He destroyed it. Everything she knew about Heaven, every detail she could remember . . . gone.

"How . . . how could you?"

Julian seemed terribly amused at her shock. "How could I? Because it pleased me, that's why. Now it pleases me to do the same to you. I so enjoy playing with fallen angels. It's sort of my hobby."

He took a step toward her just as she heard a loud crash. Julian frowned and turned around. Barlow stood behind him holding the remnants of a flower vase that he'd just used to bash the demon over the head.

"You vanquished Alexa," Barlow managed, his voice was filled with raw pain.

"Yes, I did," Julian said. "She would have been destroyed for her crimes eventually, anyhow. Giving a fallen one the Key to Heaven? Such a stupid, insipid creature, she was. And really, old man. You thought hitting me over the head was going to do *what,* exactly? I'm a *demon.*"

"Run, Valerie," Barlow yelled before he slipped back into the living room.

Julian turned to her. "Just a moment, pretty one. I'll be right back." He leisurely moved through the beaded curtain.

Val followed and pushed the curtain aside. Barlow had

grabbed a lead-crystal ashtray and backed up until he was against the wall next to the TV. Julian just looked at him, half bored, half amused.

"I'll give you a choice, old man. You can die slowly, or you can die *really* slowly. I'm cool with either one."

Val grasped blindly for something to say to stop him. "You know, now that I think about it, Nathaniel did mention you to me."

His head whipped around in her direction. "What was that?"

Oh goody, she thought. He had Nathaniel issues just as she thought he might. But, really, who didn't?

She shrugged. "Just that you were jealous of him. How hard to resist he is. How he's going to become a really important demon and you'll just toil away in obscurity for all eternity."

Julian frowned. "He said that?"

She nodded.

"Hard to resist?" he sputtered. "Perhaps when he's not wasting time feeling sorry for himself. I always see my tasks through to their inevitable conclusion. That's what I do. I'm much more reliable, important . . ." He trailed off and looked at her. "And now I have the Key to Heaven."

Val glanced down at his hand, which was tightly clenched around the key. "Well, yes, you do have a key. Whether or not it's the Key to Heaven is another story. Mr. Barlow, didn't you say you were having doubts about whether it was even real?"

Barlow just stared at her, the ashtray clutched in his hands.

She gestured with her head. "The key. Didn't you say

you tried it and it didn't work? Just a couple of sparks and then nothing?"

"Oh . . . yes, yes, I did say that, didn't I? Yes, that's right."

She watched the doubt cloud Julian's arrogant expression.

She smiled, shakily. "So that's too bad. That it's not the real Key to Heaven. Real shame that you couldn't figure that out for yourself. Nathaniel probably wouldn't have made that mistake, but he's . . . you know, special." She peered at him. "And I guess I do see what he means about being much better looking than you."

"Better looking? He said that?"

Val held up her hands. "I shouldn't say any more."

Julian looked weak and self-conscious then, just for a moment. Val wracked her brain to think of something else to say to distract him, but came up blank, since she was actually completely terrified. Her mouth was working but the rest of her had almost completely shut down. If he'd been able to destroy Alexa so easily, she didn't even want to think about what he might do to Barlow or herself.

Slowly, a smile began to spread across his face. "Stalling me, aren't you, fallen one? Nathaniel said nothing of the sort."

"Sure he did."

"An excellent try. Now where were we?" He took a menacing step toward her.

"Wait! What do you want with the key, anyhow?"

"Why should I tell you?"

She thought about that. "Why not?"

He grinned. "Very well, fallen one. I'll tell you because it pleases me to. Whoever holds the Key to Heaven, holds the balance of the universe in their hands. While I enjoy that feeling of power, I'd much rather sell it to the highest bidder. I know of one who will be quite interested in possessing it for himself."

"But I told you that it doesn't work. It's a fake key."

"Fallen angels are such miserable liars. It's a true talent to deceive one as adept at deception as myself. You may save your breath in telling me any more of your tall tales."

Valerie felt cold.

Julian stared with reverence at the golden key in his hand. "Can you just imagine what will happen when a demon walks into Heaven?"

Julian strolled away from her and toward Barlow who held his ashtray so tight as the demon approached that his knuckles whitened. "You know, I was thinking about killing the old man. But now I've changed my mind. Ask me why."

She just stared at him.

"Come on. Ask me." He waited, then sighed with impatience. "Fine. I will simply tell you. I would have killed him because that would have been enjoyable, but he's already dead. Disease is eating him up from the inside. I can see it as clearly as I can see your poorly disguised fear, fallen one."

Her gaze shot to Barlow.

Julian continued, "He has only days left. Pain-filled days. So why would I want to deprive him of that? And now that I have the key, he has no choice but to die as a human, and face what waits for him on the other side. Although I can guarantee that it won't be your precious pearly gates. You should have given yourself over to Alexa long ago, old man. Do you know what happens to a fallen angel who enters Hell without the guidance of a Tempter Demon?" He grinned. "Imagine a prison filled with vicious, hardened murderers . . . and one day the cop who put them all behind bars is thrown in to join them. A lamb to the slaughter. A slab of meat thrown to the lions. Only there is no respite. There is no mercy. It is forever. An eternity of such vileness is what you can look forward to."

"Shut up," Val heard herself say. Tears streamed down her cheeks.

Julian slipped the key into his pocket and cast his cold, blue-eyed gaze completely on her. "However, I will still enjoy taking care of you, fallen one. Just for kicks."

He came at her before she had time to register what was happening. He grabbed her shoulders and pulled her close to his face to stare into his now fiery eyes.

"Tell me I'm better looking than Nathaniel and maybe I'll show mercy."

Val blinked. Was he serious?

But before she could say anything, to either confirm or deny his request, he flinched, and looked down. "Ouch."

A rat had bitten his ankle through his leather pants, and was holding on tight.

Val raised her eyebrows in surprise. "Reggie?"

Julian's eyes widened and he let go of her. "A rat! Ahh! Oh, get it off me! Get it off me!"

He began dancing around the living room, bumping into the coffee table and armchair while continuously flicking his leg, but Reggie held on tight.

"I hate rats! So much! Foul, nasty creatures!"

You're a foul, nasty creature, Val thought as she rushed to Barlow's side and put a protective arm around the old man.

Finally, Julian managed to pry the rat's chompers out of his ankle. He staggered, sweating and harried-looking. Julian, that is. Reggie simply looked rather proud of himself as he ducked under the TV.

"Doesn't matter," the demon said, his voice a little pitchy now. He cleared his throat. "I have what I came for. When I require some entertainment in the future, I will return. You can depend on it."

He disappeared suddenly in a column of flame.

Val helped a weakened Barlow to his armchair, then knelt by his side and looked up at him with concern.

"He vanquished Alexa," he said sadly.

"I know."

His eyes had a faraway look. "I cared for her, you know. Not as she did for me, but there was something there. I'd grown accustomed to her visits over the years. Something I could depend on. She sacrificed herself to save me."

"Was he lying about what he said? Are you really sick?"

He leaned back into the chair. "It's true. I fear I have very little time left."

Val felt her eyes begin to well up again.

He shook his head. "No time for tears, my dear. You have to go after Julian."

She blinked. "And why would I want to do a crazy thing like that?"

"You must get the key back. Alexa was a fool to bring it to the earthly realm from wherever she acquired it in the first place. But what's done is done. You must find it before it's used. If you don't, then it will be the end of everything."

"What do you mean, 'the end of everything'?"

"Julian spoke the truth. Whoever holds the key holds the balance in their hands. A great amount of energy goes into keeping that very balance in check, and it is vital that it remains that way. If a demon uses the key to enter Heaven and darken it with his very presence, then the balance will be irreparably upset."

"And what's that supposed to mean?"

Barlow met her gaze. "Do the words *the end of the world* mean anything to you?"

Reggie scurried over to them. "What's going on? Who was that creep, anyhow?"

Val looked down at him. "Julian. A demon."

"Tasted like a demon."

"And how would you know?"

"He tasted like I would imagine a demon would taste. If I'd ever given that sort of thing the slightest thought before this very moment. First witches, now demons. This is one hell of a day so far."

Barlow looked at the rat. "Reggie?"

"That's right."

"You're late with your rent again."

"Oh." Reggie's eyes shifted and his whiskers twitched. "So why was I able to get rid of him with just one bite? Aren't demons supposed to be tougher than that?"

Barlow gave a small smile. "Are you trying to change the subject?"

"Is it that obvious?"

The old man sighed. "Demons have a natural aversion to that which is pure. Doves, holy water, acts of self-sacrifice . . ."

"And rats?" Val finished. "Rats are considered pure?"

He shrugged. "I don't make the rules."

"That's just weird," she said. "But let's forget about man-rat for a moment. I believe we were talking about the end of the world? Kind of important, if you ask me."

Barlow nodded. "Get the key back as soon as you can. Do whatever it takes. And you won't have to worry about the end of anything."

Her mind was working overtime. Find Julian. Find the key.

The Key to Heaven.

"And if I manage to find the key before the world explodes—"

He shook his head. "It won't explode. The earthly realm would cease to exist. Heaven and Hell would press in on either side in an unstoppable fight for dominance. A celestial smothering, if you will. And since Heaven would be tainted with the presence of a demon, the balance would already be askew. Hell would spread to cover everything. Take over everything. Until there is nothing left."

Val stared at him in shock for a moment. "Oh, is that all? Not too much pressure then, is there?" She took a shaky breath. "And, if by some miracle I find the key before that happens, then can *we* use it? Send you back before . . ." She stopped. She didn't want to finish the thought.

"If there is time. Yes, we shall use it ourselves."

Use the key and go back to Heaven. Just like that. Easy. She liked the sound of that.

"But how would I know where to start looking for Julian? He could be anywhere."

Barlow shook his head. "I honestly don't know."

Valerie immediately pushed away the first thought that

entered her mind. Nathaniel would know where to find Julian. If she asked him, would he help her? Could she risk being in his presence again if it meant potentially saving the world?

There had to be another answer. But what?

Seraphina. She could go back to Seraphina's office and have her channel Garry again. Tell him it was an emergency. If she let Heaven itself know there was a threat, then they could do something about it, couldn't they? Yes, that made sense. Perhaps all she needed to do was let Garry know and he could handle it from his end. Or at the very least help her find Julian. There was no need to see Nathaniel ever again.

Not if she could help it.

"I hate leaving you like this," she said to Barlow. He looked so old, so fragile sitting in the armchair. It broke her heart to know how ill he was, putting on such a brave front all of this time.

"Well, if you don't want to be off yet, I'm sure you have enough time to get the rooms cleaned first."

Val stood up. "Geez. This is the thanks I get for sending you back to Heaven? I'm thinking the rooms can probably wait."

He smiled and squeezed her hand hard. She bent over to hug him close to her. "I have faith in you, Valerie," he whispered. "I know you'll do what's right."

Well, she thought. *That makes one of us.*

"Hey!" Reggie shouted after her as she rushed out to the motel's courtyard. "Wait for me!"

Val stopped and turned around to see the rat bounding after her. "What?"

He was panting from his exertion. "So, where do we start?"

"We?"

He nodded his newly furry head. "I want to save the world, too. I'm morally obligated to help you out."

" 'Morally obligated'?"

"That is correct."

"You're not just looking for an excuse to avoid Claire, are you?"

"Am I that transparent?"

Val sighed. "Sorry rat-boy, but you'll just slow me down. Besides, don't you have more important things to think about? Like getting your spell broken?"

"More important than saving the world? I think not."

She blinked. "I'm just surprised you're ready to believe in everything that's been happening so easily."

"Why wouldn't I? My spooky girlfriend just turned me into a damn rat. What wouldn't I believe now? So, let's get going. Time's a-wasting."

The cool wind blew her hair across her face and she tucked it firmly behind her ears. "No, Reggie. It's too dangerous. You can't come. You need to stay here and take care of Mr. Barlow while I'm gone."

"Please?"

"No."

"Pleeeaaase?"

"Reggie!"

"Val, listen. Here's the deal. You *have* to let me come with you. I need . . . I need to prove to Claire that I'm not just a loser like she thinks. That I'm worthy of her love. Why else would she immediately assume the worst about me without even giving me the benefit of the doubt? If I do this, if you let me help you, then maybe, just maybe she'll see that I'm good enough for her. This is so important to me, you have no idea."

"No."

"Oh, come on!"

"Okay, I was just kidding on the last one. You can come. But try not to get in the way."

"I promise!"

Val hurried out of the motel's courtyard. Reggie had to run on his little rat feet to keep up with her.

Off to save the world, stop Julian, get the key, and send her and Barlow back to Heaven.

Sounded simple enough, didn't it?

No, she didn't think so, either.

Chapter Eight

———— ‿ ————

Val didn't have much money on her. Well, on her or in general, but she had enough to catch a cab to Seraphina's office just off Clifton Hill. There was an airport limo idling outside the front door.

She and Reggie were getting out of the cab when Becky emerged from the building. She noticed Val and gave a nod before locking the door behind her. She was dressed in an expensive-looking business suit and her bright red hair was back in a smooth ponytail. She held a teacup Chihuahua under one arm. The Chihuahua wore a diamond studded collar that looked more expensive than Becky's suit.

The little dog growled at Reggie who was currently in Val's arms, and he took the opportunity to snuggle closer into her chest.

"Hey Val," Becky greeted her with a smile. "Good to see you. What's up?"

Val mirrored her smile, though it felt very forced. "Going somewhere?"

"Yeah, the car's here to take us to the airport. We're off to Disneyland at her majesty's command. As if she hasn't already been there twice this year. That little girl is crazy. They honestly don't pay me enough for this job."

Val let out a long sigh of relief. Talk about timing! Another few minutes and she would have been too late. "Listen, Becky. I need five minutes with Seraphina before you leave."

"Sorry, no can do."

"What?" Val's entire body tensed up. "It's really important or I wouldn't ask. I know she's very busy. I get it. But, this is a matter of life and death. To put it *extremely* mildly."

"Valerie, melodrama doesn't suit you. I should know. I get melodrama nine hours a day from her majesty and her majesty's mother. Now I'm going to get melodrama twenty-four seven for a week while we're at the so-called happiest place on earth. Somebody just shoot me now and put me out of my misery."

"Just five minutes. Please Becky. I will owe you one. I'll even go out with your brother." Val paused, thinking about the geeky amateur wizard who seemed to drool profusely whenever he saw her. "Probably. Maybe. I'll consider going out with your brother. To a movie. Then straight home. Separately."

Becky smiled again and it looked tired. "I would if I could, really. I'm not just trying to be difficult. It's just that Seraphina and her mother already left."

Val eyed the limo. "Then what . . . what is this for?"

"For me."

Val gaped at her.

She shrugged. "Okay, it's really for Fifi—" she indicated the Chihuahua —"but I get to go along for the ride."

"She's gone?"

"Sorry. Incommunicado. Besides, she can't do any of her stuff unless she's in person."

Val burst into tears.

Becky looked stricken. "Oh . . . no, don't cry."

She took deep choking breaths while trying to compose herself. "I . . . don't know . . . what to do."

Becky patted Val's shoulder. "I wish I could help." She waited for Val to calm down, and then gave her a bright smile. "Listen, if what you need is really that urgent, you could always use Psychic Bob down the street next to the Movieland Wax Museum. Ten bucks a reading." Her grin widened. "I'm kidding, of course."

Twenty minutes later, Val sat on the other side of a dirty crystal ball and Psychic Bob. She didn't have a penny to her name after she'd paid the cab driver, so she had to force Reggie to do some rat tricks on the corner for spare change from the tourists. Made $12.51. She wasn't sure who gave them the penny, though. That was just an insult.

She handed ten of their earnings over to Psychic Bob.

"So," Psychic Bob said, his voice gruff and effeminate at the same time. He looked like a truck driver but sounded like he might know what wine would go best with beef bourguignonne. "What can I help you with today? Simple tarot card reading? Want to know when you'll meet your true love? Career questions? Ask me anything, honey. I'm here to help."

Val folded her hands and leaned over the table toward him. "I need you to channel an angel named Garry, assistant guardian of the gates to Heaven. And please hurry. This is a major emergency."

He blinked. "Sweetie, if you have an emergency I have a phone in the back. You can call 911."

"It's not an emergency those people can help me with."

"Garry, you say."

"That's right."

"Guardian of the gates to Heaven."

"*Assistant* guardian. Don't try to make him sound more important than he is—his ego is big enough already. Really he's just like a glorified receptionist. But I need to talk to him."

She'd placed Reggie gently down on the tabletop and he lay down. He'd decided not to be a part of this conversation and that was probably for the best. Psychic Bob looked uncomfortable enough without having to deal with a talking rat.

He stared at her. Bob, not the rat. Then, without another word he got out his tarot cards and shuffled them. He laid them out in a cross pattern on the table, narrowly avoiding hitting Reggie, who had to sidestep out of the way.

Psychic Bob nodded and looked up at her. "I see romance in your future. Great adventure and exciting times lay ahead for you."

"Didn't you hear me? I don't want a card reading. I want you to channel Garry—"

"Assistant guardian to the gates of Heaven. Yeah, I heard you. But I think this is better. Don't you want to know what your future holds?

Val sighed. "I already know what my future holds. Bad things if I don't speak to Garry."

"You paid ten dollars for a reading."

"I don't have time for a reading. Didn't you hear me say that this is an emergency?"

Psychic Bob stood up and pointed at the door. "Go."

"Pardon me?"

"Go," he said with his teeth clenched. "I don't have time for crazy people."

"Crazy people?" Val exclaimed. "I am *not* crazy."

"Yes, you are."

"No, I'm not."

"You must be. You come in here talking nonsense, carrying that flea-ridden creature—"

"Hey!" Reggie said.

Val coughed to cover the sound of Reggie's protest. "Just listen to me. I'm not crazy. I'm a fallen angel who needs to talk to the assistant guardian of the gates to Heaven so I can prevent a demon from bringing about the end of the world. Do you hear me? *The end of the world!* What sounds crazy about that?"

"All of it."

"You're a fallen angel?" Reggie said. "You didn't tell me *that*."

Val sighed. "When we first met I told you I was from Heaven."

"So you're trying to tell me that that's definitely *not* a strip club?"

"Did the rat just talk?" Bob asked.

"Yeah, but he's not really a . . . oh, never mind. I don't have time for this. I need to find that demon. Look, I need a psychic. A good psychic to help me out here. I can't do this by myself."

"What gives you the impression that I'm a psychic?" Psychic Bob asked.

"Uh . . . your name. Your storefront. The crystal ball and tarot cards on your table."

"Oh, those . . . those are just things. Look"—he felt under the table and pulled out a book, *Tarot Cards: The Easy Way!*—"I'm faking it. I'll admit it. I'm a big, fat fake. It's good money from the tourists and I'm currently between acting gigs. So sue me."

"You're a fake?"

He scrambled in his pockets to give Val back her money. "Take this, go somewhere else. We can just pretend this never happened. You don't tell anybody that I'm a fraud, and I don't tell anybody that you're completely insane. Deal?"

"I'm not insane."

"Honey, listen to yourself. I don't know what happened to you that you believe all of this, but angels don't really exist. Demons definitely don't exist. And, to be quite frank with you, all psychics are frauds. The world is a dull, normal, nonmagical place, and that's exactly how I want it to stay."

"Dull and normal?" Val sputtered, then pointed at Reggie. "Then how do you explain him, huh? A talking rat? Say something, Reggie."

Reggie blinked at her. "Squeak."

"Oh, that's just great. Fine, I'll figure it out on my own." She stood up from the table. "But when the world ends, just remember you'll only have yourself to blame."

"I'll keep that in mind," Psychic Bob said. "Take care now. Buh-bye."

Val grabbed Reggie off the table and squeezed him hard enough that he let out another squeak sound, this time involuntarily. She left the store without another look back.

They stood on Clifton Hill, surrounded by the tourists who braved the early winter chill to check out the many wax museums and gift stores of Niagara Falls. Each and every one of them probably felt the same way about the world as Psychic-fraud Bob did. None of them would be any help to her, either.

"Now what are we supposed to do?"

"He wouldn't have been able to help you, anyhow," Reggie replied. "He said himself he was a big faker."

"Oh, now you're talking again."

"Sorry I wasn't up to playing the part of the singing and dancing rodent, but I think he would have shut down completely then. You know, I hate to admit it, but being a rat feels very natural to me."

"I guess your outsides finally match your insides."

"Maybe that's true—hey . . . that's not very nice."

"Anyhow," she said, trying to get back on topic, "I honestly don't know what we're supposed to do next."

"So, you're really an angel?"

"*Fallen* angel."

"Fallen angel. Wow, Val, I can't believe it."

"It's true. They kicked me out."

"Why?"

She sighed. "Garry told me it was because of pride, but that doesn't make any sense to me."

"Well, that *is* one of the seven deadly sins, you know."

Val rolled her eyes. "Everyone's an expert." Then she frowned. "An *expert*. I need to find an expert. That's it."

Yeah, she needed to get Nathaniel to help her. From what she understood from Julian, they were not friends but they did know each other. He'd probably know where to find the other demon. And all she'd need to do to summon Nathaniel was probably just put her lips together and blow.

Key Largo. Oldies channel. She watched it one night last week when she couldn't get to sleep.

No. She shook her head. *No lips. No blowing. Not going to happen.*

It had to be somebody else. Anybody but Nathaniel.

Come on, Val, she admonished herself. *You're going to let your personal feelings get in the way of potentially saving the world?*

Actually, yes. Was that so wrong?

And on the subject of summoning demons, why couldn't Val just summon Julian himself? Go straight to the source. Summon him, grab the key, and all was well with the world.

She frowned at the thought. Probably because the first thing Julian would do once he saw who'd summoned him was reach out and snap her spine. He seemed like a spine-snapping kind of guy.

There had to be another relatively injury-free way.

"We need to find a demon," Val finally said out loud. "Somebody who knows where Julian might be." She shook her head. "But how would I even go about that?"

"Go about what?"

"I need to figure out how to summon a demon."

"Summon a demon to do what?" Reggie looked distracted. He was eyeing a nearby diner. "I'm hungry. Do you think we could go get something to eat? I'm having a fierce craving for some cheese."

Val gritted her teeth. "Summon a demon to help us find Julian, of course. And we need to hurry."

"Oh, it's too bad I'm not currently on speaking terms

with Claire," Reggie said absently. "Demon-summoning was one of her hobbies."

Her eyebrows shot up. "Claire can summon demons?"

He looked at her. "She used to talk about it all the time. Of course I'd just ignore her thinking it was her cute little imagination at work. But now that I've seen what she's capable of"—he sighed resignedly—"I'm thinking she might have been serious."

"We need to go see her. Right now."

His mouth dropped open, exposing his little yellow teeth. "No way."

"Yes, way. We're going to see her so she can help us."

He shook his head emphatically. "Uh-uh. Nope. If she gets another chance in her current mood she'll turn me into a *dead* rat."

"I'll protect you."

"I'd feel more protected with a thousand miles separating us."

"This isn't open for discussion. We're going. So try to act like a man and less like a rat about this, would you?"

"Squeak," he said weakly.

The lunchtime line at McDonald's was long, and it took nearly ten minutes to get to the front. Claire was behind the till, and looked at Val and Reggie with anything but friendliness when they approached.

"You have a lot of nerve coming here."

Val scanned the menu board. "I'd like a McChicken for me, and a regular cheeseburger for Reggie, please. Hold the pickles." She plunked down the money Psychic Bob had given back to her.

Claire narrowed her eyes. "Would you like fries with that?"

"Sure. Um, and a Diet Coke. Make it a combo."

"Is this to go? I hope?"

"Claire, I need a favor from you. It's an emergency or I wouldn't ask. Time is of the essence."

"Hmm, well isn't this interesting? The woman who stole my boyfriend is asking me for a favor. Well, whatever the favor is, the answer is: *screw you.*"

Val leaned closer to her and lowered her voice. "I need you to summon a demon for me."

She frowned. Then keyed in the food order and cashed it out.

"I can get off in fifteen minutes. Wait for me over there." She pointed at the tables near the kids' play area.

Well, Val thought. *That was surprisingly easy.*

They took the food tray—well, Val did—got a table, and chowed down while they waited impatiently for Claire.

She was more than fifteen minutes. More like twenty.

When she appeared, her coat was on, purse slung over her left shoulder. "Sorry. We had a fry emergency. I don't want to go into details."

"Promise?" Reggie squeaked.

Claire scowled at him and then looked at Val. "So you're serious about this, right? Or are you just trying to make me look stupid?"

"I'm totally serious."

"Then let's go back to my place."

Val stood and felt Reggie tense up. He was on her shoulder now, hiding partially behind her hair. It gave her the creeps a bit, but she was managing. Julian wasn't the only one with a rat phobia. But she didn't want to give the little guy more of a complex than he already had—besides, now that she knew rats were supposed to be "pure creatures" it should make her feel a bit different about the animal as a whole. At least Claire hadn't turned him into a tarantula.

"You have to promise not to hurt Reggie before we go anywhere with you, Claire."

She rolled her eyes. "Do you want me to help or not?"

"Of course I do. I just don't want anything funny to happen. If you can do this to him, I don't want to know what else you might be capable of."

"To be quite honest with you, I didn't mean to do that to him. It was an accident."

"Oh really?"

"Yeah, I meant to turn him into a pig."

"Well, okay. Then let's go."

"That wasn't a promise." Reggie's voice sounded strained. "She didn't promise not to hurt me."

Val frowned. "Maybe it would be better if you don't talk for a while."

Claire first took them to the grocery store down the street to pick up a few things.

"Are these used in the spell?" Val asked after a while, looking skeptically at her basket full of chocolate chip cookies, Häagen-Dazs ice cream, and a head of romaine lettuce.

"No. Why?"

It seemed as though no one understood what *emergency* meant. Val tried to be patient, but it was getting more difficult with each passing moment. Julian had given the distinct impression the key wouldn't be used for a while, but how long did that give them? And what if they were too late? She clung to the hope that Claire would be able to help her. If she couldn't, then Val was out of options.

"*I have faith in you, Valerie,*" Barlow had said to her. "*I know you'll do what's right.*"

He was counting on her. She couldn't let him down.

She wouldn't.

Chapter Nine

———— ⟋⟍⟍ ————

"So . . ." Val said after they arrived at Claire's little basement apartment. She had just seen a cockroach the size of her palm peeking out at them from behind a cookie jar shaped like Oscar the Grouch, but was trying very hard to ignore it. "Do you summon demons often?"

Not the most usual of small talk, but in Claire's case it would have to do. She'd been giving them the cold shoulder all the way back in her rusty Jetta. Despite Val's repeated assurances that she hadn't touched the woman's boyfriend, Claire refused to believe her. Reggie had taken Val's words of advice and hadn't said a single thing since leaving the restaurant. He looked a little green in the whiskers. *Serves him right,* Val thought. The cheeseburger he'd consumed had been nearly the size of Reggie's entire body. Tail excluded.

Claire was still ignoring her while she thumbed through her rather extensive collection of magic books. Some were printed by current and legitimate presses: *A Goddess's Guide to Love Spells and Casseroles, Be a Witch, or Just Look Like One, Curse Your Cheating Man—He Deserves It!* The latter looked quite worn.

On a lower shelf, however, were a few less designed covers and spines. They looked very old, weathered, and cracked. It's through these books Claire was searching.

"Here it is," she said finally, pulling out a very small black leather-bound book only slightly larger than her hand. "The silly thing hides from time to time."

"What hides?"

"The book."

Val glanced at the bookcase, then back at Claire. "The book hides? Seriously?"

There was no joking in the witch's expression. "Yes."

"Why would it do something like that?"

"Just to piss me off."

"Ah."

"So, what kind of demon do you want to summon? There's tons of varieties. They're kind of like insects, that way. There are some little harmless ones. Some cute colorful ones. Then there's the big scary ones with sharp teeth."

"Yeah, let's avoid those."

Claire flipped through the little book. "All demons have category names, but most of my research material's in Latin, and, well, I only took French in school. So that doesn't help me out very much. So, what do you say? Little, big, wings, no wings? Totally your call. We just have to concentrate on being specific. *Très specifique.* That's 'very specific' *en Français.*"

What kind of a demon did Val want to be her guide in finding Julian? Very good question.

"It would be good if it was something small"—she held her hand down at knee level—"Cute, easy to control. Speaks English."

Claire looked thoughtful for a moment. "I think I can do small, cute, and speaks English. How's that?"

"Three out of four ain't bad."

Val heard a crash and turned to look at Claire's open kitchen. "What was that?"

"That?" Claire looked over absently. "That one doesn't speak English. And it's not all that cute, either."

"It's a demon?"

"Pesky little thing, really. I was just experimenting last week, and boom.

"You summoned *that*?" All Val saw was black fur, beady eyes, and what quite possibly was a cigar hanging from its mouth. Then it flipped her the bird and disappeared in a puff of smoke.

She took a moment to compose herself. "How are you going to get rid of it?"

"I think I'm going to burn the place down and collect the insurance money," Claire said matter-of-factly while she flipped through the tiny grimoire. "Let's get started, shall we?"

Even though the balance of the known universe lay in Val's hands—talk about pressure—she was having serious second thoughts about Claire. She worried that going with the very first demon summoner she could find wasn't necessarily the best course of action, and wondered if maybe she should have at least checked the Yellow Pages first.

"Claire, I'm not sure about this."

"Not sure about what?" She'd taken an opaque blue bottle off her shelf and begun to pour white powder from it in a four-by-four circle on the carpet.

"Maybe this isn't such a good idea."

Claire stopped pouring the powder and looked up at Val with obvious annoyance. "Do you have any idea how much this stuff costs?"

"I'll pay you back. Eventually. It's just . . . are you sure this is safe?"

She grinned, finished drawing the circle, and got to her feet. Earlier she'd changed into a purple robe that looked like a housecoat Val had seen recently at Wal-Mart. But Claire seemed to be acting more "mystical" since putting it on over the McDonald's uniform.

"Nothing is safe, Val. That's what makes it *fun.*"

"It's just that I've met a couple of demons in the past couple of days"—she didn't count Alexa since she'd been reduced to a stain and a memory—"and I'm not too happy with either of them. Which is a complete understatement."

Claire frowned at her. "So you're saying you want to call this off? No summoning?"

Val chewed her bottom lip while considering other possibilities, which currently amounted to not a whole heck of a lot.

"Come on! Don't be a party pooper," Claire prompted. "It'll be fun."

"She's a little bit crazy," Reggie piped up from behind a throw cushion. "That's what I love about her."

Claire's eyes narrowed and she glared at him from across the room. He ducked back out of sight. Val was planning on trying to convince Claire to turn Reggie back into a human before they left, but she wanted the witch to be in a better mood before that subject was broached.

"First of all," Claire said after a moment, "every time I summon a demon I learn something new."

Val blinked at that. "*Every* time? How many times have you done this?"

She shrugged. "A girl's got to have a hobby. Especially when she has a cheating boyfriend."

"I didn't cheat!" Reggie yelled. "A *kiss* is not cheating!"

She ignored him. "Why don't I add in some precautions?" She pulled a small chunk of quartz crystal out of the pocket of her robe. "See this? All of the summoning power will be focused into this crystal. While I have it, the demon will have to do whatever I say. Cool, huh? Just figured that out recently. It sure would have helped with my current houseguest. Oh, and as a bonus, your demon won't be able to lie. That'll be a big help since demons are such major liars."

"Tell me about it." She thought about Nathaniel and the obviously false words he used to try to get her to come to Hell with him. As if it was a fabulous all-inclusive vacation instead of eternal damnation. Did he really think he was fooling anybody?

She frowned. *Jerk.*

"So you can fix it so the demon will obey you and can't lie."

"Isn't that what I just said?"

Val crossed her arms. "I just want to make sure I understand you correctly."

"Well, do you?"

"Do I what?"

"Understand me."

For a moment, Val stared at the eager witch. Demons were nothing to mess with. They were evil, vile, underhanded creatures, but Claire didn't seem to care too much about that. The thrill of her little hobby might get her into trouble sooner than later. If she didn't watch out, one day her enthusiasm for playing with such dark forces might end up getting her killed. Or worse.

"Cool," Val said. "Let's do it."

Claire turned off all the lights in the basement apartment so even though it was the middle of the day it was almost pitch-black inside. She lit black candles—unscented—and positioned them on the circumference of the circle. She placed the crystal at her feet just outside of the circle. Then she realized that it was too dark to read from the little book so she had to get a flashlight to hold under her chin. That kind of spoiled the mood.

Reggie refused to stay on the floor in the dark during the summoning. He was afraid the demon-on-the-loose was going to grab him and make a rat sandwich. Since Val couldn't guarantee that was definitely not going to happen, she let him sit on her shoulder after he promised not to try to look down the tank top she wore under her unbuttoned sweater. It took a full minute before he finally agreed.

Claire had a look of proud accomplishment on her face for her little circle of Hell. "Now, Valerie, go ahead and tell the circle what you need the demon for."

"I need a demon guide," Val told the circle. When the circle didn't answer back, she continued, "To find a demon named Julian who has stolen something that I need to get back."

"Good enough." Claire swished her robe and knelt in front of the powdered circle. She opened the book, and then gave Val an enthusiastic sideways grin. "Fasten your seat belts. It's going to be a bumpy ride."

"Not the Bette Davis impression," Reggie grumbled into Val's ear. "*Anything* but the Bette Davis impression."

With the flashlight propped under her chin, Claire read aloud from the little book. It was in another language, something Val didn't understand at all. Was it Latin? Didn't Claire just say she didn't understand that language? How did she even know what she was reading? And should Val be more nervous than she already was?

As a full-fledged angel in Heaven, Val vaguely remembered being able to understand all languages of the human souls who entered through the gates. And just as she'd been told that all unusual meat tastes vaguely like chicken, all languages were the same and understandable to her.

But that was then and this was now.

Even though she wasn't sure Claire understood what she was saying, she still spoke in a commanding tone, never hesitating even once. There was another container next to her—this one squat and about the size of a margarine tub—from which she scattered what looked like pink salt as a punctuation to the end of each line she spoke.

It felt like it was taking forever and nothing was happening, but finally Val felt something. A wind. As if someone had turned on a heat fan. The warm air blew through the room and swirled around the circle. The crystal suddenly began to glow.

"It's working," Claire whispered. "Now concentrate on what you want so we can find the best demon for you."

Concentrate. Okay. Val closed her eyes and tried to think about Barlow. The key. Finding Julian. Nathaniel kissing her, his body pressed firmly against hers.

No, wait, she thought. That wasn't important.

The perfect demon guide. Who would have to obey his summoner and not be able to lie.

Reggie let out a little yelp and Val's eyes snapped open.

The cigar-smoking demon was staring at them from across the room. Well, at Reggie, anyhow. And it looked hungry. Claire had stopped reading and also watched it warily.

"I'm almost finished," she whispered. "I just need to throw a last pinch of shadow salt into the circle."

"Well, let's hurry it up shall we?" Val said . . .

. . . Just as the demon launched itself at her.

"No!" Claire leapt to her feet to block its path. "You're not going to hurt my boyfriend."

"Your *boyfriend*?" Reggie piped up.

"*Ex*-boyfriend."

"*Muck-ruick soorl,*" the demon spat at her.

"How dare you!"

"What did he say?" Val asked.

"No idea," Claire replied. "But it sounded rude, don't you think?"

The demon was growling, obviously agitated that he was being kept from what it probably thought was a tasty snack. Reggie was now so entwined in Val's hair she worried she might need to cut him loose.

The demon took a step forward and Claire held out her hand. "Stop!"

"*Ollor kiiod!*"

And then two things happened at once. The demon jumped at Claire and she said some witchy Latin thing. A pulse of white light emanated from her and touched the demon, causing it to freeze in mid-jump. It looked nervously from side to side, and then . . .

The only way Val thought she could describe it would be to say it *fizzled*. Like a firecracker. Gone. The stogie dropped to the floor and Claire took a second to grind it out with her shoe before she fell forward on the carpet.

Val rushed to her side and shook her shoulder.

"Claire, are you okay?"

She was breathing, but it was shallow. Val couldn't believe Claire had that much power. She'd just vanquished a demon without any props or tools. *Holy impressive, Batman.*

She blinked up at Val, looking a little, stunned. "I just kicked a little ass, I think."

"You did indeed. A little black, furry ass."

"You need to finish the summoning. Just concentrate very hard on what you want . . . throw the shadow salt . . . and keep the crystal safe. I need to . . ." Her voice trailed off.

"You need to? You need to what?"

"Have a nap. G'night." She shut her eyes and immediately started to snore.

Terrific. Just terrific.

Val looked at Reggie, which hurt her neck a little since he was sitting on her left shoulder. "Now what?"

His eyes were very big, but it could have just been their proximity to hers. His whiskers twitched. "Did you see what she just did to that thing?"

"Uh-huh."

He scratched an ear. "I guess I got off lucky."

"I guess you did. Now, situation at hand. What should I do?"

"She could be out for hours. The woman sleeps like a log and snores like a lumberjack. Like you said earlier, we don't have that much time. Finish it."

"Right. Okay. I can do this." Val crawled past Claire to the margarine tub and grabbed a handful of the grainy substance. What had she called it? Shadow salt?

"Okay," she said, mostly to herself. "Concentrate, Valerie."

The strange wind was still blowing. A few books had blown off their shelves. A vase filled with plastic daisies lay broken on the floor. Val leaned forward and picked up the glowing crystal and squeezed the salt tightly in her other hand.

What I want, she thought. *Concentrate very hard on what I want.*

"Okay, here goes nothing." She threw the salt into the circle.

As soon as the shadow salt made contact with the inside of the circle, everything changed. The room got incredibly light, so bright that she had to shield her eyes. Then the wind seemed to switch direction. Instead of moving in a circular pattern, it moved upward, Val's long blond hair blew wildly, straight off her face. Where the circle was drawn on the carpet, flames shot out of the white powder, until they touched the ceiling to form a cylindrical wall of fire. She scrambled back to avoid the intense heat. The crystal glowed brightly in her hand, but remained cool to the touch.

What have I done? she thought with more than a little panic. *And is it too late to be having second thoughts?*

Uh, yeah.

She glanced at Claire who'd moved into the fetal posi-

tion on the floor and was sleeping peacefully while suck-
ing on her thumb.

She was going to be *zero* help.

"I hope you only thought nice thoughts," Reggie said
shakily. "And we get a nice demon."

"Me, too."

The flames cut out as quickly as they'd appeared. The
wind stopped blowing. The brightness subsided everywhere including from the crystal. The white powder circle
lay as if untouched on the carpet.

And from inside the circle Nathaniel looked out at Val
with confusion.

Nathaniel?

Hmm, she thought, feeling stunned. *Guess I shouldn't
have been thinking about him just a minute ago.*

Well, hindsight was always six-six-six, wasn't it?

Not good.

"Valerie?" he asked after a moment.

"Uh-huh?"

He cleared his throat and absently brushed off his long
black jacket. Underneath he wore a black shirt and black
pants. Looked to Val like a bit of a theme. Not that she expected to see him appear in a Hawaiian shirt. Not that she
expected to *see him.* Period. But there he was.

He smiled, but it seemed forced, as if he was confused
about what just happened. That made two of them. "I was
just looking for you at the motel. You weren't there."

"No, I'm not."

His smile faltered. "What's going on?"

"Um . . ."

Nathaniel finally looked down at the circle he was standing in. He looked at Claire, unconscious in her Wal-Mart

robe, clutching the tiny black grimoire, then again at Val with remnants of shadow salt still stuck to her palms. She slipped the crystal into the pocket of her jeans.

His eyes narrowed. "What exactly have you done, Valerie?"

She stared back at him. That was definitely the million-dollar question, wasn't it?

He attempted to move outside of the circle, but the invisible barrier created by the white powder stopped him with an audible zapping noise. He jerked back with a confused expression on his face. Then he held out his hand and lightly touched the barrier. It shimmered.

Val just watched him in silence and a healthy amount of shock, while absently petting Reggie who still sat on her shoulder. He didn't complain, but she could have sworn she heard him murmur, "Oooh, baby."

Nathaniel certainly was an extremely handsome man. Demon. *Whatever.* She hadn't been able to observe him at length before.

Tall, dark, and evil.

He stared down at the circle that kept him trapped. Then he looked at Val slowly, his gray-blue eyes shimmering with an inner fire, and a shiver went down her spine at the intensity of his gaze. Surprisingly, a smile spread across his perfect features.

"So, little angel, now that you have me all to yourself, whatever are you planning to do with me?"

"Hey, do you two know each other already?" Reggie whispered.

"Shhh." Val stared back at Nathaniel and removed her hand from Reggie, who protested a little. "If it's any consolation, I didn't mean to summon you in particular."

He nodded slowly. "I see. Just my lucky day, then?"

"Must be."

His smile widened. "I'm glad. I was hoping to see you again. I wanted to apologize for my rude behavior last night."

"Is that so."

"Yes. It's just . . . I've been dealing with some personal issues. I certainly didn't mean to take any of my . . . frustrations . . . out on a beautiful woman such as yourself."

It sounds pretty good, she thought. So sincere. So warm and friendly, and delivered in that smooth, deep voice that made her knees feel weak.

Stupid knees.

"You're lying."

"Excuse me?" He gave her innocent eyes. "I'm not lying."

Didn't Claire say that the summoned demon couldn't lie? Val was the one who threw the last bit of shadow salt into the circle. She had the crystal safely in her pocket. Didn't that mean she was in charge now? Well, there was only one way to find out.

"Can I ask you a question, Nathaniel?"

"Of course. Anything you desire."

"You've been summoned against your will and are currently trapped inside that circle there. Are you angry with me right now?"

"Furious."

Val's eyebrows went up.

He frowned deeply. "What . . . I didn't mean that. Yes, I did. I'm furious right now. I want to—" He clamped a hand over his mouth.

"What?" she prompted, though an unpleasantly cold

chill had gone down her spine at his answer. "What do you want to do?"

His eyes narrowed and he lowered his hand from his mouth. "I want to tear you apart."

"Yikes," Reggie said. "Are those actual flames in that dude's eyes?"

Val swallowed hard. He wasn't lying now. This was the truth and nothing but the truth. But it didn't change anything. He could be as mad as he wanted to be about this situation—he couldn't do anything about it.

"You need to let me out of here right now," Nathaniel said, though his expression hadn't gotten any friendlier. "You don't know what you're doing. You're in way over your head, little angel. I have given you the opportunity to come with me and you need to realize that it's for the best. *Your* best. *My* best. There is no room for argument. And there is no time for these games. None of this means—"

"Shut up." His words filled her brain up so much that she couldn't concentrate. It was like having every TV channel on at the same time with the volume turned up to maximum.

He didn't say another word.

She began pacing back and forth between the sofa and the bookcase, all eight feet of it. "Okay, Nathaniel, let's get something straight. I don't like you. But I've summoned a demon for a reason, and just because the demon I've ended up with is you doesn't change my plans."

He raised a dark eyebrow, but said nothing.

"I need you to help me find a demon named Julian. I believe you two know each other. He's stolen something from a friend of mine. Something important. I need to get it back. This is nonnegotiable. There's no time to waste. I want to leave immediately for wherever you, as a fellow demon, think he might have gone. Once I get the item back, I will release you. After that I don't want to see you again. Ever. Am I making myself perfectly clear?"

He glared at her. Then nodded his head.

"And don't even think about trying anything funny. This summoning spell binds you to me." She squeezed the crystal in her pocket tightly. "You have to obey me. And as we just proved a minute ago, you can't lie to me." The thought almost made her smile. "Got it?"

Another nod, this time slower and even less friendly than before.

"Now, Reggie." Val pulled him off her shoulder so she could see his furry face. "It's probably best if you stay here. When Claire wakes up you need to talk things through with her. You have to get her to reverse your spell."

His little beady eyes got very wide. "Are you kidding me? I know her. I figure she's got at least another two days before she feels open enough not to turn me into mincemeat. Besides coming with you gives me even more of a chance to prove to her that I'm not just a big loser. That I'm actually brave and noble. And other crap like that. I'm coming with you guys."

"No, you are certainly not coming with us."

"Pleeeaaase?"

Val frowned and moved him closer so she could look him right in his little black eyes. "It's easier this way. Trust me."

"Pleeeaaase?" He tickled her with his whiskers that time, and she rubbed her face.

"You'd rather come with me to track down a demon

who-knows-where, than stay here until your girlfriend
wakes up?"

"Without question."

Val studied the rat for a moment. He seemed very serious and sincere. Maybe it would be a good thing to take
him along. She didn't want to be alone with Nathaniel if
she could help it. Not that she was nervous about being
one-on-one with the painfully gorgeous demon, giving
him the access to now try to tempt her constantly without
a chance for her to catch her breath. Not that she'd ever
give in to temptation, that is. But was that a good enough
reason to put Reggie in danger, too?

She glanced at the demon, then at the rat, and sighed.

It was better to be safe than sorry.

"Okay, you can come."

"Hooray! I think."

She turned to Nathaniel who was tapping his foot impatiently.

"Nathaniel, this is Reggie. He's coming with us."

"Hey, Nate," Reggie said. "Is it okay if I call you Nate?"

Nathaniel crossed his arms and looked away.

"What's with the silent treatment?" Val asked.

Nathaniel glanced at her and pointed to his mouth.

She was confused. "What?"

"Oh," Reggie said. "You did tell him to shut up a
minute ago. Since he's compelled to obey you, I guess
that's what he's doing. He can't talk."

Hmm, Val thought. *I think I'm going to like this.*

With a motion of her hand, she said, "You may talk
again."

Nathaniel gritted his teeth. "You are going to pay for
this, Valerie. You have no idea how dearly."

"Do you want out of that circle, or what?"

His jaw was clenched so tightly that it looked painful. "Yes." The word was a long hiss.

"Promise me that you'll do nothing to harm me or Reggie if I let you out."

It was a struggle, but she finally heard a "Fine."

"You have to promise me. Say the words."

A deep breath now. "I promise that I will not harm you . . . or the rodent."

"His name is Reggie."

He rolled his eyes. "Or Reggie."

"Now you may have noticed that Reggie is a rat. I know that you demons aren't particularly fond of them. Is that going to be a problem?"

"I'll manage."

Val nodded. "Okay. You may exit the circle now."

She tried to look confident, but as soon as he stepped out of the circle she took an immediate step back. Claire chose that moment to roll over, her incessant snoring punctuated by a loud shout of what possibly could have been the words *Fry vat!*

The sound of her voice made Val jump. Her nerves hadn't been very good lately. She wondered if they'd ever be good again.

Nathaniel smoothly moved toward her until he was only an arm's length away. Val expected him to reach out and choke her to death, something violent. Anything. But he didn't. He couldn't. But by the look on his face he probably wanted to.

"Julian," he said. "And you're aware of the fact that we know each other *how?*"

"He told me. You two are buddies?"

"Definitely not."

He sure was tall. Val suddenly wished she was wearing heels. But for demon-tracking, she supposed her second-hand Reeboks were the best choice.

The corner of his mouth twitched. "Are you sure you know what you're getting yourself into, little angel? I am not so easily deterred from my goals, you know. And being that my goal is . . . *you* . . . this situation is perhaps not as dire as I'd originally thought. Perhaps I should be thanking you."

"Don't make me tell you to shut up again."

"We have so much in common that it's truly hard to believe. Perhaps that's why I was assigned to you."

She frowned. "We have nothing in common, demon-boy. Except for finding Julian. And if that means we have to go to Hell to find him, then that's what we're going to have to do. So let's cut with the chitter chatter, shall we?"

He began to laugh then, a rich hearty sound that moved through her body like warm water. It was a good laugh, nothing overtly evil about it. Other than the fact that she knew he was laughing at her for some reason. She didn't like it when people laughed at her. Even when they had good reason.

"What's so funny?"

He shook his head as he tried to get his laughter under control. "You think I'm going to take you to Hell?"

"Isn't that exactly what you've been trying to do since we first met?"

"That's different. That is on my terms, not yours."

She frowned deeper. "But I *command* you to."

"You can command me all you like. It's simply not possible."

"Why not? Are you lying to me right now?"

He raised an eyebrow. "I'm not lying. It's not possible for a human to enter Hell."

"There has to be a way." She hated how weak her voice sounded.

"There is a way. You must first give yourself over to me, body and soul. And that requires you to agree to do so freely"—he stepped closer—"and completely. And utterly without question." He grinned and cocked his head to the side. "My original offer is still up for grabs."

Stop staring into his pretty eyes, she told herself. *Demon. Capital* D. *Demon.*

She finally tore her gaze away from him. "Not going to happen. Take two steps away from me this instant."

He did what he was told and looked annoyed with himself. "That's not fair."

"Is there another way? How do we find Julian without going to Hell? Isn't that where demons are? Tell me. Is there another way?"

"Yes," he said, then looked disgusted. "I am hating this."

"Too bad. What's the other way to find Julian? Tell me right now."

"Most demons rarely go to the head office. That's what we call Hell." His smile returned. "Julian rarely goes there unless he's summoned, or so I've heard. He's not big on dealing with authority figures. Hurts his inflated ego to know he's just a peon."

"Then where would he go?"

"The Underworld."

Val blinked. "The movie with Kate Beckinsale?"

"No. *The* Underworld. That which lies just below the

surface of this dimension. The buffer zone between the earthly realm and Hell itself. Most demons call it home, including myself, for whatever that's worth. I know for a fact that Julian spends a great deal of time there while he plots his little self-important schemes."

"The Underworld," she repeated.

"That's right."

"What do you think, Reggie?" Val pulled him off her shoulder again to look at him directly.

"Ouch! Would you stop squeezing me like that? What do you think I am, a Beanie Baby?"

"Sorry, it's just that my neck was starting to hurt."

"Then don't look at me. Just talk. I can hear you just fine since I'm sitting right next to your mouth. I had my appendix out less than a year ago. Geez, woman."

"Sorry, okay? Now tell me what you think about what Nathaniel just said."

"The Underworld?"

"Yeah."

"Not a fan of Scott Speedman. Kate Beckinsale's pretty hot, though."

Val squeezed him. On purpose this time.

"Ow! Okay, okay. I don't know what you want me to say. If we have to go to the Underworld, then we go to the Underworld. In my book, it sounds a hell of a lot better than Hell. Hey, I just said 'hell' twice in one sentence."

Claire turned over again, clutching the grimoire like a teddy bear to her purple-clad chest. "Extra mayo, no lettuce," she announced, then punctuated the statement with a honking snore.

Val looked at Nathaniel. "Then let's not waste any more time. Let's go."

He sighed. "When?"

"Right now. How do we get there? I don't have any more money for public transportation today. Well, maybe I could piece together bus fare for me, but that's it. You'll have to come up with your share. I think Reggie can probably ride for free."

"Finally," Reggie said. "A plus to being a rat."

Nathaniel eyed the rodent, then looked at Val. "We don't have to take the bus."

"Then how do we get there? Walk?"

"Didn't they teach you anything in Heaven?" He sighed. "I said before that the Underworld is just below the surface of this dimension. All I need to do is open a doorway."

Val waited, but he didn't make any move to do so. "So go ahead and open a doorway."

"Patience, Valerie. Perhaps that's why they threw you so unceremoniously out of Heaven in the first place, don't you think? Patience is one of the seven virtues, after all."

"Nope," Reggie piped up. "She got kicked out for pride. And I'm not talking about the colorful parade."

She pinched his tail, which was met with a high-pitched squeak of pain. "Open the doorway, *now*. That was a command."

Nathaniel's breathing became labored as he stared at her, the amusement leaving his expression as flames filled his eyes. He was trying to fight her control over him, but it was a losing battle.

"Pride," he said after a moment. "I'll have to add that piece of info to your file."

"You do that. Now the doorway?"

"Very well." He turned and surveyed the room. "This will do, I suppose."

He was looking at Claire's massive bookcase, studying the shelves for a moment, then took a step back. Val saw his broad shoulders raise up as he took a deep breath. His hands moved at his sides, palms up, muscles tense, shaking with the effort of whatever he was doing.

She felt the warm air again, but this time it was different. It wasn't swirling, it wasn't going straight up. It was moving toward the bookcase, toward Nathaniel himself.

A pinprick of light appeared on the spine of one of the books. The light grew in size and intensity until it became a moving blue vortex. It narrowed and lengthened, and finally was as tall as Nathaniel was, and slightly wider. Val then watched his shoulders relax, his breathing slow down to normal. He turned to look at her, and she could see a thin film of perspiration on his forehead. He looked weary and, strangely, very human. Opening interdimensional doorways must have been very hard work, she thought.

He turned to the side so she had a full view of the dimensional doorway—a large white light with swirling blue edges. She couldn't see anything on the other side that would give her a clue where it led, which meant she had to trust Nathaniel. Trust that Claire was right about his inability to lie to her. Trust that this wasn't a one-way ticket to down below. The head office. Hell. *Whatever.*

He grinned wearily and gestured toward the light. "Ladies first."

Val hesitated, but only for a moment. She took a deep breath and placed Reggie firmly back on her shoulder. He entangled a paw into her already tangled hair so he'd have something to hang on to.

She was going to get the key back.

She was going to help send Barlow back to Heaven.

Then she was going to do the same for herself and all of this would simply become an unpleasant memory.

It would all be worth it in the end.

Another deep breath and she forced herself to walk toward the light, stopping when she got to Nathaniel. She reached out to him.

"Hold my hand?"

He frowned, hesitated, but finally took her hand in his.

They walked through the doorway. The light filled Val's vision until she could see nothing else. Claire left them with a last call of, "Sesame seed bun!"

Val hoped that was a good omen.

Chapter Ten

———～———

Welcome to the underworld.

That's what the sign said. It was the first thing Val saw as she stepped through the portal and her eyes adjusted to the bright blue sky.

Blue sky?

"This is so weird," Reggie said, voicing her thoughts. "I was expecting, I don't know, gloom and doom. Maybe drippy, slimy rock. This is not gloomy or drippy."

This Underworld bore a striking resemblance to Miami Beach. At least the one Val had seen the other day on an afternoon rerun marathon of *Miami Vice*.

She turned around to look at the portal, but it had shrunk and disappeared immediately. They were standing in the middle of a paved street and had to step quickly onto the sidewalk when a car whizzed by. It looked exactly like a red Porsche.

"Are you sure this is the right place?" she asked Nathaniel who'd stepped away from her by a good ten feet and lit up a cigarette.

He pointed at the sign. "What do you think?"

She frowned. "I can read. But I just don't believe it.

Maybe the palm trees threw me a bit. And the bright shining sun in the sky. And the beach over there."

"If you like, I can return us to where we came from. Just say the word." He smiled, but it looked forced. "Perhaps somewhere a little more . . . private?"

"No. We're staying. It's just . . . what's the word I'm looking for here?"

"It's wacky?" Reggie suggested. "Kooky? Bizarre? Not the normal way of things?"

"Any of those would do nicely."

"Is that actually an ocean?" Reggie raised a paw to point.

Val looked. Past a row of colorful buildings she could see a sliver of shining blue water. And lots and lots of tall palm trees. There were a few multicolored umbrellas on the beach for the gathered sunbathers. And was that a . . . a hotdog cart?

"Definitely wacky."

"Kate Beckinsale would fit in great in this Underworld," Reggie said. "I'm thinking black bikini, Gucci sunglasses . . . me and a bottle of tanning lotion—"

"Enough already."

"They should change the name, though. It's more like Sunnyworld. Or Tanline-land. Yeah, that works."

"I'm glad somebody's having a good time so far."

Nathaniel flicked his half-smoked cigarette against a nearby parked car. "Valerie, this is pointless. You need to release me from this ridiculous spell. Do so and I will help you find Julian of my own free will. You know I'd do anything to help you out."

"Yeah, right."

"I'm quite serious," he approached her and ran a warm

hand down her back, she turned to look into his gray-blue eyes and immediately felt pleasantly woozy. He smiled. "Then we can discuss what's really important."

"Oh," she said, but it came out a little breathy. "And what's that?"

He stroked the blond hair off her face. "You and me."

She put a hand against his chest to push him away but she felt like she couldn't move. Suddenly it was just the two of them, the only ones in the universe, and all she wanted to do was—

"Um, Val?" Reggie said into her ear. "What are you doing?"

She pulled her hand away from the demon as if she'd been burned. Then scowled deeply. "Don't do that."

"Sorry," Reggie said. "I didn't mean to interrupt."

"No, not you." She turned to Nathaniel and jabbed a finger at him. "You."

He shrugged while looking amused. "I don't know what you're talking about."

"Honestly. What you are, what you *do* makes me physically sick."

"You didn't seem so sick a moment ago."

"Aren't you ashamed?"

His smile fell. "Of what?"

"Of what you do. It's disgusting. Nothing you say or do will work on me. As soon as I get what I'm after then I'll release you from this spell. Not a moment sooner. So you'd do best to focus on that goal instead of trying to lie to me because it won't work. I know what you are and I won't be taken in. I'll never give you what you want."

"We'll see about that."

"Yes, I guess we will. Honestly, I can't believe you've

ever been successful at this before. You're so transparent. What do you get, anyhow? When you bring one of us in? Is there a reward? An employee bonus, maybe?"

The pleasantness had left his expression entirely, and his jaw clenched. "You *are* different. In an incredibly annoying way. They must have known how difficult you'd be when they assigned me to you."

"Now," Val continued, feeling a little flushed after her outburst, "I have a limited amount of time to find Julian, so you'd better hope he's here. If we're too late . . ." She trailed off.

"If we're too late, what?"

"Forget it."

"No, tell me. If it's that big of a deal."

She'd already said too much. The last thing she needed was another demon finding out about the key, especially Nathaniel.

"Well?" he prompted after a moment.

"The end of the world," Reggie piped up. "If we don't get the key it will be the end of the world. That's it, isn't it, Val? Sounds pretty damn important, if you ask me."

Val glared at him. "Be quiet."

"End of the world?" That had gotten Nathaniel's full attention. "Isn't that a bit of an exaggeration? What key did Julian steal, anyhow?"

If Nathaniel got his hands on the key she figured he might use it himself. Or he might use it as leverage to get Val to agree to come to Hell with him. No, she couldn't let him find out that they were looking for the Key to Heaven. Not a chance.

"That's none of your business," she snapped, hoping the intensity of her words would cover up the fear underneath them. "You want me to tell you to shut up again? Because I can be guaranteed that you'll actually do it."

He studied her for a moment with a mix of disdain and what could have been a bit of curiosity. "That won't be necessary. I don't particularly care what this key is."

"Good. So you were saying that you know where Julian might be?" Val glanced at a passing Austin Mini that blared Beach Boys music from its large speakers.

"No. Though I do know someone who can tell us."

"Really?" Her eyebrows went up.

"But I want something first. From you."

"You want something . . ." She frowned. "What do you mean? You're not really in a position to negotiate here, you know."

He shrugged. "Have you ever heard the saying that you can catch more flies with honey than vinegar?"

"No, and that's a stupid saying. Why would anyone want to catch flies? What do you want? We don't have much time here."

One side of his lips curled into a smile. "Kiss me. And I'll tell you how we can find Julian."

"Damn, you're good," Reggie said.

"You can't be serious." Val felt her cheeks flush with anger. Or embarrassment. One or the other.

"Very serious. Kiss me and I'll tell you where we need to go."

This was exactly why she didn't want Nathaniel to be her demon guide in the first place. Was he going to use every opportunity to try to tempt her? She'd already told him that it was impossible. But were those just words? The kiss they'd shared the previous night came back to her. *Not good at all*. Well, the kiss had been good. That was the problem This situation *wasn't* good. She didn't want to get any deeper than she already was.

"Come here," she said.

He crooked an eyebrow. "Really?"

"Yes."

He approached so close that she could feel the heat from his body. He leaned over so their lips were only inches apart, and she looked into his gorgeous eyes.

"Nathaniel?" she murmured just before their lips were close enough to touch.

"Yes, my angel?"

"I command you to take me to see the person who knows where to find Julian. Right now."

He straightened immediately and scowled down at her. "That's not fair."

"Tough."

"I'm not promising anything, you know. He might not know where Julian is."

Val crossed her arms. "So then what?"

He smiled unpleasantly. "Then I'd say you're shit out of luck."

His words hit her hard. They didn't have any time to be wrong. Barlow didn't have enough time for her to be wrong. Her eyes filled with hot tears that, before she could stop them, spilled down her cheeks.

Val turned so Nathaniel couldn't see her wipe the back of her hand across her eyes.

Reggie patted her on the cheek with his paw, but he didn't say anything.

"Let's just get going, okay?" she said after a moment, glancing at Nathaniel who looked at her as if he didn't know what to make of the crazy, emotional fallen angel he was temporarily bound to.

"As you wish."

They quickly walked down the street. To get her mind off Barlow, she tried to take in the bizarre tropical surroundings.

It was warm, too. Hot even. She wondered if it was hot because of how close they were to Hell. She was wearing warm clothes: jeans, a purple sweater over a white tank, a thick cream-colored wool coat, and now she was sweating from the unexpected heat. It was early December in Niagara Falls, cold and snowy weather, and she definitely wasn't dressed for a day at the beach.

She heard Reggie panting in her ear from the heat. Or maybe it was just heavy breathing. She never knew with Reggie.

There were other people out on the street, too. Not a lot, but some. At first glance they looked normal. People out walking their dogs, or doing some window-shopping in fancy, upscale boutiques with names like Chez Dante.

At closer glance Val saw there was nothing normal about the people in the Underworld. Though, perhaps *people* was the wrong word to use. Some looked human, but others were more like some kind of creature. Monsters, demons, out walking their little creatures, monsters, or demons. Seeing them this close up she felt fear suddenly grip her, thinking they might come over and attack, but only one monster even bothered to acknowledge their presence as they walked along the sidewalk. It tipped its hat—at least Val thought it was a hat—at Nathaniel.

"Hey Joanna," Nathaniel said. "How's married life treating you?"

"Fantastic." Joanna was about seven feet tall and the color of split pea soup. She had three eyes and what looked like three breasts to match. Unfortunately she was also wearing a two-piece bathing suit to show off her questionable figure as she watered her front lawn. "Haven't eaten him yet, so all bets are off. Ha-ha."

Nathaniel snapped his fingers, like, "aw shucks."

He caught Val staring at him and he shrugged. "Friend of mine. I was invited to her wedding."

Val tucked a long strand of blonde hair behind her ear to keep it in place in the light tropical wind. "I didn't think demons had friends. Or weddings, for that matter."

"Oh, and why would you think that?"

"I don't know. Who'd want to be friends with you, anyhow?"

"Ouch," Reggie said. "And Valerie gets in a zinger."

Nathaniel gave her a sideways glance. "There's a lot you obviously don't know about the Underworld. Or me, for that matter."

He's right about that much, she thought. "Why does the Underworld look like this, anyhow?"

Nathaniel stopped walking for a moment to take in the unusual surroundings. "Like what?"

"Like all *Lifestyles of the Rich and Damned?* All *Melrose Place* meets *The Addams Family?*"

He stared at her. "You've been watching way too much television."

"Watching TV has helped me more than you know."

"Helped you how?"

"With my adjustment to being human. I know what to expect now."

"Oh, because TV is so realistic?" He smiled. "Sure,

keep thinking that way. It'll get you far. Oh, and you should probably watch out. You know what happens to pretty girls who watch too much TV?"

Val frowned. "What?"

"They start packing on the pounds." His gaze slowly tracked down her body and he grinned. "Although, it looks like it may be a little too late."

Her hands immediately came to her waist in a self-conscious motion.

"Don't listen to him Val," Reggie said. "He's just trying to get to you. You've got a smokin' bod. Trust me, there's been more than a few times I've had to leave your presence with a strategically placed magazine in front of me, if you know what I mean."

She grimaced at the mental picture. "Gee, thanks Reggie. I think."

"It's a pleasure to ride on your smokin' hot shoulder."

They made their way a few more blocks up the road. To their left was a tall silver apartment building. Or at least that's what it looked like. *The Underworld couldn't have luxury condos, could it?* she thought.

Way kooky.

"What's here?" Val asked Nathaniel, who'd started walking so fast that she had to jog to keep up to him.

"I already told you. Somebody who might be able to help you."

"Who?"

"You ask a lot of questions."

She frowned at him and crossed her arms. "Who?" she said in a more commanding tone.

He shook slightly with the effort of fighting off the compulsion to obey her.

"His name is Donovan," Nathaniel finally said, looking supremely disgusted with himself for answering against his will.

"And who exactly is Donovan?"

"A Tempter."

"Geesh," Reggie said. "How many of you guys are there, anyhow?"

"Enough."

Great. Just great, Val thought. *Another Tempter.* After this experience, she could probably organize a softball team of Tempters. Or a wrestling team. *Mmm. Nathaniel wrestling.* Potentially shirtless.

She eyed him for a moment as he glared at her.

Jell-O came to mind.

No. No wrestling. No Jell-O.

But now she was kind of hungry.

They took the mirrored elevator to the ninety-first floor. Nathaniel walked confidently down the hallway and knocked on the door at the end.

After a moment it swung inward. From the inside of the darkened apartment, Val heard a deep voice.

"Nathaniel. Well, well. Long time no see."

The speaker slowly came into the light. Since he was a Tempter, Val knew he was going to be good-looking. She just wasn't prepared for *how* good-looking.

Damn. As in *hot* damn.

Donovan was six feet of lean, muscled perfection. He wore black silk pajama bottoms, leaving his chest and washboard abs bare. Where Nathaniel was pale, Donovan was dark. Like rich, expensive, delicious chocolate.

She had the sudden, overwhelming urge to lick him, but managed to control herself.

Just barely.

Nathaniel stared at her with an amused expression. "Donovan. I'd like you to meet someone. This is Valerie Grace."

He raised an eyebrow and extended a hand. "A pleasure." His voice was warm and deep and smooth as silk. Evil silk, that is. And very charming. She took his hand, but instead of shaking it, he raised it to his lips to give it a sensual brush that left a tingling warmth behind—which seemed to be a Tempter Demon trademark.

"Hi," she squeaked.

"Won't you both come in?" Donovan motioned with his muscled arm.

"Ahem," Reggie cleared his throat. "Aren't you forgetting someone?"

Nathaniel sighed. "Oh, and *that* is apparently named Reggie."

Donovan glanced at Val again since Reggie was still on her shoulder. But he didn't look at the rat. His gaze slowly took in every inch of her. "*Very* nice."

"Thanks!" Reggie said.

She swallowed heavily, feeling suddenly naked despite her many layers of clothing, and followed Donovan inside. He flicked on a light so she could see the apartment.

The word *plush* came to mind. Dark plush. The walls were navy. The carpet black and thick with a black sofa against the left-hand wall. There was a modular wall unit that seemed to only contain framed pictures of Donovan on its shelves. Donovan smiling. Donovan looking serious. Donovan pointing at the camera, like, "Hey camera, how you doin'?" The far wall was floor-to-ceiling window that looked out on the main street of the Underworld. The apartment was otherwise bare. *Very demony-bachelor–pad,* Val thought.

She sat down on the black, plush sofa and could have sworn she felt it squeeze her butt. If she wasn't currently in the Underworld, she'd think it was just her imagination.

"So," Nathaniel didn't sit down. He stood stiffly by the huge Andy Warhol–like portrait of Donovan hanging on the wall. "This is a new look for you, isn't it?"

Donovan smiled. And *wow,* what a smile. "You like?"

He shrugged. "Whatever it takes, I guess."

"Nathaniel, you're so cynical."

"I'm not cynical. I'm practical."

"Blah, blah, blah." Donovan turned to Val. "Don't you get sick of hearing him whine about everything?"

"You have no idea."

He laughed. "He's always been a whiner. You need to teach him how to let go of his little job issues. Stop taking everything so seriously. You look like a lot of fun, Val. Do you mind if I call you Val?"

"Not at all," she breathed, thinking that he could call her anything. Then she frowned at herself. His charm was very overwhelming, and she couldn't help but let it affect her. "But I'm not teaching him anything. We're not to-gether. This is just a one-time thing."

"I'm a big fan of one-time things."

"I just bet you are," Nathaniel said under his breath. But this time Val heard him.

"Nathaniel, don't be rude."

"Would you care for a glass of wine?" Donovan didn't seem to care that the other demon was being a jerk.

"I *am* a little thirsty," Reggie said. "So I vote a rousing yes."

Val looked over at Nathaniel.

He scowled at her. "You want wine? I thought you were in a hurry to find this key of yours?"

"Don't be such a party pooper. We have time for one glass of wine."

"Donovan would you just stop it, already? I thought you were on a forced leave of absence from tempting. She's mine, not yours, so don't get any ideas. Lay off the mind tricks, would you?"

Donovan said nothing, but grinned at him.

Val stood up, which took a couple of tries since the couch seemed to be pulling her back down. "I'm yours? Dream on, demon."

He rolled his eyes. "I wish this was just a dream. All of it."

Donovan watched their exchange with obvious amusement. "Lovers' quarrel?"

"No," they said in unison.

Nathaniel shot Val a look then glanced at Donovan. "The only reason we're here is to ask you if you've seen Julian lately."

"Let's have a glass of wine, first. Then we can talk about whatever our lovely Val wants."

"Do you have white?" Reggie asked. "Red always gives me a major headache."

"No," Nathaniel said.

Val smiled. "Where's the wine?"

Donovan gestured toward a set of swinging doors. "In the kitchen."

Val turned to Nathaniel. "Go get us a couple glasses,

would you? You don't have to have one if you don't want to." He opened his mouth to say something, but before he could, she added a, *"Now."*

His jaw clenched and he turned toward the kitchen.

"Wait a sec." She stopped him before he'd taken a step. He turned back, looking surprisingly relieved. She pulled Reggie off her shoulder getting a short protest from her whiskered friend. "Take Reggie with you."

Nathaniel walked toward her and snatched the rat away. They locked gazes for a moment and she could see flames dancing in his eyes before he turned back and walked into the kitchen.

Val sank back down into the friendly sofa.

"Quite impressive," Donovan said, coming to sit next to her. "You command him very well. I never knew he was into that sort of thing."

"Actually he hates it. But he doesn't have much of a choice."

"May I take your coat? You look awfully warm."

That sounded like an excellent idea. She peeled it off and handed it to him. He tossed it to the side of the sofa, and then stared at her chest. "And that sweater looks rather confining."

Val looked at him, into his light green eyes that stood out like chips of emerald against his dark skin. He was playing with her mind, like hypnosis. That's what he was doing—making it so she was finding it difficult to resist his charms. Demon mojo. Making her feel woozy, just as Nathaniel had.

Donovan was right about one thing, though. The sweater was very confining. She took it off. There was still a white tank top underneath so it wasn't like she was stripping naked for him.

"And that tank top." Donovan stroked a warm finger down her now bare arm. "Let's have that, too."

Mmm. Right. Stupid tank top. She started to pull at it, but stopped herself.

She frowned at him. "Wait a minute. This isn't what I came here for. I don't have time for any demon mind games. I get enough of that with Nathaniel. Now, I'm here to find Julian and supposedly you might know where to find him. Now talk—"

He pressed his finger to her lips to quiet her. And then tapped against them gently.

"Val, Val, Val . . . I said we'd talk about that after the wine."

Right. After the wine, she thought. *He did say that. Handsome Donovan said those exact words. Wow, he is so good-looking.*

"I enjoy meeting fallen angels," he breathed in a very sexy way that made her entire body tingle. "But very rarely are they delivered right to my doorstep."

For some unknown reason, her hand had moved to his thigh. Strange, that.

"How do you know I'm a fallen angel?"

He moistened his full, sensual lips with the tip of his tongue, and smiled. "I wasn't positive, but now you've just admitted it to me, haven't you?"

Val heard herself giggle. "Oh. Yeah, I guess I have."

He ran a hand down the front of her top, between her breasts, and then circled it around her waist to pull her body fully against him. "Also the fact that you're incredibly, sinfully beautiful."

Okay, that worked for her.

"Kiss me, Val. Then hand over that annoying little tank top."

She shrugged. "Okay."

He touched his lips to hers and she tried to kiss him as best she could with the limited amount of experience she had. The only other kiss she'd had was with Nathaniel. Just last night. In her motel room. Was this better? She wasn't sure. But the fact that she was able to think during it was probably a giveaway to the fact that it wasn't.

Val's mind hadn't been working at all when Nathaniel kissed her.

Donovan wasn't waiting for her to take the tank top off, he already started working it up her body. She felt his warm hand slip underneath and move up toward—

Wait a minute, she thought suddenly. *What the hell am I doing?*

Luckily she didn't have to push Donovan away. He was pulled away. Forcibly. He landed on the black shag carpeting a few feet in front of her.

Nathaniel stood next to the couch. There were two broken glasses of wine on the carpet next to him. Val looked up at him but couldn't see his eyes for all the flames that they held. His mouth was set in a thin angry line. He glared at her and she felt like she wanted to shrivel up and fade away. His furious gaze moved down to her stomach and she hurriedly pulled the tank top down to cover her bare skin.

Reggie waddled into the room from the kitchen. He looked so small on the floor, struggling to move through the thick carpet. He surveyed the damage.

"So, what did I miss?" he asked.

Chapter Eleven

Val opened her mouth to say something, some sort of explanation for why Nathaniel had had to drag Donovan off her after being alone for only two minutes. But she came up blank. Besides, Nathaniel wasn't looking at her anymore. He was looking at the other demon.

Donovan laughed as he glanced up from the floor at Nathaniel.

"This is funny to you?" Nathaniel said.

"Of course it is. I had no idea you were so possessive. You told me that you weren't together."

"We're not. She's just another assignment"—he eyed Val—"who, by the looks of things, is well over her head cold." His gaze returned to Donovan. "Stop laughing."

Donovan got slowly to his feet and brushed himself off. His amusement gradually died down. "Then what's the harm in having a little fun?"

"Show her."

Donovan's sudden frown chased away the remaining traces of amusement on his handsome face. "What did you just say?"

"Show her."

"Nathaniel—" Val began.

"Show her what you really are."

Donovan looked worried now. "There's no need for that. Don't take your job frustrations out on me. Unlike you, I enjoyed being a Tempter. How else would I get the chance to meet such beautiful women? Let's just say this was a misunderstanding and leave it at that, shall we?"

"There is a need. Show her and we'll see if your charm still works on her. Consider it a little experiment."

Donovan stared at Nathaniel for a long moment. Then he looked at Val and smiled. "Very well. I'm quite confident in my natural abilities, anyhow."

Val glanced at Reggie who was still on the floor and they shared a "what the hell is going on?" look.

Donovan closed his eyes and after a moment something began to shimmer on the surface of his perfect dark skin. An aura of some kind. Underneath it he seemed to shrink and change into something different, but she couldn't quite see what it was until he was finished. Then she could see all too well.

"Oh," she said, taking in the sight before her. "See, that's much, much different."

The demon now stood a foot shorter than she was. He was stocky. His skin was still dark, but it was more of a gray color now instead of the rich chocolate hue from before. He had a single strip of silver hair going down the center of his head. His eyes were huge, taking up the entire upper half of his face, still green . . . and definitely his best feature now. But they were overshadowed by the fact that he didn't have a nose.

He grinned. "How do you like me now, baby?"

Val looked at Nathaniel who seemed barely able to

control his amusement. He shrugged at her. "Other than his charm skills, Donovan is very adept at personal glamour. One of the best I've ever known. Wouldn't you agree?"

Donovan still wore the silk pajama bottoms. They were tight around his now ample waist and pooled at his ankles.

She forced herself to say something to the troll-like demon. Anything. "Still a hottie. You just can't help it, can you?"

Donovan shrieked with delight. "See! I told you, Nathaniel! Ha! Now, Val, why don't we spend a little more time getting to know each other, gorgeous. I have another bottle of wine on ice just waiting for us."

She nodded. "Wow. That sounds great. But first, why don't you tell us about Julian? Seen him lately?"

Donovan absently scratched his butt. "Nah, not lately. But I think they were talking about him the other day down at the one of the faery pubs. The one called the Rosebud. Yeah. I was in there with a lady friend of mine"—he waved a hand at her—"Nothing serious. Don't worry, baby, you're the only one for me now. Anyhow, I thought I heard somebody mention his name. He's a regular there. Maybe that's where you should check."

"Faery pub?" she said skeptically.

He nodded, then grinned lasciviously. "Now how about that glass of wine?"

They exited Donovan's apartment so quickly that Val left her coat and sweater behind. But it didn't matter. It was too hot for them anyhow. Besides, she wanted out of there. She also wanted the last half hour of her life back.

The thought that she'd let that little troll touch her

made her feel sick. She had the sudden desire to have a really long shower.

It was too bad. He'd been so hot.

It wasn't that she was upset he wasn't as good-looking as she'd originally thought. She just didn't like being lied to. What had Nathaniel called it? A glamour? Obviously some kind of magical cloak of beauty to cover what one really is underneath. Using a glamour was cheating as much as using the demon charm mojo. As far as she was concerned, if Donovan was a troll, then he should be a troll. He shouldn't try to be a gorgeous demon.

Speaking of . . .

She turned her head. Nathaniel was walking a few paces behind her. Reggie perched on his shoulder now. That was strange. Julian had reacted like Reggie was poison to him. She would have expected Nathaniel to behave the same, not chauffeur the little guy around as if it didn't affect him at all.

She stopped walking until he caught up to her.

"So," she said. "What do *you* really look like?"

"What are you talking about?"

She nodded toward the apartment building they'd just left. "Donovan was using a glamour to look so good. I just want to know what you actually look like underneath it all. You don't have to be embarrassed. I'm not here to judge. Just curious."

He studied her for a moment before his lips twitched into a small grin. "Are you trying to say that you think I look good?"

Val sighed and started walking again. "Forget it."

"I think I'm flattered."

"Don't be."

He caught up to her. "Just for the record, I don't use a glamour. I might use a little extra bit of charm to help me out from time to time, but with me, what you see is what you get."

She glanced at him sideways. "And I would believe that, because?"

"I already told you I used to be human."

She shrugged "You could have been an ugly human."

His grin widened. "Why Valerie Grace, I think you're attracted to me."

Val's cheeks immediately warmed and she watched Reggie's eyes widen. "Am not."

Nathaniel took in Val's flushed response with obvious amusement. "That's why I just don't understand why you're being so difficult. You like me, I like you . . ."

She wanted desperately to wipe that grin off his face. "Donovan's a better kisser. No offense."

That did the trick. His grin slid right off his face. "If you knew half of the evil things Donovan has done you would not be so glib."

"Like the things you've done?" she countered.

"You have no idea what I've done."

"I can guess."

He blinked, and studied her for a moment before replying. "I think you might be surprised, little angel. You don't know a damn thing about me. Who I am, what I've done, what I'm capable of. You know nothing. That's what I need to remember when we're together: what my assignment is. I can never forget it. Nothing you say or do can affect me, make me change my mind. Nothing."

They glared at each other.

"Okay you two," Reggie said. "Enough already. This is enough to give a rat a headache."

Val took a deep breath. "You're right, Reggie. Let's just focus on finding Julian. Then this can be over and you can convince Claire to change you back. You don't want to stay stuck like that forever, do you?"

Reggie cleared his throat. "I'm thinking a dozen roses. And a sincere, heartfelt apology."

"Who's Claire?" Nathaniel asked.

"My ex," Reggie said. "She's the witch who turned me into a rat. She also helped Val summon you. We're just like a big, happy, scary, dysfunctional family now, aren't we? Hey, Nate, you wouldn't happen to be able to reverse my spell, would you? That would save a lot of groveling on my part."

"No," Nathaniel said with disinterest. "I can't. Nor would I want to if I could."

"Meanie."

Val had one thing to say for the Underworld, everything seemed to be within walking distance of everything else. She wondered how much space it actually took up. Or if it was a magical displacement of space. And if she should be wearing some kind of sunscreen under the hot sun since she burned easily.

"You're sure you want to go to the Rosebud?" Nathaniel asked after a few minutes. Annoyance still tinged his words.

"Of course. If anyone there knows about Julian, I have to talk to them."

She was looking forward to the faery pub, actually. She loved faeries. Claire had a faery tattoo on her lower back, which she'd taken from a book about faeries she'd shown

Val when they'd still been on speaking terms. The tattooist had gotten it a little wrong, though, and had drawn the faery without a neck so it looked as if it was in a perpetual shrug.

Yes, they were pretty little faeries in that bright, colorful book. With their gossamer wings, flitting here and there. How cute. How harmless and adorable—

Nathaniel pushed open the front door of the pub.

How incredibly scary, horrible, and wrong.

Val blinked in disbelief at what was behind that door.

It looked to her as if faeries who lived in the Underworld were a little different from the ones who floated on bubbles and hung out in flower gardens.

The Rosebud resembled a hardcore biker bar on the inside. Dartboards, dark, dank atmosphere, smoke hanging heavy in the air, carcasses of odd creatures nailed to the walls. They walked into the pub through a narrow, musty-smelling passageway, pushing past what felt like cobwebs hanging from the ceiling. The bar itself was about twenty by twenty feet. Small and smelly. At a quick glance Val could count six booths and three small round tables in the middle that were carved out of rock. The bar counter had eight stools. Every seat in the house was full, but conversation and the loud, throbbing heavy metal music had stopped the moment they entered. And every eye turned to look at them.

A large, burly man with a long, stringy gray beard and a belly to shame Santa himself got to his feet so fast his chair fell and clattered to the floor behind him. He wore a dirty white T-shirt under a studded leather jacket. Grease stains marked his worn jeans. He had a fierce, unfriendly expression on his face. When he turned Val saw that his jacket had slits in it to accommodate his wings.

His pretty, colorful, gossamer wings.

He was a faery. In leather. A biker faery.

Sure, Val thought. *Why not?*

"Who the hell are you?" he growled.

Val gulped, then opened her mouth to say something. Nathaniel held a hand out in front of her. "Let me handle this."

"Oh, this should be good," Reggie said.

"What's your name, demon?" the biker faery asked.

"Nathaniel."

"I've heard of you."

"Have you?"

"Yes, a Tempter Demon, correct? By the name of Nathaniel? Oh, your reputation precedes you."

"Is that right?"

"Yeah." The faery smirked. "Heard you're one failed assignment away from getting a pair of wings of your own."

Nathaniel's eyes narrowed. "You heard wrong."

"I doubt that."

"We're looking for somebody."

"Who's 'we'?" The faery glanced at Val and Reggie.

"That's not important," Nathaniel said.

"It's important to me." A few more scary faeries stood up from their tables. "And it's important to my friends. So, hey, looks like it's pretty damn important. We don't like strangers—they make us all nervous and jittery. We don't like feeling that way."

"Well that's just too damn bad." Nathaniel moved

forward so he and the faery stood chest to chest, glaring at each other.

"I'm Valerie," she said suddenly and Nathaniel shot her a look. "And this is Reggie. Say hi, Reggie."

"Howdy."

The biker stared at her for a few very uncomfortable moments. Then he smiled. "That's more like it. Come on in, Valerie. Have a drink."

"That's very nice of you. But we don't have time for a drink."

"Now we don't have time," Nathaniel said under his breath. "*Women.*"

"Well, we *don't.*"

The biker signaled to the bartender who positioned a shot glass on the bar top. He filled it with an amber-colored liquid.

"On the house."

"Oh, well, okay then. If you insist." Val took the glass and looked at it skeptically.

"Bottoms up," the biker said.

She drank it and scrunched her nose in disgust. It tasted like nail polish remover. With just a *hint* of vanilla.

"What *was* that?" she wheezed.

"Moonshine. Our house specialty." He patted her on the back. "It's good for you. Maybe put a little hair on your chest."

"That's what I'm afraid of."

He laughed at that.

"Allow me to introduce myself to you. You can call me Bud."

"Bud," she repeated.

"My family name is Rosebud, but I just go by Bud."

Nathaniel snickered. "Rosebud. Isn't that pretty."

Bud turned around to face the demon. "What did you say, boy?"

"Just that you have a very pretty name. But all faeries do, right?"

"Who are you calling a *faery?*" His eyes narrowed.

"Isn't that what you are?"

"Maybe I don't like the way you say it."

Val went to stand in front of Nathaniel.

"Just ignore him," she told Bud. "He's just trying to get a rise out of you. I think he's looking for a fight."

"He's come to the right place. I'm sure I can take him."

"Out of my way," Nathaniel growled at her as he stared at Bud as if he wanted pluck off his wings and fry him with a magnifying glass.

"Behave yourself," she hissed. "Or else."

"Or else"—his flame-filled gaze met hers—"what?"

Val held her ground. "Or else I'll *make* you behave yourself."

He continued to hold her gaze and his teeth were clenched when he said, "You will not have power over me forever, angel. And when you don't, you're all mine."

She didn't flinch. "Finished?"

He finally broke their staring match and stormed over to a darkened corner.

Bud was studying her. "You handle him well. I'm quite impressed."

"Thank you."

"You are lovers?"

She nearly choked at that. "No. He's sort of under my control at the moment. I summoned him as my guide to the Underworld."

"Ah, your first time, I take it?"

"First and last, hopefully."

"Why? You don't like it here?"

She shrugged. "It's the *Underworld*."

"And that makes it a bad thing?"

"Not a bad thing. Just not something I need to repeat." She glanced nervously around the bar. *Okay, enough small talk.* "We're looking for another demon. His name's Julian. Blond hair, high cheekbones, hot in a completely despicable and evil way? I'm told he comes in here a lot."

Bud handed her another shot. "I know who you mean."

She looked at the shot glass of moonshine, then drank it down and wheezed again. "Smooth."

Bud smiled, showing chipped teeth—or maybe they were just naturally sharp and pointy like that. "So you're looking for Julian, eh? Did he do you wrong?"

"You could say that."

"He's got his eyes on the prize, that one. Some demons are slackers"—he glanced over at Nathaniel who was still having his pity party in the corner—"and self-pitying fools. Julian knows he needs to look out for himself."

"Why do you say that?"

"He was in here earlier for a drink to celebrate something. Happier than I'd ever seen him before."

"Did he happen to say why he was so happy?"

Bud shrugged. "Don't know exactly. But he was bragging that he has a meeting with Vaille before the big party at the mansion tomorrow."

"Vaille? Who's that?"

He raised a thick, gray eyebrow. "*Mayor* Vaille, of course. Sugar, where are you from?"

"Niagara Falls."

He frowned. "You're not from around here?"

"Nope."

"So . . . that wouldn't happen to mean that you're human, would it?"

She paused. "Technically, yes. At least for the moment."

"Damn." He glanced down at her two empty shot glasses.

Val looked at Bud—there were now two of him staring at her with concern. The two Buds would come together and then pull apart. Kind of like a kaleidoscope. It was sort of cool. She tilted her head. "There's two of you, did you know that?"

"I didn't know you were human," Bud said.

Nathaniel approached them again.

She pointed at him. "Oooh, pretty colors."

"What did you do to her?"

"I gave her a couple of shots of moonshine, is all."

"Moonshine," she repeated. "Homemade whiskey. Like on *Dukes of Hazzard*. Ride 'em, cowboy. Yee-haw!"

"No, it's *actual* moonshine. Doesn't react well with humans. In fact, I'm surprised you're still standing."

"Whaddyamean?"

Bud frowned. "What did you say?"

She grabbed his shoulder. "Whassgoingon?"

Nathaniel sighed. "What will to happen to her?"

Bud shrugged. "If she lives through the first five minutes it wears off fairly quickly after that, I think." He frowned. "Last human who did two shots actually blew up. So, perhaps you should clear out. I just had the place professionally steam cleaned."

Blew up? She didn't like the sound of that. Although

the picture in her mind made her laugh a little. Then she hiccupped and covered her mouth. "'Scuse me."

Val didn't drink much. Becky took her out last week for a few daiquiris. Becky had downed six—claiming stress from working for Seraphina as the reason behind her need for booze—and Val had one. She felt kind of dizzy after it. She'd stopped at one since she didn't like the way it made her feel.

Today was the revenge of the strawberry daiquiri.

Nathaniel rolled his eyes while he watched her sway back and forth. "Maybe this would be a good opportunity for us to break our little spell, Valerie."

"No!" She raised a numb finger and inspected it for a moment until she realized she had something else to say. "You, demon hottie, I command that you look after me and ensure I come to no harm. Nonewhassoever. No harm."

He raised his eyebrows. "Demon hottie?"

"She's drunk!" Reggie announced.

"Ten points to rat-boy"—Val jabbed her interesting finger in his direction—"rat-boy wins. Woo!"

"Asshole." Nathaniel glared at Bud. "What were you thinking?"

Bud took a step toward Nathaniel so they were chest to chest again. Val watched Bud's wings bounce gently with his movement. *Pretty.* "I want you out of here. Now."

Nathaniel threw the first punch, which Bud easily ducked, quickly coming around to pin the demon's arm behind his back. "You're just damn lucky Mayor Vaille has that Belligerent Magic Decree in effect," Bud growled, "or I'd wipe the floor with your ass right now."

In his current position Nathaniel stared at the floor. "It could use it. This place is a hole."

Bud released him. "Get out of here."

He glanced over at the window. "But it looks like the start of an unscheduled dark-time outside. We can't leave yet."

"Tough shit, demon."

Val clutched the bar to keep on her feet. "I think I'm gonna hurl."

"Now you're definitely leaving," Bud said. "Or else."

Bud's friends stood up from their tables to back their buddy. Nathaniel eyed them for a moment. "Fine. We'll go."

"Dark-time," Val repeated. "Snuggle bunny needs to tuck me in. Where're my jammies?"

"Come on, Valerie." He gripped her arm and directed her toward the door.

"It'll be okay, Val," Reggie spoke slowly so she'd understand him. "Just don't pass out on us. And try real hard not to puke. Or at least give a warning so I can hang on for dear life. We'll get you some coffee. Are there Starbucks in the Underworld?"

Bud and his friends marched them to the door, opened it, and shoved them outside without another word.

She glanced around. *Oh, so this is what he meant about dark-time. Cool.*

It was like dusk outside. When they'd entered the bar the sun was high in the sky. Val glanced drunkenly at Nathaniel. He looked around with an expression she'd never seen on his face before. It looked like he was nervous.

"Bud says Julian's seeing the mayor tomorrow," she slurred. "Mayor McCheese, or something weird like that.

There's going to be a party. I like parties. I think I like parties. I'm kinda hungry. Want some Jell-O. Maybe another drink. Maybe some pretzels, too."

"Great," Nathaniel said. "Let's get to shelter and we'll talk about it. And let's move quickly, okay?"

Her eyes felt weird. No, it wasn't her eyes. It was getting darker out. Steadily and rapidly darker.

"What's happening?" Reggie asked. "Is this normal?"

Nathaniel glanced around the empty street. "Unfortunately for us, yes."

When the last bit of light disappeared and the street lamps flickered on, Val heard the sound. A distant high-pitched squawking that raised the hair on the back of her neck.

"Whasssaaat?" she asked, clinging to Nathaniel's tense arm.

"Nightflyers. We need to find shelter immediately."

Reggie dug his claws into her shoulder. "Nightflyers? Are those, like, hawks? Birds of prey that like to eat rats?"

Nathaniel pulled Val along after him as the squawking and flapping got closer. "Worse."

"Why's it so dark?" she asked. She'd never heard of Nightflyers before. She couldn't get too excited about them yet. Also she was too drunk to care much beyond the feel of Nathaniel's muscular arm.

Very nice.

"Dark-time happens often in the Underworld," Nathaniel explained. "More often that night in the earthly realm. There are planned dark-times and some are unexpected. Like this one. Those faeries should have let us stay there until it passed. Bastards."

"*Biker* faeries," Val added, drunkenly. "With pretty wings."

"Come Valerie, there's no time to talk—"

Suddenly a dark shadow swooped over them and Val felt the whoosh of wind and the light touch of a rubbery wing against her bare arm.

"What do they want?" she asked shakily. This was real. And it was bad.

Nathaniel pulled her along with him so quickly that she was afraid she'd trip and fall since her legs already felt shaky and numb. He tried a door to what looked like a convenience store but it was locked.

"Nightflyers only come out during dark-time, they can't exist in the light. They come out into the open like this for one reason and one reason only."

"What?"

"To feed."

She didn't have to ask what they ate. They weren't running along the street because the Nightflyers had a potato chip craving.

"Can't you do something demony?"

"What does that mean?"

"Laser beams from your eyes," Reggie suggested in a quavering voice. "Or destroy them with a fiery thought."

Nathaniel glanced back at them. "You've both been watching way too much television."

"But earlier today I saw Julian vanquish Alexa. Barely broke a sweat turning her into a pile of ashes."

He turned again to frown at her. "Are you serious? Alexa? Just what is this key he stole?"

"That doesn't matter right now. Can't you do something like that? Vanquish these Nightflyer things?"

"No. I have certain abilities in the earthly realm. Powers to heal, like what I did to your ankle"—their eyes met for a brief moment—"or to destroy, like what you say Julian did." He paused to bat at a Nightflyer swarming about his head. The creatures must have claws because she saw a streak of red appear on Nathaniel's cheek. Demons bleed red? Or did that have something to do with him being human before he became a demon? His grip on her hand tightened. "But the Underworld is an official neutral zone. There is barely any magic used aside from the odd glamour. And no destructive magic at all can originate here." Which, at the moment, is a very bad thing."

"Can't you open a portal? Just so we can escape and come back later?"

He shook his head. "No time. It takes way too much concentration."

"Then we're in huge trouble, aren't we?"

Val heard Reggie's teeth chattering but he had nothing to add. Wasn't really the time for chitchat, anyhow, she thought. Maybe screaming, or crying. But not chitchat.

Nathaniel stopped running and she came to a halt, too. She looked around. Four Nightflyers had landed and surrounded them.

He stared fiercely at the creatures and pulled Val against him. "I'll protect you. Just stay close to me."

She blinked at him. "You'll protect me? Why would you do that for me?"

He turned and met her gaze for an intense moment, then looked away. "Not exactly my choice. In the faery bar you commanded me to protect you, remember?"

She did remember that. His lack of interest in her safety above and beyond the bond she'd invoked by summoning him was oddly disappointing. But she could have sworn she saw something else in his eyes—was it concern? Fear? She couldn't tell for sure. But if it was going to keep her and Reggie alive, she'd take it. She moved closer to him, holding tight to his hard, muscled arm. They turned slowly in a circle to make sure none of the Nightflyers could creep up on them.

Val felt something wet trickle onto her shoulder.

"Oops," Reggie said. "Sorry."

She shuddered. "Please tell me you didn't just pee on me."

"I'm really scared, okay? You were right. I should have stayed behind with Claire. No wait, scratch that. I shouldn't have kissed the blackjack dealer. That's where all my trouble began."

"Talk to them," Val said to Nathaniel. She still felt a bit drunk, but it wasn't as bad as it was before. She hoped so, anyhow. She needed her wits about her as quickly as possible. "You're from around here. Reason with them. There's got to be a way."

He shook his head, not taking his gaze from the leathery creatures. "They don't communicate like we do. Not anymore. You can't reason with them."

"Why are they just"—she looked at them—"staring at us?"

"They're waiting for us to run again. We're prey to them. If we don't move, their sensors won't trigger them to attack."

It felt as if Reggie was mopping at her shoulder with his paw. "So we should just stand here. All quiet and still-like. And when the sun comes up again they'll leave?"

"Excellent plan if this was a quick dark-time." Nathaniel

looked at the sky. "But it looks as if this might be an extended one. The Nightflyers have a keen sense of smell, too."

Reggie sighed. "Then I'm even sorrier about my little 'accident.'"

"You and me both. So what do we do now, Nathaniel?" Val shivered. It was cold out. No sun equaled an immediate chill and her sweater and jacket were long gone.

Nathaniel eyed her for a moment, then peeled off his leather coat and draped it over her shoulders. Reggie crawled out on top of it and glared with annoyance at the demon. Val just looked at him with surprise at the unexpectedly kind gesture.

"You do nothing but keep yourself safe. Whatever it takes. I'll have to fight them."

"Four of them? Against you?"

He turned and smiled at her, raising an eyebrow. "Are you concerned for my safety?"

She dug her fingers into his arm. "Yes."

His eyebrow rose higher.

"I'm concerned because if you get yourself eaten, then we're next on the menu."

His smile remained. "Then, my beautifully annoying angel, I suggest while I'm keeping them busy, you and your rodent escape."

He grabbed Val and kissed her fully and deeply on the lips, then let her go. "Wish me luck."

Before she could say another word he rushed one of the monsters.

Chapter Twelve

The Nightflyers encircled Nathaniel and he began fighting against them. He was tall and strong and a good fighter, but there were four of them—large, hulking, black-winged, hungry monsters—against only one of him. He would lose. It was obvious.

"I think he said something about running?" Reggie's voice trembled and she felt his sharp nails dig into her shoulder.

Val nodded but couldn't tear her gaze away from Nathaniel. He kicked one Nightflyer in its black stomach and it went down. The claws of another tore through his shirt. Every time he got a good punch or kick in against one, the other three would rally and attack again.

They were going to destroy him.

"Uh, that running thing?" Reggie said again. "Now would be a good time for that."

Val looked around for something she could use to help Nathaniel, but there was nothing. The street was dark and empty, the darkness bringing in a chill that even Nathaniel's coat over her shoulders couldn't fight.

Nathaniel swatted one of the Nightflyers away and

stared at her for a moment. "Are you deaf, woman? I told you to run."

"I know, it's just—"

"Just nothing. RUN!"

The darkness of the Nightflyers blocked Nathaniel from her view and she heard a tearing noise and a short scream of pain.

She began to run toward him, but had only taken two steps when a fifth Nightflyer landed right in her path. It was easily eight feet tall and probably weighed three hundred pounds. Its shiny, black leathery wings folded behind it. At first glance it looked almost humanoid, but on second glance . . . there was nothing remotely human about this creature. Its face was flat, as dark as the rest of it, and ugly. Black button eyes stared at her with no emotion behind them. Nothing but a mild interest in every move, every flinch she made. And the odd sense that it was very, very hungry.

"Shoo," Val said. "Go away!"

The Nightflyer cocked its thick, hairless head to the side and stared at her. She made a quick move to one side but it mirrored her movement to block her. An icy chill went down her spine. She couldn't hear Nathaniel anymore. Just the flapping of wings. Her heart unexpectedly ached at the thought of losing Nathaniel.

He was gone.

And she was next.

"Uh, Val . . ." Reggie whimpered. "What now?"

The Nightflyer licked its lips with a dark forked tongue and seemed to smile at her, showing its long sharp teeth, each one like a razor blade. It reached out with its horrible clawed hand and she staggered out of its reach, tripping over the curb behind her and falling to the ground. She scrambled backward until there was nowhere left to go.

The Nightflyer got closer and closer until it was only a few feet away . . .

. . . And exploded.

Small dry, dusty pieces of it shot out everywhere, including over Val. It felt like dirt, like someone had just thrown a ball of crusty dirt at her.

The other Nightflyers squawked and flapped their wings violently. She heard the sound of a gunshot—loud and shattering in the dark silence. The Nightflyers lifted off the ground and flew away into the sky, leaving Nathaniel's body behind. Val swallowed hard as she looked at him lying on the pavement to her left. He wasn't moving.

Then she looked back in front of her. The darkness was so thick it was like ink. Or like the gravy they served at the Downtown Niagara Diner. Thick and dark and slightly lumpy. The main lump was moving through the darkness toward her holding a big gun.

She took in a sharp inhale of breath. It was a creature, quickly approaching her, and it was even more hideous than the Nightflyers. Seven feet tall, one large eye in the middle of its forehead. Sharp claws on its four-fingered hands. Pointed ears. A wide nose and thin lips on a gray, hairless, wrinkled face.

She looked down from its hideous countenance. It wore a T-shirt from Madonna's *Who's that Girl?* concert tour. And blue jeans.

"You okay?" It rested the shotgun over its shoulder and offered her a clawed hand.

She eyed the monster warily, but couldn't take her eyes off the T-shirt. The monster looked down at itself.

"The woman is a goddess," it said. "Even back in the Sean Penn years. I'm Lloyd, by the way."

She tentatively took his hand and he helped her to her feet. She looked at his smiling face. He had sharp teeth, too. But the fact he was a Madonna fan made him less scary. "Lloyd?"

He nodded, then looked over with a frown to where Nathaniel lay. He hurried over and knelt by the demon's side. Val ran to join him.

He gently ran his clawed hand over Nathaniel's bruised and bleeding face, resting for a moment on his forehead. Nathaniel looked like he'd been run through a paper shredder for all the cuts he had on him. His shirt was torn down the front to show the bloody ruin of his chest.

"Is he . . ." Val began. "Is he gone?"

Lloyd looked up at her. "Nah. He'll be okay. Nathaniel's a trouper. It would take a lot more than this to do him in."

She felt surprised by that. "You know him?"

"Yeah, we go way back. Who are you?"

"Valerie," she said absently. "And this is . . ." She reached up on her shoulder to touch Reggie but he wasn't there. She looked frantically around the dark, deserted street. "Reggie? Where are you?"

She saw a little furry bump on the road over where she'd faced off against the Nightflyer. She ran over to see Reggie lying on his back, legs in the air. She took her index finger and pressed it against his furry chest and was relieved to feel his wildly beating heart.

"Reggie, snap out of it."

A paw twitched and he moved his furry face to the side to look up at her. "My life flashed before my eyes."

"And?"

"I think I need to do some good deeds. ASAP."

"You do that." She leaned over and let him crawl slowly up on her still unpleasantly damp shoulder before she stood. "Reggie, this is Lloyd."

"Eeeekk!" Reggie yelped. "Err . . . I mean, *nice to meet you.*"

"Likewise."

"How did you know we were out here?" Val asked. "So you could rescue us?"

"Actually, I didn't. Just doing a little Nightflyer target practice. I find that it helps me reduce stress." Lloyd picked Nathaniel up as if he weighed next to nothing. "It's still not safe outside and I'm nearly out of bullets. I think we should head back to my place. It's close by."

That was the best suggestion Val thought she'd ever heard.

Lloyd's semi-attached home was three blocks away. He fiddled with a key to open the front door, flicked on a light, and let them inside. The interior of his home was different from what Val would have expected for a one-eyed monster. Very nice, mostly a color scheme of roses and pinks. Warm and inviting. A narrow hallway led to a living room. Stairs led up to the second floor.

"Your wife decorates?" she asked. After her brush with death she was now feeling as sober as she had before their visit to the faery pub. Although, a headache had set in: an instant moonshine hangover.

Lloyd smiled and shook his head. "Nah, you're looking at a confirmed bachelor." He glanced around his place.

"Oh the pink? Can't help it, it's my favorite color. So soothing. Also, it helps to stimulate creativity."

Val followed as he carried Nathaniel up a flight of stairs and placed him onto a double bed. Nathaniel lay there very still and unconscious and broken.

She turned to Lloyd's shadowed hulk of a figure in the quaintly decorated room. "You're sure he'll be okay?"

He nodded. "Promise. He's pretty cut up, but demons tend to heal quickly. Don't worry your pretty little head."

She looked at him sharply. "I'm not worried."

Lloyd fiddled absently with a bedside arrangement of gerbera daisies. "But I thought you said—"

"I'm *not* worried."

He nodded again. "Why don't I go make some hot chocolate while we wait for him to wake up?" He left the room without waiting for an answer.

Val looked down at the unconscious demon. His severe wounds had already started to heal. She reached down to touch where a claw mark had been on his cheek and was now nothing more than a faded line, and she traced it slowly with her fingertip to his full lips as she remembered how it felt when he'd kissed her.

"Uh, Valerie?" Reggie said, still propped on her shoulder. "Would you like to be alone?"

She jerked her hand away. "No. Of course not."

With a last look at the demon, she quickly left the room, closing the door behind her.

Val sat in Lloyd's living room, cross-legged on a plush easy chair and sipped her hot chocolate. He'd put little marshmallows in it. It tasted good, soothing somehow. But it didn't take her mind off the injured demon upstairs.

He'd risked his own existence to save her life. Told her to run and leave him behind.

But only because she'd *commanded* him to keep her safe.

What difference did it make, anyhow? She'd survived. He was going to pull through. Then they'd find Julian before the stupid demon unwittingly brought about the end of the world. After that she'd never have to see Nathaniel again. As soon as this dark-time was over, she knew, at least she thought she knew—if the information Bud the biker faery had given her was accurate—where she could find Julian.

At a meeting with the mayor first thing tomorrow. Was he the one Julian wanted to sell the key to? The mayor of the Underworld?

She shook her head and took another sip of her drink. And she thought her life was complicated before this.

Lloyd came down the stairs. He'd gone to check on Nathaniel. When he saw Val was watching his descent he shook his head. "No different."

She nodded, hating the knot of concern that curled in her stomach. "Then we'll wait."

Reggie was snuggled up in a ball next to her, soundly asleep on a velour pillow. She didn't think she'd be able to sleep for a year, and that's if everything turned out okay. And if everything turned out okay she wouldn't have to sleep anyhow. Angels didn't *have* to sleep. Only if they're bored, which rarely happened.

That would have been a good thing to put in her notebook. If Julian hadn't destroyed it, that is. Her eyes narrowed at the memory. As if she didn't hate him enough already.

Stupid demon.

Lloyd sat on the sofa next to her, folding a leg under him. He leaned forward and grabbed a magazine off the coffee table.

"Cosmopolitan?" he offered.

Val shook her head. "No thanks."

"There's a good book excerpt in it this month."

"I'm happy to hear that."

"Do you read romance?"

"Excuse me?"

"Romance novels. Do you read them?"

She looked at the one-eyed gray monster. "Not especially."

"You should. I hear Trixie L'Amour's a great author. She's profiled this month in *Cosmo*."

O-kay. Val looked around at Lloyd's pink living room and noticed that there were several framed poster-sized book covers. *Love Me Forever* by Trixie L'Amour. *Ravishing Rachel* by Trixie L'Amour. *Lust in the Dust* by Trixie L'Amour.

There seemed to be a theme developing.

She looked at Lloyd. "Don't tell me."

He nodded enthusiastically. "Do you want an autograph? I have some newly printed bookmarks, too."

"You're Trixie L'Amour?"

He grinned. "Guilty as charged."

"But you're a . . ." She paused not knowing what to call him without it sounding like an insult.

"A demon."

"You're a demon? I thought you were a mons . . ." She broke off again.

"A monster?" he finished. "I'm insulted. Monsters

can't string together a coherent sentence. I have been nominated for three, count 'em, *three* RITA awards."

Val nodded. "Then I apologize."

He waved her off with a smile. "It's okay. Besides . . ." He leaned over and pulled a hardcover from under the couch to show her the back cover photo of a beautiful brunette woman. He tapped it with a clawed finger. "That's what my fans think I look like, anyhow."

Reggie snored loudly.

"But you live in the Underworld," Val said.

He nodded. "Uh-huh. Everything I do is through e-mail, so I don't have to leave unless I need to. I did one book tour, but trying to keep up the glamour spell nearly wore me out, so I keep a low profile now. Besides, it adds to the mystique."

She handed the book back to him. "Interesting."

"No, you keep that one. It's my first to hit the *New York Times* Best Seller list. Well, the extended list. But still."

She studied the cover. *Desperate Hearts* by Trixie L'Amour.

"So you're a romance-writing, one-eyed demon who lives in the Underworld," she summed up.

"*New York Times* best-selling, romance-writing, one-eyed demon who lives in the Underworld. That's correct." He grinned. "And what's your story, Valerie?"

She blinked at him. "I'm an unjustly convicted fallen angel, motel maid, on a quest into the Underworld with a Tempter Demon and a talking rat for a . . ." She paused. "For *something* important."

He shook his head. "You and Nathaniel, huh?"

"Me and Nathaniel what?"

"You're together?"

Reggie snored again, which distracted her for a second.

"No. Not other than the fact we're currently traveling together. That's all it is."

"I've never seen him protect a fallen one before. And I've known Nathaniel for . . . for a very long time."

"I guess I'm just special."

"I guess you just might be."

"So what does he really look like, anyhow?"

"Excuse me?"

"Nathaniel. He introduced me to Donovan, another demon, who was using glamour to look attractive. Nathaniel won't show me what he really looks like, denies he's using glamour at all. But I'm dying of curiosity."

"He's telling the truth."

"Really? So he's always looked so . . . so . . ."

"Dreamy?"

"I was going to say arrogantly handsome, but"—she shrugged—"that works, too."

Lloyd rubbed his four-fingered hand along his gray chin. "Did Nathaniel tell you he was once human?"

"Yeah, he mentioned it, but he didn't go into details. I figured he sold his soul to the devil or something."

He smiled again, baring his sharp teeth. "As a human, Nathaniel was tempted by a demon named Alexa."

Val choked on her latest sip of hot chocolate. "Alexa?"

"You know her?"

"Sort of."

"She's had her troubles, that one. An excellent Tempter, but not always focused. She made a grave mistake with Nathaniel."

"What happened?"

Lloyd studied her for a moment. "Perhaps I shouldn't

be telling you this. Nathaniel probably wouldn't like it very much. But . . . it *is* a good story."

She leaned forward, making sure the interest showed on her face. "And you tell it so well."

He smiled widely. "It's a gift."

"So tell me about Alexa and Nathaniel."

"There was no Alexa and Nathaniel. Or rather, there never should have been. Alexa was assigned to tempt Nathaniel's father, who bore the same name. Back two hundred years ago, Hell was recruiting fairly heavily for new demons. Hell and Heaven had a little scuffle—to put it mildly—that led to the demise of many angels and demons and when the uneasy peace was restored, the balance had to be restored also."

"Use the force, Luke," Reggie mumbled in his sleep.

Lloyd continued, "She was assigned to tempt this human with a reputation for being evil. A cold-hearted, corrupt human with no goodness in his heart. He would have made a *fabulous* demon."

"But?"

"But she came across the younger Nathaniel first. He was bedridden, dying of consumption. He didn't have much time left to live. She mistook him for her actual assignment and made her offer to him. Probably sounded pretty good, too, I'm sure. Eternal life, good looks forever, power, influence. I don't think he even considered any other options."

"What other options did he have if he was dying?"

"Dying."

"Oh."

"Once he'd been demonized, the reality of what he was sank in. Humans are rarely successful demons, I'm afraid. No matter how despicable they were in their former lives, it is rare to find one who can stomach the tasks of working for the head office. And those are the humans who are evil to begin with. Nathaniel simply had the misfortune of being born to a horrible father."

Val frowned. "So you're trying to say that Nathaniel was never supposed to be a demon. But now he has eternal life and good looks, and he's complaining? Please. Cry me a river of fire."

"Not exactly. Alexa was punished severely for her miscalculation. Nathaniel's father was to be a high-ranking demon. But his son, with no evil in his heart, but the face of an angel, was sent to the low-end ranks of Tempter."

Lloyd leaned back in the sofa and took a thoughtful sip of his cocoa.

"Well," Val said after a moment, feeling slightly stunned by what she'd heard so far. "Obviously after two hundred years he's gotten used to the job. He doesn't seem to have any issues with tempting now."

Lloyd snorted. "Is that what you think?"

She nodded.

"It's true, most wide-eyed fallen angels and other targeted humans he may have been assigned to might look at him as if he's their knight in shining armor. But he knew that what he'd been trained to tell them, that he'd be by their side forever and protect them, was all a lie. He knew that. And the guilt ate away at him."

"So why didn't he just stop?"

Lloyd placed his mug on a coaster on the coffee table. "Do you think it's that easy? Just hand in your two-week notice and leave? Well, it's not. It's called Hell for a reason, Valerie. And not because it's a super-fun place to be.

Nathaniel had as much chance at quitting being a Tempter as a fallen angel has of going back to Heaven."

Val frowned deeply.

"But he can't complain too much," Lloyd said. "There are perks. The better the demon is, the more successful he is, the more freedoms he's allowed. The higher he may be able to rise in the ranks. Unfortunately, though I like Nathaniel a great deal, he is on very thin ice at the moment. And you know what happens to ice in Hell, don't you?"

Val blinked.

"There *is* no ice in Hell," Lloyd laughed a little, before his face regained the serious expression it had to start with. "Sorry. Old joke. The point is, there are very strict rules that must be adhered to for all Tempters—including certain conduct with their assigned fallen angels. There are limits to how far they can tempt. Boundaries. Some Tempters have gone over that line, gotten to know their assignment too well, and they have been punished accordingly. To break the rules of being a Tempter Demon is a very dangerous undertaking, indeed." He eyed Val with his one great big eye. "This is his last chance. Just one more screw up on his part . . . I can't believe he would risk everything, even for one as beautiful as you."

Val clutched her mug so tightly that her knuckles were white. "What do you mean 'his last chance'?"

"I mean his last chance or . . ." He brought his two hands together to make them look like flapping wings.

Val shook her head. "What's that supposed to mean?"

Lloyd stopped flapping. "Don't you know what happens to failed demons?"

"No."

"First their minds are manipulated. There are those who are quite adept at that sort of thing. The demon will walk in behaving one way, and walk out an entirely different being. It's as if what he once was has been wiped away forever." He stood up from the sofa, walked to the window and looked out at the darkness. "That is the first stage. If that is not successful in making them behave how the head office wishes them to . . ." He trailed off.

"What?" Val prompted. "What happens then?"

He turned to face her. "They are turned into Nightflyers."

Her eyes widened with shock. "Those things that attacked us? You're kidding."

He shook his head. "Failed demons are turned into Nightflyers as their final punishment. An eternity of pain and mindless torment, and your only thought is to feed."

Reggie's legs began moving in his sleep as if he were trying to run away from something. "Claire, save me, baby! I love you!"

"And you're telling me that Nathaniel . . . is a failed demon."

"*Almost* a failed demon. The last I heard, he'd been given one last chance to redeem himself in the eyes of Lucifer. To bring in a fallen one."

"Me," she said dully.

Val couldn't believe what she was hearing. If he failed in his assignment to tempt her, he'd be turned into one of those terrible Nightflyer creatures? That he'd been made a demon by mistake?

And she was his last chance to make good on his past failures.

And yet still he protected her from the very monsters he might become in the very near future.

"You're different," Lloyd said after a moment.

"Me? Different?"

He sighed and absently thumbed through the romance novel he held. "You seem unlike other fallen ones I've come in contact with. Not that I've met very many. I was never a Tempter. I can see, though, why you've affected him. You must be very special."

She tried to think of something to say in reply, but found she was now rather speechless. Reggie took that moment to yawn, stretch each of his legs one at a time and open one black eye, then the other. "Whoa. I had some seriously weird dreams." He looked at Lloyd, then blinked. "Never mind. Maybe it wasn't a dream."

Lloyd returned to his seat on the sofa. "Anyhow, I didn't mean to turn this into 'all about Nathaniel' night. We were talking about me earlier. And my new book."

"We were?"

"Yes." He suddenly had a blue Sharpie in his hand. "How would you like it autographed?"

Twenty minutes later, after Lloyd had personalized two hardcovers and a category romance for her, Val sat next to the bed where Nathaniel still lay unconscious and studied the demon in the dimly lit room.

His bare chest was no longer a torn-up mess. It had healed almost completely and she looked at his toned, golden body for longer than she probably should have. His face had healed, too, back to its prior unmarked perfection. And he'd always looked this good, even as a human? Hardly seemed fair. It would have been easier to believe that he used some sort of glamour all this time. At least then she'd have an easy scapegoat for her undeniable attraction to him.

And that's all it was. Just a physical attraction.

Just an appreciation of his demonly male physique.

Sure. And that's why she was sitting vigil at his bedside.

That's why she'd left Reggie downstairs after insisting that Lloyd give him a reading of the first three chapters of his latest book.

Val didn't really know what to make of the demon in front of her, to tell the truth. Lloyd's insights on the inner workings of Nathaniel had turned on some major lights in her mind, but she didn't know how much to believe and how much was just made up. He was a writer, after all. It could all just be fiction. That seemed easier for her to believe than the fact that Nathaniel hated what he did and felt guilty about it. So much so that he had failed many times and only had one chance left. She was his chance. If he didn't tempt her, then . . .

She cringed, thinking that he might become one of those horrible creatures. It wasn't fair.

After another ten minutes, Nathaniel moaned softly and shifted in the bed. Val tensed as he opened his blue-gray eyes and looked directly at her.

He licked his dry lips. "You."

"Morning, sunshine."

"You've decided to torment me even as I sleep?"

"Looks like. How do you feel?"

He attempted to sit up and grimaced. "As if a group of Nightflyers attempted to have me for dinner."

"Actually, I think it was more like a late-night snack."

"How long have I been out?"

"A couple hours. It's still dark out, so we can't go anywhere yet."

"Where are we?"

"Your buddy Lloyd rode in on his white horse. Blew up one of the Nightflyers. It was pretty cool. Brought us back to his place."

"Lloyd," he repeated, and he looked immediately calmer. "Good. You'll be safe, then, for a while at least."

He stared at her for a moment, then closed his eyes again.

Val stood up. "I'll just let you rest a while."

He moved his hand out to catch her wrist. "Don't leave."

"What did you say?"

He let go of her and looked away. "Nothing. Just mumbling incoherently. Ignore me."

She sat next to him on the edge of the bed. "Why did you protect me out there, anyhow?"

"Because you commanded me to and I am temporarily bound to obey you. Remember?"

"Look at me."

He didn't move.

"Look at me," she said again, stronger.

It took him a moment, but he finally did.

She crossed her arms. "If I didn't have control over you like this, would you have left Reggie and me to die?"

His jaw tightened, but he didn't answer her.

Why was she asking him this? Because she'd finally and completely gone off the deep end? Maybe. She'd gone temporarily insane but she still wanted to know. She *needed* to know.

"Answer me, Nathaniel. You have to tell me the truth." She swallowed hard and was furious with herself that her eyes were brimming with tears. *Holy overemotional, Batman.* "Would you have let them kill me?"

A tremor went through him and every muscle in his body tensed up before she heard him choke out, "No."

"No what?"

His teeth were clenched. "No, I wouldn't have let you die."

"Lloyd told me what will happen if you fail on your assignment. If you don't get me to agree to go to Hell. Is that why? Because you were afraid of losing me before you got another chance to tempt me?"

"Lloyd shouldn't have told you a thing. It's none of his damn business."

"But he did. Now tell me. Is that why you saved me?"

"No."

"Then why? Tell me!"

"Damn you, woman."

She took a deep breath. The tears were still holding their own. None had escaped yet, but it was only a matter of time before one made a break for freedom.

"That's not a very good answer. Why not?"

He stared at her for a long moment with an expression she'd never seen before. She didn't even know how to explain it. Furious, panicked, afraid . . . all at the same time. Although, mostly the furious part.

"Because"—his eyes narrowed, and she felt the intensity of his gaze run through the length of her entire body—"I burn for you."

Val frowned at him. "You burn for me? What does that mean?"

Flames danced behind his eyes before he turned his furious glare away from her again without another word.

"Nathaniel . . ." She was so confused, growing more so every moment she sat there. She shouldn't have come in—shouldn't have allowed herself to feel such growing concern for someone whose only goal was to use her for his own gain. She should never have asked him that stupid question. He burns for her?

He had turned his face away so she could only see the back of his head. He looked so human, so not evil or anything she ever would have imagined a demon to look like. She couldn't help herself. She stroked his hair. Slid her fingers down his neck and across his broad shoulders. To prove to herself that he was real and not just an illusion.

"Please do not touch me," he said quietly, but he didn't try to pull away.

He felt like silk beneath her fingers. Warm, taut silk, and she ran her hand over his chest and along his tight abs, all the places his injuries had been. The injuries he'd sustained from protecting her. Placing himself between her and the big, nasty monsters.

Because he burned for her.

"Thank you for saving me," she murmured as her hand drifted lower.

He gasped, and he grabbed her arms, drawing her close to kiss her deeply, his tongue plunging between her lips. He pulled her down on top of him and rolled her slowly so he was on top, pressing her down into the mattress, his body a hard, hot line against her own.

"Valerie," he murmured against her mouth. "My angel."

She kissed him as if she were dying and this was all there was. Like his body was her lifeline and all that kept her from falling into the abyss. Overdramatic? Perhaps a tad, but that's how she felt. He'd tempted her. He'd damn well succeeded. She couldn't help it. She didn't care what he was anymore, what she was—just that he was with her, on top of her, against her. And he wanted her as she wanted him.

Their kiss grew even deeper, more urgent, and she moved her hands down to the back of his black pants. She'd only been human for two months, but she knew what she wanted. She wanted him. She slid her hands under his waistband and started to slide it over his hips, feeling the hot skin underneath.

He moaned, and broke off the kiss for a moment to stare down into her eyes.

"Don't you see?" she said as she pulled his hard body closer to her own. "I burn for you, too."

"Valerie, please . . . no." He turned his face away.

She tried to kiss him again. "What?"

"No, Valerie."

"Nathaniel—"

"No." He pulled away from her and pushed up into a sitting position, his back against the post at the end of the bed to stare down at her with fiery eyes. "You need to leave now."

Even though she was still fully dressed, she felt suddenly naked. Her lips tingled. Her body ached. She pushed herself up, too. Nathaniel was staring at her from the end of the bed as if he feared her.

"What's wrong?" She reached for him but he flinched.

"Nothing's wrong. We need to focus on getting your key back. There's no time for distractions. Just leave."

"But—"

"But nothing. Listen to me. I want you out of here right now."

"Tell me what's wrong." When he didn't answer, she frowned at him. "Nathaniel, I command you—"

He was off the bed and on his feet in one motion. "You command me? I've had it with that bullshit. Open your ears, damn it. I said I want you out of here *now*." He picked up the nightstand and threw it against the far wall like it weighed nothing. It splintered into a thousand pieces.

Val's throat was dry as she stood on shaky legs. She didn't say another word or even look at him again as she left the room.

Chapter Thirteen

———— ∼ ————

"He seems to be feeling better," Val announced as she returned to the living room. She'd spent a couple of minutes in Lloyd's lovely violet-colored powder room commanding herself not to cry. It had mostly worked, but her eyes were a bit red.

Reggie turned to look at her. "This guy is a great writer."

Lloyd closed the book he held. "Oh, come on. You're just saying that."

"Am not. You're fantastic. I can see it in my mind like a movie. Amazing."

Lloyd nodded. "The movie rights have been optioned. I'm thinking a young Brigitte Bardot for the lead."

"Naw. More like Jenna Jameson."

"Anyhow," Val interjected, "like I was saying. He's recovering."

Lloyd nodded. "That's good to hear. How is he?"

"He's a total jerk."

He continued to nod. "Am I missing something here?"

She crossed her arms, feeling all tense and in need of more hot chocolate. Extra marshmallows. "No. Just that he's a jerk. That's all. Oh, and as soon as this dark-time is over, we're out of here, Reggie. Just you and me. We don't need him around. He'll just cause more problems."

Reggie opened his furry mouth, but she held up a finger.

"By ourselves," she snapped. "You got a problem with that?"

He shut his mouth. "Nope. No problem, boss."

"Now," Val turned to Lloyd, "how much longer is this stupid dark-time going to last?"

He raised his one thin eyebrow. "Um. Several more hours. At least. Uh, sorry."

"Well, that sucks."

"I have plenty of room here if you want to get some shut-eye. If you want to freshen up, you're more than welcome to make use of my en suite bathroom. I have a Jacuzzi tub."

"Sounds tempting." There was that word again. "Thanks Lloyd."

Val sat on the sofa while Lloyd continued to read aloud to a captivated Reggie. She crossed her arms and listened to the tale of love and loss and redemption. It had a happy ending.

What a load of crap.

Her eyes burned when she thought about what had happened. What did she do wrong? Was she that repulsive? Maybe she was a lousy kisser. She thought he wanted her. No, she *knew* he wanted her. But just as she was all ready to . . . well, plunge right in, he'd pushed her away like she was a disgusting insect.

Women didn't like to feel like disgusting insects. It was now a proven fact.

She held her arms tightly against herself.

What's wrong with me? she thought.

Come to think of it, what was wrong with her to want him to touch her in the first place? He was a demon. It went against everything she believed in. What kind of an angel was she, anyhow? It had turned out for the best.

Nothing happened.

Good.

She decided not to give it another thought. The key was all that mattered. Time was running out for Barlow, for herself, for the world at large. She had to focus. First thing in the morning she would find this Mayor Vaille's mansion, march right in and take back what was rightfully hers. Well, *Barlow's.* And it would all work out. Just had to keep with the positive thinking.

Yeah, right.

Being that she was exhausted, mentally and physically, she must have fallen asleep on Lloyd's couch after a while, with the sound of the romance novel reading in the background. When she opened her eyes it was light outside Lloyd's bay window.

She made quick use of Lloyd's bathroom to freshen up and marched back down the stairs.

She poked Reggie, still curled up on his velour pillow. "Let's get going."

He blinked his eyes open, yawned, and got onto his feet. Then stretched out each leg before he looked at her.

"I dreamed about Claire," he said.

"And how did that go for you?"

"She was a rat, too. Seemed right, somehow. But we were together and we were happy. Thinking about starting our own rat family."

"Congratulations. Are you ready to go?"

"I guess. Are you sure you don't want Nathaniel to come with us? That might not be such a good idea, you know."

She frowned at him. "I don't care." She stood up from the sofa and turned around. Nathaniel was standing behind her.

"I *am* coming with you."

"No you're not."

Nathaniel looked at her with annoyance. "You mean to face Julian yourself, with no protection? That is the most idiotic thing I've ever heard."

"What do you care?"

"I'm bound to protect you. Whether or not I like that fact is not important. You'd walk away from that?"

Val narrowed her eyes. "Just watch me. Want to throw another piece of furniture against the wall now in a pissy show of brute strength?"

Lloyd stood up. "Is that what that noise was? Nathaniel, no more Tempter tantrums, okay? This is my house."

Nathaniel didn't budge. Didn't flinch. "I'm coming with you."

"Like hell you are."

Just as she was about to turn away from him, he grabbed her arm.

She frowned up at him. "Let go of me." she said it in her commanding tone that usually worked with him.

He immediately released her, but didn't look happy about it.

She snatched Reggie off the sofa with an audible "eek"

from him and threw him on her shoulder. "Thanks for everything, Lloyd. It was a pleasure meeting you."

"Likewise Valerie. Don't forget to check out my Web site. The new design just launched last week."

"I'll do that."

She made for the front door, opened it up, stepped into the bright sunshine, and began walking toward the sidewalk. Was she being stupid for not letting Nathaniel come with them? Probably. But having him around would remind her how close she'd been to making such a huge mistake. She didn't care what Lloyd had to say about the history of Nathaniel. He was a demon. That didn't fit very well into her heavenly plans.

End of story.

"Uh-oh," Reggie said.

She felt a hand on her arm twirl her around. It was Nathaniel again.

"Geez, don't you ever give up?"

He frowned. "Listen to me Valerie, I want to talk about what happened between us earlier. It wasn't because I—"

"Shut up," she commanded and felt an odd satisfaction that he immediately stopped talking. "I don't want to hear anything you have to say. Nothing happened. Now I want you to not move, not speak, and definitely not follow me. Got it?"

He glared at her, but seemed frozen in place.

She smiled. "That's more like it."

Turning, she continued down the front path that led to the sidewalk. A girl was coming toward her. About Val's height, with reddish hair, and a pretty face. She cocked an eyebrow.

"Hi there."

"Hey!" Reggie shouted excitedy. "That's Lisa. She was the maid at the Paradise Inn before you, Val. Hi Lisa! Long time no see!"

Lisa ignored the rat and walked right past Val to approach Nathaniel.

"Hey, baby," she said. "Remember me?"

She ran her hand along the back of his unbuttoned shirt—a new shirt, gray-striped; Lloyd must have loaned it to him since his other one was ruined—across his shoulder blades, and over to his bare chest. Val felt a sudden twinge of anger, or maybe it was jealousy that this girl was so freely touching Nathaniel. His eyes were on Val, however, and he didn't move since she told him he couldn't. His eyes flicked back to the redhead.

"Don't tell me you don't remember me," Lisa pouted.

She curled her right hand into a fist and punched him. His head snapped to the side, but he was unable to move away from the attack. A trickle of red appeared at the corner of his mouth.

The girl studied his lack of reaction for a moment. "That's very interesting. And it makes things so much easier for me."

She hit him in his stomach this time, and an involuntary "Ooof" escaped his lips. Then she hit him again in the mouth. By this time Val had closed the distance between them and grabbed the girl's arm.

"Stop it."

Lisa turned to look at Val, an angry, wild glare in her eyes before she backhanded her across the face.

"This has nothing to do with you, bitch. This is between me and the demon. I'm here to vanquish him. But first I want to kick his sorry ass."

Val held a hand to her stinging cheek and narrowed her eyes. "I'm the bitch?" Before she realized what she was doing, she threw her fist through the air, clipping the girl across her cheekbone.

"Oooh, girl fight," Reggie said from Val's shoulder. "Me likey. Why don't you put me down so no rats get inadvertently harmed in the making of this hot action."

"Ow!" She held her face and glared at Val. "This has nothing to do with you. He needs to be punished. Mind your own business."

"This is my business." Val glanced at Nathaniel. "He's with me."

She jabbed a finger in Nathaniel's prone direction. "You don't know what he did. What he's capable of."

"You'd be surprised."

"Just let me vanquish him."

Val considered that, but only for a moment. "No, I don't think so. Nathaniel, I've changed my mind. You can move and talk again."

His hands clenched into fists, fire appearing in his furious gaze as he looked at the girl. "I don't know who you are. I've never seen you before."

She laughed and turned to Val. "He doesn't recognize me. After what he did to me, he doesn't recognize me. Isn't that bloody typical of a Tempter Demon."

Lloyd appeared at the doorway, wearing an apron and holding a plate of brownies. "Is there a problem out here?"

"I'll say there's a problem out here." Lisa pointed at Nathaniel. "He's the one responsible for sending me to Hell. He tempted me and then turned his back on me like it meant nothing to him. And now I'm back to destroy him."

Val frowned at her. "Are you trying to tell me you're a fallen angel?"

"Once was. Now I'm personified vengeance."

"Is that a title or something?" Reggie asked. "Like 'Greased Lightning'?"

"They don't know I've escaped." Lisa looked around nervously. "I don't know how much time I have before they drag me back, but I'm going to use the time I have for revenge. And there's only one monster I want revenge against."

"I don't remember you," Nathaniel said simply.

"That doesn't make it better. If anything, the fact that you can't remember me . . ." She sniffed before she pulled it together again. ". . . Makes it worse. Much worse. That I meant nothing to you, not even to remember what you did to me."

"I remember you," Reggie said. "You used to do the nicest hospital corners on the bedsheets. It's really an art."

Nathaniel glanced at Val, but she didn't meet his eyes. She watched their exchange with growing apprehension. Lisa had escaped from Hell? She didn't even know that was possible. And now this girl wanted revenge on the demon who sent her there in the first place. Made sense to her, but she wouldn't let it happen. Not today. She figured this made everything Lloyd had told her null and void. Nathaniel had obviously succeeded in tempting before. And to think, he didn't even remember the poor girl?

"Listen, Lisa." Val approached her cautiously, but she didn't make a move to attack. Lisa's eyes were brimming with tears and Val put a hand on her shoulder. "Nathaniel's an unforgivably heartless bastard."

Nathaniel cleared his throat. "I don't know if you're helping matters."

"Quiet," she said over her shoulder, and then turned back to the girl and felt a huge flood of sympathy toward her. Just an innocent fallen angel who didn't know better than to say yes to a handsome demon. She felt betrayed. Betrayed and abandoned, with eternity to regret her decisions. "I get how you're feeling. I'm a fallen one, too."

Lisa looked at Val skeptically. "Is that why you're here? Is he taking you to Hell"—She glanced around their surroundings—"via the scenic route?"

"Not exactly."

"Then what are you doing together in the Underworld?"

Val sighed. "He's sort of helping me."

She actually laughed at that. "A Tempter Demon helping a fallen angel? That doesn't happen. It's against the rules."

"Well, I guess there's a first time for everything. Look, like I said, what he did to you wasn't right. But he's a demon. That's his job." Val glanced at him again and he met her eyes but didn't say anything. "He doesn't have a choice. I could go into the whole 'balance' lecture I've been hearing lately, but bottom line, it's out of his control what happens to us after we're tempted. But at the end of the day, it's our decision. You're the one who said yes."

She frowned deeply. "Why are you defending him?"

"I'm not. I'm simply trying to show you things aren't quite as black and white as you think they are." She looked at Nathaniel. "Do you have anything you want to say?"

He raised an eyebrow. "I don't remember this woman." At Val's look of disbelief, "I *don't*. She must be lying."

"And what would she have to gain by lying?" Val shook her head and turned to Lisa. "So . . . what are you going to do now?"

She sighed and looked around the street to see the neighborhood's demons now emerging from their homes to go about their daily demon business. Dark-time was officially over. No more worries of becoming a passing Nightflyer's tasty snack.

"I plan on getting back to the earthly realm. Before they find me. I have a plan."

Lisa made a move to walk away. Then she stopped, turned around, and kicked Nathaniel hard in the groin. He collapsed to his knees, groaning in pain.

Lisa turned around to smile at Val. "It's not a vanquishment, but it just felt so good. And Nathaniel, word to the wise. If you break any more rules, especially with her, you're going to be in serious trouble. More than you already are."

Val opened her mouth but couldn't think of anything to say to that. Lisa walked down the sidewalk without looking back.

"Well," Reggie said. "Ain't that a kick in the nuts."

Val tried hard not to smile and waited as Nathaniel rose slowly and uncomfortably to his feet. "You okay?"

He glared at her. "Never better."

"You really don't remember her?"

"No."

"I suppose you forget a lot of the fallen ones you tempt. Kind of an out-of-sight, out-of-mind thing, right?"

He shook his head and looked away. "I remember each

of my assignments. They're burned into my memory, every last one."

"From guilt?"

Nathaniel shot a look at Lloyd who stood at the doorway to his town home. "You need to keep your mouth shut about my business."

Lloyd shrugged. "But it's such a good story. I can't help it."

Val crossed her arms. "So why don't you remember Lisa?"

He watched the fallen angel in the distance before he met her gaze again. "I have no idea."

"So," Lloyd said, "if you all are certain the morning violence is over, would anyone care for a brownie before you leave?"

"Mmm, brownie." Reggie was nearly drooling.

Nathaniel and Val hadn't stopped staring at each other. She couldn't figure him out. He was an enigma. Everything he did, everything he said. He was like one of those fortune cookies that was so vague it could mean anything. Best thing was to forget the message and eat the cookie.

Wait a minute.

"I'm coming with you," Nathaniel said firmly after a moment. "And no, Lloyd, I don't want a brownie."

"But I added chocolate chips."

"Yum!" Reggie waved his paw. "Me, me."

Val stared at the demon in front of her. The good-looking one, not the grayish, single-eyed one with the plate of brownies. Nathaniel was still under her power. The summoning crystal was still safely in her jeans pocket. She had to put aside her personal issues with him. It would serve her better to have him at her side when she found Julian.

"Fine. Let's just get it over with, then." She marched past Nathaniel to grab two brownies off the plate. She broke one in half and gave it to a very grateful Reggie.

Then she walked down the path to the sidewalk. She turned around. Nathaniel wasn't moving. "Are you coming or what?"

He sighed. "You commanded me not to follow you earlier. The whole 'don't talk, don't move' thing?"

"Oh." She waved her hand, not that it did anything—but it just felt right, somehow. "You may now follow me."

He started to trudge down the driveway, walking a little funny after the damage done to his groin. Not that it mattered. He didn't seem to have a use for that equipment anyhow, as proven earlier in the bedroom.

She frowned as something Lloyd said earlier twigged her memory.

"There are very strict rules that must be adhered to for all Tempters—including certain conduct with their assigned fallen angels. There are limits to how far they can tempt. Boundaries. Some Tempters have gone over that line, gotten to know their assignment too well, and they have been punished accordingly."

Then she thought about what Lisa had just said.

"If you break any more rules, especially with her, you're going to be in serious trouble."

Val stared at Nathaniel for a moment until it finally clicked for her. *Holy celibate monk, Batman.* Was that what had happened? He wasn't allowed to . . . go any farther with a fallen one? It was against the demon rules? Was that the real reason why he pushed her away?

"What?" He frowned at her wide-eyed expression.

"Uh . . . nothing. Nothing at all."

Talk about irony. A Tempter who couldn't allow himself to be tempted.

"Okay, angel, now you're giving me the creeps. What's with the stare-a-thon?"

"Nothing." She looked away. It didn't matter. Only the key mattered. If they didn't find it today, then nothing would ever matter. "Julian's seeing the mayor. We need to go to his mansion."

"And that's the sum total of your plan?"

She bit her lip. "It's simple. Go to the mansion and get Julian to give me the key."

He laughed. "Just when I think you're so much more worldly than the others, you show your true naïveté. Julian will not allow you to march up to him and demand anything of him. He's seen you before. He'll know what you want and obviously he doesn't want to part with this stolen key you say he has. Is that a fair assumption?"

"I guess."

"And as for the mayor's mansion, you have no idea what you're walking into. I've been there before. Mayor Vaille has been assembling a small army of demons for his own personal use as bodyguards. Here's my plan, since yours will do nothing but blow up in your face. We go to the mayor's party. I have an open invitation so he'll assume I'm also there to discuss employment opportunities. You will pretend to be my woman."

"Your *what*?"

His grin widened. "My woman. An evil witch from the earthly realm who is on vacation here in the Underworld with her"—he glanced at Reggie—"familiar."

"*Evil* familiar," Reggie added. "Oh the power. I can just *feel* it. Being a rat is so freeing."

"But aren't rats supposed to be pure?" Val asked. "That's what Barlow told me, anyhow."

Nathaniel shrugged. "Looks like it depends on the rat. Your rodent has no effect on me."

"You want me to pose as a witch? Why do I have to pretend to be something I'm not?"

"Because if Julian sees you he'll immediately realize something is up. And if the mayor finds out you're a fallen angel whom I didn't escort directly to Hell, he'll be suspicious, too. And you don't want the mayor to be suspicious. It would be very detrimental to your health."

They swiftly walked past a demon home with three demon children running through a sprinkler on the front lawn. *Cute,* Val thought. *Sort of.* "Who is this mayor guy anyhow? What does he do?"

He ran a hand through his dark hair. "Mayor Vaille is—how should I put this?—very *particular* with what he wants. He was once second-in-command in Hell, but he wanted too much power, got all greedy, so he was demoted. Put in charge of this desolate wasteland as a punishment."

Val glanced around her. Palm trees waved in the warm tropical breeze. The ocean waves lapped at the shore of the white sand beach. The sun shone brightly in the perfect, cloudless sky. She could smell the salt of the ocean in the air.

"Yeah, looks like quite the desolate wasteland to me."

He smiled, but his eyes were strangely sad. "Have you learned nothing from your trip here? All is not as it appears. Glamours are not isolated to improving one's personal appearance. If one has the power and the resources, as the mayor does, it can be stretched much further than that. Much, much further. The mayor enjoys beautiful things, be they real or not."

Val looked around again. A convertible drove by that contained what looked like two bikini models in the backseat and a handsome surfer dude in the front.

"Are you trying to tell me that everything I'm looking at right now is just another glamour? All the trees, the beach, all of this? It's all fake?"

Nathaniel stopped walking and crossed his arms. "Do you really want to know?"

"Yes. Absolutely."

"Me, too!" Reggie squeaked.

"Then come here."

She hesitated for a moment, then walked to where Nathaniel stood on the sidewalk next to a beautiful, blooming crab apple tree.

"Turn around," he told her. "I can remove the glamour for you to see what the Underworld truly is. It's one of the few powers I can use here. You'll see why I don't use it very often."

Val turned around and felt him press his body against her.

"Nathaniel, I—"

"Shh, you wanted to know the truth. Have you changed your mind?"

"No."

He slid his hands up her arms, and, avoiding Reggie on her shoulder who'd chosen to be temporarily quiet as a mouse, he covered her eyes with his hands. He was so close that when he whispered, his lips grazed her ear. "You can't always trust your eyes to show you the truth."

He removed his hands and Val blinked in horror at what she saw before her.

Mile upon mile of gray, jagged rock spread out before her eyes. The sky was dark and swirling with white veins of lightning that appeared every few seconds. There was a cold, bone-chilling wind that whipped the hair off her face. Nathaniel held her waist as she stared at the true Underworld. Barren, cold, dangerous—a feeling of despair filled her as she looked at it. And emptiness.

There were gray creatures crawling along the rocks in the distance, eyeless beasts, and she could hear the flapping and distant squawking of the Nightflyers. A lump of fear formed in her chest.

"Do you see, Valerie?"

She turned around in his arms and looked up at him, her eyes filled with tears that began to streak down her cheeks. This was his true home? This is where Nathaniel had to live? This empty, cold, soulless place with only a veneer of glamour on top of it to make it bearable?

"Make it go away. Please."

He nodded and wiped her tears gently away with his thumbs. "As you wish."

He covered her eyes again and when his warm hands moved away, the glamour was back. The Underworld again looked like a bright, shiny, happy place full of warmth and sunshine.

But now she knew it was all a lie.

"Is it over?" Reggie said from her shoulder with a

tremor in his voice. "Good golly, Miss Molly, please tell me it's over."

"It's over." She rubbed her arms to chase away the chill that filled her body. "We're okay. Open your eyes."

Val looked at Nathaniel. He looked unhappy. Was he sorry he showed her the no-holds-barred truth? Showed her that his existence was not as glamorous as she may have believed? That underneath it all was pain and loneliness and eternal suffering, just as Lloyd had said? She reached for him but he pulled away, and instead presented her with a killer smile.

"Anyhow," he said. "Time's a-wasting. And the mayor's mansion is only a few blocks away. Let's get going."

Val swallowed hard. "Okay."

"First, though, I think I need to do a little glamour on you, little angel."

She frowned at him. "Glamour?"

He grinned. "Evil witches need to have an evil witch look, don't you think? Not an innocent, naïve, blond angel look."

She looked down at her jeans and tank top. She flicked away an errant chocolate chip that had attached itself to her otherwise clean clothes. She ran a hand through her slightly tangled blond hair, feeling self-conscious now.

Nathaniel stepped back from her and moved his gaze slowly down her body, much as he'd done the first time she'd met him in the alley after the mugger had attacked her. His gaze finally met her own and he raised an amused eyebrow.

She flicked her hand. "Fine. Make me look different, then, if you think it will help."

Val felt a sudden wave of warm air touch her and then it was gone.

Nathaniel grinned. "Done."

"Wow, Val," Reggie breathed.

She slowly looked down at herself. She was now wearing a skin-tight leather corset over a low-cut, *very low,* black lace top. Her newly ample chest was pushed up to nearly her chin. An equally tight black leather miniskirt that barely covered her butt, and thigh-high leather high-heeled boots finished the outfit. She moved a long, red fingernailed hand up to her face.

"What did you just do to me? Does my face look different?"

Nathaniel smiled. "That's an understatement."

She moved over to the window of a nearby store to stare at her reflection. She looked like a complete stranger. A drop-dead gorgeous stranger with a Pamela Anderson body, way too much makeup and long, long bloodred hair. She raised a high, penciled-in eyebrow at the rat on her shoulder. He was wearing a little leather biker cap.

"Well," Val put a hand on her hip. "That's definitely different. This is your idea of the perfect woman, I assume?"

"No, my idea of the perfect woman is . . ." He stopped talking for a second and eyed her. "Yeah, that's right. This is exactly what I like."

"Then let's get going," she said, thinking about the key. "Julian won't know what hit him."

Chapter Fourteen

———— ⌇ ————

I am evil, Val told herself as she tried to get into her Elvira-Mistress-of-the-Night-like character. *An evil, large-breasted witch who's up to no good. No good at all. And who wears too much makeup. And very uncomfortable thong underwear.*

The mayor's mansion was at the end of the Miami-esque main strip of the Underworld. Behind it was nothing. Literally nothing, which Val found quite strange, since she never knew what nothing looked like until she saw it. The mayor's gated estate made her immediately think of Hugh Hefner's Playboy Mansion, which she'd seen on *Entertainment Tonight.* She'd thought for an old man he sure had a lot of gorgeous babes surrounding him. Maybe he, too, was a fallen angel and those were all of his buxom blond Tempters.

She suddenly felt like they were being watched, then noticed that at the side of the gate was an eye. A large eye-ball about the size of a beach ball mounted on a metal pole. When they neared the gate it turned to look at them.

"And *you* are?" it asked blandly. But, since an eyeball

on a pole didn't have a mouth to speak, Val simply heard the voice projected around them.

"We're here to see Mayor Vaille," Nathaniel told it.

It blinked. "Are you here for the party?"

"Oooh, that's right. There's a party," Reggie said.

Nathaniel glanced at the rat on Val's shoulder, then back at the eye. "That's right. My name is Nathaniel."

The eye moved so Val was in its sight. "And *you* are?"

She swallowed. "The name's Claire," she said, having decided that it was a good name to use. Easy to remember and after all, Reggie's girlfriend was also a witch. "I'm with the demon. I'm an evil witch."

The eye immediately closed up.

Nathaniel grimaced and turned to her. "You should know that evil witches don't typically go around telling everyone that they're evil witches."

She shrugged. "Sorry. I'm new at this evil thing."

"You're not evil. Don't even try to act like it. Just be very quiet. Pretend you're mute."

The eye reopened and looked at them with disdain. "The mayor is pleased you could make it. Though, since you didn't have the courtesy to RSVP, there may not be enough refreshments for you and your . . . guest. Next time, try to follow procedure."

The gates opened and they walked inside. Val turned around to watch them close up again, locking with a bone-chilling click. Her heart pounded hard against her ribcage.

"Okay," Nathaniel said. "We go in and find Julian. Approach him when he doesn't expect it, doesn't recognize you, and get your key. Then this will all be over. Simple."

"Not simple." She looked at him warily. "How do I know you won't just tell everyone who I am?"

"I won't."

"But how do I know that for sure? Only hours ago you didn't want to help me unless it was in line with tempting me, and now you're doing me this big favor? What gives?"

He sighed. "Can't you just accept it without over-analyzing it?"

She shook her head. "What assurance do I have that you won't just go in there and blurt out to the mayor what I really am? Lloyd told me you're on real shaky ground with your job. Maybe you want some extra Brownie points?"

He looked exasperated with her. "I'm going to have to have a very serious discussion with Lloyd and his tendency to run off at the mouth. You know, if you're that concerned about my intentions, you could just command me not to say anything."

Val immediately brightened. "Oh. Right. I totally forgot about that for a moment. Okay, Nathaniel, I command you not to tell anyone who I really am." She let out a long exhale and smiled. "There, I feel much better now."

His lips twitched and he studied her for a moment. "You like that, don't you?"

"Like what?"

He turned away. "Forget it."

"No, tell me what you were going to say."

Nathaniel turned back around with an amused expression. "Dominating me."

Val's eyes widened. "Excuse me?"

"You like being the one with all the power. Making me

do what you want whether or not I like it. Having your way. Being a bossy little bitch." The smile disappeared and flames suddenly flared in his eyes. "Do you have any idea what I plan to do once I'm free of your little spell, angel?"

She didn't like the way he was looking at her. Not at all. She didn't say anything back to him but an icy chill went through her. She definitely didn't want to know what he planned to do.

But she was obviously in the minority.

"What?" Reggie asked curiously. "What will you do?"

The demon's eyes flicked to the rat on her shoulder, then back to Val. "Never mind."

Reggie moaned. "Oh, brother. You're all talk, you know that? You're not going to do anything bad to her, and you know it."

His eyebrows went up, and he casually ran his hand through his dark hair. "Is that right, O wise rodent? And why would you think that?"

"Because you're totally in love with her."

"What did you just say?" he hissed.

"In love. With her. Did I stutter?"

Val could barely hear Reggie with the blood rushing through her ears.

Reggie chuckled, the sound cutting through the absolute silence. "Yeah, Val, I'm serious. It's kind of cute, actually. The two of you arguing all the time but it doesn't mean a damn thing. Just sexual tension. I learned about that from Lloyd's books. You should see how Nate looks at you when you're not paying attention. It's like he's . . . eeek!"

Nathaniel snatched Reggie off her shoulder and held

the rat up at eye level, squeezing harder than necessary. She couldn't see his eyes for the flames that filled them now.

"I think I've had enough of you," Nathaniel said in a very cold voice. "Nonstop chatter, telling your lies, making snide comments, whatever you can say to fill up the silence. Are you afraid of the silence, my little friend? Are you afraid of what you'll hear when your mind is still? That you're a failure in life, in love, and that nobody gives a damn if you live or die? That you've been reduced to the sum total of your parts? A pathetic sewer dwelling lifeform that needs to be exterminated? I think I can help you out there. Put you out of your misery."

"Val!" Reggie squeaked as Nathaniel squeezed him harder.

She stormed at him and punched him in the shoulder as hard as she could. Her hands were clenched so hard that her glamourized long red nails bit painfully into her palms. "I command you to put him down right now. Do it!"

Nathaniel shook with the effort of trying to fight her power over him. He didn't release Reggie.

"Put him down!" Val's voice raised a level and she saw the demon actually flinch as if the words caused him pain.

Finally, slowly, Nathaniel leaned over and released Reggie to the ground. The rat limped over to where Val stood. Nathaniel looked at her again, his eyes still filled with fire, his breathing uneven. His lips a thin, angry line.

"He lies," he said. Then he turned away and continued along the path to the mayor's sprawling mansion. Val watched him go for a moment before she gently picked Reggie up.

"Are you okay?"

Reggie was breathing hard, shaking, and his teeth chattered. "Methinks the demon doth protest too much."

She frowned deeply at him. "Stop provoking him."

"By telling the truth?"

"It's not the truth. He can't stand me."

"He's crazy about you."

"You're the crazy one." She paused as she waited for her flushed cheeks to cool down a bit. "Besides, FYI, he's a demon. I'm an angel. Well, ex-angel, anyhow. It doesn't happen. Got it? And even on top of all that I've only known him for a couple of days."

"That doesn't matter. In Trixie's books, they fall in love at first sight. Maybe you two are soulmates! Oh," he sighed. "How romantic. Although I think he may have broken one of my ribs."

Without another word to further provoke Reggie's ridiculous notion, Val followed behind Nathaniel as he made his way to the tall front doors of the Playdemon Mansion. She looked around at everything from the well-manicured hedges, to the rolling green lawn, to the interlocked driveway that had a Jaguar, a Mercedes convertible and a Rolls-Royce parked in front of the house. Anything to distract herself from what had just happened.

Nathaniel appeared to know exactly where he was going as he stormed through the grounds. Val trailed behind him as he bypassed the front door and walked through a vine-covered archway leading to the rear of the mansion. Everything about this place seemed so real to her. Like on that *Miami Vice* show with the big, expensive, flashy drug dealers' houses that had a tendency to blow up at any given moment.

But it wasn't real, Val reminded herself. None of it.

None of the prettiness of it, anyhow. The visual of the gray, jagged rocks flashed in her mind. How did they do it? Keep up the façade so perfectly? Had it always been this way?

The archway led through to the most beautiful pool she'd ever seen. Not that she had much to compare it with the out-of-order, leaf- and snow-covered one at the Paradise Inn. She had seen commercials for high-end resorts in the Caribbean and this pool was torn right out of one of those. Blue, blue water. There were two stunningly beautiful women sunbathing topless. A shirtless man carrying a drinks tray delivered a couple of umbrella-topped cocktails to them. They laughed and giggled and flirted with him. Beyond the pool she could see the ocean, sparkling like diamonds under the perfect sky.

Oh, and the big, fat slug. She couldn't forget about that.

Definitely *not* beautiful, she decided. In fact, it was repulsively ugly reclining on a chaise longue under a large umbrella. She'd recently seen *The Return of the Jedi* and the slug-creature immediately reminded her of Jabba the Hutt. Only smaller and a little less sexy.

Nathaniel stopped walking at the edge of the pool and waited for her to catch up. He turned his head in her general direction but didn't look at her. "Let me do the talking."

"Okay."

"No argument?"

"Nope."

"Good." Then he looked at her, his gray-blue eyes cautious but currently flame-free, and he forced a smile to his lips. "Remember, we're supposed to be together."

She waited for a comment from the peanut gallery, aka: Reggie, but there was nothing.

Smart rat.

"Just one question," Val said and Nathaniel sighed immediately.

"I knew it."

"It's just"—Val lowered her voice—"that isn't the mayor over there, is it?"

He glanced at the slug. "Yes. Why?"

She shrugged. "It's just that . . . he seems so concerned with how things look by his house and the rest of the Underworld, why doesn't he, I don't know—"

"Use glamour on himself?"

"Well, yeah."

The corner of his mouth curled up. "He can't."

"Why not?"

He glanced at the mayor who didn't seem to have noticed their arrival yet. "Like I told you before, Mayor Vaille was second-in-command in Hell itself until he got a little too ambitious and power-hungry. Lucifer didn't like that too much, to say the least, so Vaille was demoted to overseeing the Underworld."

"The Underworld that looks like Miami Beach."

He nodded. "Part of the mayor's punishment was an inability to perform personal glamour."

"So that means that he can make everything look good except himself?"

"Precisely."

"He must hate that."

Nathaniel smiled and shook his head. "Have you ever heard the story of the emperor's new clothes?"

"Wasn't that a Disney movie?"

"That was *The Emperor's New* Groove," Reggie piped up. "I have it on DVD. David Spade's my hero."

Nathaniel gave Reggie a withering look. "In 'The Emperor's New Clothes,' the ruler is naked but his underlings have convinced him he wears beautiful clothes. He is unaware of his own humiliation until someone points it out to him." He paused. "The mayor has convinced himself, and no one has argued with him, that he is very desirable and attractive."

"You're kidding."

"So, it would be best if you say nothing that may belie that delusion. Understand?"

Val took another look at Jabba and grimaced. "What if it just slips? What if he says 'Don't I look good today?' and I say, 'For a slug you look good.' What then?"

"Then," Nathaniel looked away, "you would count yourself lucky if you only lost your tongue."

"Nathaniel!" The mayor finally noted their presence, and waved his flipper-like appendage. "Come here, my boy."

Nathaniel slipped an arm around Val's waist, which took her by surprise and steered her toward the mayor.

The mayor extended a flipper and Nathaniel dropped to one knee and kissed it. "I'm so pleased you could make it to my party. To what do I owe this unexpected pleasure?"

"The pleasure is mine, great one." Nathaniel rose to his feet. "I wanted to come by and tell you personally that I have been giving your generous offer of employment much serious thought."

"And? Will you join me?"

The way the mayor was eyeing Nathaniel made Val think he left off the "in the hot tub," part of the proposition.

"Like I said, I have been giving the matter much thought."

"That is not an answer. Things are brewing, my demon friend, a great opportunity has only today presented itself, and I would relish the chance to have you on my team."

"What opportunity is that?"

The mayor raised a lump of flesh on his forehead, which could have been his eyebrow. "That's privileged information. But join me, and you will be one of the privileged few." His gaze tracked along Nathaniel's form and came to rest on Val.

"This is . . . *Claire*," Nathaniel said. "She is with me."

"I see." His lump of eyebrow traveled higher. "Do I smell human? A *human* in the Underworld? Nathaniel, I'm shocked at your audacity."

"She may be human, but she's striving to be so much more than that. She is a practitioner of black magic."

The mayor nodded. "Ah, a witch. Very nice. Very nice, indeed. Welcome, my dear."

Val wondered how an evil witch might answer him. "Thanks a bunch."

"I enjoy magic very much, myself," the mayor continued. "Would you do a demonstration for me?"

A demonstration? Val's eyes widened. *Of magic?*

She swallowed hard. "Do you have a deck of playing cards handy?"

Nathaniel laughed. "Claire, don't tease. Great one, forgive her, please. Her magic is so dark, so malicious in its nature, that none of what she does can be demonstrated here since there is that Belligerent Magic Decree you so wisely put forth."

"Yes, yes, of course, you are right." The mayor eyed

Val and she tried to eye him right back. Evil witches didn't get intimidated by Underworld bosses. If there was a handbook for evil witches, that would be on page one.

Fallen angels, on the other hand, were intimidated very easily. And often. At least *this* fallen angel was, she thought.

The mayor nodded at her. "Your familiar is very well-behaved. An interesting choice, I must say. It must ensure that all but the bravest demons will stay away from your business."

"Excuse me?"

"Your familiar." He waved a flipper at her.

Val looked at Nathaniel.

"Squeak," Reggie offered.

"Oh, right. My familiar. Yeah, he's . . . quite well-trained, actually. Not housebroken, though, but what can you do?"

"Squeak?"

"Well, you're not."

The shirtless waiter delivered a drink to the mayor who was unable to pick it up, so he stood there while the mayor sipped it from the tray with a long, bendy straw. When he'd sucked the last of whatever the oddly puce-colored liquid was, the waiter wandered back toward the topless women.

"This party will be quite the event," the mayor said. "It was originally simply one of my regular bashes, but now I'm celebrating."

"What's the occasion?"

The slug shrugged. "It has to do with the privileged information I spoke of before. But a word from you could change all that. I would love to have you in my folds. Err . . . I mean, have you in *the* fold."

"I would enjoy"—Nathaniel seemed to shudder ever so slightly—"discussing it further with you."

The mayor eyed Val again. "In private."

She took a step back. "Yeah, you guys talk. I'll just go snag a drink and leave you two at it."

Nathaniel held eye contact with her for a moment before he went to grab a nearby lounge chair, pulling it up alongside the mayor's chaise.

Not that she was one to judge, but it was quite obvious that the mayor preferred handsome demons to sexy evil witches.

Can't say she blamed him. It. *Whatever.*

Val backed away until she was out of earshot. She was putting a lot of faith into the fact that Nathaniel wouldn't give her away. She felt fairly assured he wouldn't, what with the whole "command" thing, but either way it was a risk she had to take. If it meant finding Julian and getting the key, then it was worth it. Then straight back home to Barlow. She'd been gone long enough already.

"So what do you think about that, Reggie?" she whispered. "So strange. I so want out of this crazy place."

"Squeak."

"That's cute, but you can talk now. At least for a moment. I guess familiars don't usually talk. You're doing a good job. Have you been practicing? Sounds like a very realistic squeak."

"Squeak, *squeak.*"

She frowned. "A sound which is now getting on my nerves. Would you just knock it—"

Reggie bit her.

"Ow!" She pressed a hand to her neck and stepped back . . .

Into something firm.

She turned around slowly.

"Well, well," Julian stood there looking at her, from stiletto heels to rat. "Aren't we a pretty one?"

Val opened her mouth but found that she'd lost her voice—perhaps forever this time.

"Please, allow me." He reached forward and took her hand in his, pulling it away from the little wound Reggie had made while he'd tried to warn her that frigging *Julian* himself was standing behind them, wearing an expensive-looking dark blue suit with a white, partially unbuttoned shirt. Looking very nice and appearing to not be afraid of Reggie at all. No, he seemed very calm, cool, and collected. For a demon with low self-esteem and a hidden rat phobia, that is.

Julian looked at her neck, and then touched the wound with his index finger. She felt a familiar tingle . . . the same feeling she got when Nathaniel healed her broken ankle in the alleyway. He smiled at her. "All better."

Val forced herself to not try to pull away from him in disgust and fear. He didn't know who she was. She looked completely different from when he'd last seen her at the Paradise Inn—after he'd vanquished Alexa and stolen the key. However, he looked exactly the same. Tall, ice blond, high cheekbones, and his arrogant "Aren't I hot?" mask was firmly in place.

"Thank you," she finally managed to say and raised her eyebrow in what she hoped looked like a flirtatious gesture.

"I don't believe we've met before."

"I'm Claire."

"Julian."

"My pleasure."

He smiled a bit wider at that. "Not yet. But it certainly could be. In so many ways."

"So . . . are you here for the party?"

"Of course." He glanced over at the mayor and Nathaniel. "What is *he* doing here?"

"Excuse me?"

"Trying to make his move?" he sneered. "Too bad, so sad." He tore his gaze from Nathaniel to look at Val again. "Are you here with *him*?"

She tried to play dumb. "Him who?"

"Nathaniel."

"Oh." She glanced over. "Yes, I am."

"You deserve much, much better than him."

She smiled at him and forced herself to touch his arm. "I totally agree."

His lips twitched with amusement. "Claire. Beautiful Claire. I do believe I'll enjoy getting to know you. And showing you all the ways I could satisfy you better than that poor excuse for a demon could."

He moved to grab a drink from a passing tray and his shirt opened a bit. His pale but muscular chest revealed something else. On a long gold chain around his neck he wore the Key to Heaven.

Chapter Fifteen

The Key to Heaven. Right in front of her, less than an arm's reach away.

She must have stared at it a little too long, since Julian looked down at himself. He touched the key and she thought he meant to tuck it back inside his shirt, but he pulled it all the way out.

"Pretty isn't it?"

"Very."

He lifted it so it lay flat on his hand. "Do you see? There are words etched into its surface. It's an incantation."

"So you're saying that it's a magic key?"

His smile widened, although she did notice his gaze flick nervously for the briefest moment to Reggie. "A magic key. Yes, it is. And very powerful. Do you like power, Claire?"

"Who doesn't?"

He shook his head. "No, that is not a proper answer. Do you like power?"

She met his gaze. "I'm a witch. An evil one, that is. I absolutely adore power."

He closed the small distance between them and took

the key, tracing the end of it down her neck, along her collarbone, and down her chest to the ample cleavage that spilled out of the top of the corset. "Then we will get along just fine."

He let the key drop back into place under his shirt and continued his exploration of her chest with the tip of his finger. She froze in place, unable to do anything about what was happening.

"Unhand her," a voice said from behind her.

Julian smiled, but his eyes were focused on Val's glamourized body. "Nathaniel. So good to see you again."

"She's with me."

Julian's eyes flicked to Val's. "He's like an incessant little insect buzzing around my head. It's been buzzing for nearly two hundred years, but I'm hoping it won't for much longer." His hand moved to boldly cup her left breast.

Nathaniel moved beside them and grabbed Julian's wrist. Their strength must have been equal as Julian's hand didn't budge.

Reggie growled and shifted position on Val's shoulder. Julian's hand shot back like he'd been burned.

"Your animal is very protective," he said.

She glanced at Reggie from the corner of her eye. "It's probably his little leather hat. Makes him feel like a bodyguard."

"Mmm." He turned to Nathaniel, shook his head and clucked his tongue. "Nathaniel, jealousy does not become you."

"Julian—" Nathaniel shook his own head "—you're an asshole."

"Such a brilliant comeback. But what else could I expect from a halfling?"

Nathaniel didn't reply to that.

"A halfling?" Val said. "Isn't that like a hobbit? Nathaniel, have you been holding out on me?"

Julian smiled. "A halfling is an impure demon. Something less and unworthy. Something terribly sad and pathetic."

Nathaniel ignored Julian and looked at her. "Are you okay?"

Julian snorted. "What is this? Nathaniel concerned with someone other than himself? Claire, you must be truly special." He moved in and whispered in her ear. "I will so enjoy taking you away from him."

Nathaniel pushed Julian so that he staggered back. "I told you to keep your hands off her."

Julian cocked his head to one side. "If your actions didn't amuse me so, I would make you very sorry."

Nathaniel faked a yawn.

Flames flashed in Julian's eyes but they quickly died down as a smile snaked across his face. "I think you will be one of the first I destroy."

"Is that so? You and what army?"

"The army of my choosing. I will surround myself only with those who please me, and you have never pleased me."

Nathaniel looked at Val. She'd been watching their tennis match of verbosity with a tight feeling in her chest—and it wasn't just from the corset. "He's always been full of himself, this one. Cocky son of a bitch."

Julian laughed, then ran a warm hand down Val's bare arm, making her skin crawl.

"I told you to unhand her." There was no more lightness to Nathaniel's words.

Julian held her gaze.

"Nathaniel, don't get possessive," Val said, knowing
full well that the only way to get her hands on the key was
to cozy up to Julian, even if the thought of it made her
sick to her stomach. "You don't own me. I can talk to anyone I want to."

"Oh, yes." Julian moved closer to whisper again in her
ear. "I do think I like you."

Nathaniel grabbed his arm, pulled him physically
away from Val before his fist connected with Julian's face
with a loud smacking sound. "Don't make me repeat myself again."

Julian held a hand to his mouth, then pulled it away to
look at the blood. "No finesse. No class. Just like the former human you are. Sad, really. Once I thought you had
so much potential—almost equal to my own—but you've
proven time and time again that you are lacking in so
many ways. Especially recently. And one so lacking as
you could never hope to be a part of what is about to happen here tonight."

"A part of what?" Nathaniel's eyes narrowed.

Julian studied him for a moment, then smiled thinly.
He pulled the key from under his shirt and held it in his
hand. "This."

"What is that?"

"This is the universe in the palm of my very hand." Julian stared down at the golden key with total reverence.
"The beginning and the end. The balance of light and
dark. Solidified power for me to wield at my whim."

Nathaniel looked at it for a moment. "That's funny. Looks like just a key to me."

"You have no vision. It is so much more than just a key. This is Lucifer's own *Key to Heaven*."

Val felt her stomach sink as she glanced at Nathaniel. He stared down at the harmless-looking key in Julian's hand.

"I don't believe you."

Julian smiled. "We shall see, won't we, what is to be believed. Or rather, I shall see. When *I* open a gateway to Heaven tonight. Won't they be surprised to see the likes of me in their lily-white realm? To do a little—how should I put it?—*remodeling* of their terribly exclusive club. The mayor has agreed to compensate me greatly for my efforts."

"Is that what this is all about?" Val asked, hoping the tremor in her words wasn't too obvious. "The party? It's recruitment for your little demonic episode of *Trading Spaces*?"

"It is a coincidence that the cream of the crop of the Underworld are at the mayor's party tonight, but it is a lucky coincidence, I'd say." His gaze slid down to her chest. "And you are more than welcome to join me, my lovely witch. I can show you what a demon of true power is capable of."

Her mind was working overtime. In a really messed up sort of way, this was the perfect situation for her. But she needed to get him alone. If he let her be a part of his plan, half her battle was already done. He was playing right into her hands.

Big boobs really did *pay off in getting men to do what you want,* she thought. *Who knew?*

"I would love to be a part of this." She sidled closer to the blond demon, and hooked her arm through his. "However can I repay you?"

"I'm sure I can think of something."

Nathaniel scowled at him. "You want her only because she's with me."

A grin tugged at Julian's lips. "Maybe a little. Would that hurt you? Imagining me enjoying her and she, me?"

He laughed. "I don't think any woman has ever enjoyed you, Julian."

"You will not get a rise out of me."

"No, actually I've heard that nobody's gotten a rise out of you in over a hundred years." Nathaniel paused. "Have you ever thought about trying Viagra?"

"That's very amusing." Julian said, then glanced quickly at Val. "And completely untrue."

She shrugged. "Whatever you say."

"I can prove that it's a vicious lie."

"Trust me, not necessary. Look, I want to know more about this"—her gaze flicked uneasily to Nathaniel—"Key to Heaven. Sounds fascinating."

Julian stroked the key but still looked a little disturbed that his demony manhood had been questioned. "Did I mention that it is solidified power?"

"Uh, yeah, you did. Where did you get it?"

He blinked. "What difference does that make?"

"How do you know it's really the Key to Heaven? Maybe it's just an ordinary key that someone sold to you under false pretenses. One of those *Antiques Roadshow* mishaps."

He raised an eyebrow. "You amuse me."

"Goody."

"It is real. I am certain of its . . . *realness.*"

Val absently started to pet Reggie, just to see the nervous shift in Julian's eyes. "I'm just saying that if I'm going to dump my current boyfriend to follow you around like a rock-star groupie, I at least need some sort of reassurance that you're not just blowing hot air. No demon pun intended."

He raised an eyebrow. "Are you asking for a demonstration of its power?"

Is that what it sounded like she was asking for? "Yes, that's right. Can you open up a gateway to Heaven to show me? Even if it's just a tiny, rat-sized one."

"Squeak!"

He shook his head. "I'm afraid not."

Nathaniel snorted. "See? I knew it."

Julian glared at him. "I will open a doorway only when the mayor is ready for me to. But the time is nigh. Oh yes, the time is nigh."

" *'The time is nigh'?*" Nathaniel repeated. "Who talks like that?"

Val shot him a look. "So it will definitely be soon. At this party."

"Yes, very soon."

She eyed the golden key, feeling a great wave of anxiety wash over her. If only she could hold it in her hand, just for a moment. "Can I touch it? Uh, the key, I mean."

Julian stared at her so long and hard that she was certain her glamour had slipped and he was looking at the real her—recognizing her from Barlow's living room—and was seconds away from reaching out to snap her neck like a candy cane. But he didn't. She still looked like Skanky the Bad Witch.

Finally he spoke. "I'm not sure that would be wise."

"Why? Don't you trust me?"

"Should I?"

She forced a devilish smile to her lips. "Absolutely not."

He mirrored the expression, then slipped the chain from around his neck and pressed the key into her palm. "Then of course you may touch it, my lovely witch."

The moment the key touched her skin she could feel its power. She wasn't magical. She wasn't even an angel anymore. She was completely human. But she could still feel it humming up and down her arms, filling her with a sense of goodness, and peace, and happiness. Plus, she felt a great sense of ownership. The key was meant for *her.*

She could run. Right then. Go all Gollum on them and run away with the key in her possession. She looked around the pool to see that more partygoers had arrived. The mayor was now surrounded by four muscular men who seemed to be paying him the attention he desired. The topless girls had put on tight, colorful party clothes. Julian stood in front of Val, and Nathaniel was only a few feet away, his arms crossed, his expression guarded and slightly annoyed.

She wouldn't get five steps from Julian. There was no chance.

She reluctantly handed the key back to him, feeling ill at having to continue with the façade.

"Nice," she said. "You're very lucky to have it. Did you have to kill the previous owner?"

He smiled at the question. "No. But the old bastard doesn't have more than a couple days left. I could see the cancer eating away his insides. If I killed him it would have just put him out of his misery . . . so why bother?"

Val clenched her fists at her sides.

"You know who should be a part of this?" Nathaniel glanced around. "Alexa. Maybe she'll be here later. You seen her around lately, Julian?"

Julian's expression didn't change. "No. Haven't seen her in quite some time. Keeping herself busy in the earthly realm I imagine. Perhaps she's mistakenly recruiting more useless humans to join the demon ranks."

Nathaniel opened his mouth, but Julian didn't let him say anything. "I'm needed elsewhere." He slipped the key back over his head and Val saw it fall beneath his shirt. "I look forward to speaking with you later, Claire."

She nodded and smiled before he breezed away without another word and disappeared inside the mansion.

Nathaniel eyed her. "Can I speak with you over there?" He nodded toward a palm tree away from the growing noise of the party crowd by the pool.

She swallowed. "Sure."

"Holy crap," Reggie said after he let out a rat-sized sigh of relief. "Sorry I had to put the bite on you, Val. He was very . . . what's the word I'm looking for here?"

"Evil?"

"No, that's not it."

"Full of himself?"

"No, I'm thinking of something . . ."

"I don't know."

"I've got it. He was just so, so . . . blond. Do you think he colors his hair, or does he have, like, Swedish demon heritage?"

Val rolled her eyes. "You couldn't think of the word *blond*? I'm blond."

"Not at the moment you aren't, gorgeous." He nestled

closer into her red mane. "But, gee, your hair smells ter-rific."

She lifted Reggie off her shoulder and placed him down on the ground. "You've just talked yourself out of riding privileges for a while."

"Oh, come on," he whined. "It was a compliment!"

She moved toward Nathaniel out of earshot of the rest of the partygoers. He stared at her with annoyance as she hobbled over on her ridiculously high heels.

"Why didn't you tell me?" His voice was quiet.

"Tell you what?"

"About the key, of course."

She shrugged. "What was I supposed to have told you?"

"The truth."

"You wanted me to tell you we were looking for the Key to Heaven?"

"Yes."

Val rolled her eyes. "Look, I know we haven't been keeping a score card here, Nathaniel, but in case you've forgotten, you're a *demon*. I didn't tell you what we were looking for because . . ." She trailed off as she searched for the right words.

He crossed his arms. "Because you don't trust me."

She nodded. "Precisely."

"I see. And the fact that your power over me keeps me from being able to lie to you—that wasn't a consideration in letting me know what we were up against?"

"I don't know how far that power goes. Or how long it will last. I couldn't take the risk that you'd try to take the key for yourself."

He nodded, jaw clenched. "And now you are willing to

throw yourself shamelessly at that self-obsessed asshole in order to get what you're after."

"If I have to. Yes."

"You're a fool."

Val crossed her arms and felt her face begin to flush again. Only this time it wasn't from embrassment, it was from anger. "I don't need to explain myself to you. I'm doing what I have to do for Barlow, okay? A good friend of mine who is also a fallen angel. He's dying, just like Julian said. I need to use the key to send him back to Heaven before it's too late. And even aside from that, I need the key back so Julian doesn't have a chance to use it. The damage he'd do by gaining access to Heaven will destroy everything. Like, we're talking major high-budget universal damage."

He looked away, toward the sparkling swimming pool surrounded by the Mayor's beautiful guests. "Finished?"

"Not even slightly. But on this subject I am." She leaned against the palm tree, feeling slightly exhausted from her speech.

"And what about you?"

"What *about* me?"

"Will you use the key for yourself? Send yourself back to Heaven?"

She paused. "Probably."

Nathaniel scoffed at her. " 'Probably', she says. You *know* you will."

"That's really none of your business."

"You *are* my business, remember? If you succeed at going back to Heaven . . . I fail."

She felt a chill at the thought. "I can't help you there. That's just the way it is."

"So you're going to all of this trouble to save the world like some comic book heroine. Save your friend. And then maybe, just maybe—if there's time—save yourself."

"That's right."

"That's so selfless of you."

She stared at him for a moment, not liking his sarcastic tone. "I guess it is."

He laughed and shook his head. "You're fooling yourself. None of the other stuff matters to you. You're getting the key for yourself and only yourself. So *you* can go back. Just like the so-called good deeds you tried to do in Niagara Falls these last couple of months. You think you were doing them because you were trying to help the greater good? No. You were doing it to earn your heavenly Brownie points so they'd forgive you and take you back. Face it, angel, you're just as selfish as the rest of us. And just as big a liar."

She narrowed her eyes. "How dare you say that to me!"

"Because it's all true. You've been selfish in this whole thing just so you come out the winner. Even if your idea of winning is to go back up to your safe little predictable cloud and get back to your easy, perfect existence, doing whatever it is you did up there. No risk, no excitement, no rush. Just same old, same old. You have been given the chance to do something different for a while as a human, but you're too damned scared to embrace it." He turned away from her.

She grabbed his arm to make him look at her. "I'm too scared to embrace being a human? You're . . ." She glared at him. "You're too scared to *embrace* a human."

He shook his head incredulously. "What are you babbling about now?"

"Earlier, remember? You pushed me away? I get that it's against the rules. That you can't get too close to one of your assignments. I figured that out all by myself, even without Lloyd's help. So don't talk to me about being scared when you're obviously the one who's petrified."

He glared back at her, his eyes stormy gray. "You have no idea what you're talking about."

Val felt so frustrated, she couldn't help what came out of her mouth next. "What is this?"

"What?"

She bit her bottom lip before continuing. "Are you just playing games with me—is all of this just to make me feel something for you so you can use it against me to save yourself and your job? Or does this mean something to you?"

He sighed but his harsh expression didn't change. "You are driving me insane. I just called you selfish to your face and now you're getting all psychoanalytical on me?"

"Why can't you just answer a question without making me force you to?"

He glared at her.

She crossed her arms. Her face had become incredibly hot and it wasn't just because of the bright Miami-like sun in the sky. "Fine. Be that way. I want to know what this means to you. Why you haven't tried harder to get away from me. Why you've sort of stopped trying to tempt me at every given opportunity. Why you're helping me to get the key back. And what you meant when you said you burn for me. I command you to tell—"

Nathaniel pushed her up against the palm tree and

covered her mouth with his hand. His eyes were full of flames, but he didn't look angry anymore. He looked scared. "Don't say anything else, Valerie. Just don't. Trust me when I tell you that this is not the time or the place to get into this discussion. There's too much at stake for both of us. He shook her a little harder than necessary and frowned. "Do you understand?"

His expression began to soften as he stared into her eyes. She nodded and he removed his hand.

He held her in his deep, bottomless gaze and the rest of the world fell away. There were only the two of them. She felt things for him that she shouldn't have been feeling. He was a demon assigned to tempt her. She couldn't let herself forget that. It was wrong for her to be near him, close to him, feeling this way. Big-time wrong.

But she sensed his loneliness, his pain, his desperation. Was everything Lloyd told her true? Was Nathaniel tortured daily by his horrible duties as a demon, without even the hope of freedom, without ever being with someone he burned for?

Her heart swelled, which, considering the size of her glamourized breasts, was no small feat.

"Just try to trust me if you can, my angel," he murmured and leaned closer to her, until their lips were nearly touching.

"Val!"

She heard the shriek and turned to look over by the pool.

Reggie had wedged himself under a lounge chair and there was a large leopard-spotted cat crouched next to him reaching out a paw in an attempt to grab him.

Val pushed Nathaniel away and ran over to the pool. The cat hissed and swiped at her as she moved between it and Reggie. She knelt down and offered a hand to her be-spelled friend. He climbed up, quivering with fear.

"My life flashed before my eyes again," he said with chattering teeth. "It was the extended, unrated DVD version this time. Not good. Not good at all."

"Sorry to hear that. But it's okay now. You're safe. Well, as safe as we're going to get around here."

Val glared at the cat and followed the thin gold-chained leash up a pair of long, long . . . looonnnggg tanned legs.

"Your familiar talks," the legs said in a low, sexy, accented voice. Val looked up even higher. The speaker was actually the gorgeous woman attached to them.

She had waist-length black hair, golden skin, and amber-colored eyes. She wore a leopard print bikini to match her cat that could have fit in a small, overnight delivery envelope. The bikini, not the cat.

"Yes, he can," Val replied. "He's like that singing and dancing frog in the Bugs Bunny cartoons." She placed Reggie on her left shoulder where he found a chunk of red hair to hide behind. "I don't appreciate your cat almost having him for lunch."

She smiled. "Perhaps you should keep a better eye on the things you cherish." Then she all but dismissed Val as Nathaniel approached. "Nathaniel. I was told you were here. I'm so pleased."

"Yasmeen," he said evenly.

And then she walked right up along the edge of the swimming pool to Nathaniel and kissed him on the mouth. Val blinked. French-kissed. With tongue and everything.

"Have you missed me, darling?" It sounded more like *dah-link*. *Like Zsa Zsa Gabor*, Val decided. Only more evil.

Nathaniel glanced at Val then back to her. "Very much."

"Yasmeen has missed you, too. Yasmeen is worried about you, *dah-link*. She hopes you will follow through on your latest assignment as soon as possible. She may be able to help you get a promotion, if you do."

"Excuse me," Val said.

Her amber eyes tracked to Val as if she'd just noticed a fruit fly buzzing nearby. "Who are you?"

"I'm Nathaniel's evil witch girlfriend. Got it?"

Her thinly arched eyebrows slid up. "Is that so?"

"Yeah, it's so."

A bemused smile twisted on her full red lips. "And what did you wish to ask Yasmeen?"

"Do you always talk about yourself that way?"

"What way?"

"In the third person. It's rather distracting. Well, that and sticking your tongue down Nathaniel's throat a moment ago. Don't do that."

Yasmeen cocked her head to the side and studied her for a moment, her gaze raking down Val's glamourized body, taking in every inch.

"You are human." She turned to the demon. "Nathaniel, *dah-link*, I knew things were dire, but I had no idea you'd gotten so desperate. You should have contacted me and I could have taken care of you much better than any human can. As you well know."

"After Lucifer promoted you, you've been at the head office for so long, I wasn't sure if I'd ever see you again."

She smiled. "Yet here I am. I always am looking for new challenges, new excitement."

"New risks?" Nathaniel said, and his gaze flicked to Val.

"Most certainly. Existence is boring without a certain level of unpredictability and risk."

"I absolutely agree."

Val frowned at him, but was ignored.

"We will spend much time together being . . . spontaneous." Then she eyed Val. "He is mine, human. Always has been. And as soon as he once and for all accepts what he is without reserve, and the power that I can bring him, he always will be."

"Bitch!" That was from Reggie.

Val forced her expression to stay blank and bored despite the heavy fist that just pulled out her heart and pounded it into the ground. "Yeah, well, maybe I'll go see what Julian's up to. You see one hot demon you've seen them all."

She laughed. "Silly one, be my guest. Julian is hopelessly insane, power-hungry, and rumor is that he's as impotent as a garden hose."

"Then how is he any different from Nathaniel?"

That got his full attention. His lips twitched and he almost smiled, but managed to stop himself. "I'm not *insane*."

Val shrugged. "Two out of three, then."

Yasmeen turned her gaze back to Nathaniel. Honestly, Val thought, the woman looked at him like she should be wearing a I'M NATHANIEL'S NUMBER ONE FAN T-shirt or something. It was really pathetic. Well, it would be pathetic if she wasn't as gorgeous as a European supermodel from Hell. As well as practically naked.

"Yasmeen must go take care of some business," she purred. "But let us have large amounts of sex later. When you have rid yourself of the short, disproportioned human."

Val adjusted her glamourized boobs. "You're just jealous. You're lucky I can't use my evil witch powers around here."

She fixed Val with an icy gaze. "And you as well."

Then she walked away showing them that her leopard print bikini was, in fact, a thong.

"I've never been so scared," Reggie said. "Or so incredibly turned on in my entire life."

Nathaniel looked at Val and shrugged. "She's a demon."

"No kidding." She watched Yasmeen disappear into the mansion, and then started to laugh.

Nathaniel frowned. "What's so funny?"

Val shook her head. "I'm so unbelievably naïve that it's ridiculous."

"What are you talking about?"

"I was feeling all sorry for you before. I thought that you . . . that whole thing about not being able to 'be with' anyone or you'll break the rules and be punished. I thought . . . forget it. I'm such an idiot."

His frown deepened and he crossed his arms. "There *is* a rule that a Tempter cannot be with his assigned fallen angel."

"It really doesn't matter."

"It *does* matter."

"No, it doesn't."

"Yes, Valerie"—he grabbed her arm—"it does."

"I command you to let go of me."

He did and then stared at her. "I don't care what she made it sound like, Yasmeen and I—"

"I command you to stop talking about this."

He shut his mouth. "Very well. But you just need to know that she means—"

Val pushed him into the pool with a big, loud splash and turned away to go in search of a fruity drink with an umbrella in it.

Chapter Sixteen

—⁓—

"I don't know how mature that was, Val," Reggie said as he gnawed at the piece of pineapple that decorated her third piña colada. "But it sure was funny."

They sat on a lounge chair a short distance away from the noisy party. The Underworld was currently experiencing a planned dark-time—Val had been told by a passing waiter that it was only to last for ten minutes—and patio lanterns were out, lighting up the pool area. Several large, demony men had shotguns and were taking target practice at the few Nightflyers that had dared to come too close. Val found it extremely disturbing to watch, knowing that the creatures had once been demons like Nathaniel. But the alcoholic beverage was helping her cope. A bit.

She'd searched around for Julian so she could continue working on him. All she needed was for him to let her hold on to the key for a while. Then as soon as she got out of his sight she would simply escape with it in her possession. But he was nowhere to be found, at least at the moment. As each minute passed she got more and more nervous that her plan was so flimsy it would fail miserably.

Maybe I shouldn't have had that third drink, she thought.

Nathaniel had called her selfish before. Was he right? Did she only want the key for herself? To go back to Heaven and back to her predictable, risk-free existence? She'd always thought that would be the pleasant side effect after she'd helped Barlow and saved the world. But as far as it being her main reason for going through everything she'd gone through . . .

Was she being selfish? The thought made her feel ill. Maybe she was a horrible person deep down and all of the poison was now coming to the surface.

Like the "pride" thing. She'd never known that was one of her flaws. It hadn't even occurred to her that there had been a real reason for her expulsion from Heaven until it had been pointed out to her. Even then, it seemed like an unlikely reason.

But maybe it wasn't. Maybe she didn't deserve to be an angel at all.

She had committed the deadly sin of pride. She was selfish. And now she feared for her own safety if Julian caught her trying to take the key.

I am a wimp, she thought dejectedly as she slurped at the bottom of her drink. *A selfish wimp. With incredibly large breasts.*

Reggie poked her with his paw. "Don't look so glum. Have another drink."

She pushed the glass away. "No. I think I've had enough. Of all of this. I just want to go home now."

"Hey, remember when I said that when you're not looking, Nate's always staring at you like a little lost puppy dog?"

"I don't remember you putting it quite like that, but yeah, I guess so."

"He's doing it right now. Over by the mayor."

Val looked over just in time to see Nathaniel turn his gaze away. His clothes were still damp from his unplanned swim in the pool. He hadn't spoken to her since, or come near her.

A band had set up on the other side of the pool and they were playing music that reminded Val of the Gipsy Kings CD Barlow sometimes played in the manager's office. Flamenco-sounding, only these performers all looked like short, fleshy green Muppets. Short Muppet monsters that could shake a mean maraca. She kept her eyes on the mansion, through the darkness, waiting for Julian to make another appearance.

The band stopped playing after their most recent song—"She Bangs" by Ricky Martin—and Yasmeen approached the microphone.

"Welcome, *dah-links*," she said. There was still that hint of an accent Val couldn't place in her voice.

Bitchylvania, she thought. *Or maybe Bitchachussets. Yeah, that's it.*

She felt like she was dealing with her dislike for Yasmeen quite well. In a seething, unpleasant, eating-away-at-her-insides kind of way. Why didn't Val like her? Was it because she knew she had carnal knowledge of Nathaniel? But that would be ridiculous and completely petty.

Also, terribly, terribly accurate.

"I know you're all wondering what our big announcement will be, what the mayor has in store for all of us, don't you?" Yasmeen breathed into the microphone. She'd slipped a cover-up over her teeny bikini. A see-through cover-up.

Was that an oxymoron? Val wondered.

Speaking of morons, Nathaniel had begun to move closer to where Val was sitting. She didn't look at him.

"Well," Yasmeen continued, "you're going to have to wait just a bit longer for the big announcement. But it won't be long now."

Julian seemed to appear from nowhere to join Yasmeen on the stage. Val sat up in her chair as he grabbed the microphone.

"Yes," Julian said to the crowd. "It will be well worth the wait, I promise. In the meantime, Mayor Vaille wishes you all to enjoy the party. And I just wanted to say, doesn't the mayor look fantastic tonight? Your personal trainer is doing wonders for you, great one."

The entire crowd of gathered demons glanced over at the slug for a silent moment. Then everyone cheered.

"Thank you, my boy," the mayor said. "Sven does have a way with free weights. He's a big brute with the cardio, though."

Julian smiled. "It's paying off. Now, if you'll excuse me, I have an important matter to attend to inside." He stepped down from the stage and began to move toward the mansion. Yasmeen went to sit by the mayor's side and the band started up again.

Val couldn't tear her gaze away from the blond demon. "I have to go after him." She stood up from her seat but Nathaniel caught her wrist. "There's not much time left."

"Please don't. It's dangerous."

She tried to pull away. "I need to get that key."

"Julian is evil."

"Yeah, I already figured that out all by myself. But there's no other way."

"I'll go with you."

She shook her head. "No. He doesn't like you."

"The feeling's mutual."

"That's just it. If I can get him alone . . " She didn't really know how to finish that sentence.

Nathaniel's eyes narrowed and his grip on her wrist increased. "Not a good idea."

Julian was almost at the mansion. She had to keep him in sight so he couldn't disappear on her again.

She met his gaze and forced herself to sound commanding. "Let go of me. Right now."

He did, but didn't look happy about it. Yasmeen approached them at that moment, and while Nathaniel's head turned to her latest accented proposition, Val slipped away and hurried toward the mansion, trying to move quickly and quietly past the pool and along the cobblestone pathway.

Julian had stopped to talk with an eight-foot-tall creature covered in blue fur, so Val hung back for a moment and tried her best to look calm. His ice-blond head didn't turn in her direction. She didn't want him to notice her until they were somewhere private. He slipped inside the mansion and she followed.

He again stopped to talk, this time with a big guy with faery wings and a leather jacket with the word SECURITY in silver studs on the back.

"What?" Julian exclaimed after the faery said something in his ear. "Impossible. How did she get past security?"

The faery shrugged and had the decency to look embarrassed.

"What's going on?" Reggie whispered.

Val jumped and clutched her chest. "You surprised me. Shhh. I forgot you were there for a moment. You're so quiet."

"Oh, look. They've got Lisa!"

Val's gaze moved to another leather-jacketed faery who held the girl who'd attacked Nathaniel outside of Lloyd's house in his grip. She looked absolutely terrified, but her chin was lifted in defiance.

Val's eyes widened. "Oh no."

"How did you get in here?" Julian leaned over to look at her closely.

"Forgot my invitation. Just wanted to have a look around." Lisa's voice was strong, but shaky. "See what all the buzz is about."

Julian laughed. "Right. Well, what's done is done. This is good, in a way. We could use a little more entertainment tonight. The mayor so enjoys a good sacrifice."

The girl cringed as Julian clipped her gently under the chin. "Don't look so upset. It's an honor to be sacrificed to Mayor Vaille. Entire ancient cultures used to do it on a daily basis. He misses that, I think." He nodded to the faeries. "Tie her up somewhere safe for the time being."

They nodded and dragged Lisa away in the opposite direction. Julian continued down his hallway.

Val began to follow the faeries.

"What exactly are you doing, Val?" Reggie whispered.

"I don't know."

"Aren't we after Julian?"

"Yes, but . . ." She swallowed and stopped walking for a moment. "I can't let them hurt her."

"But—"

"Shh. Just be quiet for a minute, would you?" Her brain hurt. She could do both. She'd help Lisa and then get back to Julian before it was too late.

Lisa had looked so small and defeated. Not like the butt-kicking girl she met in front of Lloyd's house.

"I don't mean to be the voice of reason here," Reggie's small voice whispered. "Because that's so not me. And I like Lisa a lot, but do you think it's the first time they've done something like this? Or the last time?"

The hair on Val's arms stood up at the horrible thought. "I'm not here other days, or I'd try to do something then, too."

"It's because she's a fallen angel, isn't it?"

"I don't know what you mean."

"Yeah, you do. It might be at a subconscious level, but you know exactly what I mean. You want to rescue this ex-fallen angel who got tempted and taken to Hell because you look at her and see you."

She stopped walking for a second and turned her head to see Reggie's whiskers twitch. "I what?"

"You think what's happening to her could very well be happening to you. So by helping her in a way you're actually helping yourself. Does that make sense?"

Val frowned and began walking again. "Not even remotely."

She felt Reggie shift position on her shoulder. "Well, I kind of confused myself somewhere along my line of thinking. But this is still a bad idea."

"Maybe I should just leave you right here in case Yasmeen's pet is looking for a snack later."

"You wouldn't let that happen to me, would you?"

"Just watch me."

He shifted again. Nervously. "We should definitely find poor Lisa. And rescue her. It is the right and noble thing to do."

"See?" Val braved a smile. "Now you're talking."

The faeries stopped and opened a door, and the two of them disappeared inside with their struggling prisoner. Val waited with her back pressed against the wall, barely breathing, until the door reopened and the faeries exited, shutting the door behind them. They began walking in the opposite direction to Val but then one of them stopped and turned his head a little as if he sensed something. She stopped breathing completely and crushed herself up against the wall, hoping the loud banging of her heart wouldn't give her away. After a long moment, the faery continued to walk away.

"Whew," Reggie breathed. "That was a close one."

With her back still against the wall, Val slid along until she reached the closed door, freezing at every little sound, even if it was just her stomach telling her that a brownie and three piña coladas did not meet all of her daily dietary needs. Then she wrapped her hand around the handle and turned it, expecting it to be locked and surprised that it wasn't. It turned easily and she pushed it open a crack to peer inside.

It was a bedroom, large and ornate with a great round bed in the middle. The room was in shadow, but she could see that Lisa was on the bed, tied up and helpless. She looked over her shoulder to check if anyone was coming down the hallway but she and Reggie were completely alone. She slipped into the room and silently closed the door behind her.

"Lisa," she whispered. The girl's shoulders tensed. Her

hands were tightly tied behind her back and attached to her feet with the same piece of rope.

Val searched the darkened room with a sweeping glance. Was someone waiting in the shadows just for the opportunity to jump out at her? That would be just her luck. She thought she'd probably deserve it with how careless she was being.

But the room was empty other than Lisa, Val, and the shivering rat on her shoulder. This was a demon party meant for the darkest, nastiest creatures around. No one would expect there to be a rescue attempt. Lisa wasn't anything more to them than a mild diversion, probably on par with a tasty, but quickly forgotten hors d'oeuvre.

When Val got to the bed she reached out a hand to touch Lisa's shoulder. The girl jumped and tried to scramble farther away.

"It's okay, I'm not going to hurt you," Val whispered. "I'm here to help you."

She made a mournful sound, muffled from the gag in her mouth. Val tried to untie it but Lisa cringed farther away from her.

Val frowned. "It's me. I'm not going to hurt you."

The scared look in the girl's eyes didn't go away. Val couldn't understand it. They'd just met a short time ago when Lisa tried to drive Nathaniel's gonads into his throat. Didn't she remember?

Oh. Val looked down at herself. *Right. The glamour. Forgot about that.*

Not that the high heeled boots or the corset had gotten any more comfortable, but she hadn't been staring at herself in the mirror every five minutes, so she'd nearly forgotten what she looked like.

"It's me, *Valerie*. We met earlier. Nathaniel, remember? I'm a fallen one, too?"

Lisa looked confused.

"This is just a glamour, so don't worry, okay?" Val continued. "I'm here to help you. Now hold still so I can get this thing off your mouth."

She reached out with her long, sharp red fingernails, but this time Lisa didn't move, though she did look scared. Val worked on the knot for a moment—it was pretty tight—and finally got it loose enough to pull it away from the girl's mouth.

Lisa swallowed a couple of times. "My hands."

It took Val longer to get those knots untied and she ended up breaking a nail in the process. She didn't usually have long nails, but she could now see why breaking one could make you mad—it just ruined the whole look.

"Are you okay?"

"No." She still seemed confused. "Why do you look like that?"

Val looked down at her cleavage, then back at Lisa. "Um, Happy Halloween?"

Lisa just stared at her.

Val shifted her feet nervously. "I needed to get in here and I couldn't let them see who I really am. This is temporary."

"You looked better the other way."

"I agree," Reggie said from Val's shoulder. "Although I don't mind the twins."

"Twins?"

"Yes, your two round and beautiful"—his whiskers twitched—"*eyes*. Yes, your eyes are lovely."

Lisa frowned. "Your familiar is talking."

"He's not my familiar. Although, I think he's getting a bit too familiar, truth be told."

"Lisa, gorgeous, it's me. Reggie."

She fixed him with a blank look.

"From the motel?"

"Oh . . ." She nodded slowly. "Right. The rat from the motel. I remember you now."

"See?" Reggie said proudly. "I'm unforgettable."

"Why are you helping me?" Lisa asked.

Val shrugged. "Why wouldn't I help you?"

She gingerly rubbed her rope-burned wrists. "I didn't expect this. You're putting yourself in danger."

"Seems to be what I do these days." Val didn't say it as a particularly good thing.

"But I tried to barbecue your boyfriend earlier," A grin pulled at Lisa's mouth. "If I get the chance I might try again."

"He's not my boyfriend."

"Seriously?" She raised an eyebrow. "The way he was looking at you—"

Val held up a hand to stop her. "So I've been told. But it doesn't mean anything. Maybe he just tends to stare off in the distance and sometimes that distance is me. I don't know. What I do know is he isn't my boyfriend."

She shook her head. "I don't understand why he brought you here, to the Underworld. It goes against all the demon rules."

Val sighed. "I'll tell you if you really want to know, but not here. Let's go . . . somewhere that isn't here and we'll chat, okay?"

"Deal."

Val grabbed Lisa's hand to help her off the bed,

snatched her boots from the floor, and they moved toward the door. Val pressed her ear to it. Reggie pressed his ear to it.

"Hear anything?" she asked him.

"Nope."

She opened the door and looked out. Nobody was there. She beckoned for Lisa to follow her quickly and quietly down the hallway.

"Okay," Lisa whispered. "What's up with you and Nathaniel?"

"He's my guide to the Underworld. That's all."

Lisa looked at her curiously. "How did you manage to convince a demon to be your guide?"

"I summoned him." They turned a corner. The carpeting was red and plush and the walls were lined with generic, but expensive-looking oil pointings in gilded frames.

"That's it?"

"Pretty much."

"Doesn't sound like something a demon would appreciate. Being forced to take orders from a fallen angel." She paused. "He hasn't tried to get away from you?"

"No," Val answered immediately.

"That's very strange."

Val shot her a look. "He has to do what I command him to. It's part of the summoning spell. He's bound to me. Whether he wants to be or not."

Reggie snickered but didn't say anything.

"That's very industrious. Summoning a demon," Lisa said. "And you're only just fallen?"

"Two months." Val was quickly growing weary of this inquisition.

"Two months without being tempted?"

"Nathaniel's also my Tempter." After a moment, she added, "So far unsuccessful."

She nodded. "I heard that about him. His complete failure at being a demon."

Val's lips tightened. "He succeeded with you, didn't he?"

"Oh looky," Reggie said. "A door."

"Okay," Val said. "Consider yourself rescued. Now beat it."

Lisa smiled. "Thanks."

"You're welcome. Now shoo. And don't get caught again. One rescue per night. That's the rules."

She opened the door and Val felt the tropical breeze from outside blow her hair back off her shoulders. "I'll remember this. See you later," she said, then winked and slipped out of the mansion, closing the door with a soft click behind her.

"See you later," Val repeated, slowly turning back around so she could start retracing her steps through the mansion. "Reggie, I don't want to see that crazy girl again, if I can help—"

Julian stood behind her. "Claire. What are you doing in here?"

Chapter Seventeen

———— ⌒ ————

Val forced a smile and tried not to release her bladder at the sight of the blond demon.

"What am I doing in here?" she repeated, and placed a hand on her hip. "Looking for you, of course."

Julian arched an eyebrow. "Is that so?"

"Yeah, that's so." She reached out to tap his chest. "You've been avoiding me."

"I haven't been avoiding you. I simply had some important duties to attend to."

"Well"—she tried to look as seductive as she could, but thought it probably came off looking a bit constipated—"your duty is to take care of me now."

She moaned inwardly. *Your duty is to take care of me?* That was probably the dumbest thing she'd ever said. And she'd said a lot of dumb things in her two months as a human.

His eyes lit up. Literally. "It would be my pleasure."

"It wasn't easy getting away from Nathaniel, you know. He's very possessive."

His gaze slid to Reggie on her shoulder and she could

see an edge of nervousness in his expression. "As is your familiar. It is giving me the evil eye."

There was a sudden ringing noise. Julian seemed annoyed and pulled out a cell phone from his jacket pocket to glance at the display screen.

"Please excuse me for a moment," he said before he flipped it open and held it to his ear. He moved a little away from them. "Yes?"

"Reggie," Val whispered, trying not to move her lips.

"Yeah?"

"I need to get Julian alone so I can get that key away from him and I can't do it when you're around."

"Why not?"

"He's scared of you."

"I'm tingling with power."

"Well . . ." She pulled him off her shoulder and set him down on the ground. "Go tingle somewhere else for a while."

"But—"

"No buts. I don't have time to discuss this with you. It's now or never. Just go outside. Find Nathaniel. He'll keep you safe."

"That guy hates me."

"It's him or Yasmeen."

"I love Nathaniel."

"Go."

"I don't want to leave you alone with Julian."

Val glanced over at the demon on the cell phone, then down at the rat. "Just go. I'll be okay. There's no time to argue."

Without giving him a chance to say anything else, she turned her back and walked toward Julian who was finishing up his call. He closed the phone just as she hooked her arm through his. "Let's go somewhere private so we can get to know each other better."

He smiled. "Excellent idea."

"Who was the phone call from?"

"Head office. That's how they get in touch with us these days. Rather modern, don't you think?"

"Absolutely. Is that one of those camera phones?"

He patted his pocket. "No, not in the budget. The head office is notoriously cheap, but the phone keeps them from having a direct feed into my mind. Can be a painful thing at times."

"I'd imagine it would be."

He led Val to an empty room that contained a long, plush red couch and huge bed that she eyed uneasily. "So, what did you want to know about me?"

How can I get that key away from you? "Everything."

He smiled. "That's very flattering."

How can I render a demon unconscious with a mere thought? "You're just so interesting."

His smile widened. "I try."

And how do I open a portal back home to the Paradise Inn? "And incredibly handsome."

He nodded in agreement. "You are as smart as you are beautiful, Claire."

"So . . . why do you hate Nathaniel so much?" She sat down on the couch, as opposed to the bed, and tried to look comfortable.

He crossed his arms. "I don't hate him. It's more of a festering distaste, really. So much potential, and he squanders it with his silly morals. He could use his power to be truly great, but just his mere presence reminds me of his weakness. I despise weakness. Just because Yasmeen favors him doesn't mean anything. He will pay for his shortcomings very soon. His latest assignment has yet to be successfully tempted. I met her. She, too, is weak. If he cannot tempt even her then he has no chance."

Weak? Val's shoulders stiffened.

He came to sit very close to her on the couch. "Tell me how you met him. It is unusual for him to express interest in a human. Unprecedented, in fact. I didn't know he was able to express interest in anything other than his own self-pitying reflection. You must be very special."

"You have no idea."

"No, I'm quite sure that I don't. So tell me, how did you meet the halfling?"

"Blind date."

Julian laughed at that. "No, seriously."

"Okay. Actually, I was attacked in an alley. He happened to be going past at the time."

He leaned back into the sofa. "And he rescued you? How terribly quaint."

"No, I reduced my attacker to a pile of ashes and Nathaniel seemed impressed by my abilities."

"I can well imagine he would be. Have you always been so powerful or has this been something you have come by in recent years?"

"I'm a self-made evil witch," Val said. "Had a lousy childhood, got picked on in school by bullies . . . went to the bookstore and shoplifted a few witchcraft books to learn about black magic so I could extract my revenge on those who did me wrong. You know, the usual story."

He slid closer to her. "You do amuse me."

"I'm so glad. Now enough about me. Let's talk about that lovely key you have there."

He slipped a hand inside his shirt and pulled out the chain. "What would you like to know about it?"

"Can I wear it?"

He smiled. "I'm afraid not."

Strike one.

"When are you planning on using it?"

"Very soon." His lips curled into a self-amused grin.

Val tried to choose her next words wisely. "It just seems a dangerous thing, a demon in Heaven. Wouldn't that upset the balance? Maybe shift things so much that everything would get all messed up?"

His smile held. "Probably."

She tried not to frown at his reply. "Don't you care?"

"Should I?"

She shrugged noncommittally. "The earthly realm does have its benefits, you know. If it's destroyed, then think of all the things you'd be missing out on."

"For example?"

"Lots of things. Movies, art, food, you name it. Also some humans are worth saving. Like me, for example. You'd be willing to destroy all that for the rush of walking into Heaven?"

"Absolutely."

"Just checking."

"But don't worry, my lovely witch. You will not be inadvertently destroyed. I fully intend for you to be at my side." He studied her for a moment as she tried to keep her face as blank as possible. "Can I tell you a little secret that may explain my interest in the key?"

"Are you sure I can't try it on, even for a minute?"

"I'm quite positive."

Strike two.

He moved closer to her so his leg pressed against hers. "Now, no one knows this. Not Nathaniel, not Yasmeen, not the mayor. No one."

Val swallowed. "What is it?"

"My mother was a human. She was a witch who was eventually burned at the stake during the Inquisition. Evil to the core. The blackest soul imaginable. You remind me of her a great deal."

"I'm flattered." She leaned back into the couch. "And what about your father?"

He paused. "My father expects a lot of me. He gave me the position of Tempter in hopes that I would work my way up to a more lofty position. He gave me no extra assistance. In fact, I believe he's hindered my progress any way he can. I should be working at the head office by my father's side, instead of being stuck where I am. It's beneath me—the child of true evil itself."

Val felt a chill go down her spine. "Your father is . . ."

"Lucifer," Julian said matter-of-factly. "He met my mother while on vacation. Knocked her up. Left her to fend for herself. Finally acknowledged me after her torture and death, although he wasn't happy he had a halfling for a son." His bottom lip quivered. "I'll never be good enough for him."

"Uh . . ."

"But now . . . with the key, *his* key that he lost so long ago, I'll be making a name for myself. And if I end up destroying the earthly realm? He won't be able to ignore *that,* will he?"

"Of course he won't."

Julian sniffed. "I just want my daddy to love me. Is that too much to ask for?"

Oh boy.

He started to cry then and opened his arms to her. She grimaced before letting him hug her tightly and sob uncontrollably on her shoulder.

This guy has issues, she thought.

And he also had the key, now pressed firmly against her ample, glamourized chest. This was her chance, presented now in an unexpected, rather drippy way. He wouldn't notice if she just shifted position a bit, and slipped the chain over his head . . .

There was a knock at the door. "Julian are you in there?"

Strike three.

Julian straightened up, pushed Val away from him, and wiped his tear-dampened face as the door opened slowly.

A breath caught in Val's throat as she saw who it was. Donovan, the demon she'd met when they'd first entered the Underworld. Tall, dark, and evil . . . a surface glamour that covered the ugly troll underneath. *Small Underworld.* "Oh there you are, man. I've been looking all over for you."

"What do you want?" Julian's voice caught on the words. He sniffed.

Donovan cleared his throat. "Your sacrifice escaped."

Julian leapt to his feet. "How did this happen?"

"Don't know." He glanced at Val but she didn't see any recognition in his green eyes. When he'd met her she'd been less redheaded evil witch, more blond fallen angel.

"We'll have to do a check for her. The mayor will expect a full report."

"Already started." Donovan pulled a metal object that looked like a TV remote control from his belt loop and tossed it at the blond demon, who caught it one-handed. "If you're not too busy, Julian, we could use your help."

Julian sighed. "I suppose."

"Dude, have you been crying?"

"No!" He wiped absently at his damp cheeks. "What a ridiculous thing to suggest."

Donovan glanced at Val again. "Hello there, beautiful."

She pasted a slightly shaky grin on her lips. "Hello yourself."

"Do we know each other?"

She gave him a quick up and down look. "I'm sure I'd remember someone as incredibly gorgeous as you."

He grinned. "I suppose that you would."

"She's Nathaniel's woman," Julian told him as he flicked a switch on the remote control. "For the time being, anyhow."

Donovan frowned. "That's odd. I just saw Nathaniel yesterday. He was with a—"

Val stood up and pointed at the remote control. "So what does that thing do?"

"This is a spell-checker," Julian explained. "After the mayor put forth his Belligerent Magic Decree to avoid any more unpleasant assassination attempts, these are used to make sure that everyone complies. It'll reveal any spell, and hopefully lead us right to our little escapee. She might be hiding behind a simple glamour. Allow me to demonstrate."

He pointed the remote at Donovan in front of the doorway and a red beam of light hit him. Immediately his glamour dissolved and Val could see the tiny, dumpy gray troll that he really was.

"Hey!" Donovan said. "Don't do that. It tickles."

He stepped out of the beam and immediately regained his tall, perfect stature. He looked a little pissed off at Julian, who was grinning widely.

Val's heart was beating so loudly that she was sure it would throw off the band's rhythm outside by the pool.

A spell-checker? she thought frantically. *Here? Now? I have to get the H-E-L-L out of here before—*

"And what about you, my lovely witch. Are you truly so beautiful?"

The red light shone in Val's face, momentarily blinding her. She blinked and looked down at herself. Tank top, jeans, long blond hair visible past her shoulders. Reeboks on her feet.

Oops.

She blinked up at Julian who was looking at her with confusion that slowly melted into recognition. He moved the beam away and her glamour fell back into place.

"You," he said. "I know you."

Val cleared her throat. "Claire. Evil witch. Dating Nathaniel. Up to no good, no good at all. Remember?"

"No more lies." Julian waved his hand and she felt a warm breeze touch her, wiping the glamour away permanently.

Donovan wagged a finger at her. "*You* were the one with Nathaniel. At my apartment. You left your sweater and coat there."

Val nodded slowly. "Yeah, would you mind popping those in the mail for me sometime? That would be great."

"She's a fallen angel," Donovan told Julian. "She's in the Underworld because she's looking for you."

"And why ever would that be?" Julian fingered the key around his neck as his eyes narrowed at her. "Hmm, I have absolutely no idea."

"Probably for that Key to Heaven you have there," Donovan offered.

"I was being facetious, you moron."

"Oh."

Julian fixed her with an icy glare. "Almost had me, didn't you? Now let me take a wild guess. You were the one who helped my little sacrifice escape?"

Val looked away, then forced herself to meet his furious gaze. "So what if I did?"

He narrowed his eyes. "Believe me, I am going to make things very uncomfortable for you now." He took a step toward her.

"You first," she said, and drove her knee into his groin as hard as she could.

He blinked and fell to the ground, gasping for breath.

"Ouchy." Donovan winced with sympathy. "That wasn't very nice."

Maybe Val couldn't vanquish him, or even hurt him very bad, but after what she'd seen Lisa do to Nathaniel, she knew she could cause a little damage.

But not nearly enough.

He staggered back up to his feet and backhanded Val across her mouth. "You're only making things worse for yourself. Perhaps you can take the place as our entertainment for the mayor. Seems only fair, doesn't it?"

He grabbed her arm, hard, and dragged her toward the door.

Donovan looked at them.

"Move," Julian commanded.

Donovan blinked, grinned stupidly, then fell to the ground.

Nathaniel stood in the doorway with his arms crossed, head cocked to the side. "You have been monopolizing my woman for way too long. I don't think I like that very much."

Julian stared down at Donovan's unconscious body, then looked at Nathaniel. He snorted. "Your *woman* is a fallen angel."

Nathaniel glanced at Val and she saw him blink as he noticed the blood trickling from the corner of her mouth. "Get the hell out of here!"

"No," Julian said. "I'm quite serious."

Nathaniel took a step toward him. "I was talking to her." He punched Julian in the face, and turned to her as Julian lost his grip on her arm. "Get the hell out of here, Valerie."

"But—he's still got the key. I have to—"

"I'll take care of that. Are you going to argue with me every time I ask you to do something?"

"And Reggie! I don't know where he is."

"He's the one who told me that you were being an idiot by getting Julian alone. He's around. Don't worry about him."

"But I can't just leave you here."

"Go get Lloyd. Tell him what's happening. But *go*. In a few moments, Julian will be the least of our problems when the rest of security gets here. Just leave while you still have the chance."

Julian came at Nathaniel with the couch raised above

his head, his eyes fiery. "I've been waiting for this for longer than you'll ever know, halfling."

"I've never much liked that expression." Nathaniel rushed him and the couch splintered against the wall.

Val heard footsteps pounding outside as security approached. With a last glance at Nathaniel and Julian beating the crap out of each other, she turned and ran away.

It was a straight run to the entrance of the mansion and back to the pool area. Nobody gave her a second glance even though she must have looked like a wreck and was practically hyperventilating.

She'd managed to put everything she believed in, everybody she cared about, in jeopardy. Nathaniel had been right. She was selfish. She'd risked everything, stormed into the path of danger without a coherent plan just so she could save the day. Get the key. Do her good deed to end all good deeds to get the chance to go back to her fluffy white cloud where—as her continually fading memory served—everything was safe and happy and perfect.

But all she'd done was make things worse.

She ran all the way to Lloyd's house and collapsed to her knees on his front lawn. She began to sob.

Worse, she thought. *Everything was worse now. Much worse.*

And it was all her fault.

The door creaked open and Lloyd looked out. He wore a pink apron. *Has he been baking more brownies?* she wondered. *Yeah, he was going to be a whole lot of help.*

"Valerie?" Lloyd peeled off his oven mitts. "Are you okay? What happened? Where's Nathaniel?"

He came down the steps and helped her to stand up. She didn't say anything yet, she was crying so hard she couldn't speak, so he directed her into his house and closed the door behind them.

"It'll be okay," Lloyd assured Val. "But I need to leave right now. He was right to tell you to run."

"It won't be okay. Nothing will be okay."

He looked anxious. "He told you to come get me, did he not? There's a reason for that. I wasn't always a romance writer, you know. I put my time in at the head office before I earned the right to a simpler existence. But I still have connections. Trust me, if you can."

She rose to her feet. "I'm coming with you."

He shook his head. "No, you'll stay here. You've been through enough already. Besides, you'll just slow me down."

"But Lloyd, I—"

"Nathaniel was right about you. You are a pain in the ass."

Val's eyebrows shot up. "He said that?"

Lloyd sighed. "I think it was implied. Just stay here. I'll be back as soon as I can."

With a last look he hurried out of the house and closed the door behind him, leaving Val alone.

She nearly wore a line in the pink carpet from pacing back and forth for an entire torturous hour without a word. She couldn't just stay there and do nothing. She finally decided to go back to the mansion herself. Whatever happened, happened, but at least she'd know she gave it a shot. That she'd tried to find Reggie. Tried to help Nathaniel. Even if it was too late.

It couldn't be too late.

She rushed over and opened the front door to leave.

Nathaniel stood on the other side. Val's eyes widened at the sight of him.

He shrugged. "And *that's* what he gets for calling me a halfling."

He stepped past her into the house while she simply stared at him.

"That asshole," he continued, "has always caused me grief. Two hundred years and all I hear is whining from him. And I'm the self-pitying loser? I think not. It's too much. It's just seriously too much."

Val finally found her voice enough to say, "He's Lucifer's son, you know."

"That explains a lot, actually."

She swallowed hard. "You're okay."

"You seem surprised."

"No . . . it's just . . ."

She tried to restrain herself, but suddenly threw her arms around him and hugged him tightly. When she finally let him go, he looked at her with shock.

"Do you have the key?" she asked.

"Are you sure you're all right?" He blinked at her. "I . . . uh . . . wasn't sure you'd be here."

"Forget about me. What about the key? What about Reggie? Is he okay?"

"I couldn't find him. But he's fine. I'm sure he is. The party's still going strong, so he's fine for a while."

"You couldn't . . ." She took a shaky breath. "We need to go back."

"Excuse me?"

"We have to go back. To the mansion. We have to find Reggie."

"You'd risk your neck for that rodent?"

She glared at him. "He's not a rodent. He's human. I never should have brought him along in the first place. It's all my fault. All of this is my fault."

He sighed. "Honestly Valerie, I've never met anyone so vain."

Her mouth dropped open. "I can't believe you've got the nerve to call me vain. After everything I've been through today."

"See? *I, I, I, I.* It's all about you."

"But—"

He grabbed her arm. "Do you seriously believe that everything that has happened, from Julian's theft of the key to Reggie's current unknown location, is all your fault?"

She nodded. "Of course it is."

"And that's why you tried to get Julian alone? In the hope of stealing the key right from underneath his nose?"

"I almost had him."

"No you didn't. You're fooling yourself. Had you tried to take the key from him, he would have ended you without a second thought. I have no doubt of that."

She stared at him fiercely for a moment before her shoulders dropped. "You're right. But at least I would have tried. Instead of being a big old chicken who runs away at the first opportunity."

"A very beautiful, incredibly annoying chicken," he said, with a small smile.

She eyed him warily. "Are you trying to cheer me up?"

"Is it working?"

"Not even close. So what are we going to do now?"

He raised an eyebrow. "You're asking *me*?"

"At the moment I'm extremely open to suggestion."

"Very well. Here's my suggestion, my little angel. I will return to the mansion, find your friend, and deliver him back to the earthly realm where he can work out his domestic issues with his girlfriend."

"Okay. So what about me? What am I supposed to do?"

"You will go back to your home."

"The motel?"

"No." He paused. "Heaven."

"Oh, *that* home. Right. And how exactly do you propose I do that?"

Nathaniel pulled a long gold chain out from underneath his gray-striped shirt.

Val stared at him, gaping at the golden key the demon now wore.

Chapter Eighteen

———— ∽ ————

Nathaniel's lips twitched with amusement at her shocked expression.

"How?" Val said. "But, Julian had it, and now you . . . did you fight him for it?"

"Julian would have fought me to the end of time for this, I believe. But he couldn't once he was unconscious. I simply removed it from around his neck."

She reached out to almost touch it, but then pulled her hand back again. "The key."

He looked down it. "This is the correct one, I hope."

She nodded. "It is. Definitely."

"I can feel its power. It hums against my skin."

Before she could say another thing, Nathaniel slipped the chain from around his neck and held it out to her.

"Here."

Her gaze flashed up to meet his in shock and amazement. "You're giving it to me? Just like that?"

"Wasn't that the reason for this trip to the Underworld in the first place?"

Her hand moved up to twist nervously through her hair. "Well, yeah. Of course."

"Then take it."

"Aren't you afraid of what's going to happen to you by helping me like this?"

He stepped closer to her and took her hand in his to place the chain and key into it.

"The key is yours. Don't worry about me."

She looked up at him. "Why are you doing this?"

"Do I have to have a reason?"

Val's heart beat so loud and fast she thought it might burst from her chest. "For this? Uh, yeah, you do. Not that I'm not happy about it, don't get me wrong. But look, I've known you for precisely three days. Has it even been that long? In that time I've pissed you off, you've pissed me off, I summoned you and have been bossing you around for the longest two days of my human life, you tell me the first moment you're free you will make me pay dearly for the unpleasantness I've put you through, and now, after all of that, you hand me exactly what I've been searching for? When I know very well—thanks to Lloyd—what major trouble you're already in with head office. Yeah. I want to know why."

He turned toward the door. "I need to go find your rodent."

Val grabbed his arm. "I command you to give me an answer, Nathaniel."

His shoulder twitched, and he turned around to stare flames at her. "Don't do this."

"Why? Just tell me why."

"I've given you the key because"—he grimaced—"I want you to be happy."

Val's eyebrows shot up. "Say what?"

He glared at her. "Happy. You. Being happy. So now that you have the key you can go back to Heaven."

She stared at him, then blankly at the key in her hand as she tried to process what he'd just said.

He studied her stunned reaction for a moment. "You'll notice that you didn't have to command me to give the key back to you."

She blinked. "I did notice that."

"Then stop making me want to wring your neck and just go. Use your key. Go back to your fluffy white cloud."

"It's not like that."

"Whatever." He met her eyes. "Just be happy, Valerie."

"You really want me to be happy?" She looked down at the key again.

"How many times do I have to say it before you'll believe me? Yes."

"Why?"

He shook his head. "You ask a lot of questions."

She stared at him for a moment longer and wondered if she should command him to tell her why. But instead she took a decisive step toward him and threw her arms around his solid frame to hug him tightly to her. "Thank you."

He wants me to be happy, she thought with amazement.

Nathaniel, a Tempter Demon, whose assignment it was to lure her, a fallen angel, to Hell . . . wanted her to be happy. And he was willing to risk his own existence to ensure it.

She frowned and stepped back from him. How did that make any sense? He'd only known her three days and he was willing to risk that much?

He looked at her uncertainly.

No. Scratch that. He must want her gone. That was all it was. Had to be.

Out of his life. Out of his hair. And not along for the ride to rescue Reggie.

"No," she finally said.

"What do you mean, *no*?"

Val slipped the chain over her head and felt the comforting weight of the key drop against her chest. "Here's *my* plan. You glamour me up again and we go back to the mansion and get Reggie. Then we *all* go back to the motel. I can't go anywhere until I get back to Barlow."

He shook his head. "You're not going back to the mansion."

"Why not?"

"I have to explain this to you? Julian isn't vanquished, I'll have you know. He's going to be looking for you, glamour or no glamour, and now he knows I've taken the key he'll be looking for me, too. And you tell me that he's Lucifer's son, a little piece of information I wish I'd known before I just beat the shit out of him. You want to walk back into that?"

"I don't see that I have any choice."

"You do have a choice." Exasperation colored every one of his words. "I'll find Reggie. Trust me."

She felt her bottom lip start to quiver. "It's my fault Reggie's stuck at the mansion in the first place. I don't care what you say, it's *all* my fault."

She covered her face with her hands and started to cry. She knew she was a nervous wreck. *Prozac, here I come,* she thought.

Nathaniel grabbed her wrists and pulled them away from her face. "Stop crying."

She continued to blubber.

"Damn it, Valerie. Stop crying."

She momentarily put the floodworks on pause and looked up at him.

His frown was very deep. "You've gone after this key with everything you've got. Listen to me. Do you know how amazing that is? You're just so filled with light and life I can barely believe you're real. No one else I've ever known in my entire existence could make me go from despising them to adoring them in less than three days."

She blinked back a tear. "Huh?"

"You heard me."

"No, I don't think I did."

"Valerie, you make me feel . . ." He trailed off and frowned.

"Feel what?"

He glared at her. "Just *feel.*"

"Why are you looking at me like that's a bad thing?"

He let go of her. "Because it is. The whole demon/angel thing? Not good. I don't want to feel this way. But I can't help it anymore."

"So that's why you want to get rid of me?"

"What are you talking about now?"

Val sighed. "You want me to use the key so I'm not around anymore."

"I want you to use the key so you can be happy."

She frowned. "Can we rewind a little? Seriously, I'm really confused—"

He grabbed her shoulders and pulled her to him and kissed her deeply.

He adored her? What was he, crazy or something?

Just then, she heard a cell phone.

"Um . . ." She pulled away a little and looked up at him. "I think your pants are ringing."

Without moving his gaze from her face, he reached into his pocket to pull out the small phone, then quickly glanced at the call display. He pressed a button and slid it back in his pocket. "They can wait."

"You don't want to get in any more trouble than you're already in." She frowned again, thinking about Julian's cell phone exchange with the head office earlier. "So, now what do—"

He sighed. "What more do I have to do to prove myself to you?" He kissed her again.

She pushed against his chest, feeling dizzy and unsteady on her feet. "Look, buddy. Reggie's not going to wait at that mansion forever, you know. We're talking priorities here. I don't know what you think you're doing, but I—"

Third time was the charm. She finally shut up.

He lifted her into his arms and carried her up the flight of stairs without another word.

Reggie could keep himself occupied at the mansion till the cavalry rode in, she thought. He was a self-sufficient rodent, after all.

Nathaniel explored her mouth fully and completely before he moved down her body in hot, electric lines. Val wasn't thinking about anything anymore. It didn't matter where they were. Heaven, Earth, the Underworld, Hell. She was with him. He was with her. And it felt so right. So perfect.

This is Heaven, she thought.

Oh.

No, wait. That *was Heaven.*

"Valerie . . ." Nathaniel moaned just before he met her lips again.

"Uh-huh?"

"Is this okay?"

"Oh . . . *yeah.*"

"Good." He smiled at her, his mouth only a couple of inches from her own.

She raised an eyebrow at him. "You're sure you're not going to stop this time? Maybe throw another side table? You want to just get it out of your system?"

He leaned back to look down at her, his eyes were dark with desire now . . . no flames need apply. "Not unless you want me to stop."

"Um. Nope." She ran her hands through his hair, down his back. "It's all good."

"Good." He moved down to kiss her neck, her collarbone, and—

She grabbed his face and pulled him up to meet her gaze again. "Nathaniel . . . what about the rules?"

"What *about* the rules?"

"Aren't you worried they're going to find out?"

He stared down at her and smiled. "I don't care about the rules anymore."

"That's not a very good answer. Nathaniel?"

"Yes?"

"Is that your cell phone again?"

"Ignore it."

"But aren't they—"

"Just ignore it." He kissed her slowly and deeply, and then pulled back again to stare into her eyes as she held his handsome face in her hands. "Oh, and Valerie . . ."

"Mm-hmm?"

He nuzzled close to her neck and his lips grazed against her ear. "Remember that 'adoring you' thing I mentioned earlier?"

"Uh-huh?"

"I lied about that."

She immediately tensed up and a breath caught in her throat. "What?"

"I don't adore you. I . . ." He leaned back for the barest of moments to capture her gaze in his suddenly uncertain one. "I . . . *love* you."

She smiled and wrapped her arms around his neck. "Nathaniel?"

"Yes?"

"I love you, too. Now shut up already."

There was a moment of complete and utter bliss, of two bodies, two souls becoming one. A taste of Heaven . . . before it all shattered.

Nathaniel screamed and clutched at his head before he slid completely off the bed and onto Lloyd's hardwood floor.

Val clutched the bedsheet to her, her eyes wide. "What's wrong? What are you doing?"

She watched his chest rise and fall with his labored breaths. "Shit," he managed. "Shit!"

"What? Talk to me!"

He scrambled for his black pants, now in a ball at the

end of the bed—he was searching for something. He pulled out his cell phone and stared at it, then swore loudly and threw the phone against the wall where it shattered. Then he clutched his head again and screamed.

Val was beside herself by this time. What was happening to him? Everything was fine, and wonderful, and well, damn near perfect only moments ago when they'd made love, and now he was freaking out. What was going on?

He scooted back into the corner and held his knees to his chest. "I honestly didn't think they'd find out about us. Stupid. I'm so stupid. Oh Valerie, I'm so sorry."

"What?" She practically fell off the bed and crawled to his side. She grabbed his arm but he pushed her away,

"No . . . don't touch me . . ."

"What's going on? Please! Nathaniel, tell me."

He looked at her then, a half-crazed look in his eyes. "Head office. I . . . I didn't answer their call. And now, they're—"

He screamed again and clutched his head.

Val's entire body shook as she helplessly watched him suffer.

He calmed down enough to say, "They're . . . summoning me. Right now." He pressed his hands against his head. "They're in here. But I can't move. I can't leave this place or you." He met her eyes. "Please . . . you have to help—"

He convulsed and curled up into the fetal position.

She stared at him, tears streaming down her cheeks. Hell was summoning him. They knew he'd just broken the rules by making love to her. Shit. *Shit!* And he couldn't move, he couldn't answer them because he was still bound to her.

"Nathaniel." She gently touched his back and he flinched as if it caused him additional pain. "I can fix this. I can. Just try to hold on."

Where was it? She stood up on shaky legs and tore through the room looking for her jeans. The summoning crystal Claire had given her. It had to be there. Where the hell were her jeans?

She looked up. *Oh. Um, okay.*

She yanked her jeans off the ceiling fan and said a silent prayer that the summoning crystal hadn't disappeared during the course of the day. She honestly couldn't remember the last time she'd touched it. For the first little while during their trip to the Underworld she'd touched it in her pocket regularly to reassure herself that Nathaniel was still bound to her. But over the last few hours she'd completely forgotten about it.

Please. Please, let it still be here, she thought frantically.

She slid her hand into the pocket as she heard Nathaniel gasp in pain. The sound made her physically hurt. *There. There it is.* She exhaled deeply with relief as she wrapped her fingers around the cold, hard crystal and pulled it out. She squeezed it and frowned as she looked over at Nathaniel. His body seemed almost distorted, as if he was being reflected in a fun house mirror. Stretched. Like he was being pulled in two different directions. He cried out again in agony.

"Valerie!"

She clutched the crystal tight enough to hurt. "I release you! You are no longer bound to me!"

But nothing happened. He continued to suffer, but managed to look up at her through pain-filled eyes. "It's okay, my beautiful angel. If this is to be my end, then I will accept my fate—" He gasped for breath and yelled, "Shit! I take it back. Valerie—damn it—do something! Do anything!"

"Okay! I'm trying!"

She squeezed the crystal even tighter. "Just release him. Let him go. Now. I demand it!" She stared at him. "I don't know what to do. Claire never told me how to break the summoning."

She tried again. And again. But no words she said seemed to make a damn bit of difference. She couldn't bear to watch him suffer any longer. It was going to drive her mad with grief. She felt an anger such as she'd never felt before well up inside of her, spilling over as she failed and failed again. Time after time. Her words were just words. They had no power to save him from this. She wasn't a witch like Claire. She had no power to stop this. He was being destroyed right in front of her.

And again, it was all her fault.

Val swore, so loud she thought she felt the house shudder under her feet and, frustrated, she threw the crystal as hard as she could against the wall.

The crystal shattered and fell like sparkling dust—like the shadow salt that had bound him to her in the first place—to cover Nathaniel where he lay curled up on the floor.

She saw his shoulders immediately relax, and he swallowed. His chest rose and fell with his labored breathing. He pressed a shaking hand against the hardwood floor and pushed himself halfway up to look at her. A small smile began to form on his beautiful face and she knew the pain had gone. It was okay. *He* was okay. She let out a long, shaky sigh of relief.

"You had me scared there for a minute."

"You're incredible, Valerie," he said, and reached out to her. "Thank you—"

His face contorted and he screamed again, then vanished in a column of flame.

Chapter Nineteen

———— ⸿ ————

Val sat with her back against the bed, eyes wide and glassy, staring at the place Nathaniel had just been. She raised a trembling hand to pull her messy, tangled hair off her face.

What the hell just happened?

She took in a deep breath and heard it shudder through her chest.

Nathaniel.

Then she stood up and gathered her clothes, dressing quickly and methodically.

Punished. They were punishing him because of what just happened between them.

She looked at the bed and wrapped her arms around herself, trying to stop from shaking.

She wasn't crying. Not yet, anyhow. She was in too much shock.

At her neck, she felt for the key on the gold chain. She took the stairs down two at a time and by the time she got to the front door it opened in front of her. Lloyd filled the doorway and looked at her with a strange expression on his one-eyed face.

"Lloyd!" she managed and her voice cracked on the word. "I need your help. There's no time to waste. Nathaniel, he was here already . . . and we . . . well, never mind what we did, but I think he's in huge trouble with the head office. I have to go back to the mansion and I need you to glam me up so I can get in without—" She stopped talking and stared at him for a moment. "Lloyd? Why are you looking at me like you just ran over my dog?"

His bottom lip quivered and a great big tear dropped from his great big eye. "I'm sorry, Valerie. I . . . I didn't mean for anything like this to happen."

"What are you talking about?"

Lloyd suddenly stumbled. As he fell to the floor in front of her, she saw that he was actually pushed.

Julian stood behind him. He stared at Val in silence for a moment, and then smiled widely.

Her stomach dropped.

"Nathaniel's in trouble with the head office, is he?" he said. "Does that mean that I spy with my little eye . . . a big fat slut?"

Her jaw clenched. "I'm not fat."

He chuckled. "Even after everything that has happened, she still has a way about her, a true *je ne sais quoi*, wouldn't you say, Lloyd?"

Lloyd hadn't risen yet from the floor. He said nothing, but glowered up at the blond demon.

Julian crossed his arms. "Now, Valerie, I believe we have a little unfinished business to take care of, don't we?"

She didn't make a move. "What are you talking about?"

"My key."

"*Your* key? You know, I'd always heard the story that it

was Lucifer's key. I wonder what he'd have to say about you taking over ownership without even consulting Daddy first?"

Julian's smile disappeared. "You should hope you never come face-to-face with him to find that out. Now kindly give it back to me."

She frowned at him. "Why do you think I have it?"

He raised a blond eyebrow and said nothing. His foot begin to tap impatiently.

Val shrugged and tried to remain as calm as she could. "I don't have it. The last time I saw it, it was around your neck. Now leave me alone."

"I want my key." He actually stamped his foot as he said it.

"I don't have it."

His eyes narrowed. "Nathaniel took it from me."

"And that means what?"

"That he more than likely gave it to you, perhaps around the same time that your legs were tightly wrapped around his waist."

She slapped him. She regretted it as soon as it happened, but couldn't control herself. She would have rather beaten him into a pulp if she could, but a slap would have to do for the time being.

He pressed a hand to the side of his face. "Only a few short days is all it took to get you on your back? Sad, really. No wonder they were so eager to throw you out of Heaven."

Lloyd had slowly gotten to his feet and listened to them in silence. "You don't know what you're talking about, Julian."

"Is that so?" Julian snapped. "I'd advise you to shut

your mouth. Seriously, Lloyd. I remember when you were once a fierce and loathsome demon. And now? You're a writer of silly, meaningless stories."

Lloyd frowned deeply. "They're not silly. And they do have meaning. They're about the power of love."

Julian scoffed. "They have turned your brain to jam. Sweet, runny, useless jam." He turned to stare at Val again. "But I'm getting off topic, aren't I? I came here for the key. I have been very patient up till now, I think. Now, give it to me, fallen one . . ." He smiled cruelly. "Or else."

"She doesn't have it," Lloyd said. "Just leave her alone, you impotent bastard."

Julian turned his attention again to the one-eyed demon. Val thought he was going to say something, another dig, another insult, but instead he hit Lloyd, a blow so hard that it sent the demon flying across the room into the far wall, breaking one of his cherished framed book covers. Lloyd slid to the floor, unconscious.

Her gaze shot back to Julian as he closed the distance between them and pulled her firmly against him. He wasn't as tall as Nathaniel, actually he was only a few inches taller than she was, so their eyes were close to the same level as he stared at her with his fiery gaze. He slid his hand down to squeeze her ass.

"So, Nathaniel wanted a piece of this, did he? I wonder why. Let's have a quick taste, shall we?"

He crushed his lips to hers and she felt pain and revulsion all at once. When he backed away with a self-satisfied smile on his face, she hit him again, as hard as she could. He didn't even flinch.

He licked his lips. "Not bad. However, I've never been one for sloppy seconds."

Then he grabbed both her wrists in one hand so she couldn't fight him and slid his other hand down the front of her tank top until his fingers curled around the key. He pulled it out and looked at it with a greedy gleam in his eye.

"Naughty little angel, you lied to me. You did have it." He yanked it to break the chain, then slipped it into his pocket.

Val struggled against him, but considering he'd just launched Lloyd across the room with a single punch, she knew it was a lost cause. Still, she wasn't about to make it easy for him.

"Now"—he still held her wrists effortlessly in his grasp—"whatever shall I do with you?"

She glowered at him but didn't reply.

His smile widened. "I'm sure I'll think of something suitable."

He let her go, just long enough to strike her across the side of her head. She felt pain, saw stars explode, and then darkness spread across the world.

Val opened her eyes slowly, but it didn't change anything. It was too dark to see. Where was she? She didn't know, but she did know that she was tied up—her hands behind her back, feet bound at the ankles. She lay on a soft surface. A bed.

She tried to raise her head, but pain shot through her.

Not good.

"Hello?" Her voice cracked on the word. She wondered how long she'd been unconscious.

This was all wrong, she thought. It wasn't supposed to go this way. She was supposed to come to the Underworld and easily get the key. Go back to the Paradise Inn and use it for her and Barlow, lickety-split. A to Z in a couple of hours. But everything had gone wrong. Horribly, horribly wrong. And now she was just waiting there until Julian decided to kill her. Like one of those stupid, big-haired bimbos who always got into trouble and needed *Magnum P.I.* or the *A-Team* to come to her rescue.

But this was real life, not TV. And Julian was going to kill her.

Not that I have anything to live for anymore.

She snorted into the mattress. Could she be any more dramatic?

Her mild laughter turned to self-pitying sobs after a moment.

She was going to die. Slowly.

Then she heard a sound. A quiet click as the door behind her opened. It was Julian, she knew it. He was ready for her. She tried to pretend to be asleep, but her heart was beating like crazy, her breathing uneven. She'd never felt so helpless. Just like one of those lobsters staring plaintively out from the tank at Red Lobster—her favorite restaurant other than McDonald's—begging not to be picked.

The floorboards creaked. Then there was no sound for a few moments. She strained her ears to hear anything, deciding that maybe it had only been her imagination. Maybe—

A hand clamped down over her mouth and she screamed against it, but the sound was muffled.

"Shh," a familiar female voice said. "Be quiet, or they'll hear you."

She tried to turn around. "Lisa? Is that you?"

"In the flesh. Talk about déjà vu, huh?"

"Where the hell are we?"

She laughed softly. "Interesting choice of words. We're in the mayor's mansion."

"Oh no. Not again."

"Yeah. Just when you think you're out . . . they pull you back in."

Val brightened. "*Godfather* quote. Nice."

"Now hold still and I'll undo these ropes."

She heard another voice. "Val? You okay?"

Val tried to turn around again. "Reggie?"

"In the fur."

The ropes slipped off her hands and Lisa started to untie the ones at her feet. Val's eyes were adjusting to the dim lighting enough to see the outlines of bodies. Lisa's small, shapely one, and Reggie's small rat one sitting proudly on her shoulder.

"You're not dead!"

"Shh!" His tail twitched. "We'll all be dead if you keep screaming."

She lowered her voice. "I'm not screaming. I'm just so happy to see you."

"There," Lisa announced. "You're free."

Val rubbed her sore wrists. "What are you doing here at the mansion again? I thought you would have been long gone by now."

She shrugged. "I had a little unfinished business to take care of. I sneaked back and saw Julian drop you off earlier. I've been waiting for everyone to clear out so I could come in and repay you for saving my ass earlier. Are you complaining?"

"Not in the slightest." Val slipped off the bed and stood

on shaky legs. Her head throbbed from the hit she'd taken earlier from Julian.

"Come on." Lisa grabbed her rope-burned wrist and pulled her toward the door. Before Val had a chance to gather her thoughts, she'd opened it, and they were making their way down an abandoned hallway.

Val asked, "Where are we going?"

"Oh, I guess I should give him back to you now." Lisa stopped and gently picked Reggie off her shoulder before placing him on Val's.

"Thanks for the ride, sweetheart," Reggie said.

"Anytime."

"Really, you mean that? Because I just might be in the market for a new girlfriend soon. It would be a rebound thing, but I don't see why we couldn't make it work."

"I don't date outside my species."

Reggie nodded. "Can I get your number anyhow?"

Lisa rolled her eyes. "Is he always like this?"

Val managed to grin at that. "Pretty much. But you didn't answer me. Are we getting out of here?"

"Soon. Like I said, I've got a little business to take care of."

"And that would mean—?"

Lisa shushed her again and started walking, keeping close to the wall, ready at any moment to slip inside a room if someone started coming their way.

"So, Val," Reggie said, "last time I saw you, you were hot-tailing it out of here and Nathaniel was giving Julian a ride on the pain train. You probably didn't see me."

Her heart sank at hearing Nathaniel's name.

Reggie continued, "I hung out under a potted plant for a while, then slipped out. I've been checking this place out ever since. It's big. Especially at my current size. Even if I was normal-sized I think it would still seem huge. Anyhow, I wasn't panicking. I knew you'd come back for me. Of course, I thought you'd come back of your own free will, not trussed up like a Thanksgiving turkey, but I'm not complaining. I'm just happy to see that you're okay." He paused. "So where's tall, dark, and gruesome?"

She swallowed hard.

"Val? Where's Mr. Moody? He-who-hates-the-rat? Demon-boy? Hello?"

She swallowed again and tried to find her voice. "He's gone."

"Do you know where he went? I thought he was bound to us. Well, to you, anyhow."

"He was. I released him."

She saw his whiskers twitch out of the corner of her eye. "You released him? Why?"

"Just had to."

"You just *had* to release him? But he's our ticket out of this hole." His voice had gotten pitchy. "Remember? The whole bookcase-turns-into-dimensional portal deal? I kind of wanted it to be a two-way ride. It's one thing to be stuck as a rat. I have to say I'm actually starting to enjoy it a little, especially the riding around on gorgeous women's shoulders part. The view from up here is spectacular, if you know what I mean. And I mean cleavage city. But I'd rather be a rat at home, than a rat in the Underworld. Hey, maybe that will be the title of my autobiography. I like it. It's catchy. Val?"

She shook her head. "We're going to have to find another way out, I think."

Lisa touched her shoulder. "Are you okay?"

Val felt a hot tear slip down her right cheek. That's where it had been. Just building itself up until she had an audience for her eventual blubbering. *Great.*

"He's gone."

"Where did he go?"

"They summoned him back to . . . to Hell. And since he was still bound to me it was tearing him up—causing him major pain being pulled in two different directions. So I . . . had to release him. I had no choice."

Lisa frowned. "I don't understand. Punished for what?"

"Nathaniel's been a bad boy, I guess," Reggie said. "Geez, Val, what did you do, sleep with him, or something?" He laughed.

Val didn't.

Reggie stopped, "Oh shit. You slept with him. Val! I'm shocked. And incredibly turned on at the same time."

"Me, too," Lisa said, then frowned. "The shocked part. I'm in no way turned on by imagining you having sex. Seriously. I draw the line at Angelina Jolie."

"Oooh. Angelina Jolie," Reggie murmured. "But, back on subject. What happened? You've only known him for a few days, right?"

She shrugged. "I don't want to talk about it."

"Did he force himself on you?" Lisa asked.

"No. If anything, I may have forced myself on him a little bit." She almost smiled. "I'm not normally so . . ."

"Experimental?" Reggie offered.

"No."

"Erotically inclined?"

"Reggie—"

"A naughty little monkey?"

"Could you please not help me? I'm happy you're alive Reggie, but please be quiet."

"Sorry."

Her head ached. "Look, he said things to me. I said things to him. He told me that he loves me."

Lisa's eyebrows shot up. "He said that? And you believed him?"

Val frowned. "This subject is officially closed. I don't want to discuss it any further with either of you. Got it?"

"It's gotten," Lisa said.

She waited for a response from the rat before she turned her head to try to look at him.

"Beyond gotten," he said, raising a paw. "But for the record, I don't think he was lying. Who could possibly know you and not love you?"

Val's eyes brimmed with tears at that. "That is the nicest thing I think anyone's ever said to me."

"I know, I've used that line before. Works like a charm."

She sighed. "You *are* a rat."

"A rat who loves you."

Val continued to follow Lisa through the hallways of the mansion. "I got the key, you know. Nathaniel gave it to me."

"You did?" Reggie said. "That's great. And furthermore, then what the hell are we still doing here if we have the Key to Heaven?"

"You have the Key to Heaven?" Lisa repeated with surprise.

"I did, but Julian took it again. If it's here in the mansion we have to get it back."

"I'm getting sick of this stupid key," Reggie said.

"Shhh," Lisa commanded from over her shoulder. "Be quiet you two. We can't let them know we're here."

"Who's they?"

She stopped walking and Val practically slammed into the back of her. They were near a set of glass doors that looked out at the area where earlier Val had been drinking piña coladas and pushing Nathaniel into the pool.

Good times.

There was a small gathering of demons and other strange beings on the patio. Julian stood on the stage and he didn't look happy.

"Why?" he was saying into the microphone, but it sounded like he was mostly talking to himself. "Why isn't it working?"

Val gasped as she saw the golden key catch the light from the patio lanterns. Julian was trying to use the key to enter Heaven.

Right now.

Chapter Twenty

Val watched with horror as the mayor waved a flipper-like appendage at Julian. "Try again. I've always found incantations to be particularly tricky."

Julian sighed. "Perhaps you're right. I'll give it another shot." He brought the key closer to his face and read the ancient incomprehensible words etched into its surface. When he was done, he looked up expectantly.

Nothing happened.

He stamped his foot like a little boy who didn't get his lollipop.

Yasmeen approached the stage. "Perhaps your pronunciation is off. Let me try." She reached for the key but Julian held it out of her reach.

"No. It's mine. Back off, bitch."

She put a hand on her hip. "You're such a self-involved idiot, Julian."

He pouted. "Takes one to know one."

Yasmeen glanced over at the mayor. "I have no time for this foolishness. At your leave, great one."

The mayor looked at her for a moment, then nodded his head. "As you wish, my dear."

She vanished in a column of fire.

"Come on," Lisa whispered and grabbed Val's arm to pull her outside, closer to the group of demons by the pool and stage.

"Are you crazy?"

"Probably. But I have a plan to get your key back."

"You're definitely crazy."

She grinned. "Consider yourself lucky the key doesn't work for Julian."

"Is it his pronunciation?" Reggie asked. "I always thought incantations were in Latin. At least Claire's always sound Latin." He sighed. "It's all Greek to me."

Lisa shook her head. "It's a much older language, even older than Latin."

Val frowned. "I don't even remember telling you about the key before a minute ago. How do you know so much—"

"Shh." She pulled Val down until they were completely hidden behind the pool bar. If Val stood up, Julian would be looking directly at her. Though, currently he was too busy staring angrily at the key in his hand to pay attention to anything else.

She glanced at Lisa. "If you're such a surprise expert on the subject, then tell me, why isn't it working for him?"

She licked her lips and smiled, but it looked more mischievous than genuine. "The Key to Heaven will only work for a fallen angel, of course."

"What?"

"It's true. Haven't you heard the stories?"

"Yeah, but not that one. I thought it was supposed to be an all-access pass. Anyone could use it."

She shook her head. "Anyone can go through the doorway once it's opened, yes. But the words must be spoken by a fallen one. Lucifer was originally a fallen angel, you know. And it is his key. Makes sense."

Julian had just finished reading the incantation for the fourth time with zero success. His face flushed red with anger and flames danced in his eyes—and it was an unhappy dance.

Val frowned. "How long do you think it'll be before he figures that little tidbit of information out?"

"With Julian? Could be a few centuries."

"You know Julian?"

She shrugged. "Doesn't everyone?"

"He told me that he's Lucifer's son. That he's doing this to get Daddy's love and approval. Or something like that."

She almost laughed at that. "He should have just bought a card from Hallmark."

Suddenly Julian yelled, and for a horrible moment Val was reminded of Nathaniel suffering on the floor of the bedroom before he was taken away from her. But Julian wasn't being pulled anywhere. He wasn't in any pain, at least not physical pain.

He was just frustrated.

"I don't know what I'm doing wrong! This should work. I should be walking into the pristine palace as we speak."

Val frowned. *Pristine palace? What a dork.*

In the meantime, a few more demons had made their excuses and wandered off. Time was precious, even in the Underworld.

The mayor looked extremely disappointed for a moment, but then he seemed to brighten slightly. "Let's take a break and bring out the fallen angel for some entertainment, shall we? I need a good laugh. Plus, I'm a little bit hungry. Just don't tell Sven that I cheated on my diet."

"Not yet," Julian whined. "Let me try one more time."

The mayor sighed. "Very well."

He tried. He failed. Val stifled a laugh at his obvious misery. Then he had a literal hissy fit and threw the key on the ground and made a big show of stepping on it and grinding it into the stage with his foot.

"Stupid key!"

"Let me down, Val," Reggie whispered. "I think I have an idea."

"That is never a good thing to hear."

"Just let me down."

She picked him gently off her shoulder and put him on the ground. He looked up at her. "Wish me luck."

Val opened her mouth to do anything but wish him luck, to stop him from whatever stupid idea had drifted into his gumball-sized brain, but he was gone. And he was headed for the stage.

"He's very brave," Lisa said. "For a talking rat."

Val helplessly watched Reggie's small, furry body dart from covering to covering, weaving in and out between lounge chair legs. If a demon glanced in his direction, he'd freeze in place until it was safe to move again. It was like watching a rodent version of *Alias*. She held her breath and clutched Lisa's hand.

"Val," Lisa whispered.

She didn't tear her gaze from Reggie. "What?"

"If anything goes wrong here, promise me you won't look back. That you'll just run."

"I promise. Same for you. But I'm not going anywhere without Reggie."

She smiled. "You're a good friend to him. And to Nathaniel. It's so strange that you care for him despite what he is."

"Nathaniel . . ." Val's voice trailed off. "I'll probably never see him again."

"No. You probably won't."

She looked at Lisa sharply. "Not exactly helping."

"You'd rather I lie to you? Trust me, the truth is always better than lies. Better than all these false surfaces." She glanced around. "Like this ridiculous place. The truth is painful, it's shocking, and it's rarely easy . . . but it will open doors you never knew were there before."

"Shh."

Reggie slowly crawled up the steps to the stage. The key lay four feet away from where Julian stood talking to the mayor. The last couple of demons, and one angry-looking biker faery started to drift away.

"Mayor Vaille," Julian began. "Great one, I'm so, so sorry. I can't tell you how much I wanted to make this work."

"Maybe you were fooled. The key is a phony?"

Julian looked appalled by the suggestion, then thoughtful, then sheepish . . . and then back to being appalled. "No, it's real. I can feel its power."

"Then what you are saying is that you are a failure."

He opened his mouth, then closed it. "No. I will figure out why it's not working. Then I'll open the doorway and go in myself. Once it's open we can enter at our whim. It doesn't need to be tonight."

The mayor sighed. "But it would have been so cool for the party."

"Another party, then."

"Perhaps we should have waited for Nathaniel. He may have been a great assistance to us in this matter."

Julian laughed. "Nathaniel is a fool. *He's* the true failure. Such power at his grasp and he refuses to use it to his full potential. Such a waste. Especially now."

"What do you mean?"

"Nathaniel has turned soft. He's at the head office right now answering for his many shortcomings. The next time you see him, I doubt you'll even recognize him. No"—he smiled—"I greatly anticipate seeing what they'll do to him."

The mayor shifted position on his chaise and yawned.

"Yes," Julian continued with a gleam in his eye, "aside from his continual failure at tempting, he has allowed himself to be manipulated and seduced by his current assignment. And you know very well that is against the rules."

The mayor smiled a bright fan of sharp teeth. "I came up with that rule myself. Originally it was only a little inside joke at the head office, but it seems to have stuck. And let me guess, he broke my rule with the fallen one he was with earlier? The one you have tied up as we speak?"

"Yes."

The mayor grimaced. "But she was so . . . trampy. All that fake red hair, and the inch of makeup. Those large, unruly breasts. She didn't seem that enticing to me."

Julian shook his head. "That was only a glamour. Underneath she is as pure, as good, and as beautiful as any fallen angel I've ever seen."

Aw, Val thought. *That was actually kind of sweet.*

"That is why I will take great pleasure eviscerating her.

The screams of anguish I shall coax from her beautiful lips will be music to my ears."

Not sweet.

The mayor chuckled. "So our boy Nathaniel finally indulged himself with a fallen one, did he? Good for him."

"Good for him?" Julian huffed. "I bend over backward with this key and he gets a 'good for him'?"

"This was only an amusement to me, anyhow. And I am no longer amused. Perhaps I'll go plan my next party." He looked thoughtful. "Though, another band next time. Today's was somewhat . . . lacking. Their version of 'La Bamba' was so weak. I may have them vanquished for displeasing me."

Julian just stared at the mayor blankly as he was all but dismissed from his presence. Val noticed with a sinking feeling that Reggie had finally reached the top step and was panting hard from the exertion. Then he darted across the stage toward the discarded key, picked it up gently between his little yellow teeth just as Julian turned around.

Reggie froze in place.

"I think I will try a couple more times," Julian said.

The mayor sighed. "If only the key came with an instruction manual."

"Yes, if only." Julian glanced down to where he'd thrown the key. It was gone. His eyes widened and he scanned the area, but before his gaze could rest on the galloping rat, Val saw Lisa rise up next to her and step out from behind their hiding place. She reached out a hand to stop the girl, but it was too late.

"Hey," Lisa said. "Remember me, you little bastard?"

All Val could do was watch helplessly as Lisa stepped

out fully from behind the bar. Julian stared at her also, the key momentarily forgotten.

"However could I forget?"

Lisa smiled.

"I'm pleased to see you."

"Are you? And why's that?"

"Because now I not only have one fallen one waiting in the wings for me to take out my frustrations on, I have a backup. Which is good since I'm extremely frustrated."

Instead of cowering at the intensity of his slightly wordy threat, Lisa took a few steps closer to the stage. "Come and get me."

Julian grinned, then leapt off the stage.

"Excellent." The mayor clapped his flippers. "At last, some decent entertainment!"

Reggie finally reached Val and she took the key from between his teeth. The chain was long gone so she slid it under her tank top and into her bra for safekeeping. She picked Reggie up and stared at Lisa, who was standing in front of the extremely frustrated blond demon.

What could she do to help her?

There was too much to lose if she did something stupid. Well, stupider than normal, anyhow. *Too much.* She had the key. Her only hope now was to go back to Lloyd and hope he had the power to open a portal for her to get back home.

"If anything goes wrong here," Lisa had said only moments ago. *"Promise me you won't look back. That you'll just run."*

Val had promised. But it still didn't make it any easier.

Keeping as low to the ground as she could, she ran back to the mansion's doorway and slipped inside. Turning her head one last time, she saw Julian standing only inches away from the girl who seemed so small and delicate in front of him. So brave. So foolish. But Val wasn't going to let Lisa's sacrifice go to waste.

"We're out of here," she told Reggie.

"Not a moment too soon."

The key would only work for a fallen one? In that case, only a matter of minutes remained before Val could put the last two months behind her once and for all. Everything would be the way it was supposed to be. Barlow and herself officially out of danger's way. A perfect ending.

She felt the tears on her cheeks. *Yeah, really perfect.* But she wouldn't think about that right now.

Focus. Have to focus.

She turned the next corner and skidded to a halt.

Nathaniel leaned against the wall, smoking a cigarette.

Val's mouth dropped open.

He smiled. "Miss me?"

She just stared at him. "Nathaniel, is it really you? I thought . . . that you were . . ."

"In trouble?"

"Well, yeah."

He shrugged.

She exhaled deeply, feeling a huge weight lift from her shoulders, leaving behind a giddy lightness. "I didn't know what happened to you. But you're here. You're okay. And you look . . ." She smiled at him. "You look great."

"Thanks." He flicked his cigarette away.

She moved closer to him. "I was so worried. But I should have known you'd handle yourself just fine. Now, we're getting out of here. I'll explain everything later."

Nathaniel glanced at Reggie, then back at Val. "Where are we going?"

"Home. And we're going, like, *now.* Come on." She reached for his hand, but he pulled away and crossed his arms.

"Aren't you going to *command* me to come with you?"

"Huh?"

His eyes narrowed. "Command me. Like the well-trained puppy you're used to. Or perhaps you'd prefer to force me to tell you the truth?"

Val blinked. "We don't have time for this—"

"Did you happen to know that every time you commanded me to do something it caused me pain? And you want to know something? I don't care too much for pain, angel."

Uneasiness settled over her. "Yeah, well, I promise to make it up to you."

He smiled thinly. "Yes, I just bet you would."

"Remember that thing I just said about no time? I kind of meant it. Now come on. Don't be difficult." She tried to grab his wrist but he twisted away from her

"I'm not going anywhere with you."

Val glanced nervously over her shoulder. There was only a matter of minutes, if that, before somebody would be along the hallway. "Excuse me?"

"It's over." He smiled and cocked his head to the side. "But it was fun while it lasted. For, oh, ten minutes or so."

She frowned. "What—?"

His gaze moved to the rat. "Reggie, you would have been so proud of me. All it took was a few flowery words and—well, let's just say she's certainly no angel underneath it all."

Val's mouth opened but she couldn't find the words to speak.

"Don't talk about her that way," Reggie said, low and edgy.

"What way? I'm only speaking the truth. So typical. Honestly, they're all the same. Women. When a man tells her what they want to hear, they'll give it up. Anything. Cease being themselves and become a plaything." He shrugged. "Not that I'm complaining, of course."

Val's jaw was clenched so tightly that it hurt. "What did they do to you at head office?"

"I can't wait to tell Yasmeen all about it. Now, *there's* a woman who knows exactly what I want. A little risk, a little unpredictability, and might I add . . . amazing in bed. Not all timid and inexperienced like you were, angel. Amusing, but in the end, a waste of my precious time."

"I said," Reggie spoke louder, "don't talk about her that way. You don't deserve to be breathing the same air as her, you pathetic demon piece of shit."

Nathaniel cocked his head to the other side, looked at the rat for a moment, then in one motion flicked him off Val's shoulder. Reggie fell to the floor with a painful sounding "ooof."

She turned her stunned gaze to the demon. "I don't care what they tried to do to you down there. You need to fight it. They've messed with your mind. Lloyd told me about it. It's . . . mind manipulation. Like brainwashing. This isn't really you."

"But it is me, angel. I thought you always wanted the truth? Or was it only the truth you *wanted* to hear? Too bad. You let me tempt you. And it was so easy. Admit it."

He grinned. "Don't try to tell me you didn't enjoy it. I know you did."

"Shut up."

"Make me. I don't love you. Never did. It was all a ruse to get you to say yes to me. Got it? Do my words sting, angel? The truth hurts."

Val stared at him. Then she gathered Reggie, now limping and staring daggers at Nathaniel, in her arms and stood tall to face her Tempter. She tried to summon something within herself, channel her hurt feelings into rage, bring fire into her own eyes to stare him and his razor-sharp words down. To hurt him back.

But she couldn't.

A tear slipped down her cheek. "I don't believe you."

He frowned at her. And his expression softened for a split second before tensing again. He straightened his back and raised a dark eyebrow.

"Well, that's your problem, isn't it?" His eyes narrowed. "Now I believe I gave you something earlier to hold on to for safekeeping? The key? Forgive me, but I'll need to take it back before I go ahead and take you to Hell."

She stiffened. "Forget it."

"The head office wants it. I'm now compelled to obey them, and only them. Got it?"

"Oh, I got it all right."

"Now." He stepped closer. "The key?"

"No."

His expression darkened. "Give the key to me."

"Nope."

"Give it to me."

"No."

He sighed, and grabbed her upper arm tightly. "I'm sick of playing these games. I won't ask you again. Give it to me now."

"Okay."

Val kneed him hard in the groin as Lisa did earlier. As she'd done to Julian. Practice made perfect. He immediately released her. Then she lashed out with her fingernails, the best weapon she had available—other then her lethal knee—to slash at his perfect face. Then, one hand pressing Reggie protectively against her chest, she started to run.

"Valerie!" Nathaniel called after her, and his voice sounded angry and pained. "Come back here!"

She didn't turn. She didn't answer. She simply ran. She turned the next corner and skidded to a halt when she saw Lisa in front of her.

"Val!" the girl yelled and waved her arms wildly.

"Come on." Val ran over and grabbed her wrist to drag her along toward the front doors. She didn't have the time to ask her how she'd managed to get away from Julian. They'd both escape. Together. But as she grasped the huge handle to the front door of the mansion, she felt Nathaniel clamp his hand down on her shoulder and turn her forcefully back around.

A line of blood showed above and below his left eye from where she'd scored him with her fingernails. Between, his eyes were fiery. Fierce. Angry. His grip was so tight she knew she wouldn't be able to get away from him now. He could easily take her and Lisa back out to Julian. He could take the key.

How had the head office managed to change him so greatly?

She met his fiery gaze and held it as they stood at the doorway.

"Nathaniel," she said, and noticed her voice was so choked up that it hurt to talk. "I need to tell you something."

"Is that right? Well, spit it out, angel."

She blinked. "I still love you."

The flames strengthened in his eyes for an excruciatingly long moment until it hurt just to look at him, and then extinguished completely. He frowned deeply, and his grip on her arm increased. Then he closed his eyes and she felt warm air and a shaking of the world around her.

After a moment he opened his eyes and released her. "Go."

She frowned. "What do you mean?"

He nodded at the doorway and she looked behind her. There was a swirling blue portal there now.

It hadn't been there a moment ago.

Lisa grabbed her hand. "Come on."

Val tried to touch Nathaniel, but he moved out of her reach. "But, I need to—"

He glanced over his shoulder then back at her. "For once, just once, do what I ask. There's no time to argue. They're coming. Go!"

She looked at him, one last time, and then turned and leaped through the waiting portal.

Chapter Twenty-one

———————— ‿‿ ————————

"I think we're just damn lucky that wasn't a portal to Hell," Reggie commented as Val and Lisa ran up Niagara's Clifton Hill. "I mean, Nate wasn't exactly acting like his usual uncharming self, was he?"

After more than a day in the strangely tropical Underworld, the earthly realm felt positively frigid to Val, who was only wearing her jeans and tank top. Well, it *was* December, an easy thing to forget when hanging out among palm trees and beaches, even if it was all fake. Running like a crazy person back to the motel was definitely helping to warm her up a bit.

She didn't bother answering Reggie. She had to save her energy for the single-minded goal of getting back to the Paradise Inn and using the key. Thinking about anything else—*anything else*—was just going to throw her concentration off.

For example, she wasn't going to think about Nathaniel and what just happened at the mansion. His cutting words doing their damage to hurt her, to shake her confidence in him, and then at the last moment, something returned. It was obvious he'd been given behavior modification as punishment for breaking the rules—that was why he'd been so cruel and heartless. But if so, why did he let her escape . . . even creating the portal himself to allow her to escape?

See? she thought *Thinking about stuff like that is only going to slow me down.*

Also, thinking that as soon as Julian knew both she and Lisa had escaped from the Underworld and had the key, he'd be coming after them with a fiery vengeance.

Nope. Not going to think about that, either.

"Where are we going?" Lisa panted.

"Back to the motel. We've got to get to Barlow."

Val tried to clear her mind, but it kept racing as fast as her feet. Was she running *to* something or *away* from something?

Here, she'd thought she'd been so in control of what was going on. Just like the glamour on the Underworld, on Donovan, on herself to become an "evil witch." She'd been fooling herself. All of it was false surfaces. She'd never had any control at all. She thought she could control Nathaniel through the summoning spell? He was a demon with a mind, an agenda, of his own. Maybe opening the portal was just another way to tempt her. To gain her trust after it had almost been lost completely. After all, no matter what Lloyd might have told her, she really had no idea how many assignments he'd had before her in two hundred years of being a demon? Hundreds at least. Probably thousands. Why did she think she was any different? Any more special than the rest?

Lucifer was probably laughing at her right now. As well as everyone else at the head office. At the stupid angel who'd fallen for a gorgeous demon.

Not a story Trixie L'Amour would be telling any time soon.

So she kept running. And desperately hoped for a sign.

A little of that divine intervention would be really cool right now, she decided.

With Lisa right behind her, she slipped past a parked car and crossed the street. She heard the squealing tires and froze, staring stupidly at the big, black limo that lurched to a stop only inches from turning her into a frozen pancake.

The back door opened and slammed shut. She saw red hair and a fancy Chanel suit quickly come toward her.

"Val!" Becky called. "Are you trying to get yourself killed?"

Her heart pounded so loud she could barely hear anything. Lisa skidded to a stop next to them. She could hear Reggie panting on her shoulder, which, since he hadn't been running at all, was a little disconcerting.

"You almost hit me!" Val exclaimed.

"You almost deserved it running out like that and not looking both ways. Geez. You practically gave me a heart attack. Sweetie, you're shaking like a leaf. And FYI, it's *winter.* You're a total candidate for *What Not to Wear* in that outfit."

Becky waited for a reply but Val had nothing. She glanced at Lisa.

"Where are you two headed?"

"To the Paradise Inn," Lisa told her.

"I'll give you guys a ride. Come on." Becky put her arm around Val's shoulders and steered her toward the limo, directing her into the backseat.

Seraphina sat on the opposite seat looking at her. Her

hair was done in perfect blond ringlets. Her arms were crossed. She wore a yellow outfit with a cartoon duck on the front with the words GOING QUACKERS.

"I want McNuggets," she said.

"That sounds like a plan," Reggie murmured. "Running for my life makes me so hungry."

Lisa joined them in the limo. Val shook her head and glanced at Becky. "We have to get back to the motel right now. It's urgent."

"You need to learn how to relax—I should give you the number for my masseuse. He seriously has the fingers of a Greek god. We'll drop you off, don't worry. As soon as we stop at McDonald's for her majesty."

Val blinked at her. "What are you doing here, anyhow? Didn't you just leave for Disneyland?"

Becky shrugged. "Yeah, like a week ago. Thank God that torture is finally over. She made me go on Space Mountain eight times. In a row! They actually ran out of barf bags. I'm so glad we're finally back. Besides, I still have a ton of Christmas shopping to do."

Val's mouth had gone completely dry. "Did you just say you were gone a week?"

"Yeah. We left a ago week today."

A week? Her eyes widened. It hadn't been a week. It couldn't have much more than a day . . . two at the most . . . even though that time felt like an eternity. But back here an entire week had gone by?

"Her mother's at the spa to recover from the trip," Becky said, eyeing the little girl warily. "I'm way stressed and we were only gone a week. And when I'm stressed, I eat. If we were gone any longer I might have come back weighing six hundred pounds."

"McNuggets!" Seraphina whined. "I want my Mc-Nuggets."

Becky sighed. "Okay, just hold on a minute, would you?"

"NOW!"

The limo drove up the road to McDonald's and Becky climbed over Lisa to get out of the car.

"Reggie," Val said softly.

"Yeah?"

"We're going in."

He nodded. "Where you go, I go. Lead the way."

They slipped out of the limo and left Lisa in the car with Seraphina who began telling her all about her Mickey Mouse experience, and ran up the stairs to the restaurant.

"This is good, actually," Reggie said. "I'm so hungry I could eat . . . something large and unruly. Not that that is any different from a normal day."

"Claire," Val called as she ran through the front doors.

"On second thought," Reggie said. "I just lost my appetite."

Claire was cleaning out a nearby garbage can. She looked up as they approached.

"Well, well. Look who's finally returned. I don't think you could have left my place in more of a mess. That was a real treat to wake up to. Steal my man and trash my home. Way to go."

"Yeah, good to see you too, Claire."

She put a hand on her uniformed hip. "How did it go, anyhow? Did you end up summoning a good demon?"

"It went okay. I guess," Val said, knowing that was a big fat lie. "A good demon? That's debatable."

"Was he small, hairy, and destructive?"

"No." She sighed. "Tall, dark, and a major hottie. But I don't have time to go into the details. I just needed to return something to you."

"Oh?"

She pulled Reggie off her shoulder and handed him to Claire.

"Hey!" he protested.

"What's this?" Claire asked.

"Your boyfriend. Now forgive him, change him back into a human, and start dating again. Somebody needs to have a happy ending today."

Reggie's whiskers twitched. "Val, what are you doing to me? She's going to kill me!"

Val shook her head. "She won't. She's crazy about you. If she wasn't she wouldn't get all jealous. Look Claire, bottom line is that me and Reggie didn't do anything. Believe it because it's the truth. He can be a dumb guy and he's made some questionable choices, but underneath it all he loves you. He told me so a bunch of times. He's been so wonderful and brave since we left, you would be so proud of him. I know I am. So just turn him back and live happily ever after, okay?"

Claire frowned at her, and then she looked at the rat who stared back at her in rigid anticipation of her answer.

She shrugged. "Okay."

Val was surprised. "Well, that was easier than I thought it would be."

"But Val—" Reggie began.

"Yeah?"

His whiskers twitched. "Does this mean I'm never

going to see you again? You and Lisa are going back to the motel to use the key?"

She nodded.

He sniffed. "I'll miss you."

"I'll miss you, too."

"But I know it's what you want—to go back home."

Val swallowed hard and thought about the word for a moment. "Right. Home. I do want that."

"Maybe I'll start praying more often. It'll be cool to talk to you even if I won't be able to hear you answer me."

She opened her mouth to tell him it didn't work that way. Not on her level anyhow, to the best of her faulty-memory knowledge, but she decided not to. "Sure, any-time. Thanks for everything, Reggie. You've been a great friend." She nodded and then turned to leave.

"Wait . . . Val?"

"Yeah?"

"I just want you to know . . . Nathaniel's a damn fool if he doesn't realize how great you are."

She kissed her fingertips and tapped him on the top of his furry head. "Take care of each other, guys. I'll miss you."

With a last look, she left McDonald's, slipped back into the limo and met Lisa's concerned gaze.

"It's just us now," Val said.

Lisa nodded grimly.

"Fry?" Becky offered.

"No thanks."

Seraphina blinked at her from the facing seat. "I know you. You're the angel."

"You're the what?" Becky asked incredulously.

"She's an angel."

Becky smiled patiently. "No she's not. She's my friend Valerie."

"Actually, she's right." Val rubbed her temples gingerly. "I'm a fallen angel. Just got back from the Underworld where I had to retrieve the Key to Heaven. I had a brief fling with a handsome demon, rescued a fellow fallen angel, and now we have to get back to the motel so I can take my boss back to Heaven before Hell catches up to us. So let's get this limo moving, shall we?"

Becky stared at her for a moment, then burst into laughter. "You are such a hoot. We should go out more, maybe clubbing or something. Oh, and by the by, my brother is still talking about how much he wants to go out with you. Come on . . . the two of you would make a beautiful couple. Well, you'd be the beautiful one. He could be the Superman expert. Still, a good match. Did I mention that he drives a black Trans Am?"

Val thought about Becky's comic book lovin' brother. He would give her a lot less grief than Nathaniel had. She had no doubt about that.

She forced a smile. "I'll keep it in mind."

Or, in other words, *Not on your life.*

The limo pulled away from the curb and Val stared out of the window as she formulated her plan. Reggie was safe now. She only had Barlow and Lisa to worry about. If all went well they might all be hanging out at the . . . She frowned. She couldn't remember anywhere she used to hang out in Heaven. What did she do Up There for fun? It wasn't just a big fluffy cloud like Nathaniel had said. There was form and substance to her existence as an angel. She did things. She knew other angels, like . . . what was his name? The assistant to something-or-other.

And they knew her. They were all one big happy family in Heaven.

But she couldn't remember the specifics. It was gone. And she didn't have her notebook as a backup anymore.

Didn't matter, though, she thought. Not much longer and it would all come back to her.

Forever.

"Fallen one," Seraphina said. "Look at me."

Val closed her eyes and tried to ignore the brat.

"Be polite," Becky said sharply. "And don't call Val that. Finish your apple pie. Use a napkin. You're getting the filling all over your Gucci poncho. Do you have any idea how much that costs to dry clean?"

"Fallen one," Seraphina said again, calmly.

Val opened her eyes to look at the little girl. Her eyes were fully white and she stared at Val with all the creepiness that only a nine-year-old with massive psychic powers could have.

"Uh, yeah?"

"Do you have it?"

She was about to ask what Seraphina was talking about, but had a funny feeling she already knew.

"Yes, I do."

"There is very little time left. Allow no one to distract you from doing what you feel in your heart is right. *No one.*"

"Who are you?"

"There is little time—"

"Yeah, you already said that." Val leaned forward. "Listen, whoever you are, I've had one hell of a day. I don't need any additional pressure, got it?"

Lisa leaned forward. "What if I—"

"Silence," Seraphina hissed and Lisa promptly shut her mouth. The white eyeballs turned back to Val. "It will only work for a fallen one."

She sighed. "Old news. Now I don't know who you are. But I've had it up to here with these cryptic messages. None of it helped me, you know. There was no fragments of light falling to the ground or otherwise."

"That is because it already fell. A very long time ago."

"Whatever. Also, just so you know, I'm pretty sure that the darkness prefers the darkness. Not that he had much of a choice in the matter. So everything you told me before was all crap. I'm on my very last nerve ending today, so why don't you leave me alone? The weight of the world is on my shoulders right now and I'm afraid of throwing it all away by mistake."

The corner of Seraphina's mouth twitched with amusement. "Excellent. I believe the right choice has already been made."

Val frowned and she leaned forward to stare at the little girl. It was then that she noticed the light from her eyes wasn't just white, it was pure and perfect and filled her with a sudden sense of peace and rightness.

"Boss?" she said so softly she could barely hear her own words. "Is that you? Please, tell me what you want me to do!"

Seraphina's eyes went back to their normal bright blue and she took another bite of her apple pie, completely oblivious to what had just happened. Val glanced at Becky who stared back at her with wide eyes, a fry dangling from her lips.

"What the hell was that?"

"The pain that is my life," Val told her just as the limo

pulled in front of the Paradise Inn next to a police car. Val eyed the cruiser curiously and grabbed Becky to give her a quick hug before she and Lisa got out of the limo. "Thanks for being a friend. I'll miss you."

Becky nodded. "Okay then. I'll give you a call. Maybe we can catch that new Brad Pitt movie next week."

Val smiled at her. "Yeah, sure."

Without waiting to watch the limo pull away, she dragged Lisa with her straight to Barlow's office. A uniformed police officer emerged from the interior of the office. He held up a hand to them as they approached.

"Can I help you two?" he asked.

Val tried to look past him into the darkness of the manager's office. "Is everything okay? I need to talk to Mr. Barlow. He's the manager here."

He nodded. "You must be Valerie Grace?"

"That's right." She and Lisa exchanged glances. "How do you know that?"

"You're mentioned in Mr. Barlow's papers. We've been looking for you."

She swallowed hard and felt her heart begin to sink. Lisa reached down to grab her hand and squeeze it. "Where is he?"

The officer's brow lowered for a moment. "I'm sorry to tell you that Mr. Barlow passed away a short time ago. The coroner just took away the body. Looks like natural causes." He produced a business card. "Here's where he has been taken. I'm very sorry for your loss."

Val's bottom lip trembled. "He can't be gone. Not yet. I just got back."

"I'm sorry." The officer nodded grimly, then headed toward his cruiser.

"Val," Lisa said. "It's going to be okay."

She pushed Lisa out of the way and ran inside the office, past the beaded curtain. Silent. Empty. Barlow was gone. She had the key but it was too late to help him.

"Sorry," she said to the empty room, the empty armchair—her heart a heavy, aching thing in her chest. "I'm so sorry. I tried. Really I did."

Val closed her eyes, and let herself start to sob. What was the point? Of any of it? It was too much. She went through all of that for nothing.

Nothing.

Val felt a hand on her arm and opened her eyes. Lisa looked at her with great concern. "I knew Barlow," she said. "And I know one very important thing about him."

Val sniffed. "What?"

"He'd still want you to use the key. To go without him. To save yourself. I know he would."

Go without him. A breath caught in Val's throat. She was right. That's exactly what Barlow would want for her. She could still go. She and Lisa.

She reached down into her top, into her bra, to pull out the object that had caused so much pain, so much stress, so much . . . hope.

The key.

Once she got back to Heaven she could find somebody, talk to somebody. Barlow had only been gone a short time. It might not be too late to still save him. But she had to go now. He'd had faith in her. He believed in her. And she wasn't going to let him down again.

It was her brand-new plan—she figured she was probably at Plan Z by now—and she clung fiercely to it. Go back to Heaven and do what she could from there.

And she was taking Lisa with her.

"We're leaving," Val said. "Fasten your seat belts. This may or may not get bumpy."

Bette Davis, she thought. *Sort of. Reggie would be so proud.*

Val held the key close to her face and turned it in the dim lighting while she read the ancient—but strangely readable—words etched into its surface. She felt the power hum through her, the essence of the golden key coursing up her arm and through her entire body. When she'd finished speaking, she hardly remembered saying anything at all, what the words were or if they made sense. But at that moment power filled her with a feeling of peace and goodness, equal to the light that emanated from Seraphina's eyes. The power seemed to solidify and grow larger until she felt like a glass of water about to spill over or shatter into a thousand pieces. And when it finally felt too much, the energy streamed out of her in a single line of power, hitting the far wall of Barlow's living room, in the corner where the rabbit-eared television sat. It trailed up from the floor, six feet high, then across, then down. The outline of a door. Val watched in awe as the inside of it began to grow opaque, glowing until it was nothing but a rectangle of glimmering light in the dark room.

She let out a long, shaky breath.

Not bad for a first try if I do say so myself, she thought wearily.

"Val," Lisa said from behind her.

But Val was busy looking at the doorway of light. Only a few steps away. So close and all that had happened to her would become a fading memory.

A tear slipped down her cheek.

"Val," Lisa said again. "I think we have a bit of a problem."

"Let's get a move on," Val said. "We don't know how long it's going to stay open."

There was a sound then. A jingle, like the bell on the door to the manager's office. A cold draft of air swept into the room.

Val turned around to look at Lisa and felt her stomach sink down, down, down . . .

Well, hell.

"You were so right, Nathaniel," Julian purred as he stepped through the beaded curtain. "She is *terribly* predictable, isn't she?"

Chapter Twenty-two

———— ᴖ ————

Nathaniel entered through the curtain and stood next to the grinning blond demon. He stared at Val with an expression that looked like . . . disappointment? *Right,* she thought. Disappointment that she was oh-so-predictable. So naïve. So stupid.

Three out of three.

There was nothing in his expression to indicate he was there to help her. Nothing at all. The behavior modification must have worked after all. The Nathaniel she'd gotten to know over the past few days was gone forever.

She exchanged a worried glance with Lisa and turned back to the glowing doorway. *Note to self: Must remember to make sure no demons are present before opening a gateway to Heaven.*

"I command you to close," she said to the glowing light. She shook the key in its direction. She knew it wouldn't work, but figured it was worth a shot.

Julian laughed. "Nice try."

Val shrugged. "Not really. But thanks for saying so."

"No, I'm very surprised, fallen one. That you just made it so easy for me. For us." He glanced at Nathaniel, then back to her. "Looks like your little spell over the halfling here is definitely over, isn't it? He isn't exactly riding in on his white horse to save you now."

Nathaniel just continued to stare at her, expressionless. Blank.

She swallowed. "White horses are overrated."

Julian's grin widened. "I truly thought you'd make it more difficult before you did exactly what I would want you to. You see, a little bird told me that only a fallen angel could use the key."

"A little bird?" Val thought about that, then frowned.

"Yes," Julian continued. "A little bird that flew away before I had the chance to cage it properly."

Val glanced at Lisa who shrugged back at her. "I was trying to buy a little time so I could escape. It actually worked."

Julian scowled at her. "Yeah, well, you turn your back for one moment . . . Plus, I was kind of distracted with the mayor and . . . oh, never mind. You won't escape again. Now, back to the matter at hand." He gazed at the doorway of light. "Pretty isn't it? Though I did organize a little something in case you weren't willing to open it."

Val stomach was in knots. "What do you mean?"

To her left there was a sudden flash of fire and Yasmeen appeared, smiling.

"Ow, that's hot . . . *ouch!*" a familiar voice yelped.

Behind Yasmeen was Reggie, no longer a rat, but a man as he was before. He was naked, and held two McDonald's food trays—now slightly melted from the trip there—against his front and back to cover his nakedness. Claire stood next to him clutching his arm and staring around the room with fear as naked as Reggie's body.

"Reggie!" Val exclaimed.

"Val?" His gaze darted around the room. "This isn't good, is it?"

"Not even slightly."

Julian looked them up and down. "Now that you've already opened the doorway, I don't need them, do I? What should I do with them?" He turned. "Nathaniel? Any thoughts?"

Val's uneasy gaze moved to the other demon and she watched as the corner of his mouth twitched into an unfriendly smile. "I can think of many things. Reggie, remember how I promised I could put you out of your misery? That offer is still available."

Reggie blinked. "Uh, gee, thanks for the offer, Nate. But I think I'll pass."

Val's eyes narrowed. "You touch him and you'll be sorry."

Nathaniel turned to her with the smile still in place, but he didn't say anything.

"Now." Julian took a step toward the doorway of light and rubbed his hands together. "Time to get this party started."

She stepped in front of him. "Julian, listen to me. You can't go through there. You'll shift the balance and it'll destroy everything. The earthly realm, Heaven, Hell. *Everything.* You hear me?"

He raised an eyebrow. "How incredibly exciting. Don't you think so, Nathaniel?"

"Absolutely."

She shot the other demon a dirty look. Yasmeen had slipped an arm around his waist and stared at him as if he were the greatest thing since sliced bread. Really bad analogy, Val thought. But she was too busy freaking out to come up with something good.

Julian was just about to walk into Heaven and obliterate everything up by his mere presence.

And again . . .

All her fault.

She was sensing a theme. The theme of Valerie Grace. Throwing everything away that she cared about because of her stupid, selfish, predictable behavior.

"Val—" Lisa said shakily. Val glanced over at the girl with her bright eyes and pale skin—a desperate look on her face as she waited for Val's next move.

Julian smirked at her. "The funniest part of all of this is that you honestly thought you had a chance. Thought you could use my father's key. Did you ever think about what would happen if you wandered back into Heaven without an official invite? Would they greet you with open arms? What kind of existence would an angel have who wasn't welcome there? But you're *not* an angel, are you? You're just a sad, frail, predictable woman who would throw it all away when her hormones kicked in. Nathaniel probably didn't even need the behavior modification at all. Perhaps all the time he was simply playing you for the little tramp you are." He laughed coldly. "My hat's off to him, too, because he even had me fooled. Didn't you, Nathaniel?"

Julian turned around and was greeted with Nathaniel's slamming fist. He was hit hard enough to be launched across the room, hit the wall and slide down to the floor.

"Yeah, I *did* have you fooled, didn't I?" Nathaniel said. Then he crossed the room to grab the stunned Julian and hold him down against the faded beige carpet. "Valerie, go now. There's no time to waste."

She closed her now gaping mouth. "What the hell are you doing?"

"No time for explanation. Just consider this your white-horse delivery. Better late than never. Go back to your home. To Heaven. Go now!"

Lisa was at her side, staring at the doorway, which glowed as bright as it had when it had first appeared.

Julian began to fight against Nathaniel and Yasmeen stared at the two demons as if she didn't know what to make of this strange turn of events.

Val's breathing was coming hard and rapid. What was Nathaniel doing? she thought frantically, but then realized it was kind of obvious. He'd just given her the chance she'd been looking for all of this time. Two long months stuck as a human and this is exactly what she'd been hoping for. The only thing that had kept her going when the going got tough.

"Come on," Lisa said as she moved toward the glowing doorway.

Val grabbed her arm to stop her from going any farther. "Just a moment."

"What?"

"Valerie, what are you doing?" Nathaniel pressed Julian hard into the floor.

"Let me go, halfling!" Julian's voice was muffled by the carpet. Val suddenly wondered when the last time was it had gotten a good vacuuming. Not from her, that's for sure.

"Val, now's your chance," Reggie yelled. "What are you waiting for? This is what you've wanted all along."

"The weight of the world is on my shoulders right now and I'm afraid of throwing it all away by mistake," she re-

membered saying in the limo ride over there, speaking to whomever it was that Seraphina was channeling.

"Excellent," they'd said. *"I believe the right choice has already been made."*

Was that the boss? she thought. Was that God himself who was speaking through Seraphina helping her to find the answers she sought? And if so, couldn't he have spelled out the answer for her instead of making her have to guess all the time at what the true meaning was behind the words?

It never worked that way.

"You're right. All of you," she said suddenly. "And Nathaniel, about what you said to me in the Underworld—I *am* selfish. All my good deeds, whether or not I really realized it, I was doing for bonus points. Trying to get back to what I knew. Where it isn't scary or lonely. Where I felt wanted and safe and cared for and knew what to expect. I didn't mean to lie to myself, but that's just what I did. And my selfishness, all my meaningless lies have led to this very moment. Right here, right now."

"Valerie," Nathaniel struggled with Julian. "I don't know how much longer I can hold him. You must go while you still have the chance."

She nodded "The thing is—I just wanted to let you know that you were wrong about one very important thing about me, Nathaniel."

"Oh?" His gaze locked with hers. "And what's that, my beautiful angel?"

"I'm not predictable."

She threw the key at the doorway and it passed through and disappeared to the other side. In the barest of moments, a split second, it closed like a bright blind, a line of light that was there for a moment, then gone the next as if it had never been there in the first place.

She blinked with surprise. She hadn't been sure it would work, but figured it was worth a shot.

Julian screamed, long and loud and she saw Nathaniel fly away from him as he got to his feet, flames in his eyes, so bright it hurt to look at him. More than normal, anyhow.

"You bitch!" he said, his voice pitchy. "You threw away my key."

Val took a step back. "I didn't see your name on it."

He stormed toward her, hands clenched, but Nathaniel rose up behind him and grabbed him by the back of his jacket and the two of them staggered through the beaded curtain, then crashed through the manager's office window and out to the courtyard outside. Val was about to run out after them when Yasmeen stepped into her path. She looked angry, upset, and confused. Mostly the confused part.

"You," she began, her brow lowered enough that Val could tell she was a few hundred years overdue for Botox treatments. "You are human, yes?"

"Looks like."

A quick glance past the curtain showed that Julian and Nathaniel were going at it outside in demon to demon combat. It actually looked to Val more like a bar fight than what she'd expect from two supernatural beings, but she supposed that fists were a more manly way to deal with conflict than laser beams from one's eyes. Although, definitely not as cool.

Yasmeen's eyes narrowed. "And yet he defends you."

"What's your point?"

"Nathaniel is *mine*. He's always been mine. If it wasn't for me, he'd be nothing."

Val crossed her arms. "And again . . . your point?"

Yasmeen's eyes turned fiery and Val decided right then and there that she was sick and tired of looking at flames in people's eyes. It just wasn't right. It made her go all teary and in need of large doses of Visine.

The demon's expression darkened with pure hatred and her eyes reflected Hell itself. "I am going to *destroy* you."

Val gulped. "You mean we can't be best friends?"

Yasmeen stormed toward Val.

Reggie suddenly leapt forward and grabbed Yasmeen's arm, succeeding in dropping the tray that covered his butt. "Don't touch her, you bitch."

She raised an eyebrow. "How quaint." She flicked a finger at him and he flew across the room, his remaining McDonald's tray and all.

"Excuse me," Claire said softly.

"What now?" Yasmeen turned to her.

"Nobody beats up my boyfriend except me." Her eyes narrowed and Val felt a wave of energy jump off her. Yasmeen gasped, stared at Val for a last frozen moment, and . . .

. . . Fizzled out.

Vanquished by the fast-food witch.

Claire collapsed to her knees on the floor. "That shit sure takes it out of me." She fell to her side, closed her eyes, and immediately started to snore.

Reggie scrambled for the handmade afghan that was draped across the armchair, wrapped it around his waist, and stared down at his girlfriend.

"My beautiful snookums saves the day." He glanced up at Val. "I really have to make sure not to piss her off anymore. She is one scary woman."

Val glanced over at Lisa in the corner, then turned to run outside. Julian had Nathaniel pinned to the ground over by the pool, his hands tightly around Nathaniel's neck.

Nathaniel ground his thumbs into Julian's eyes who then screamed and let him go. They scowled at each other.

"You are so whipped," Julian snapped. "It's sad, really."

"You're just jealous."

"Yeah, I'm so jealous. Not!"

Lisa touched Val's arm. "Why, Val? Why did you stop me from going through the doorway?"

Val turned to look at her. Poor Lisa who'd gotten a raw deal and regretted being tempted. Who just wanted a second chance.

She shrugged the girl's hand away.

"Fallen angels are fallen for a reason," Val told her. "And sweetie, I've learned way too much in the past couple of days about false exteriors. So why don't you quit the act?"

Her eyes widened. "I don't know what you're talking about."

Val just fixed her with an icy glare. "Drop it. I saw your flamey eyes inside—you must have lost your concentration or something. Had me going, too. I thought you were a fallen angel all this time. I should have believed Nathaniel when he said he didn't remember tempting you. Because he didn't, did he?"

"Val," Reggie said off to her left, struggling to keep his afghan up. Behind him the boys continued to fight and verbally taunt each other, though neither seemed to be winning. "Why are you being so mean to her?"

Val sighed. "I've had a really lousy day."

Lisa smiled then, just a small smile that blossomed into a full-fledged grin. "You are wrong about one thing, Val."

"Oh? And what might that be?"

"I *was* once a fallen angel."

Lisa shimmered as her glamour shifted, and she became taller, broader, thicker. Her red hair turned blond, so bright in color that it hurt Val's eyes. Her feminine features became masculine. And perfect. He was incredibly handsome, but . . . there was something about the way this man looked. His beauty was so acute it was nearly painful. Looking at him didn't fill Val with light, it filled her with dread, and goose bumps formed on her arms. Though it was already cool outside and a few snowflakes were drifting down from the clouds above, a deeper chill now spread across the motel grounds as she faced the being in front of her. His eyes were all fire as he stared at her and Val got the strange impression that this is how his eyes always were. All of the time.

"Damn," Val finally managed to say.

Lucifer shrugged and looked down at himself. "You don't like?"

She swallowed. *Hard.* "Um, I guess I'm just a little speechless."

"I tend to have that effect on people."

Reggie cleared his throat nervously. "This is just like *Scooby-Doo.* Only evil and really scary."

"I thought Lisa used to be a maid here," Val said after a moment.

"She was. I believe she eloped with her boyfriend to

Montreal. I thought the glamour would help me get a little undercover work done."

Her feet didn't seem to be working anymore. Not that she could have run away from freaking *Lucifer* if she tried. But it would have been nice to have had the option. "What kind of undercover work?"

He glanced over at the two demons who hadn't noticed the major change to the cast of characters yet. "It's not easy being me, I'll have you know, Valerie. You know Donald Trump? All the businesses he oversees? That's nothing compared to what I have to do. So many employees to keep an eye on in case they're up to something. That usually takes most of my time. Your side isn't the only one interested in keeping the balance, you know. I like things just the way they are and I work hard to ensure it stays that way. However, every now and again there is something too interesting added into the mix that requires me to take an extra look. You, for instance."

Val frowned. "Me? What for?"

"You because you were a fallen angel without a crime. That so rarely happens, it's a national event when it does."

"She was thrown out because of pride," Reggie offered, hiking up his afghan toga. "It's a deadly sin, though I guess you probably already know that. Um. I'll shut up now."

Val nodded. "It's true. There's apparently paperwork and everything."

Lucifer laughed and it sent chills down Val's spine. "Pride? Is that what they told you?"

"Well, yeah."

"And what about him?" Lucifer nodded toward Nathaniel.

"What about him?"

"He has aided you instead of tempting you. That doesn't happen, either. Yet another sign that you are special. For others like Alexa who were slightly drawn to the goodness they found in a fallen one, much as a moth is drawn to a flame, I considered it a passing fancy. I allowed her the slight indiscretion since her other work was exemplary, but Nathaniel." He clucked his tongue. "A failure from the moment he was originally brought to me. I should never have given him the many chances he's squandered."

Val felt cold at his words. "Please don't hurt him."

A cold grin tugged at the corner of his mouth. "I grow tired of this foolishness." He turned to the two fighting demons, brought his hands together and then pulled them apart. The demons went flying in opposite directions.

"Cool," Reggie observed, though he'd taken more than a few steps back from Val and Hell's head honcho.

"Now," Lucifer turned his glare back to Val, though his smile remained, "you should know I'm very displeased with you. You threw away my key. Do you know how long I've been looking for that thing? *Very* annoying." His gaze shifted. "Oh, look. Here comes my pathetic excuse for a son."

Julian stormed toward them, but skidded to a halt when he saw who was there. "Daddy?" he squeaked.

Nathaniel glanced uneasily at Lucifer, but slid a protective arm around Val's shoulders. "What's going on here?" he asked stiffly.

"What's going on is that you've been a naughty little demon," Lucifer said. "And you, too, Julian."

Julian shifted his feet nervously. "But aren't demons supposed to be naughty?"

"Well, yes. Of course they are. But not when they do it behind my back." Lucifer turned to Val and the flames blazed even brighter in his eyes. "Now, I believe we were discussing my key?"

Val swallowed hard. "You know, until just the other day I always thought the key was a myth. Imagine my surprise when it turned out to be true. Weird, huh?"

Lucifer nodded. "A myth, you say? Sort of like the small piece of Heaven that allegedly fell off and dropped to the earthly realm?"

"Yeah, like that."

"That happens to be true, too."

Her eyes widened and she moved closer to Nathaniel's tense body. "Really?"

"Yes, I find it hard to believe you don't already know it to be a fact." Lucifer glanced around at the motel. "Since we're currently standing right in the middle of it. Can't you feel it? Its purity and goodness makes my skin crawl. Perhaps it is for the best I didn't pop back to Heaven to say hello to my old . . . *friends*. Though, the look on their holier-than-thou faces would have been well worth the visit. Yes, the Paradise Inn. Do you get the sad attempt at an in-joke some angel with nothing better to do thought of? *In Paradise?* This is a place I have never paid any heed to, since it is but a useless piece of Heaven. But still, it's mildly irritating."

Val glanced at the rickety plastic furniture, the snow-covered pool, the run-down rooms, the flaking paint. "I don't believe you."

Lucifer sighed. "Tell me, why did you come here after your fall?"

"Because the address was written on a piece of paper," Val said, as if that explained everything. Then frowned. "In the wallet Heaven provided with the cash and the birth certificate to help me get started."

"Coincidence?" Lucifer smiled. "I think not. There's no such thing as coincidence. Tell her, Barlow."

Val's mouth dropped open as she saw Bartholomew Barlow walk briskly and with purpose over to stand next to Lucifer.

"Hello, Valerie, my dear."

She brought a trembling hand to her mouth. "But . . . but that police officer told me you were dead."

He smiled. "Oh, I am. As a doornail. But I can't leave until I finish up a bit of business."

She felt her eyes fill with tears of joy to see him again. "I was so worried. I tried to do what I could to get the key. And I did. I brought it back, but you weren't here. Mr. Barlow, I screwed up. Big time. It's all my fault."

He shook his head. "No, you did just fine. You passed with flying colors."

"What are you talking about?"

"The test. To find a worthy successor for me."

Val felt so confused. "What are you talking about? A successor for what?"

Barlow glanced warily at the original fallen angel. "What Lucifer told you is correct. The Paradise Inn is a very small piece of Heaven. Too small to do any damage by its shift to the earthly realm, but it requires a guardian. And for fifty years that guardian has been me. People are drawn here for a reason, because they need to be here, just like you. Even without that slip of paper, I have faith that you would have found your way eventually. I have helped the travelers who seek shelter here find whatever answers they seek. It's my job, and it's a very important one. But now my time is at an end. The inn will only accept a human guardian and since humans have naturally limited lifespans, it was time for the next guardian to arrive."

"Me?" she squeaked and glanced at Nathaniel who looked very surprised by this news. But not as surprised as she was.

"Yes. You were chosen because you displayed the necessary assets to become a human. Curiosity, love, fascination. An interest in all things shown during your interactions with the humans you helped guide into Heaven. Plus, I believe you were Angel of the Month not so long ago. It is a great honor to be chosen, Valerie. You should be very proud."

"But that's a deadly sin," Reggie piped up.

Barlow smiled at him. "It depends how the pride is displayed, and it is not always a fault but an asset. Val was chosen specifically and I have great faith that she will do an excellent job as guardian of the Paradise Inn."

Val was trying to process everything he was saying. "So are you trying to tell me that the whole thing was just a test? The key and everything I've been through?"

He shook his head, then smiled to show a spray of wrinkles around his kindly eyes. "No. Though it certainly helped establish your desire to do the right thing—the selfless thing—even at high cost to yourself. Had you gone through the doorway it would have stayed open for Julian to follow. Only by throwing away your one chance to return to Heaven—the key itself—were you able to close it with no harm done."

"So if Julian had gone through the doorway—"

"The world would most certainly have ended. Don't doubt it for a moment."

"Oh."

"That would have been so cool," Julian said sadly.

"Excuse me," Lucifer said. "If we could concentrate on the more important thing here? Me?"

Julian knelt down and lowered his head. "Yes, Father."

"Get up, you little bastard."

Julian scrambled back up to his feet.

"You"—Lucifer's flame-filled eyes narrowed as he gazed at his naughty little boy—"stole my key from the fallen one, then without even telling me, tried to use it yourself."

"Yes, but—"

"I'm not finished. You vanquished Alexa, one of my favorite employees, despite her shortcomings, and you sided with that ugly slug Vaille of all demons for a grasp at power."

Julian swallowed. "In my defense, I did it all to gain your favor."

"Silence."

"Yes, Daddy."

"Don't call me that." Lucifer's gaze tracked to Nathaniel who had been silent all this time though he hadn't moved from Val's side. "And *you* . . . even before your introduction to this woman, your job performance has been weak at best. Do you have no taste for temptation at all?"

"Sir, I can explain—"

"Do not interrupt. Two hundred years and I've smelled

the guilt you harbor for your assigned duties from dimensions away. And to so easily allow yourself to be summoned, to aid this fallen angel on her journey to the Underworld, disappoints me more than I can express. Many times you had the opportunity to end her, to leave her, but you didn't."

Nathaniel moved his hand down and captured Val's, squeezing it tightly but not saying a word in his own defense.

"You knew the rules and you chose to break them. You were given behavior modification and that has obviously failed. There is one last punishment suitable for one as failed as you. Yes? Is that what you want?" Lucifer shook his head with disappointment. "It is not enough that I must control all that is below, but I must keep tabs on my lowliest of employees? I'm very annoyed with the both of you. Answer me this, why did you do it?" He looked at Julian first.

His brow lowered. "For power."

Then to Nathaniel, who locked gazes with Val. "In the beginning, I felt I had to do as she wanted. I couldn't resist the summoning. But then it was more than that. I felt something I hadn't for as long as I can remember—not even when I was human. *Hope.* That there was something more. Something bigger for me than the existence I'd thought there was no escape from."

"So"—Val felt a big lump form in her throat at his words—"you didn't really mean all those cruel things you said to me at the mansion?"

His jaw tensed. "They tried to modify my behavior, and initially it did work. I wasn't as I am right now when I saw you in the hallway of the mansion. But I snapped out of it finally. Thanks to you."

A smile twitched at her mouth. "Then I'm sorry I scratched your face like that. Shouldn't that be healed already?"

He touched his face and flinched. "Well, I guess I sort of deserved it."

"Glad you agree."

"Hope?" Lucifer interjected. "That's why you did it?"

Nathaniel nodded. "Yes."

Lucifer nodded and smiled, then looked at Val as the smile faded from his painfully beautiful face. "Wrong answer."

Nathaniel and Julian both screamed and Nathaniel let go of her. She stepped back from him, eyes wide, as the two demons disappeared in columns of flame.

Val's mouth fell open and she gaped at Lucifer. "What did you do? I helped rescue you at the mansion. Isn't that worth anything?"

He laughed. "You think you rescued me? Foolish girl. How else was I supposed to gain your confidence? I could have made you believe anything I wanted you to."

"Don't hurt him," she managed, each word painful as it left her mouth. "Please. I love him!"

He shrugged. "I guess I'm just not that much of a romantic. Go figure."

He disappeared.

What? What just happened? She stared frantically over at Reggie who looked just as shocked as she did. Then she turned to Barlow. He was starting to fade away; she could see right through him to the other side of the motel.

"I'm sorry, Valerie," he said sadly. "Lucifer is cruel and heartless—always has been—but it's for the best."

"But, Nathaniel—" she choked out the words.

He shook his head and looked at her kindly. "You have a greater purpose to fill now. Try to forget him for no demon is worth your tears. Always remember that I have great faith in you, Valerie. I always have and I always will."

He faded away in a glimmering light before she could say anything else. The last thing she saw was two large white wings spread out behind him, and then . . . he was gone.

It was just Val and Reggie in the courtyard then, as the snow drifted lightly to the ground. Everyone else was gone. Gone forever.

She looked at him.

He looked at her.

She waited for him to say something funny, to make her laugh, but he just shook his head sadly. "Sorry, Val."

She nodded and felt a tear slip down her cheek. "Me, too."

Chapter Twenty-three

———————— ✺ ————————

She never thought she'd see him again, and when she did—when he rose above the hill to look down upon her with her long blond hair blowing in the New Mexican breeze—she breathed a great sigh of relief.

He beckoned to her, and she ran to meet him, throwing her arms around him.

"I love you," he said.

"And I you."

"Nothing could keep me away. No world vast enough, no mountain tall enough, no villain evil enough. We were meant to be together, always and forever.

Yes. Always and forever, she thought as their lips met in a kiss that felt like Heaven.

Val closed the book, stared at the back cover of Trixie L'Amour's glamourized black and white photo, and threw the hardcover across the room where it knocked her artificial Christmas tree over.

Who reads this crap? she thought. *Seriously. Happy endings are for wimps.*

But then she got up from behind the check-in desk, dutifully walked over to pick up the book and gingerly brushed it off. Then she propped the tree back up and straightened out the lights before she went back to sit behind the desk.

Two weeks had passed since the proverbial torch of looking after the Paradise Inn had been passed to her. It was Christmas Eve, and she'd strung a bunch of lights around the motel to make it look as festive as she could—just like the other motels she'd observed around Niagara, only hers looked better, she thought. Barlow had said that pride was an asset sometimes. And her Christmas lights were really cool if she did say so herself.

She had a Harry Connick holiday CD cranked up and was nibbling at a piece of fruity Christmas cake—courtesy of Becky—and drinking a glass of milk.

One thing about being a human she definitely didn't like—not that she was keeping a list anymore. After all, she'd accepted her new position as guardian of the Paradise Inn with open arms. *Christmas cake sucked.* But she ate it because she knew Becky had made it herself. Val was invited over to her place for Christmas dinner the following night. Becky was still clinging to the false hope that Val would hit it off with her brother. And who knew? Maybe she would.

Not.

Val had spent the last two weeks trying to keep her hands and mind busy. Signing the paperwork that turned ownership of the motel—not to mention Barlow's sizeable savings account—over to her was surprisingly easy.

One might almost think it was all preordained, or something. No questions asked.

Since then, as if to acknowledge Val as the new guardian, the inn had sort of . . . perked up a bit. Stopped looking so weathered. The sign out front that appeared not to have changed since the fifties, one day updated itself to look modern and shiny and new. The pool, still covered with a tarp and a layer of snow, had grown in size, become kidney-shaped with a slide and everything. Just waiting for the summer. Waiting for the snow to thaw. For a new season to begin.

It might have something to do with the revitalized look, but at the moment the motel was completely full. Zero vacancies. Val's clientele turned out to be everything from a completely normal family of four vacationing from England, to a depressed wizard who hadn't come out of his room in a week, to a tiny, maraca-playing demon who was in hiding and looking for a new band.

She tried to be as friendly to all of them as she could. Letting them know that she was there if they needed anything. If she could help out in any way.

Reggie and Claire were thinking about getting engaged. He'd been trying to be on his best behavior, but Val wasn't really sure how well that was working out. When she'd seen him the day before, Claire had just turned him into a weasel.

And then there's me, she thought.

Good old unpredictable, slightly selfish, moderately prideful, Valerie Grace. The owner/operator of a slice of Heaven called the Paradise Inn.

All alone on Christmas Eve. And feeling very, very

sorry for herself after reading eight romance novels in a row.

Lloyd had sent over his entire backlist as an early Christmas present. Val pulled out the next Trixie L'Amour from under the desk and opened it up to page one.

The bell above the door jingled.

Oooh, she thought as she started reading. *A Regency this time. Nice.*

She felt a draft of cold air.

"Sorry," she said without looking up. "We're all booked up. There's another motel right next door. Free shuttle service to the casino and everything."

"Valerie . . ."

She looked up at the sound of his voice to see Nathaniel standing at the doorway.

A breath caught in her chest.

He smiled and it looked like it hurt a bit. She noticed a pinkish scar where she'd scored him across the eye with her fingernail. He touched his face when he saw where she was looking.

"I know. It didn't heal."

"I'm sorry."

"Don't be."

"What are you doing here?"

He flinched, as if wounded by her curt words. "They threw me out. Of Hell. I'm human now. Just like you."

"He made it sound like you were going to be punished."

He smiled. "Lucifer finds different ways of punishing his employees. Being a human is my punishment. I believe Lucifer considers that a worse fate than being turned into a Nightflyer. Believe it or not, Julian was rewarded and given a promotion because of his—"

"Evil ways?"

"Yeah. Also a little nepotism goes a long way. I guess I'm just not evil enough for them."

"You can be evil when you try to be."

He grinned. "You're just saying that to make me feel better."

"Maybe a little."

"So, listen," he said, and met her gaze. "I didn't really know where else to go. So I'm here. I know you probably hate me after all the ways I screwed up. But . . . I love you Valerie. So much. I don't know what I'd do without you."

Val just stared at him in silence, so he continued. "I honestly didn't know anything was missing in my existence before I met you." He frowned. "Well, I knew something was wrong, but I didn't know what, other than the fact that I hated what I did. I figured that was my fate. An eternity of despair, but that was just par for the course. When I was a human before . . . before all of this . . . I didn't have a very good life then, either. So when I got the chance to become something more, I took it, thinking that might ease my pain, that it might fill the empty hole inside of me, but it didn't. It only got worse."

He paused, looked away for a moment, then met her gaze completely. "And then I met you, and everything fell into place. Even though it was an uncomfortable place that scared the shit out of me, it felt so right. I think I loved you before I ever met you. No one else has ever . . . touched me the way you did. Your bravery, your stubbornness. It's you, Valerie. You are my light."

She continued to stare at him, then blinked and looked

down at the motel ledger. "We're seriously all filled up. There's no vacancy. It's the holidays—big tourist time, you know."

He pressed his lips together. "Yeah, I figured. I just wanted to make sure you were okay. I guess I'll leave you alone and not bother you anymore then." He turned away and pushed the door open. Val felt the cold breeze again as she continued to study the check-in ledger.

"Oh, just a moment," she said. "There does seem to be one room available."

He turned. "Oh?"

"Yeah." She looked up. "Room seventeen. Is that okay?"

"Room seventeen. But—" he frowned—"isn't that your room?"

"Is that going to be a problem?"

A slow, cautious smile appeared. "No problem at all."

She nodded. "Good. Now there's only the matter of payment."

The smile faded. "I don't have any money. Hell doesn't even spot us a couple of bucks when we're thrown out. But, just give me some time—"

Val shook her head. "No, that won't do at all. I suppose I'll have to put you to work. I could use the help around here." She moved out from behind the desk. "You don't mind being bossed around a bit, do you?"

He stared at her for a moment, then a grin slowly spread across his handsome features. "I guess that all depends on who's doing the bossing around."

"Then I think we can come to an understanding." A wide smile suddenly appeared on Val's face. "I love you, too, Nathaniel. And I've missed you so much. Now I command you to kiss me. Right now."

He took a step forward, then stopped and frowned. "Wait, there might be a problem."

"What?"

He grimaced. "I think I may be coming down with a cold. My nose is all stuffed up. I'd probably just give you my germs. I may even sneeze on you."

Her smile widened. "What's life without a little risk?"

He smiled back, and then gathered her into his arms to give her a kiss that felt as good as Heaven itself ever could.

Well, she thought, *pretty damn close, anyhow.*

About the Author

Michelle Rowen currently lives in Mississauga, Ontario, with an evil cat and a poster of Hugh Jackman. By day she's a slightly stressed out graphic designer, and by night she pens comedic paranormal romances—originally only to amuse herself. *Angel with Attitude* is her second novel. She'd love to hear from you! Seriously, she would. Reach her by e-mail via her Web site at www.michellerowen.com.

The lady is a vamp . . .

Sarah Dearly,
the lovable fanged princess
from *Bitten & Smitten*, is back!

Turn the page
for a preview of
Michelle Rowen's next novel,

Fanged & Fabulous

Available in mass market Spring 2007.

Jogging is great exercise. Running for your life—even better.

Or, at least that's what I tried to tell myself.

It was the new jogging suit I'd bought at half price that did it. I felt all *J Lo* in my fuchsia velour, out for a quick, late-afternoon jog. Feeling good in the cold but fresh February air with my newest pair of very dark sunglasses firmly in place.

I guess I shouldn't have smiled at the cute young guy by the hot dog cart outside of my apartment building. Firstly, because, hello? I'm *taken*, thank you very much.

Secondly, because of the whole "fang" situation.

That never goes over very well with vampire hunters.

Next thing I know, instead of getting some much-needed aerobic activity—surprisingly enough, a diet of diluted blood is *not* calorie-free—I was high-tailing it through a nearly deserted nearby park with a hunter on my Reebok-clad heels.

I shot a look over my shoulder. "Leave me alone!"

"Stop running, vampire," he replied.

I eyed the wooden stake he had in his left hand, and then picked up my pace, darting past a couple of speed walkers who didn't give us a second glance.

Two months had gone by without seeing a single hunter. Two *very* good months. It couldn't be hunting season in Toronto again so soon, could it?

"I'll catch you," the hunter shouted from a few steps behind me. "So why don't you stop running and save me some time?"

I jumped up as we passed an overhang of evergreens and grabbed a nearby icicle. Then I stopped abruptly and spun around to face him with the sharp piece of ice in my hand. He skidded to a halt, almost slamming right into me, and looked at me with confusion. "You stopped."

"I'm trying to be more proactive these days. Come near me and this—" I indicated my drippy weapon "—is going through your eyeball."

He was still cute. Probably in his early twenties, with fashionably spiky dark hair, a thin but attractive face, brown puppy-dog eyes. He wore a black leather jacket over . . . beige Dockers?

I could take him.

"Proactive?" He raised an eyebrow, and shifted the stake to his other hand.

"Yeah, that's acting in advance to deal with an expected difficulty. I looked it up. It means that instead of running like a chicken with my head cut off—pardon the cliché—I will confront my attacker and deal with the situation in a calm yet forceful manner."

"You're smart for a vampire," he said.

I almost smiled at that. "Really?"

"A vampire who's about to die."

I tensed and curled my other hand into a fist. I'd been going to self-defense fitness classes with my best friend Amy for over a month. It was true that only four lessons at an hour apiece probably weren't going to earn me any major ass-kicking awards, but I felt a little more confident about my current situation. A *little*.

Proactive with a capital P. That's me.

"What's your name?" I asked the frat-boy.

"Chad."

"Seriously?"

"Yeah. Why?"

"Is that short for anything?"

"Yeah, it's short for I'm going to kill you now." He frowned. "Why are you still talking?"

He kicked the icicle out of my hand. It shattered on the ground next to me. I blinked down at it.

Well, that's not good.

I held up my hands. "Look . . . Chad, just walk away now. You *do not* want to mess with me." I thought of the first move I'd make. I'd go for the groin. Always a good place to start. And end.

"Let me tell you a little something . . ." he paused expectantly and raised his eyebrows.

"Sarah," I offered.

"*Sarah.* The only reason you're still talking is because I'm allowing it. I might not look it, but I've dusted over a dozen vamps, this year alone."

I swallowed hard.

"Well, if you've killed that many," I said, much less confident now. "You should know it's not really dust. It's more like goo."

"Whatever." He looked down at the stake, ran his thumb along the sharp tip, and glanced over at me. "Now let's get this party started."

Hell, he looked fairly harmless what with the Dockers and all. Guess you can't judge a man by his casual, stain resistant pants anymore.

I turned and ran, but before I got more than a few steps, I felt his hand clamp down on my shoulder, stopping me in mid-flee. He spun me around, then brought his hand down to my collarbone and shoved me hard so I stumbled back and fell to the ground in a heap. I scrambled back a few feet and looked around. We were all alone. Why were we all alone? Where were people when I needed them?

"I'll make it quick." Chad winked at me. "If you stay nice and quiet for me."

Yeah, like that was going to happen. "Are you aware that you're the bad guy?"

This stopped him, but his stony expression didn't change. "What?"

"Vampire hunters are evil, homicidal bastards who kill for the fun of it. They're the bad guys. Vampires are completely harmless. Like adorable, pointy-toothed bunnies."

He laughed a little at that and stepped closer. "Yeah, right."

I held up my hand and slowly rose shakily to my feet "Do you ever stop to look at the big picture? Do you know what you'd be doing if you murder me?"

"*Slay*, you mean."

"No, don't try to make it sound all pretty. You'd be *murdering* me. Just because you think I'm a monster. But I'm not a monster. I'm just a little dentally different from you."

"You drink blood."

I made a face. It sounded so gross. "This is true. But it's provided by willing donors. There's kegs of the stuff, hopefully sanitized and homogenized or whatever they do to make it clean and disease-free."

"You're an undead creature of the night." He jabbed the stake in my general direction.

I looked up and pointed at the sky. "Sun's still up, isn't it? And I'm breathing. Heart's going all pitty-pat. Seriously, you need to read up a little on the topic."

Chad sighed heavily. "So you're saying that everything I've been told all my life, everything I believe—it has all been a lie. That I haven't been doing my job as a citizen of the world by ridding it of bloodsucking monsters, I've actually been killing innocent people."

I nodded enthusiastically. "Bingo!"

He snorted. "You're funny. That's almost enough for me to let you live, but you know what? Not going to happen."

Bingo denied.

I tried to scramble away from him, but he grabbed my fuchsia covered leg and pulled me back, until he was completely on top of me, pinning my arms under his knees so all I could do was thrash from side to side like a wounded seal. He grabbed my face and squeezed, making my mouth open up so he could inspect my fangs. He ran a thumb over one of them.

"I usually take these from the young ones I slay. Got myself a nice necklace now."

I sank my teeth into his hand as deep as I could, and he pulled it away with surprise and a sudden yelp of pain.

He smacked me across the side of my face and glowered dangerously. "Shouldn't have done that, vampire."

"You touch me again and my boyfriend is going to rip your lungs out," I hissed.

"Yeah?" He smirked and looked around from his position on top of me. "I don't think I see your boyfriend anywhere. Or anyone else for that matter. It's just you and me."

"He's a master vampire and he's not a big fan of hunters. Lungs? Ripped out? Do I need to repeat myself?"

"A master vampire? In Toronto?" That got his attention. "There's only one that I've heard of."

"That's him. Do I need to mention the ripping out of lungs again?"

His raised stake seemed to wilt slightly, and his brow furrowed. "Did you say your name was Sarah?"

"So what if I did?"

"Sarah *Dearly*?"

I struggled to get out from under him but he had me pinned too firmly. "Get off me, you bastard."

Surprisingly, he did. As if there were wires attached to his body like a marionette, he sprang back from me to his feet. He gazed at me with a deep frown while I slowly got up and brushed myself off. I glanced at him warily.

"Sarah Dearly," he repeated. "The master vampire's girlfriend."

"How do you know my name?"

His eyes widened. He breathed in a deep breath of cold air and let it out slowly before he spoke again. I saw the frozen air puff out in front of him. "Everyone knows about you."

"Everyone?"

"The Slayer of Slayers." He said it under his breath and took a step backward.

"The what of the what?"

"Two months ago . . . the massacre at the vampire lair. You killed so many hunters . . . so many . . ." his voice trailed off and he brought a hand to his mouth.

I was confused. What was he talking about? "The vampire lair? What massacre?"

"Your name is legendary." He took another step back and hit the thick trunk of a tall oak tree next to a park bench. "I . . . I . . . should never have . . ." His eyes shifted back and forth and I noticed the hand that held the stake was shaking. "Please, spare me. That whole thing earlier, me acting all tough . . . that was an act. The other hunters . . . they're so mean, and they all think I'm weak. I was just out for a hot dog and a Coke, that's all. Please, don't hurt me. I was kidding about the fang necklace! Really!"

Two months ago was the hunter/vampire show-down at the Midnight Eclipse. That was my boyfriend (sounds like a silly thing to call a six-hundred-year old vampire—but that's what he was) Thierry's secret vampire bar that had been lo-cated through a door at the back of a tanning salon.

It was true that the night in question was a major deal, that a lot of people got hurt, both hunter and vampire, and that I may have . . . possibly . . . sort of . . . had to kill a hunter named Peter, jerk that he was. But that had been pure self-defense—and something I was still feeling great gobs of greasy guilt from, even though he'd majorly deserved it. And it had been with a gun, not with my bare teeth as Chad seemed to indicate with the fearing-for-his-life expression on his now sweaty face.

Now I was legendary?

I took a step toward him and he fell to his knees, the stake clattering to the ground. He put his hands together and began to pray in barely coherent whispers. With a shaky hand he reached inside his shirt to pull out a heavy silver cross and held it up.

Let's just nip this in the bud, shall we?

I closed the remaining distance between us, reached forward and yanked the cross from around his neck. His eyes widened in fear. I inspected the cross. Pretty. And shiny. I slid the chain over my head and let it drop to my chest.

I grabbed his shirt and pulled him up to his feet, easy to do since he was like a rag doll now. I brought him close enough that our eyeballs were only inches from each other.

"I will let you live . . . *today,*" I said, calmly and dangerously, as I let him go. I used to aspire to become a world-famous, well paid actress, so I just called on that questionable ability to give my words a little extra weight. "But if you or your friends come near me again, I shall bathe in your blood."

Ew. Did I just say that? How disgusting.

But it seemed to get my point across. Chad was now the one scrambling backward, nodding like a lunatic, saying "Yes, yes, I promise," over and over again. Then with a last look of fear—the intense kind one might have before investing in adult diapers—he turned and ran from the park like the proverbial bat out of hell.

I leaned over and picked up the stake from where Chad the vampire hunter had dropped it and studied it for a moment. I had to go find Thierry, tell him what just happened here and what, if anything, I should do about it. If anybody would know, he would. He just wasn't going to be too happy about it.

Slayer of Slayers, huh?

I threw the stake into a nearby garbage can.

That new little nickname was *so* going to come back to bite me in the ass.

THE DISH

Where authors give you the inside scoop!

♥ ♥ ♥ ♥ ♥ ♥ ♥ ♥ ♥ ♥ ♥

From the desk of
Sue Ellen Welfonder

Some characters wrap themselves around an author's heart and hold fast, claiming their place and beguiling, until the author agrees to write their book.

Kenneth MacKenzie, the hero of **UNTIL THE KNIGHT COMES** (on sale now), is such a character. Indeed, he has haunted me since my very first book, **DEVIL IN A KILT**, winner of the 2001 *Romantic Times* award for Best First Historical Romance. Kenneth's father was the villain in that book and, although he was quite dastardly, he also possessed a certain undeniable charm. So much so that I always regretted not being able to redeem him. But I could give him a bastard son, a hero just as dashing as his roguish father but worthy of becoming the Keeper of Cuidrach, the proud inheritance Clan MacKenzie reserves for the most valiant amongst the clan's by-blows.

Darkly seductive, Kenneth first appeared in my previous book, ONLY FOR A KNIGHT, but this one is his.

Now he must claim his birthright, Cuidrach Castle and the Legacy of the Bastard Stone. And although he is well able to do this and more, he is not at all prepared to have his heart claimed by the enticing and mysterious woman who so unexpectedly greets him when he arrives at his supposedly deserted keep. Together, they must face a maze of secrets, betrayals, and a very determined enemy before they can surrender to the redeeming power of love.

Readers wishing for a peek at Kenneth's world might enjoy visiting my Web site at www.welfonder.com to see photos of Kintail and even the famed Bastard Stone. I happened across just such an unusual sea cliff while visiting Scotland during the writing of this book. Seeing it warmed my heart and convinced me that Kenneth and Mariota would indeed find their happy ending.

With all good wishes,

Sue-Ellen Welfonder

www.welfonder.com

♥ ♥ ♥ ♥ ♥ ♥ ♥ ♥ ♥ ♥

From the desk of Michelle Rowen

Angels and demons and talking rats. Oh my!

The best part about writing a paranormal romance novel is that *anything is possible*. If I get an idea for a book and think, "This is a little weird. I haven't seen anything like this before," that's actually a *good* thing.

On the surface these stories may appear different and otherworldly, even bizarre . . . but I think the reason for the genre's immense popularity is that it acts as a mirror to our own lives, reflecting themes that are sometimes easier to look at if presented in a more fantastical manner.

My fallen angel in **ANGEL WITH ATTITUDE** (on sale now) isn't *just* a fallen angel: She's a girl who simply wants to go back home. She doesn't understand what happened, and will do anything in her power to make everything okay again. My demon isn't just a demon: He's the good-looking bad boy who's way too easy to fall for. Underneath his tough, snarky exterior, though, is a man who hates his existence, but is afraid to make a change (the devil you know vs. the devil you don't—only in this case it's *literal*). He knows he's living a lie, but he needs somebody to restore his faith in himself, humanity, and . . . *sigh* . . . love.

Together they discover that appearances are not always what they seem; that there are no easy answers in life; that the most difficult journey isn't always one of distance, but one we take within ourselves; and that having a witch girlfriend who thinks you're cheating on her is a good way to get yourself turned into a rat.

However, that last one's really just common sense.

Happy Reading!

Michelle Rowen

www.michellerowen.com

Can't get enough
vampires and dragons and witches?

Bitten & Smitten
BY MICHELLE ROWEN

"A charming, hilarious book!
I'm insanely jealous I didn't write it."
—*MaryJanice Davidson, author of* Undead and Unwed

Doppelganger
BY MARIE BRENNAN

"I can't wait for her next book!"
—*Rachel Caine, author of* Windfall

Kitty and The Midnight Hour
BY CARRIE VAUGHN

"I enjoyed this book from start to finish."
—*Charlaine Harris, author of* Dead as a Doornail

Out of the Night
BY ROBIN T. POPP

"A stellar job of combining intriguing characterization
with gritty suspense, adding up to a major thrill ride!
—*Romantic Times BOOKclub Magazine*

Working for the Devil
BY LILITH SAINTCROW

"A unique and engaging mélange."
—*Jacqueline Carey, author of* Kushiel's Avatar

*Want to know more about romances at
Warner Books and Warner Forever?
Get the scoop online!*

WARNER'S ROMANCE HOMEPAGE

Visit us at www.warnerforever.com for all the
latest news, reviews, and chapter excerpts!

NEW AND UPCOMING TITLES

Each month we feature our new titles
and reader favorites.

CONTESTS AND GIVEAWAYS

We give away galleys, autographed copies,
and all kinds of fun stuff.

AUTHOR INFO

You'll find bios, articles, and links to personal
Web sites for all your favorite authors—and
so much more!

THE BUZZ

Sign up for our monthly romance newsletter,
and be the first to read all about it!